Gillian Slovo was born in South Africa in 1952. In 1964 her family was forced into exile. They settled in London, where Gillian Slovo still lives. Since the birth of her daughter she has been writing full time and is the author of three detective novels featuring her character Kate Baeier as well as *Ties of Blood*, her first novel set in South Africa.

The BETRAYAL

GILLIAN SLOVO

Published by VIRAGO PRESS Limited 1992
20–23 Mandela Street, Camden Town, London NW1 0HQ

First published in Great Britain 1991 by Michael Joseph
a division of the Penguin Group

A CIP catalogue record for this book
is available from the British Library

Printed in Great Britain by Cox & Wyman Ltd, Reading, Berkshire

For Andy

Sometimes it happens that history and fiction collide. So it was with *The Betrayal*. When I started writing the book, Nelson Mandela was in prison, the ANC was banned and I had not been in the country in twenty-six years. And then, a week after I finished it, I was in South Africa watching Mandela walk the length of the Johannesburg offices of a legal ANC. And so the book is set firmly in 1989, placed at the point where the past and the present met inside South Africa, a book about what had gone but a book also about what might one day be.

My thanks to Gavin Cawthra, Mandla Langa, Marius Schoon, Joe Slovo and Elaine Unterhalter for answering each and every question I threw their way. The fiction I have made of their suggestions and of the facts they supplied is, of course, entirely my responsibility. Thanks also to Caradoc King and Susan Watt for their generous and constantly available help.

Soweto, 1985

The light blocked everything. Because of its brightness the man could make out neither the colour of the sky nor the thorn-bushed escarpment in front of the shack. Inside was shadow, and the mahogany of his hands had turned to darkest black. All was monochrome, bleached out by the light, and all was unearthly quiet.

But then he heard it. A thin cry, the cry of a bird high in the sky. An eagle, he thought. He was about to twist his head up through the cracked glass, in an attempt to spot the bird, but then he realized that there was no point. There could be no bird of prey circling the skies above Soweto, there would not be one.

The cry he had heard was an illusion conjured out of a childhood long ago deserted. It came back sharply, that day in his youth. On that day the light was also bright, the sky almost white. He remembered shading his eyes with one hand and peering into the dazzled beyond at a small hillock in the distance and at a figure on that hillock. He had heard the bird's cry then and the shout that followed it.

He had looked up, up high into the sky, searching out the bird. The light had been strong then too, burning a white line across his eyes, a white line on which tiny black spots danced, a line so dazzling that his eyes were forced shut. Another shout and he had opened his eyes and raised his head again, looking across parched grassland with its burnished reds and browns, looking at the small hillock. His friend had been there, standing on its top, one arm held high in the air, index finger pointing.

1

He had followed his friend's finger, had followed a line which seemed to join up with it, until finally he saw it: the bird, its wings spread far, soaring gloriously above the earth.

He remembered, more clearly even than the sight, the feeling that had overcome him then, the feeling of awe at its magnificence and of exhilaration too – of exhilaration that something could be so proud and still so free. He had stood motionless on the ground, dwarfed by the bird's world and by the immensity of the shimmering white sky.

He had watched the bird until it was no longer visible, and as he did so, his body seemed to grow until it became the frame, not of a youngster, but of a man. He had begun to run, straight towards the hillock, stretching his legs, running long and hard into the arms of his friend. He remembered that firm flesh, warm and strong as they embraced. He remembered the first thrill of that touch.

And he recalled something else: how, on that day and in that moment, he had promised himself that when he grew to be a man he would join that eagle. I too will be fearless, he had told himself, I too will be free.

Now Victor, the full-grown man, stood by the window of the shack and smiled grimly. Since that day on the veld he had learned only too well fear's secret underpinning and had also learned how illusive was freedom. Yet he did not feel bitter. He looked back upon his life and for the most part he was satisfied: the man had kept his pledge to the boy and to the eagle in himself. The man, at least, had lived.

And now, he suddenly thought, now I am truly free for freedom stands alongside death – to look the one in the face is also to possess the other.

I'm free, he thought, at the same instant as he saw the sign he had been waiting for, the sign that he'd been dreading. He saw it, almost as if it had been foretold, a movement in the distance, a flash of silver, a quivering of some greenery and then an artificial stillness.

I'm free, he thought, and, drawing the gun up to the window, he broke the pane of glass, lined his eyes along the barrel, and began to fire.

2

The Week Before

CHAPTER ONE

South Africa 1989

The man came out of the café and stood still for a moment, looking around. His glance was nervous – a dart in all directions – until it changed to something other. What had started as a shiver of his eyelids spread down a neck to become a quake before finally reaching feet whence it was translated into motion.

Standing opposite, Alan Littell watched the man lope off down the road. He moves like a puppet, Alan thought, a puppet on a string and a stupid one at that – the man must have discarded his brains along with his loyalty. For despite his cursory stab at counter surveillance, he had failed to spot Alan and then, having taken only the most superficial of precautions, he seemed to forget all about security. He walked down the pavement, weaving in and out of the crowds, chewing at something wrapped in a piece of paper. His bite was anxious – he was the type who ate under stress – but still he didn't glance even once across the road where he might have caught Alan mirroring his steps.

The man's carelessness amazed Alan. It made him wonder anew whether his own conclusions might not yet be proved ridiculous. Surely the man could not be involved in the dirty dealing Alan suspected him of? Surely he would be more vigilant if he really had turned traitor? Frowning, Alan continued to follow but more reluctantly.

The man slowed down and finally came to a halt outside a music shop. Jazz audible even across the road issued from the shop, but the man seemed unmoved by it. He hesitated by the doorway, uncertain, wiping grease from his chin with the back of a calloused hand, darting his eyes around.

Alan, suddenly alert, stepped back into the shadow of an awning. Confidence returned. He was right, he knew he was. This man, this former comrade, had gone over to the other side. Even from afar Alan could smell the fear upon the man's breath and see the shiftiness that sprang from the deeper wells of treachery.

The man moved suddenly. He swerved round and darted across the road, heading straight for Alan. It was an unanticipated, surprising, alarming move. There was no time to take evasive action and nowhere to go. As the man headed closer, Alan cursed himself. It was a trap, he thought, there are others in the street, and they are after me.

He muttered one short, condemnatory swear word. How could he have been so stupid? How could he have lulled himself into a sense of false security, mocked his prey while all the time it was he who was the hunted?

The full knowledge of his danger calmed him. He pushed his thoughts away, forcing his years of experience in the field to overtake them. He must discard self-recrimination – it could only make him vulnerable. He pulled himself up tall, and, while he continued to look straight at the man, his hand went to his pocket to clasp the cold steel inside. He was ready for anything.

But there was no need to be ready. The man had noticed nothing amiss: he came within five feet of Alan and then swung away. Alan sagged back against the wall, drained not by fear but by the absence of action. Only after a few, long seconds could he find the energy to turn his head and watch the man. The smile that settled on his face was bitter. It was no trap, he thought, no trap at all. The man was too far gone for that, so preoccupied with his own betrayal that he had failed to recognize his comrade and his nemesis.

Alan did not bother to pursue more closely for he knew already where the man was headed. This was the second time that Alan had kept this very vigil, the second time that the man had led him to this same street in the middle of Johannesburg's Hillbrow. Alan could afford to wait and when, and only when it was safe he would easily track the man and get final confirmation of what he had long suspected.

Standing still, he allowed his mind to range backwards to the beginning and to the incident that had brought him to this place. He had been inside South Africa on a dangerous mission – his job to place a series of rocket launchers – and hadn't slept for days. When he had spotted the man, whom he recognized vaguely from the camps, he'd almost ignored him. If he had done so, he would have been following procedure: fellow ANC combatants must never greet each other unless absolutely necessary.

But the man's behaviour had verged so close to the hysterical that it had mesmerized Alan. The man, known to Alan by his nickname, Slim, was parodying a picture of unconcern and doing it badly. Slim had been out on the street, Alan in a car some yards away. As Alan watched, Slim had begun to laugh – so raucously that his laughter had turned heads. And every subsequent movement had been likewise exaggerated. He'd nodded his head too frantically, he'd shaken his companion's hand too furiously and then, when he was walking away he had done so jerkily as if in slow motion.

Alan had followed Slim – just for the hell of it – and had seen Slim start to run as soon as he turned the corner. At that moment two questions raised themselves: why was Slim so nervous and who was he running to? Alan had no time to investigate then: he couldn't jeopardize his mission for a hunch. But Slim's behaviour had intrigued him and he hadn't let it go.

On each return visit Alan had watched Slim. On each return visit he had gathered a further piece of the puzzle. It was easy to spot the tell-tale signs: meetings furtively arranged, passwords, exchanges of information, dead letter boxes and payments – these were the easiest to catch. What he had found was more, much more, than he expected. What he'd found was that Slim was not alone in his treachery: he was associating with three of Alan's former comrades – one a well-known turncoat, one who had disappeared inside the country and was presumed dead and the last, a man with a reputation so tarnished that the ANC seldom used him.

Four of them, altogether: four of them working for the enemy. Four of them, whose every recent mission had been a disaster and who acted without consulting HQ. Four of them identifying ANC personnel to the South African police. Four of them involved in acts of provocation and betrayal. Four of them with more to back them up.

Four of them and Alan alone knew it. He had not informed the ANC, nor even hinted at his suspicion. He had kept the information to himself, hugging it close. He'd told himself that his silence was an ethical one – that in these times of hectic change he had no right to point a finger at a comrade without also having the proof. But he knew this was rubbish: the truth was that, if the men were indeed traitors, then he, Alan Littell, wanted to expose them. He wanted to be the one – and he needed to be.

Alan blinked. Slim had reached his destination, one of a row of apartment buildings, overcrowded and tarnished with over use.

Alan watched Slim disappear inside, his shoulders heaving by the door as if, having reached base, his burden of anxiety was already beginning to fade.

When he was sure that Slim must be halfway up the stairs, Alan strolled towards the building. He stood outside and looked up smiling. This was the location of their safe house, Alan was almost positive of this. To double check he must wait, a night if necessary and to the day beyond it, wait and watch each of the four come and go, seeing their arms laden with food, seeing the parade of women dressed in deep purple and black who swaggered in beside them. It would be tedious to do this work, but Alan had never shirked from work. His reputation in MK, the ANC's army, had been earned by dint of hard application and tenacity for details. This mission, self-appointed though it was, would be no exception.

But then Alan's smile widened for he remembered something about those apartment blocks. It was always possible, he thought, unlikely but worth checking all the same. He strolled slowly to the building, through the narrow doorway and into a dingy lobby that stank of urine.

The outline of what had once been there – that sense of slightly impoverished gentility – was still in evidence, altered completely, however, by the sheer press of numbers. As Alan took one step into the gloom he was met by a wall of sound issuing from every

8

one of the building's orifices. Doors would open and voices be released from them, snatches of conversations, of arguments, of shrill singing and deep rumbled threats all of them reverberating across the dingy space. Alan waited until the confusion in his ears had abated and until his eyes had become accustomed to the dark. He saw two children across the lobby, two children dressed in knee-high trousers, dividing a packet of lifesavers between them. They were sitting underneath a sign: 'Only one family per apartment' the sign proclaimed. 'Absolutely no children'. Beside the children was a desk, and on the desk a book. A man, his eyes glazed, sat behind the desk, one pudgy brown hand resting on the book.

Alan walked up to the desk, stopped and pulled the book towards him. The caretaker's hand was limp and it slid off, coming to rest almost by accident by his side. He slowly raised his head to look at Alan but his eyes refused to focus. The sweet smell of *dagga* issued from his breath and his head drooped down again.

Alan glanced at the last signature on the book and his pupils dilated, making their cold blue deepen. For there, without any attempt to disguise it, was the name of his prey. Like all members of the ANC, Slim had a variety of different names and yet he had used the one by which he was known within the ANC military. 'Slim,' he had written. 'Slim, visiting Jakes'.

If Slim had been so foolish, Alan thought, then maybe the others had too. He turned the pages of the book, looking through the preceding days. And sure enough the other names were there, all four of them, all four of them pretending to visit Jakes while all four of them were living here. Alan's night-time vigil was no longer necessary.

When he re-emerged into the fierce light of day, Alan's eyes were narrowed not only against the sun, but against the thoughts that crowded in on him. The four had made no attempt to hide their identities and that could only mean one thing – that they felt themselves secure. They had high-level protection, Alan thought, and he shivered. For the second time that day he wondered whether it was he who was about to become the fall guy.

But then, as he began to walk away, his brow cleared. Of course

9

they must have protection (they had after all been turned by the security branch), but there was another explanation for their bravado – that it stemmed not from real security but rather from stupidity. Feeling themselves safe they had grown passive and thrown caution to the wind: feeling themselves invulnerable they had made Alan's job easy. For a moment he hated them for their carelessness. He despised them for what they did and for the ease with which they threw off their hard-earned training. He had known one of them in the camps and he remembered the beads of sweat on his former comrade's black face, the perspiration appearing now in hindsight as treachery itself.

Alan shook himself. He could not afford to inhabit his past, he must dwell only in the present. Life changes, he thought, life changes. He walked down the streets of Hillbrow, bombarded by a multitude of boastful signs, of massage and beauty parlours, balconies of wrought iron with glimpses of faded flock wallpaper behind them, of grubby lace curtains, and of the bulk of humanity, mainly black, that flowed down the streets and in and out of myriad shops and cafés. He walked past the site of the Fontana supermarket and, pulled once more into the past, he remembered how long ago he and his friends – sheltered, white suburban offspring – had come here as students to buy late night coffee and exotic donuts. He remembered how grown up he had felt then – merely because he was up so late. In those days Hillbrow had been white, zoned off and segregated. Now Africa had begun to reclaim it.

Criss-crossing the streets, Alan reached Hillbrow's centre. He strolled through the gates that lead to Joubert Park. The place was overflowing with nurses on their lunchtime breaks, courting couples, children darting in and out, snatching bravely at drunks who sprawled across benches. Alan took a seat away from them, absorbing the transformation in the once immaculate botanical gardens as a flurry of different languages hit at him from all sides. South Africa, he thought, you've changed. Hillbrow is the beginning, and de Klerk the beginning of the end. He shook his head, no that wasn't true: the ANC was the beginning and the ANC the end.

The end of you – the words shot out at him. Who had once

uttered them? Oh yes, it came unbidden, that face to the forefront of his mind. A large face, burnt red by the sun, with flaming hair above it. Captain Gert Malan, that was the name that matched the face, the name Alan would never forget. He had met Malan only once but he would never be able to throw off the impression of the sheer intelligence of the man, nor the almost brutish sadism that seemed to lurk behind that mind. Captain Gert Malan, a malignancy that pursued Alan.

Alan stood up and the image of Malan lost its potency. If South Africa was in the midst of vast sea changes, he thought, then Malan would be the first to drown. He smiled again. He had no cause to worry: he would soon be gone from here, headed not for Zambia but for Tanzania. A strange destination for one on active duty but that's what the courier's decoded message had clearly meant. Alan shrugged. There were people in Dar, he knew, who could not leave the country and who had information to impart. And anyway, it suited Alan's purposes. In the relative calm of Tanzania he would have time to prepare his case, to tie up the details he had collected, to nail down what he had so painstakingly uncovered.

In the meantime there was one more thing he must do, one more visit he must make.

CHAPTER TWO

As soon as Captain Gert Malan surfaced, six young officers surrounded him, jostling with each other in their attempts to congratulate him. They were, he thought, like over-fed calves, their faces tanned a ruddy brown, their big bones pumped by muscle, their sparkling teeth marshalled for inspection. He imagined nudging them and watching as they tumbled one upon the other, legs and arms flailing in a playful heap. So vibrant was the image, so full of possibilities, that he even lifted his hand to give the first push.

He controlled the hand. It would do his reputation no good to show impatience. Dissimulation – that's what he needed.

Dissimulation came easily to Malan. He took the proffered hands and shook them hard, harder than they expected, and he smiled while they laughed, and nodded while they boasted. He stood, apparently enjoying himself, agreeing that it was a great victory to have broken an ANC group operating from this small *dorp*.

'I will go back to Jo'burg content,' he told them, 'content in the knowledge that together we've delivered a blow to the ANC's power in the country.'

As he talked of returning to Johannesburg, the words transformed themselves into necessity. He gripped his briefcase to his side, an image of what lay in it, beckoning. He was assailed by a sense of urgency. The year 1989 was a turning point, a year when the battle for South Africa might be lost or won; it was a turning point and Malan was at the crux. There was no time to waste.

Muttering one final word of empty praise, he detached himself from his honour guard. He gave a genial wave as he strode from the police station, a formerly imposing man whose physique had diminished as the red of his hair had faded, but whose intellect remained as sharp as ever.

He climbed into the back of his waiting car. Shifting from one rump to the other he glanced up in time to see his driver kick at the back door. Without looking at the man, Malan flung out an arm. Flesh blocked metal and then, while Malan looked away, his driver gingerly secured the door. As the car began to move off, he closed his eyes, waiting, expectantly, for sleep. But the niggling pain in the small of his back prevented him from surrendering himself and, instead of drifting off, he began to think of what lay there – there in his briefcase.

'Sir?'

Malan opened his eyes and blinked. He had fallen asleep after all, fallen so deeply asleep that he hadn't even noticed when the car arrived in the underground garage of John Vorster Square. He scowled as he intercepted his driver's look of concern.

'What's your problem?' he demanded.

Without waiting for a reply, he bent his head and swung one leg out of the car. The movement pulled sharply at the base of his spine. He leaned heavily on the leg and thrust himself upright. He stumbled and grabbed for his driver's arm but as soon as he had regained his balance he pushed the man away.

'That will be all,' he said. 'Get some rest.'

He walked to the lift, ignoring uniformed policemen who, on seeing him, stopped and saluted smartly. He did not need to call the lift, it was waiting there and the junior officer inside it jumped out and held the door. Malan walked straight in and pressed the single button. The lift didn't stop. It had only one destination – the tenth floor, headquarters of the South African security police.

Malan's throat was dry as he nodded to the policeman who released the turnstile. He summoned up in his imagination the smell of fresh coffee, the smell and the taste as well. He'd put the coffee on his desk, he thought, and make sure he was comfortably seated before savouring the first glorious sip.

But he never reached his office, nor sank into his chair. A few steps away from it, and an underling informed him that Colonel Jansen was expecting him.

Malan shrugged: better, he thought, to get it over. He knocked on Colonel Jansen's office door and entered.

Jansen rose to meet Malan. A tall man in his early fifties, the Colonel was sleekly dressed. In a blue suit with ties and socks to match the steel grey of his hair, Jansen looked dry, clean and pressed – the perfect bureaucrat, in fact. 'Congratulations, Captain,' he said. 'A good job, efficiently done.' He waved his hands in the direction of a chair.

Malan licked his parched lips and yawned.

'You need some rest,' Jansen suggested.

'If I needed rest,' Malan replied, 'I would have gone home.'

Jansen raised an eyebrow. 'A good job,' he repeated. He paused, flicked his eyes down to his desktop as if something waited there to prompt him. The desk was bare. 'So good,' he said with a smile, 'that I'm having trouble keeping you.'

Malan blinked and with that one movement threw off the fatigue of his last forty-eight hours. Danger – he felt it coming.

'We at the centre have coped with the increased workload imposed by the Emergency,' Jansen said.

That's right, Malan thought, we've coped.

'The outlying regions,' Jansen said, 'have not been as successful. They're requesting reinforcements.' He stressed the last word, stressed and paused on it. 'I've drawn up a list,' he continued, 'and naturally your record speaks for itself. Your name is at the head.'

So that's it, Malan thought, Jansen's planning to bury me in the *veld*.

'I wouldn't, of course, release you on a permanent basis,' Jansen said. 'You're too valuable. But a few months in selected districts should elevate standards nationwide.'

A few months in selected districts, Malan thought. A few months that will stretch into a few years, right up to the time when I'm due to retire.

'What do you think?' Jansen asked.

Malan bit down on the obvious retort. This indeed was

14

danger and he must be careful. He kept his face stiff, his eyes coldly polite. 'Ja,' he began, 'some of the outposts need improvement.' He counted silently to five. 'It's a question,' he softly said, 'a question of who to send.' He looked down at the floor. 'A younger man,' he suggested, 'would benefit from the experience.'

No dice. 'A younger man would not have an ability to command as you do,' Jansen said.

'True.' Malan bit the corner of his lip. 'There are, however, my continuing operations. Some of which I can't possibly offload.'

'You wouldn't be cut off, you know,' Jansen said. 'You would have almost immediate access to all information. In addition,' he raised his voice theatrically. 'In addition I will give you special powers to override existing channels.'

Special powers, Malan thought, channels overridden! So Jansen was serious. He straightened his back. 'Moving from Jo'burg would make access to my most important contacts difficult,' he said. 'Difficult and perhaps even impossible,' he concluded.

Jansen knew precisely what Malan meant. He frowned. 'Ah yes, your contacts,' he said. The frown deepened. 'Your contacts have been curiously silent lately have they not.' It was a statement, not a question.

Malan smiled. He could afford to. 'We've been working on something big,' he said.

He could afford to smile, but nevertheless his equanimity was partly forced. The timing of this revelation was not of his choosing and timing had always been important to Malan. But Jansen was looking at him expectantly.

Ah well, Malan thought, I've been preparing for months. 'I have the papers here,' he said.

They were in his briefcase where he kept them, constantly within grasp. He opened the case, removed the file and pushed it at Jansen. As Jansen began to read, Malan was assailed by a loathing so strong that it was almost physical. It was a feeling that he was accustomed to suppressing but that, in the silence, he allowed himself to savour. Jansen, he thought, you're a designer policeman – even your muscles have been purchased wholesale from a gym.

Jansen turned a page.

Your path was smooth, Malan thought, from university straight to the top. You don't know what it's like to struggle.

Another page, Jansen was reading rapidly now.

You talk of how much you value the team, Malan thought, but you do all you can to undermine it.

Jansen looked straight across the desk, straight at Malan. There was something in that look that was uncharacteristic. Something that spoke of uncertainty. Malan pushed all emotion aside and prepared himself for what was to come.

'Interesting,' Jansen said.

Interesting, Malan registered. Perhaps, he thought, Jansen has read too quickly. 'I am in the process of identifying the armed enemy unit,' he explained. 'When I do this, I can ensnare them. With surprise on my side, I plan to turn some of them.'

Jansen's lips twitched but Jansen, Malan saw, did not smile. 'You have evidence of who they are,' Jansen said, 'and of what they've done. But not where they are.'

'I'm waiting for the final report,' Malan said. 'I expect it imminently. It will contain all the details.'

Jansen nodded and turned away, pointing his head at the window as if he were lost in profound thought. 'Tell me, Gert,' he eventually said.

Malan heard this, the first ever use of his Christian name, and his attention was redoubled.

'Tell me,' Jansen repeated, turning his head to the front again. 'Do you really think the ANC is still serious about the armed struggle?'

Not this again, Malan thought. 'Yes,' he said out loud. 'Yes, I do.'

Jansen shrugged. Here it comes, Malan thought.

'Umkhonto hasn't launched anything big for some time,' Jansen said.

'Umkhonto hadn't done anything much before hitting Sasol,' Malan countered. 'When the refinery blew it took us all by surprise.'

'Sasol,' Jansen said. 'Sasol was a long time ago. Things have changed since then.' Jansen softened his voice and smiled almost

16

enticingly at his junior. 'Look around you, my friend,' he suggested, 'you will see how much they've changed.'

Things have changed – that's what a thousand Jansens were saying these days. They phrased it in the past so as to eliminate others from their shady deals. They phrased it grandly to hide the fact that behind such sanguine statements they were trembling at the sight of a few headstrong people waving the black, green and gold of the African National Congress.

'We have to stabilize the political situation,' Jansen continued. 'We must embark on an orderly process of change.' He looked across the table, his watery eyes momentarily strengthened by an emotion which bordered on the messianic. 'Face it, man,' he urged, 'things are changing.'

Things are changing! It made Malan want to laugh. What Jansen really meant was that his people, de Klerk's bright new breed, were making sure that things looked as if they were changing. The world had turned against South Africa and suddenly Jansen and his ilk had lost the stomach for confrontation. With their flowery words and insincere smiles they were trying to hide the truth which was that they were no longer interested in catching terrorists – only in releasing them.

'De Klerk is right,' Jansen continued. 'Our country desperately needs to undergo a process of normalization. If we remove our most pressing social problems we will in one stroke remove the need for revolution. Things will change, mark my words they will.'

Things will change: they phrased it so and then they called themselves the new realists. They made policy on their feet – releasing Rivonia trialists, talking about ending the Emergency, and even, amongst themselves, about negotiations. They were desperate, that was it. They described themselves as forward looking but they were merely hungry for power. And their hunger, Malan thought, was so intense it scared even them. They talked and talked to conceal their fear and all the while it was men like Malan who kept them safe.

Jansen's voice, less speculative now, pulled Malan back from his reverie. 'I guarantee you', Jansen was saying, 'that by the end of the year Mandela will be released.'

17

Mandela, Malan thought, that's impossible. But then an image shadowed this thought – an image of Mandela's closest friend, Walter Sisulu, as he stalked the streets of Soweto. Mandela will be released, Jansen is right, Malan realized. But so what, he thought.

'Mandela is more reasonable than those in exile,' Jansen said.

Mandela, reasonable, Malan thought telegraphically.

'He'll split the ANC and the country will follow him,' Jansen said. 'The armed struggle will become a thing of the past.'

Reasonable – the man they'd once called enemy number one! It took some effort to push back the hiccup of mirth that rose in Malan's throat. But it wasn't funny, it was pathetic, Jansen believing his own propaganda. Jansen had fallen for stories of splits in the ANC, and of terrorists handing in their guns and walking up to the negotiating table. How could he? It was beneath contempt.

'A thing of the past,' Jansen concluded.

There was no point arguing: only the facts would do. 'I'm a practical man,' Malan said. 'Look again at my evidence and you will see that this Umkhonto unit I've identified is poised to strike. They've already been implicated in a number of necklacings.'

'Hearsay,' Jansen quickly said.

'When we have their location,' Malan continued, 'we'll have it all.'

Jansen's eyes narrowed, this time visibly. ' "We",' he said. 'I'm glad you talked of "we".' His voice was loud. 'When you have the location,' he said. 'You will, of course, inform me.'

'Of course.'

But Jansen did not leave it there. He raised his voice another notch. 'I am ordering you to inform me,' he said. 'Before taking action.'

Malan swallowed hard. It was an outrage: Jansen ordering him – Jansen pointing out the chain of command to him.

He swallowed again, this time to control himself. 'Of course,' he repeated softly.

'That will be all,' Jansen said. 'Thanks for coming in, Gert.'

And then having had the last word, Jansen felt it necessary to add something else. He timed his question carefully. He waited

18

while Malan manoeuvred himself out of the chair, while Malan walked to the door, while Malan put his hand on the knob. Only then did he speak.

'Are you sure you can trust Zonda?' is what he said.

Malan sat in his office and smiled. With this last dig, Jansen had given himself away. Jealousy, that's what motivated Jansen. Jealousy at Malan's contact with Zonda. It rankled with Jansen that Malan, with Zonda's help, had been at the centre of the department's most successful moves to halt ANC infiltration. Jansen hated Malan but he could not get rid of him because Zonda was Malan's creation and because, with Zonda at his side, Malan's feats were legendary. Jansen would never have a spy as good as Zonda. Jansen would never have a spy that good and so he wanted Zonda out of commission.

Oh yes, Jansen hated Zonda and he wanted, desperately, to denigrate him. But what Jansen wanted would soon be unimportant. When Zonda supplied Malan with the location of the terrorists, he would inform Jansen. And then there would be nothing that Jansen could do, nothing to prevent Malan from victory. Nothing at all.

Malan took a swig of coffee and began to scan quickly through the folder on his desk. It was all ordinary information – outcomes of interrogations, reports from agents, lists of those who had arrived in South Africa – particulars of what had occurred in his absence. He lifted the phone and dialled his home number.

Ingrid answered almost immediately. She always answered the phone in the same way, breathlessly as if she'd been interrupted in the midst of strenuous activity, and she always gave their number before her hello.

'It's me,' he said.

Her voice grew more certain as he had known it would. 'Gert,' she squealed. 'When did you get back? When are you coming home?'

He glanced at his watch, told her he would be with her in a couple of hours and then asked how she'd managed during his absence. As she began to reply he scanned the lists on his desk. Nothing there, he turned first one page and then another.

19

'And then he did it anyway,' Ingrid was saying. 'What do you make of that?'

He heard her speak but didn't answer. His eyes had stopped on a name, a name amongst many on a routine airport list. He blinked and looked again. Surely he had misread it?

'I mean the cheek of it,' Ingrid said indignantly.

He'd got it right first time. There it was, the name – Sarah Patterson – with a passport number to accompany it. Malan could check the number, he could do so hoping he was wrong, but he knew this would only confirm his fears.

'Gert?'

His fears that this was the same Sarah Patterson who had come into the country.

'Gert?'

The Sarah Patterson he had never met.

'Gert. Are you all right?'

The Sarah Patterson who should not be here.

He spoke loudly into the phone. 'I'll have to ring you back,' he said.

The receiver dropped straight down. Sarah Patterson had come into the country and he hadn't expected her. Which meant only one thing. Something had gone wrong. What he needed to know was how badly wrong. He picked up the phone and methodically he began to dial.

CHAPTER THREE

Looking neither to left nor to right, Sarah Patterson walked straight past the police station. She walked as if she were completely unaware of her surroundings, as if familiarity had rendered them invisible. She walked, in short, like any other white South African woman who found herself walking only because she was between shopping malls.

But the truth couldn't have been more different. For Sarah had worked hard on her apparent unconcern and now she was involved in a different kind of work – she was counting. Conscientiously spacing each step so that the intervals between them were identical, she paced the pavement surrounding the police station, measuring it. Only when she had turned the corner did she stop.

She lowered her shopping to the ground as if she were giving herself a much deserved rest and then, out of her handbag she withdrew a small diary. She opened it to a day somewhere long in the future. On this page, on its extreme left underneath two numbers, she noted down two more. She used no words to remind herself of what they meant. She had no need for words. She would never forget that there written in sequence were: the distance between the police station and the building opposite it; the distance between the police station and the bus shelter; the distance between the left hand corner and the centre door of the police station; and, finally, the number of paces between this same point and the corner on the right.

Sarah knew such attention to detail was unnecessary but she was by nature a perfectionist. Whenever she did anything, she did it thoroughly, a virtue which had earned her a first-class degree in England as well as early promotion to a school's head of department. And now that she was in South Africa she continued to stick to her elevated standards, checking and rechecking her observations, constantly alert to anything she might have overlooked.

She picked up her bags again and walked full circle back to her car. Opening the boot she threw her shopping inside. She closed it again, reflecting, with relief, that this was the last time she would need these props. She climbed into the car and turned the key. The engine, along with the car's tinny radio, sparked into life. Music issued out of it, loud discordant music, accompanied by a voice singing gracelessly in Afrikaans. She flicked a switch and the voice was abruptly cancelled. She put the car into gear and moved it slightly, aiming it for a file of slow moving traffic. She allowed herself one backward glance. There it stood, the police station, a squat modern building with its long, narrow windows and high ramps, an ugly building, a place of pain. As she nudged her car into the midst of others, she shivered at the thought of the chain she'd started. It was hot inside, hot as hell. Unrolling the window, she breathed a sigh of relief. She stretched forward and flicked the radio on again, turning the volume up high. The voice had been joined by others just as loud, all repeating one short phrase over and over again. Sarah joined in, imitating their jagged pronunciation, singing without understanding the song's meaning or caring about it. It fitted her mood, that song, and the words were irrelevant.

She was singing lustily, loudly, when she noticed something, a blur on her right. Her voice faltered as she glanced to her right. She saw a motorbike, a policeman astride it. He was keeping pace with her – leaning over to look straight in.

Sarah was immediately transported into another space, into the vision of arrest and incarceration that she'd daily been expecting. She breathed in and tried to calm herself: no matter what happened she must remain in control.

The music sounded out alone, its disharmony drilling its way into her head. She wrenched at the dials, yanking the volume knob so hard that it came off in her hand. A crackle of radio interference took over. With the flat of her hand she banged at the casing and then there was silence. A silence broken only by the pulsing blood around her temples. A silence which she endured, waiting for the inevitable, her mind blank.

The policeman winked at her, once only. And then, as she continued to watch him, hypnotized, he rose in his seat, pushed himself forward and he was gone, leaving only fumes as a reminder that he'd once been there.

The bastard, Sarah thought, he was looking down my cleavage.

That bastard, she thought, and she laughed out loud. She laughed again, first in relief and then in a kind of euphoria. I've finished, she thought, and I've survived. She pushed her right foot down, gunning the engine as if she could clear the queue in front of her this way.

But the traffic was slow and her eyes remained focused on the image of the police station in her rear view mirror. The place tugged at her, almost as if it were trying to pull her back. She drove automatically, watching, fascinated as it grew smaller, watching until she could no longer distinguish it from its surrounds. She need never see it again. She need never see it again unless, of course it was chosen as a target – in which case she would recognize its husk on the front page of a newspaper. If the ANC did bomb it, she thought, the policeman who's just passed, and the others – the ones I've been watching – some of them might die.

She shook the thought away. She was only one of many involved in similar reconnaissance and the time for armed struggle was rapidly passing. They'll probably never bomb mine, she thought. Mine – it wasn't so odd a thought, for the police staton did feel a bit like hers. For five days she had been watching it, working out its routine until she felt as if she controlled it. She would stand across the street, look at her watch and then say to herself, the next shift is due – and they would arrive. She would see the back of a retreating officer and know whether he would or would not stick to security drill. She knew what time they ate breakfast, how soon 'elevenses' followed, when they had lunch. She knew it all.

And now it was time for her to go.

I'm finished, she thought, and as she drove into the distance the pull of the police station gradually diminished. She drove and drove, humming to herself, thinking distractedly of this and that, without coherence or the need for it.

She had been driving for some considerable time before she came to. She looked up and it dawned on her that she was lost. Until that moment Johannesburg had seemed defined by only two locations – the one where she stayed and the one where the police station was sited. But now she was elsewhere. She looked around her, searching for a reference point. There was nobody in sight and the odds were that nobody would appear to help her out. She saw a name plate on a free standing wall ahead and she kerb-crawled her way to it. Once there, she stopped and took her map from the dashboard shelf.

Bryanston – she saw that she was in Bryanston! By some unlikely coincidence she had driven to the place where Alan had been brought up. She looked down at the map and pin-pointed her location. It was almost unbelievable. She had never been to Bryanston and yet she had landed only one street away from the Howards' house. Well, this she could not resist. She would not deliberately have travelled here but now she had stumbled across the place there was nothing to stop her inspecting it.

She drove around the block. There it was, the house on the corner, the house surrounded by high walls. It was just as Alan had said – a forbidding exterior muted by two vines, one with red and one with purple flowers, which cascaded down until they almost touched the ground.

She got out of her car and walked up to the gates. They were tall and imposing, black with intricate patterns, a hefty lock worked in as part of the design. She peered through two of the vertical bars. She was looking a a scene that was familiar even though she had never seen it before. It was familiar because Alan had described it and described it accurately. She'd assumed that childish eyes might have exaggerated the scale but the place was every bit as grandiose as he'd recounted.

From the gate swept a wide driveway, its white chipped granite set in brick sparkling in the sun like a crystalline sea. The driveway was lined by two rows of tall elms, regularly spaced and leading to the house – a huge Spanish style hacienda all white stucco and elegant wrought iron. On the right of the driveway, and stretching almost as far as Sarah could see, was a carefully clipped lawn, English in its neatness although even from the distance the coarseness of the grass betrayed the continent in which it flourished. The grass was interspersed with flower beds, overflowing with riotous colour but obviously well cared for: it ended by the side of a large oval swimming pool. Beyond the pool Sarah could just make out the outline of a glass building (the changing rooms and greenhouse extension) and then lines of trees – Girlie Howard, she remembered, listed fruit growing as one of her hobbies.

Not bad, Sarah thought, not bad at all. A palace, just as Alan had said it was.

And, she thought, if it amazes me, I who have travelled the world, then how it must have intimidated the young Alan. No wonder he never recovered from the shock of the transition.

The thought brought with it a vague sensation of disquiet. No, that wasn't right, it wasn't the thought – something else had made her uneasy. It was a slight movement at the periphery of her eye, something high up which intruded. An insect she thought, flying into vision.

She looked up and saw that the movement came not from an insect but from a video camera, which was planted at the top of the gate and swivelling in her direction. Its partner, on the other post, was already trained on her. At the camera's monitor, she thought, might be Girlie Howard, Girlie alone and walled in, looking out nervously on a world that passed her by. Girlie Howard. Sarah could not afford to meet her. How would she explain what she was doing here? How would she bring the name of Alan to her lips without accusing this woman who was now old? No, it would not do to meet her, it would not be right.

She turned from the gate and got back into her car. With one last glance at the house, she restarted the car, did a U-turn and made her way back to her rented house.

It had suited her needs well, this house, and it was furnished and decorated to a standard far in excess of what she'd grown used to, but this time, when she walked in, it looked different and somewhat tarnished. It's the comparison with the opulence of the Howards' house, she realized as she stood by the doorway. She stood quite still as she'd been taught to do, letting her eyes range from one wall of the open-plan arrangement to the other, checking that everything was as she had left it. Everything was in its place, even the postcards that she had half-written but never sent, and the nearly empty mug of cold coffee on the kitchen counter. It was the maid's day off, she remembered, that's why the place looked unkempt.

Her muscles relaxed. I'm free she thought as she stepped into the living room and she experienced the sheer jubilation of that thought. I'm free, she thought, it's over. She stood in the middle of the floor, stock still for a moment, and then, throwing her arms wide above her head, she launched herself into the air.

'Yippee,' she shouted. 'Yippee!'

Over and over again she jumped, higher and higher, as her lungs expanded and her head grew dizzy. Still she kept on jumping and still she kept on shouting, revelling in this explosion of an energy that had been too long dammed. Higher and higher she jumped, until reaching the limit of her own ability, she suddenly flopped down. She was limp, dazed, purged of her celebration. She lay on the floor listening to herself gasping for breath.

By the time her breathing had calmed she was suffering badly from the heat. She walked over to the nearest window and flung it open. Outside it was as close as in, without a hint of a breeze, and with a heavy summer perfume hanging there, ready to insinuate itself into her synapses. She shut the window abruptly and thought longingly of the bedroom and its air conditioner. It beckoned at her, the cool and the bed with its crisp sheets, and sparkling white bedspread.

Why not? she thought. I can do what I want.

She walked towards it, aware only of how tired she suddenly felt, and it cost her an effort to make the tiny diversion necessary to switch on the air conditioner. When she had done that she breathed a sigh of relief, threw herself on to the bed and was asleep almost as soon as she closed her eyes.

*

26

She awoke four hours later. No soft wakening this, no gradual emergence into consciousness. She was hit instead by an abrupt, frightened alertness. Her body was covered in sweat. She gasped for breath, struggling her way out of sleep but dreading at the same time what awareness might bring her. I'm not alone, she almost screamed, I'm not alone.

She forced her eyes open. There was no one there, no one at all. The heat weighed down on her. The air conditioner, her brain dredged up the memory of it. She stumbled out of bed and made her way towards it. The air was thick around her, thick as egg yolk and cloying at her. She shook her head, shaking inertia from it, her thoughts jostling one upon the other in their effort to order themselves.

The air conditioner had a fail-safe mechanism, she remembered, in case an insect got trapped inside. She pulled the plug from its socket and poked her hand into the mechanism. Her hand came out black but when she replaced the plug, the machine whirred back into life.

She looked at the bed, at the cover on the floor and at the rumpled sheets. She had been dreaming, she realized. Memories of the dream had gone but they'd left a sour taste in her mouth, an apprehension that something had gone wrong, a premonition that she would be caught.

It was only a dream, she told herself. It woke me up because it was only a dream.

She turned away from the bed but stopped abruptly. The dream hadn't been what disturbed her – not the dream alone. A sound, that's what came into her head, a sound. The dream had not awakened her – loud banging had done that. She was suddenly overtaken by something stronger than fear – by absolute, relentless terror. She stood by her bedroom door, willing herself to move away from it but unable to do so. Somebody was outside, she knew that for the truth, somebody waiting to pounce on her.

Alan, she almost cried, where are you? Alan, come and help me.

Alan wasn't there. He'd warned her to keep away, had pleaded with her and shouted too in his attempt to stop her from volunteering. He couldn't help her now. She took a step and then another, and another until she had reached the kitchen.

She looked out of the kitchen window. Night had fallen while she slept, fallen abruptly as it did in this part of the world, wiping out both the brightness of the day and the red intensity of sunset. Suburban houses similar to hers flanked both sides, their welcoming lights illuminating their porches.

The terror no longer lingered, it was memory alone. It was my neighbour banging his car door, she thought, that's what woke me up. She did not know whether she believed the thought, but she no longer really cared. A door, an insect or something else had dragged her from sleep and now she was awake. She opened the fridge and felt the luxury of cold air hitting at her skin. She yawned and old sleep dragged down on her.

I'll have a shower, she thought. I'll feel better then.

She turned away from the fridge and walked back towards her bedroom. Halfway there she passed a low table and saw, lying on it, her airline ticket. She stopped and frowning picked it up. She had not remembered leaving it there, surely it should be elsewhere? She shrugged and opened it and saw, folded in it, the numbers of Jo'burg BA offices. They'd given her those, she remembered, in case she suddenly needed to change her flight, in case she had to get out quick. She looked at the paper idly and she thought for a moment of dialling one of the numbers. Her mission was over after all, she had no need to wait a further three days, and no inclination to act the tourist. She took a step towards the phone.

And then she laughed. It was too late to phone the office, they would be closed. And besides there was no point in changing the arrangements. She was tired, that was all, and unable to think logically. She had slept too early and awakened too abruptly. She would put the ticket away in the drawer where she should have stored it in the first place. If tomorrow she still felt inclined to go, she could do so.

In the meantime, she would have a shower, make a salad and then sit outside and savour the night.

CHAPTER FOUR

They had found Sarah Patterson. It had taken them days but they'd eventually found her.

Malan frowned as he scanned the surveillance reports. Nothing, nothing of use. She'd parked once in the general vicinity of a police station, but so what? She hadn't returned to it and neither had she done anything else suspicious. All she'd done, in fact, was go shopping, drive to Bryanston and then back to her rented house, and then sleep, eat and sleep again.

She wasn't in South Africa as a tourist, Malan was certain of that, but he was also certain that they'd found her too late. She was due to leave in a few days – booked on a BA flight to London. Her inaction must indicate that she'd already completed her mission.

Malan scrutinized the catalogue of her movements again. Bryanston, what the bloody hell was so enticing about Bryanston? This was the second report he'd received in as many weeks of a visit there – the second where all the visitor did was look and leave. Malan turned over the page. The man who'd been following Sarah was one of his finest, and if he said she'd done nothing of significance in Bryanston then Malan believed him. So her visit must have been pure nostalgia – made more sickening by the fact that it was somebody else's memories she had visited.

Psychological mumbo-jumbo, Malan thought and nodded to himself. His face cleared.

But then, pushing all thoughts of Bryanston away, he frowned once more. He had other, more pressing matters to consider. And the first of these – the question of why Patterson had entered the country – continued to nag at him. She was after all a side-kick, an onlooker in the theatre of revolution, not an actor. She should have stayed backstage.

Yet here she was in Jo'burg. It made no sense. And something else made no sense and it was more important – the question of why Malan hadn't known she was coming. He should have been warned. If his network had been functioning properly, he would have been warned.

Colonel Jansen's voice echoed distantly in his mind. What was it Jansen had said? Oh yes, Jansen had asked Malan if he was sure he could trust Zonda.

Malan thumped his hand hard down on his desk. Of course he could trust Zonda. His hand began to throb and as he waited for the anger and the pain to slowly drain away, he nodded his head. The same explanation came to him and he knew that it was right. Jansen was jealous of him and Jansen was trying to undermine him. Jansen was a politician who didn't know how to deal with men like Malan. Jansen was probably even a secret atheist, threatened by Malan's dedication to the church.

Yes, Malan thought, that's it. But then his smile faded. He could not afford to grow complacent, he must be on his toes. For something apart from Patterson was worrying him – something other. An 'other' that was hard to categorize because it also rested on silence, on a dearth of messages passed, on an uneasy quiescence that seemed to have descended on the country. Jansen would laugh at Malan for thinking so, but such a lack of action, such a passivity on the part of the armed wing of the ANC, convinced him that there was trouble brewing.

The only time things had been so comparatively quiet was before Sasol. Malan was haunted by a premonition that another Sasol was in the offing, that another explosion was about to throw the security forces into a state of confusion, a confusion that they could ill afford.

There was a knock at the door.

'*Kom,*' Malan growled.

A young policeman opened the door, stood on the threshold and saluted. Malan held out a hand. The policeman hurried forward and put a message in it.

Malan read the paper and scowled. 'Ag, I've got no time to see him now,' he snapped. 'Tell him I'll meet him at the usual place in two days' time.'

As the policeman left his office Malan leaned across and pulled a set of files closer. A sharp pain ran the length of his leg, followed by several more radiating twinges. Malan waited impatiently for the spasm to go: this was happening too often these days, he reflected – he must get Ingrid to arrange an appointment with his doctor.

The pain diminished as he had known it would. He opened the top file. Inside was a pile of photostats, photostats of photographs taken in different countries.

He glanced at the first in the series. It was of a youngish woman dressed in jeans and a simple blouse. She was smiling straight at the camera, a trifle nervous as if she was not quite sure what she was doing there. She was a pretty enough woman, the Captain supposed – if you liked that type. He did not like the type and neither did he need to read the caption. He knew her well enough – she was Sarah Patterson. He pushed the photo to the bottom of the pile.

The second picture was of two people caught in the same year as the first. Patterson was standing beside a young man, in the middle of a line of people. Captain Malan looked at the caption. 'London December 16th, 1980' it said.

'December 16th,' some idiot had added, 'is the commemoration of the founding of the ANC's army, Umkhonto we Sizwe.'

Malan studied the photo. The man was Alan Littell, Sarah's lover of (at that time) almost one year's standing. His mouth was open and his fist was up in the air, clenched in a militant salute. Acting, thought Malan, they're all actors. He moved on, flicking through the series. What he saw was a catalogue of Alan and Sarah – sometimes together, sometimes apart. He pushed Alan's face to the periphery of his vision and concentrated on Sarah. As he turned the photos over, reviewing almost ten years of pictorial documentation, he noticed something that he had previously missed – he noticed Sarah's right arm.

In 1980 it was firmly by her side. In 1981, when she stood by an open grave, it had made its way halfway to her shoulder as if it

31

were struggling for air. In 1984 the arm was raised but the fist incompletely closed. And in 1988 final victory: the fist was up there high and proud and this time it was firmly clenched. Her face had hardened for that last picture. Perhaps it was on that day, Malan thought, that she'd decided to commit herself.

Sarah Patterson: he cursed the name. She was a stupid woman, involving herself in affairs that did not concern her. Stupid, but she had cost him dear. It was she who had him doubting Zonda, who had him doubting the very basis of his work.

I have no other choice, he realized, I have to pick her up.

Jansen would object: Sarah was British and Jansen had issued instructions that, at this delicate juncture, foreign nationals, especially British nationals, should be handled with care. Jansen would object, but Malan was confident that he could override him.

That decided, Captain Malan jumbled the pictures of Sarah and Alan up and pushed them to one side. He was left with only one photo – a precious one taken in an ANC camp. A group picture this one and blurred. Malan let his eyes range along the line-up. Alan Littell, a determined outsider, had positioned himself as usual on the margins. He was staring, not at the camera, but at some point in the distance, his eyes unfocused, as if he was wishing himself elsewhere.

Malan's gaze was drawn towards the centre where Victor stood. A myth in MK, the ANC army, and the South African one as well, Victor was at the centre of some of MK's most daring deeds, a man supposedly as faithful to his own as he was a threat to his enemies.

Malan had never met Victor but he had seen him dead. He had found it hard to forget the expression on the corpse's face, that combination of pride and defiance, evident even after a hail of bullets had done their work.

Malan blinked. Standing to Victor's right was the man known only as Peter. A dark horse this one, a limited personality who did his job well. How well was evidenced by the rumour that Peter had long been operating inside the country and yet, despite the fact that there was this picture of him, he had not been caught.

He should have been, Malan thought. That was the trouble with the security game: one was always at the mercy of the incompetence of other branches of the police force.

Malan glanced to Victor's left. There stood Thabo Mjali – the one who got away.

Malan smiled. Thabo would be shocked at hearing himself so described. He was, after all, rotting on the Island. But Thabo should have been dead. The fact that he survived was pure bad luck – bad luck and not a little incompetence. Malan made a mental note to reiterate to the authorities his instruction that Thabo be carefully monitored.

Except, Malan thought, except it might be too late. He was assailed again by a premonition that something big was about to blow. The ANC, he was convinced, was on the move, preparing for something that could prove more embarrassing than the recent defiance campaign. He knew that he was right: knew it with all his might.

And yet he had no proof. The sense of frustration that descended on him every time he thought about it, made him want to scream.

He did not scream. The Captain was a man who never screamed. Instead he slowly inched his way up until he was standing, waited patiently until the spasm subsided into a bearable ache and then re-seated himself. He pushed the bell.

A uniformed policeman entered the room. 'Coffee,' Captain Malan said.

He waited until the man returned. When he was again alone, he took one slow sip, enjoying the first jolt of caffeine. This night of all nights he needed to be completely alert. He drank until he had finished and then he laid the cup carefully to one side.

CHAPTER FIVE

'Thabo Mjali,' Captain Malan wrote.

Racial Group: Black.
Age: 43
Present whereabouts: Robben Island.
Sentence: life.
Release date: –
Visitors: immediate family – sister, brother.

Malan stopped writing for a moment and considered the man. Mjali was a particularly dangerous brand of terrorist. He came not from a 'movement' family like so many in the ANC. Instead he'd been one of those politicized by Steve Biko's Black Consciousness Movement. All well and good – Malan had never considered Biko's outfit much of a threat. But then, after Biko died, Mjali had joined the ANC. That made him worth watching; he had his roots in two camps and he could help form a bridge between them.

He did just that, pulling his former allies into the ANC's army. He himself was sent for training, a man slightly too old for the camps and a man, therefore, who might be expected to rise in the hierarchy. Mjali, however, had never been made a commander. The reason, Malan conjectured, could have been that Mjali was too outspoken and, on top of that, his black consciousness roots might have made working with whites difficult. Whatever the reason, Mjali had not seemed unhappy to follow rather than to lead. A close friend of Victor's, he'd shown himself willing to obey instructions – not least on the day when he'd been captured.

Those were the bare bones of the man: those and the fact that he could expect to die in prison. Malan received sporadic reports on Mjali, the most recent saying that Mjali was growing increasingly preoccupied, maintaining a distance between himself and the warders and fellow prisoners alike.

Thabo, Malan suddenly thought, are you plotting against me? Is that why you're so preoccupied?

As soon as the bell had sounded Thabo Mjali had sunk into unconsciousness. On the Island the need to sleep (and therefore survive) was paramount. For in that desolate place life was hard. The prisoners had to be dragged from bed by alarms: by those and by the need to wash, dress and eat the lukewarm *mealie-pap* in a race against the *sjamboks*.

And yet Thabo didn't look as if he were securely asleep. He was lying down and his eyes were closed but his eyelids kept fluttering as if a battle was raging in his body. His left arm was flung out with violence, hitting at iron and flailing back on to his body again, a constant motion of unrest.

Thabo was dreaming but what he was experiencing was not merely a dream. It was a visitation, a sequence of events one after the other, a horrific and inevitable unfolding, from which he fought ineffectually to escape.

It started innocuously enough. At dawn in the country. The four of them together, his commander, Victor, and two others whose names he could not bring himself to remember. The two anonymous figures were leaving. Thabo and Victor stood by the door and watched them go, saw them walk awkwardly up the dirt track, shaking off sleep with every step. In the dream, Thabo, with a premonition of what was to come, nearly cried out to call them back but Victor stopped him.

Victor placed one hand lightly on Thabo's shoulder. 'To work,' he said, and then he shut the door.

To work! that's what Victor had said in real life, but in the dream Thabo knew that the work, the planning and the scheming, had already been done. It was Victor's fault. Thabo was not to blame. His arm jerked out again, protesting.

The dream moved on. Thabo watched himself walking down

35

the narrow paths, twisting and turning and finally reaching his destination. He watched his hand, a younger, uncalloused hand, remove a brick and stare into a cavern. He watched his young self smile at what he saw and, in watching, he knew that the smile would soon be banished. He watched helpless as he doubled back alert to any strange occurrence.

He did it by the book, he was sure he did. He was not to blame.

The final sequence of the dream arrived.

'No,' Thabo yelled.

Thabo in the dream did not shout, not then at least. Thabo in the dream walked on, quickening his pace as he neared the shack. Ten yards, that's all he had to overcome. Ten yards and the dream might end differently.

He couldn't manage that short distance. The time had come, within the dream, for him to shout.

'No!' he shouted, when the arms grabbed hold of him. 'No!' as a sack was tied around his head, 'No!' as he was pulled roughly back towards their house.

The sack was removed and he saw policemen gloating at the nearness of their victory. He saw them crawling to their holes, cocking their rifles, lifting their hands to hurl grenades at Victor.

And then the unexpected happened. Thabo heard the first gun firing, but it came not from the enemy but from the house. Victor was too smart for them! Victor had been prepared! Thabo heard a muffled sound and the man beside him fell, letting go of him, allowing for one short moment the thought that he could run to Victor, that together the two would fight until the end, that, in blood, they would leave a mark on their country that would never be obliterated.

Another hand pulled him back, a hand that forced his head towards the house, which made him watch as his commander was annihilated, shot and then burned to death.

Even though that was bad enough, the dream was not yet over. The worst was still to come. From the ashes of the house, Victor emerged. Victor with his head held high, still holding an AK. Victor in all his strength. Through the ranks of police Victor trod – alone, impregnable.

Through the ranks and up to Thabo he walked until he stopped in front of his comrade and held out his hand. That hand touched Thabo's shoulder and Thabo felt its warmth.

The dream fooled him, now, as it always did. 'You're alive,' the dreamlike Thabo told Victor.

Victor smiled. He opened his mouth. He said one word, not said it, but projected it across the field of death.

'Traitor,' he said and smiled again.

But this time, where once had been a mouth came only blood, gushing from an open wound. The hand gripped Thabo, not warm now but cold as ice. 'Traitor,' Victor said.

'No.' Thabo twisted and turned away from the touch, struggling to free himself from the accusation. The hand gripped down into his shoulder bone, it was stronger than he, it was possessed with the power that must have come straight from the devil.

'No,' Thabo screamed again. He grabbed the hand and wrenched it from him, pushing with all his might to rid himself. The pressure was suddenly released and he heard a bang.

'For God's sake,' a voice said.

He sat up abruptly. The dream had let go of him, he was no longer caught up in its ugly past. He was in his cell, on his bunk, looking down at a man on the floor. The other inmate was a short distance away, poised at the door, his hand raised to bang on the heavy steel.

'I had a dream,' Thabo said.

The man on the floor got up. He shook his head in sorrow. 'You had a dream,' he said. 'I tried to shake you out of it.'

'I'm sorry.' Thabo did not know where to look or what to say. 'I'm sorry.'

The man came up to him, held out his hand, but withdrew it when he saw how Thabo flinched.

Thabo turned to face the wall. He shut his eyes. 'I'm all right,' he muttered.

CHAPTER SIX

Captain Malan drew a line under his account of Thabo's life. He
tore off another sheet.

> 'Peter,' he wrote.
> Surname: unknown.
> Racial Group: Black.
> Age: mid thirties
> Present whereabouts: unknown? Transkei?
> Present Activities: Suspected courier.

Peter was waiting. His crossing had been trouble-free, and once in
Swaziland he was theoretically safe. But he did not feel secure.
The security police thought nothing of breaching the border in
pursuit of their quarry, and, on top of that, there was always the
possibility of encountering the Swazi police. They shot first and
asked questions later, especially of a man who stood so close to
the border in the dead of night. They were too untutored to
decode the message but they would more than likely hand it
straight over to the South Africans.

And that could mean disaster. Peter had been a courier for long
enough to guess when something was important. He knew that his
information was potential dynamite made more important by the
fact that he had sniffed out something else. An action was in
process, an important action – he was certain of it. The signs had
all been there: in the increased number of times that he was called
to guide new people into the country, in the accelerated pace of

38

correspondence, in the hint of urgency that infused the words of his commander.

He glanced at his watch and saw by its luminous dial that he had five minutes before he must turn back. Once safely on the other side he would get some sleep, he thought, and then return to base. If something big was up then he had better be prepared. He laughed to himself, imagining what it might be. Then he looked at his watch again. Three minutes left. They would go slowly if he was too conscious of them. He returned himself to his thoughts.

It had been a long time, he thought, since he had relaxed his guard, since he had spent an evening without once gazing at his watch. It had been years, as far back as his time in the camps. The faces and the names of his comrades there came flooding back to him. He had been the lucky one: he had lasted. Victor and Thembi were both dead, Thabo imprisoned, Wentworth . . . it was not worth thinking about Wentworth.

Yes, Peter, thought, I have been the luckiest of them all. Except, that is, for Alan Littell.

Peter had never liked Alan. The man pretended to be a comrade but he kept himself aloof. There was a part of Alan which was locked up, a cold calculating part. When Alan had sung with them, when he had joined into the dancing of the *toyi-toyi*, Peter had been watching. And he had come to a certain conclusion: Alan was not one of them, he was merely imitating them. Alan was not sincere. He wasn't.

But nobody would listen to Peter. Even after Alan destroyed Thembi, they refused to listen. HQ dismissed his observations lightly, joking about growing paranoia. When Peter pressed the point, HQ rebuffed him, implying that his criticism was a product of mere jealousy. The whole thing had done Peter's standing in the movement little good and he'd been forced to drop it. But now they would all have to listen for in his breast pocket lay the proof. He was finally vindicated.

Except that it was time and he must go. During their training they had many rules drilled into them, and the one about meetings had proved invaluable. 'Never stay longer than ten minutes after the deadline,' the instructor had said. 'To do so is to expose yourself.'

Peter had no choice. He would have to go. Heavily he turned, knowing in his heart that the information he had was vital. He took a step towards the border.

It was then that he heard the sound, a twig cracking from behind him. He whipped round in time to see a dark shadow emerging from a nearby screen of low scrub. Peter cursed. His contact must have been waiting there for some time, observing him. This was not good. Peter hoped the man wasn't going to report on him.

'About time,' Peter said.

His contact nodded and looked him square in the eyes. Peter glanced away but then, knowing that he was only piling further suspicion on himself, he forced his face into a bland neutrality, took the letter from under his pullover and thrust it at the other man.

'It's important,' he said. 'Immediate transmission.'

The contact nodded, received the letter and folding the envelope in two, put it in a trouser pocket.

'How's it going man?' he asked.

The tone was friendly and Peter relaxed. He shrugged. 'Not bad,' he said. He looked up at the sky, which was already losing its blackness. 'We better part,' he said.

The other nodded and held out his hand. Peter shook it rapidly in the three fold motion of the MK handshake. Then he walked away. But his lapse in the bush dogged him as he recrossed the border. He should have been watching more carefully. That was the trouble with personal grudges, they took your mind away from the essentials.

Well, Peter could now forget Alan. He had done his duty, it was up to them to decide.

CHAPTER SEVEN

The first glimmers of daylight were pushing through the darkness by the time that Captain Malan had finished with Peter. His search had been unsuccessful. He had trawled through all the files, searching for clues, for something, anything that might pin-point Peter's whereabouts, but had failed. Now the sun was about to rise and he must stop. He placed Peter's file on top of the others and turned back to his pad.

'Alan Littell,' he wrote.
Racial Group: White
Age: 35
Present whereabouts: Tanzania? (refer to TS/AL/351/B)
Present activities: ???

He didn't bother writing more. He could have, he could have written a book, because of all files in his possession he had studied Alan Littell's the hardest. There was no reason to add to what had been written, no reason at all.

Alan Littell was dangerous, that much was clear.

Malan had studied Alan but it was a long time since he'd read Alan's life in Alan's words. Perhaps, he thought, perhaps now's the time to look at it again. Perhaps it will teach me something.

From the back of Littell's file he withdrew a photocopy, yellowing with age. He could no longer remember how he had obtained it – through some junior in the London office, he supposed, life histories being amongst the easiest items to get hold of. He cast his eye down the first few lines:

Name: *Alan Littell*
Date: *16 June 1980*
Subject: *Life History*

He smiled grimly to himself. It came flooding back to him, the memory of this document – its confessional style, its flowery use of language and its *näveté*, which bordered on the pathetic. The whole thing reminded Malan suddenly of the old days – neither better nor worse, those days, but more predictable.

And Alan Littell's biography, written during those times, was certainly predictable. Malan closed his eyes and tried to remember how it had begun. Oh yes, he had it: 'I was born.' That's how it started.

He looked to the text:

'*I was born in a country that was not mine,*' he read, '*and this simple fact has haunted me for most of my life.*'

Malan sighed and moved on to the second paragraph. '*I realise how this might sound,*' he read. '*I know only too well how strange it must seem that I, a white South African, an educated white South African should say that South Africa never belonged to me. And yet it is true. Until the day that I finally made my choice, the day that led me to the writing of this statement, I had never felt part of South Africa: I simply never felt that I belonged.*'

Malan sniggered. That's how progressive whites had talked in those days – about belonging and not belonging. Next would come the philosophical gloss, straight out of NUSAS-speak.

'*Perhaps this fact*', Malan read, '*is at the core of the tragedy of our country, that many feel as I have done and yet few can admit to it.*'

It was worse than he had remembered, and even more self-indulgent. And what kind of biography was it anyway? Where were the facts? He turned the page.

At last: '*I was born in 1954 in Mayfair, Johannesburg.*'

Now the bit to start the tears flowing: '*I never knew my mother – she died giving birth to me. I lived for my first twelve years with my father, and my experience of him was of an almost total absence of contact.*'

That's a good one, Malan thought. He let his eyes run down

the page. Mayfair, Johannesburg, that's where Littell had been born – a place that Littell grandly called, *'not a pale imitation of its London namesake but instead its very opposite, its dark side.'*

That means, Malan thought, that Littell was poor and that he hated being poor. Poor and English in an Afrikaners' suburb. Listen to this: *'I lived alone with a father who could never throw off the shadows of his own misery. We were surrounded by other poor whites: Afrikaans speakers for the most part, whose only rallying point was rancour at the wealth of our country, so near and so unobtainable.'*

The next paragraph was so syrupy it made Malan sick. *'My father never raised a hand against me,'* Alan had written, *'his was the sin of omission rather than of ill treatment. For the most part, he left me to my own devices. He made sure that I was clothed and fed; as I grew older, we would share the labour of the house – such as it was. We lived in what can only be described as squalor.'*

The details of their income or lack of it came as a relief after that. Littell skirted the minutiae, while making it clear that his father was a failure, working only when the landlord threatened to evict them and getting sacked as soon as the threat had passed.

But Alan Littell, the young saint, managed to preserve his sanity throughout all this.

'Not that I was bitter – I left that to my father. He blamed the world for his troubles, kaffirs, *Boers, Jews and above all his own countrymen – the English who had abandoned him.'*

At first the young Alan spent time on the street, furious at his difficult father, but the mature Alan had found the resources to forgive. *'Looking back on it,'* he wrote, *'I suppose that my father's problems could have been physical rather than psychological. He suffered from continual ill-health and our circumstances did not allow us to seek competent medical treatment. In addition, my father had an unnatural fear of doctors, caused perhaps by my mother's death. He would dismiss any concern I might express as to his extended bouts of coughing, choosing to rise from his sick bed and stumble uselessly around the house rather than subject himself to my anxiety. As a result I stopped thinking about his mortality.'*

And now for the punch line, Malan thought: *'His death, which occurred when I was just twelve years old, came as somewhat of a surprise.'*

A surprise, Malan thought — that's one way of putting it.

His smile faded as he read the next phase of Littell's life.

'I loved my father: he was all I had, and yet of those first days following his demise I can only remember the fear about what would happen to me.'

The twelve-year-old Alan, Malan read, had wanted to stay in Mayfair. But the twelve year old was not consulted.

'The decision was made that I should go and live with Jack and Girlie Howard. And so I was summarily removed from my environment and taken to Bryanston.

'I now know that by white South African standards the Howard's house is not particularly ostentatious. But at the time it dazzled me. I was desperately unhappy, at sea in this bright new world and the Howards' behaviour did not help. I experienced the sensation of being an alien and my every move seemed to provoke irritation concealed behind seemingly endless forbearance.

They were probably like Jansen, thought Malan, and the first twinges of sympathy for Alan Littell entered his consciousness. He pushed them aside.

Not that I blame Jack and Girlie,' he read. *'They were kindness itself and they did what they thought right. And, in a way, I am grateful to them for their care, and indeed their love. They were a childless couple who tried to pour into me all their ambitions to raise another human being. What happened subsequently could be said to be their fault and yet they had no other choice. They were merely, I was later to understand, trapped in the South African dilemma as surely as were the bigots of Mayfair. . .'*

Malan's patience was at an end. Feeling slightly disgusted with himself he shoved Alan's autobiography away. He no longer knew why he'd bothered to read it: the last thing he needed at this point was to feel sorry for one of his suspects.

He arched his back. From somewhere, from a distant place, something screamed a protest. He twisted his wrist and glanced at his watch, seeing what he had not been conscious of because his blinds were drawn.

It was daylight already and he had not slept.

Pushing himself upright, he inched his way towards the door. He would get home to Ingrid, take a few hours' sleep, wash, shave and then visit his doctor on his route to work. The files could stay lying there until then. He had time.

Day One

CHAPTER EIGHT

Zambia

There is a room located near to Lusaka's open-air market. On the day that Peter's message arrived, the windows of that room were closed: closed as a security precaution although this had the added advantage of blocking the stench of urine from the streets. It was not so easy to get rid of the noise. In the distance came the sound of methodical banging as someone hammered tin sheeting into the shape of a roof: superimposed on this were two women's voices raised in shrill acrimony.

A man, his gait unsteady, one hand gripping a bottle of Castle beer, climbed the stairs towards the room. It was dark on the stairway and when he reached the first landing he missed his footing. He fell and his beer fell with him. Cursing wildly he felt around for it.

A light clicked on.

The drunk looked up startled. At the top of the next flight he could just make out the shape of a young man – the details obscured by the fact that this man was in darkness, whereas a 100-watt light bulb was shining directly into the eyes of the drunk.

The drunk shaded his face with one hand. 'Greetings, my "bro",' he said weakly.

The man above him shook his head. Once only.

The drunk got unsteadily to his feet, holding his beer high. 'Share and share alike,' he said.

The young man moved towards the drunk. His action was almost imperceptible but there was something in his manner that made the drunk suddenly afraid. Dropping the bottle he stumbled

49

down the stairs, back towards the safety of daylight. The bottle came clattering after him but he did not stop for it.

If he had, and if he had looked back, he would have seen the young man had returned to his post. He would have seen the young man lean against the crumbling wall, his eyes seemingly closed. And perhaps even the drunk would have known that the man's slumped posture hid the presence of an automatic weapon and that his drooped eyelids masked an alert state of watchfulness. His job was to guard the room.

Inside the room the air was thick with smoke. The people in the room ignored the sounds outside: they focused instead on each other and on their collective need to reach a decision. They were surrounded by files to which they each continually referred, searching the paper as if therein lay the answer.

In front of each of them lay a single sheet of paper, an identical photocopy of the message which Peter had sent to Headquarters. The message was what had prompted this meeting. One message which had the power to pull the group from everyday concerns; from meetings, dreams and petty squabbling. Eyes kept being drawn to it.

'*Theo walked down the Bryanston street,*' it read. '*My contact saw him turn and bump deliberately into a man. Second man identified by my contact as known police agent. Contact witnessed an exchange of envelopes before the two men parted. Theo drove to a bar and spent some time there. Contact not in position to further pursue.*'

They all knew of Theo's identity – they had been told of that. Theo was Alan Littell. Alan, a member of MK, recently out of South Africa, a man that they needed badly to trust. And they all knew something else. They knew that if what Peter's contact had seen was accurate, and if Alan Littell was indeed an enemy agent, then *La Valenta* must be recalled.

La Valenta, the brave, an apt name. *La Valenta* a boat carrying what might be the last of the ANC's active combatants into the country. Combatants not only of the highest calibre but men chosen for their wiliness and for their patience as well. Forty trained soldiers sent not to start a war, but to sit and watch for the first signs of one. Forty men who would not lose their combat readiness and who would never, ever betray their role. Men charged with the duty of forming an underground so deep that even their closest comrades would never learn of its existence. Forty men whose job might one day be to safeguard the future of their country: who would build resistance in case de Klerk's uneasy smile slipped to the glint of a fox.

In that room above the market there were differences of opinion about the boat and the purpose for which it was being used. But in that room, no matter what each person felt of the boat, they all agreed on one thing. If someone had betrayed them, if the boat was exposed as it entered South African waters, then the ANC would be plunged into a chasm so deep that it might never emerge. If the boat failed, no not failed, if the boat was intercepted by the regime it would bring demoralization, disorder and international disapproval.

The chairman, a member of the ANC's national executive council, cleared his throat. 'We have three possibilities,' he said. 'Number one,' he held up an index finger. 'Comrade Peter's contact is mistaken.'

A second finger joined the first. 'Number two, Comrade Peter's report is accurate but there is an innocent explanation for Alan Littell's behaviour.'

'Number three,' a third finger was raised. 'Comrade Peter's report is accurate and Alan Littell is working for the enemy. In which case . . .' he turned the three fingers towards his forehead and made a clicking sound with his teeth. He did not smile.

'We are in the process', he continued, 'of checking with Comrade Peter the reliability of his report. We know that Alan was recently in South Africa – he left there a day ago and is now in Dar. What we don't know is what Alan was doing in Bryanston. So shall we start with the second option? He was there on our behalf.'

'Impossible.' The man from security didn't even bother to look up. 'The meeting was accidental?'

The man from the military shook his head glumly. He held up one of his many pieces of paper. 'All combatants are required to report fully on their activities inside the country,' he said. 'In his last report Comrade Alan didn't mention he'd visited Bryanston.'

The man from security sucked at his teeth, loud enough for them all to hear.

His counterpart in the military responded indirectly. 'We must guard against a tendency to condemn our cadres without proper evidence,' he said sternly. 'What we have here is a report of an apparent exchange of envelopes: dubious evidence on which to condemn a man.'

Battle had been joined.

The man from security lifted a file and brandished it in the air. 'Comrades,' he replied, 'this is not personal. I am merely doing the job with which I was entrusted.' He slapped the file down hard on the table. 'We know that this is not the first time that Alan Littell has come under scrutiny,' he said and paused as he looked around at each of his companions in turn. Having got their complete attention he dropped his voice. 'We know that matters have gone as far as a trial,' he concluded.

'But Wentworth was proved to be the spy.' Despite her resolution to keep out of this age-old battle Zandile found herself protesting vehemently. She lowered her voice. 'Wentworth admitted as much,' she said.

The man from security grimaced. 'They sometimes send them in pairs,' he said. 'We've had cases where ten men from one small town were enemy agents – a group like that backs each member up, making it almost impossible to check their life histories.' He grabbed the file and waved it in the air again. 'There are several other unexplained leaks, all of which have, in some way, involved Alan Littell.'

'And many successful missions involving him,' the man from the military said.

Quickly was the reply delivered, 'Which could equally mean that his masters are protecting him.'

'Deadlock,' said someone in the room, someone who preferred not to claim his words. There was silence. The chairman shook his head.

'How much does Alan know?' Zandile asked.

'Officially he's been told enough to cause anxiety,' the security man replied and his tone was even, 'although we could still control the situation. But unofficially, if he is a spy, he might have gathered enough to hang us all.' He started to tap his fingers on the scratched wooden surface of the table.

52

'Not us,' Zandile thought, 'but forty of our men.' As the tapping filled the room she knew that every person in it was thinking something similar. If Alan Littell was a traitor, if Alan Littell had betrayed the movement then . . . no, it was too painful even to contemplate.

'Ag this boat's a blerry waste of time,' the man from security suddenly exploded with wrath. 'And it's dangerous as well. We never should have committed ourselves to it.'

'What would you like us to do? Take de Klerk at his word? Lie down and wait for him to kick us? Give up because the *baas* seems to be having a change of mind?'

The security man glared across the table and began to rise, his breath coming rapidly. Zandile shivered.

'Comrades, enough.' Their chairman's voice rose over the room so loudly that even the din from outside seemed momentarily to abate. He dropped his voice slightly. 'We have made a decision on the boat,' he said. 'And we will, as usual, stick by our democratic decisions. Let us not waste time: let's explore the overall picture. Beginning with Alan's training.' He looked slowly around him. 'Who was Alan close to and where are they now?'

The man from security resettled himself and opened a file. 'Comrade Victor was his commander,' he said, as he tapped on the table. 'He was killed in action. Others include: Comrade Thabo, on Robben Island; Comrade Peter, underground; Comrade Thembi, no longer with us. Robert Wentworth,' he looked up from the file and his eyes flickered around the table, registering each of his companions. 'We all know what happened to Wentworth.' He began to tap again, drumming out a message of disaster. 'Littell's former instructor', he continued, 'is in Angola and the lines of communication are down. There are not many others: Littell has always been a loner.' He closed his file. 'But of course,' he said quietly. 'There's Sarah Patterson.'

Although his voice was carefully neutral, his meaning was clear. He had been against sending Sarah into the country, arguing that she was ill suited for the task and that, furthermore, she was too emotionally involved with Littell. He had only agreed after a considerable amount of pressure had been brought to bear.

'It doesn't look good,' he concluded.

'What about Alan's autobiography?' the chairman asked.

The man from security pulled some papers from the file. 'There are two,' he said. 'The first dating from the time of his entry to MK and the second written during the last trial. We could find no contradictions between the two, no evidence at all against Littell – except for the fact that somebody betrayed Victor. We assumed that somebody was Wentworth.'

'Is Littell well liked amongst the men?' This from the man from the national executive.

'Some like him,' the man from the military said quickly, 'some don't. Comrade Peter didn't.

'So it could be a private vendetta,' Zandile interjected.

'Comrade Peter is one of our best couriers,' the man from the military said glumly. 'We have never been given cause to doubt him.'

The chairman turned to Zandile. 'When does *La Valenta* leave?' he asked.

'Tomorrow.'

'And it will take five days to get there?' He didn't wait for confirmation. 'Can it be recalled at any moment?'

Zandile nodded. 'Communication will be open until almost the last hours. After that comrades inside will be in radio contact.'

'What happens if we delay for a week?'

Zandile shook her head. 'It would have to be at least another month,' she said. 'The tides must be right. And we'd also have to recall the insiders, which would lead to all kinds of complications. It's possible but let's not pretend it won't be difficult.'

The chairman looked around the table. When nobody spoke he took one last drag of his cigarette and made as if to stub it out. But then he changed his mind, reaching instead for another from the pack, and lighting it on the old. Only then did he speak.

'I think it is agreed that we must take Comrade Peter's message seriously,' he said. 'We cannot afford to jeopardize the mission by ignoring it. In addition I hope it is understood that we will recall the boat rather than risk the lives of more than forty of our men.' Murmurs of assent greeted his statement. He lowered the cigarette. 'On the other hand,' he continued, 'this mission is important. We only abort it if we have to. Which leaves us, I think, with one option. I'd like to suggest that we launch *La Valenta* as planned and at the same time urgently explore all avenues. That means we must convene a tribunal of inquiry into Comrade Peter's allegation, and investigate Alan Littell. The time is short: we have six days to decide. It should be enough.'

He looked around the room, waiting for comment. None came. 'I take silence as consent,' he said. 'Which means we should move immediately to the appointment of the members of the tribunal, locate and detain Alan Littell, and begin the collation of evidence. I will now entertain suggestions as to the head of the Tribunal.'

A silence descended on the room. From one side of the table a name was muttered but quickly withdrawn. Each of the occupants of the room was sorting through the lists in their head, cancelling those who were too far away, or too busy, too hasty in their decisions, or too slow.

'Rebecca Moisia,' Zandile suggested.

'It should be someone from security,' the man from security interjected. 'This is too important to risk on a beginner.'

'Comrade Rebecca is hardly a beginner,' Zandile protested.

The man from security shrugged. 'Her field is administration,' he said. 'She's a former schoolteacher.'

'Who runs a department,' Zandile protested again.

'A sub-department of the department of information,' the man from security corrected. 'Hardly training in combat is it? We need somebody with real experience.'

The chairman held up his hand. 'At our last conference,' he said, 'we passed a resolution saying that, in the interests of fair play, members of tribunals should no longer be drawn from the ranks of our security section. We must abide by this resolution, even in a case as pressing as this one. Only by remaining true to it can we safeguard the democracy of our movement. Security will, of course, be consulted throughout.'

The man from security held his tongue.

'I second the name put forward by Comrade Zandile,' the man from the military said.

'Any objections?' the chairman asked. 'Any further nominations?'

He waited a beat and then he levered himself up, stubbing his butt into the overflowing ashtray. 'We're agreed then,' he said. 'In future communications on this matter are an absolute priority – all sections to be informed. I will inform Comrade Rebecca of our decision. Now we must select the other members of the tribunal.'

Having done that the chairman coughed hard again and then, bent almost double, he walked from the room. As Zandile followed him she felt a hand on her shoulder. She turned and smiled.

'A good suggestion,' the man from the military said. 'Rebecca is a just person. She will do the job well. Thank you.'

'I hope Rebecca thanks me,' Zandile joked.

The man did not smile. 'I hope she makes the right decision,' were his parting words.

The suitcase landed on the floor with a dull thud. Its contents spilled chaotically out.

'Stupid,' Rebecca Moisia said. She gritted her teeth in an attempt at self-control. With her clipboard wedged firmly under one arm, she stuffed the errant clothes back into the case and then continued to pack. Every now and then she would stop and add to the list on the board.

Shortly afterwards she tripped and dropped another armload of clothes. She stamped one foot hard on the ground knowing as she did so that the dropping of clothes was irrelevant. Her anger came from elsewhere: she had been furious ever since they had pulled her out of her briefing session. They had no right and no consideration. If they'd at least given her some notice she might have been able to impose a rough semblance of order on her department. But no, the leadership had insisted that she leave immediately. She had had no time to delegate tasks, to check and double check that they could manage without her, to try and lessen the sense of abandonment her staff would surely experience. And more important than all this was her certain knowledge that she was unsuited to this new job. She was an administrator, not a judge; a middle-ranking cadre who dealt in newspapers and the certainty of the printed not in the murky possibilities of betrayal.

She grew more furious as she thought of it. If only they would leave her alone to get on with the job to which she had been appointed. That was the trouble with the movement: there was altogether too much switching and changing. No one was ever allowed to develop a field of expertise.

'Stationery,' she thought. She added the word to her list and then immediately crossed it out. She went over to her desk and opened a drawer, pulling a precious ream of blank paper from it. This she thrust into her suitcase, resentfully, but with resolution. There was no telling under what conditions this investigation would take place. She had learned from bitter experience never to take anything for granted and never to travel unprepared.

As she bent to retrieve the fallen clothes there was a tap on the door.

'Enter,' she instructed.

Zandile walked in. 'Packing?'

Rebecca sighed. 'We're going to have to work day and night,' she said. She stood up. 'So I thought I'd take a few changes of clothes.'

They're very unlikely to have any woman's available there,' Zandile commented.

That's all I need, Rebecca thought. Zandile's scoring another point in her battle against men. Rebecca did not voice her thoughts. She was in no mood to start up their old argument. Zandile's obsession was boring and, as far as Rebecca was concerned, destructive at this point in their struggle.

'I'm glad you were chosen,' Zandile said.

Because I'm a woman, Rebecca thought. Once more she bit back a bruising reply. It isn't Zandile's fault that I've been chosen, she thought. It isn't anybody's fault. Except perhaps Alan Littell's.

She guillotined the thought. She must not even contemplate this possibility: not yet, not before she had the facts. 'I'm in a hurry,' she said briskly.

Zandile dropped a sheaf of papers on Rebecca's single bed. 'Alan Littell's first biography,' she said. 'Plus other background material.'

Rebecca nodded.

'And I thought you might be interested in the names of your fellow tribunal members,' Zandile said. 'Albert Kana is one . . .'

Albert Kana, thought Rebecca, an uninspired choice, although not a disastrous one. Albert was one of the old guard, a stalwart who was at least methodical in his thinking even if a trifle slow.

'. . . Dlamini the other,' Zandile concluded.

Rebecca shivered. 'Dlamini? Not Jabulani Dlamini?'

'Yes,' Zandile's voice faltered under Rebecca's glare. 'Jabulani. He will act as NEC observer and give advice when necessary. Don't you think he's up to it?

'Oh, Jabulani's clever enough,' Rebecca said bitterly. And then, even though Zandile was still watching her, she closed her eyes. She closed her eyes and remembered when she had last spent time with Jabulani. She remembered the tenderness that had grown between them and the recriminations that had followed. She remembered, oh so clearly, the look on Jabulani's face when she ordered him out of her bed, out of her room, out of her life.

She remembered it all as if it had happened yesterday. But it was years ago and their paths had crossed only temporarily since then. Now they would be together, alone, isolated, unable to get away. She shivered again. She opened her eyes and glared at Zandile, who was standing there foolishly opening and closing her mouth.

Get out, Rebecca nearly said. But she stopped herself. Zandile could not know what had happened between herself and Jabulani and Zandile was, after all, a friend.

'A terrible thing to happen,' Rebecca said sympathetically.

'If it has happened,' was Zandile's reply.

'Do you mean . . .?' Rebecca stopped in mid-sentence. What was she thinking of? She should not discuss the case before it had even started. She looked at her watch. 'I've got twenty minutes before my car arrives,' she said. 'I might as well make a start with these.'

Zandile nodded and smiled wanly. 'Can I do anything?'

Rebecca thrust the clipboard at Zandile. 'Take this to my department if you don't mind: it's the proof of our next editorial.

On the changes in press freedom. Ask them to make at least an attempt to stick to it, will you?'

She sat on her bed and picked up the first of the papers. She was already reading when Zandile closed the door.

CHAPTER NINE

Tanzania

Dar es Salaam, Tanzania: a house on the outskirts of the city. A shabby, sprawling house in an area that had once, long ago, known better times. A house like all its neighbours, with overgrown bougainvillaea cascading down a broken fence; a house whose doors and windows were open wide for ventilation; a house guarded by a banana tree, whose tattered green fronds dropped over a crumbled concrete veranda. In that house were seven men, all ANC members, all members of the ANC's army, all waiting for further instructions. And one of them was Alan Littell.

Alan was seated by a table just inside the house. He was surrounded by his companions but isolated from them. A couple of them were dozing on the floor beside him, another was by the window cleaning his gun and the remaining three were on the veranda absorbed in an edgy card game. Alan knew none of his comrades would take kindly to being disturbed and so he suppressed his rising whoop of joy. He settled for a wide, and private, smile.

He glanced down at the photos he had spread in front of him – photos of four men. I've got you, he thought, I've got you. He'd finally done it: he'd unmasked them. They'd been clever (or their masters had), but no one can escape detection forever. The evidence, all stored in Alan's mind, was incontrovertible.

Four of them and Alan alone knew it. He sat quite still and smiled at the beauty of it. He held their fates in the palm of his hand. He had tracked them down, worked out where they stayed, how they co-operated, whom they had betrayed. He had them.

He smiled and tore their photographs into tiny pieces, which he scattered in the waste paper bin. He felt little sympathy for the men. They were contemptible, he thought, betraying friends for chicken feed, trapped by their own weaknesses and keeping each other company so that they would never have to face themselves. I should set fire to these pieces, he thought, as he looked down.

The bin was metal and when he kicked out at it, it fell on to the wooden floor with a resounding bang.

The men in the house acted instinctively. The one who had been cleaning his gun turned, dropped to one knee and zeroed in on the doorway. At the same time one of the sleeping men grabbed his gun from under his shirt, jumped straight upwards with it in hand and started to turn around the room, aiming it in all directions, half asleep but ready to fire.

The three on the veranda, the card players, saw what might happen and ducked. From under the table one of them called.

'Comrades: all clear,' he shouted.

Both men inside dropped their guns by their sides and both smiled a trifle sheepishly. They were all too trigger-happy, they told themselves, unused to being armed in Tanzania.

Alan sat still, completely still. A bead of sweat trickled from his hair onto his forehead, and then down his nose to hang suspended at its end. He made no move to wipe it away. Despite the smiles the men would be angry: he knew as well as they that it was not only unwise but also dangerous to kick a metal bin.

But Alan was saved from their wrath. From the floor a sleepy voice spoke. 'What's happening?' The bewilderment in the voice was palpable.

One of the card players rose to his feet. 'Ag, man, lucky it wasn't the Boers,' he said. 'You could sleep your way through a full-scale invasion.'

The card player laughed and then all the men joined him, Alan included, laughing at the comical expression on the face of their comrade on the floor, and laughing, as well, to expel their fear. They laughed together, boisterously, and the more they laughed, the more they each stoked the others' laughter.

They laughed themselves into a shared joy and then over into the other side: into sorrow. Their laughter rose into the air, high up into a roof which had once been timber and was now tin, rising until it reached a peak. And then abruptly their laughter subsided. In the silence that followed they looked at each other, slightly ashamed, and when they looked at each other it was difficult to know whether the tears on their faces came from happiness or from a profound well of pain.

Someone's foot sounded on the path.

It's for me, Alan thought, before he even had time to look up.

A figure appeared on the veranda steps, a figure pursued by another and both blocked out the sun.

It's for me, Alan thought, as he watched two men, two men from security, standing in the doorway. It's for me, he thought, as the man on the left gestured to him.

'Please come with us, comrade,' said the man.

Then and only then did Alan experience shock.

The motor boat had stopped only for the briefest time before speeding away. Its driver had told Alan to wait, saying that transport wasn't yet available and that he'd be picked up by the road in a couple of hours' time. Alan hadn't asked for any further details. He had rolled up his trousers, got out of the boat, waded through the warm water, and onto the land. He hadn't asked and neither had he turned when the motor revved up again. He'd let the boat go without a parting word, he'd waited in fact for it to go.

He needed to think. He needed to be alone.

He could not, however, shake off the feeling that he was not alone. He looked around him. On the beach no living thing stirred. In the distance he could see the lights of a restaurant and occasionally a fragment of conversation drifted along the blackness and reached his ear distorted. No other sounds, save perhaps the sudden rustling of a palm leaf in the breeze, were discernible.

And yet Alan still felt himself observed.

It wasn't possible. His brief journey by sea must have jangled his nerves – that after all was the point of it, that's why they had chosen this route when the road would have been so much quicker. They were trying to disorient him and it was working: he was imagining things. It had happened to him before, it was inevitable and one had to learn to expect it. In two hours, he told himself, I will be picked up and in two hours it will all become clear.

He walked up the beach towards the light. When he reached the glass doors of the restaurant his gaze was pulled inside. There were couples seated there, laughing, happy couples. Alan stared at them as if he were once more a child, a child glimpsing a lifestyle that he never would attain.

Sarah. Her face came to him suddenly.

He missed her so. What he wouldn't give to have her here, to be sitting at the restaurant laughing and joking as if they had not a care in the world.

He shook himself, walked around the glass until he found the door and then he entered. Leaving the jollity behind him, he walked through the restaurant and into the reception area. There was a telephone there, tempting him. He walked straight past it.

But before he could leave the place, he felt himself pulled back, unable to resist the phone. Like a man in a dream he went to it, picked up the receiver and began to dial. One digit, two digits, three — each one bringing him closer to Sarah. He hit another number. He paused.

It was no good. He must not phone her. He replaced the receiver and walked quickly away, out of the place, through the parking lot and to the road. Once there, he sat on a low wall, put his head in his hands and began to wait.

They picked him up an hour later, three of them in a jeep. They treated him politely but they did not look him in the face. When he asked where they were going, they shrugged. When he requested that they stop they complied, but got out with him and waited until he had relieved himself. Their attitude to him was one of deliberate neutrality, neutrality tinged with suspicion. He did not try to make conversation, not even to draw out from them their destination. He leaned back and closed his eyes.

The road was bumpy and Alan couldn't be sure whether it was this fact alone that kept him awake – or whether he was right to suspect that, every time he was about to drop off, the man next to him jogged at his elbow. He gave up on sleep. He opened his eyes but didn't bother trying to identify landmarks. Tanzania was unfamiliar to him and, besides, the sky had clouded over and the night covered everything with its dull black shadow.

The journey stretched on into time. They drove down dirt tracks, weaving their way so as to avoid obstacles in their path, ploughing across an empty land. They had come well prepared, and at one point they stopped and poured petrol from a can in the back into the tank. Alan's apprehension intensified, but he forced his breath into a semblance of regularity. If this was an endurance test, well, then he would survive it. He would be prepared.

And then they stopped abruptly. At a nod from the driver, Alan got out. He stretched and looked around him. Directly in front of him were three low buildings, rudimentary constructions made from corrugated iron, which stood alone in what seemed an otherwise empty landscape. The terrain was flat, extending into the distance, flat and brown with only the occasional, low plane tree and the ugly electricity cables, breaking the monotony. Except, Alan suddenly realized, he was wrong: the land was not empty. Behind the three buildings, almost concealed from sight, were tents laid out in neat rows. There were even signs of elementary horticulture – patches of land fenced off from the rest. Inside them green shoots were pushing their way to life.

Alan rubbed his eyes. He wasn't used to missing such obvious detail, he must be more tired than he realized. He yawned and looked to the horizon. The night was almost over and the sun was beginning to rise. He felt no joy at the impending end of his long night.

He heard the jeep start up again and he resisted the urge to turn and call it back.

'Pull yourself together,' he said out loud.

As the word 'together' sounded in the night the door of the

central building opened. A woman appeared. He recognized her immediately although he didn't know her well. She was Rebecca Moisia, a middle ranking member of the ANC, a woman renowned for her dedication and her toughness. He remembered her not only because she was well known but also because of what she'd once said about Thembi.

He must truly be tired to think of that. He straightened his back and watched as she headed straight for him.

'Welcome, comrade,' she said. Her face was stern. 'If you wouldn't mind following me.'

'Comrade' she'd called him – then it couldn't be that bad. He walked behind her, feeling the cramp drift from his muscles. And with this sign of life returning, came anger. How dare they treat him like this? How dare they? The boat, the wait on the beach, all had been part of a ridiculous charade meant to break him down. And why him? He had done nothing wrong.

Nothing except . . .

He had hidden his knowledge of the four traitors, that's what this must be about. This idea, and it must be the right one, brought with it not fear, but a warm feeling of consolation. He had hidden their names, and of course that had been wrong. But it was an error easily remedied. His explanation – that he had wanted to be sure – would eventually be accepted and then how impressed they would be by what he'd done.

'Close the door,' a voice instructed.

The voice was rude and Alan's anger returned. He knew it was misplaced and, worse, that it was destructive: it would only bring him further trouble. Taking a deep breath, he shut the door. Calm down, he thought.

He had meant to project an unperturbed air but when he turned towards them a bright light seared through his fatigue, partially blinding him. His eyes shut automatically. Holding an arm up to shade himself he forced them open again.

The light was switched off. He blinked and readjusted to the gloom. He saw that Rebecca was seated in the centre of a long table. She was flanked on either side by men, grim, unsmiling men.

She stood up. 'My name is Rebecca Moisia,' she said. 'My companions are Comrades Jabulani Dlamini and Albert Kana. We are here to ask you some questions.'

From her tone Alan knew that the questions would not be about the traitors, that they would instead be about him. This should have come as no surprise, it was the inevitable end to the journey. And yet Alan did feel surprise. Surprise and self-contempt. He realized that, throughout the long journey, he had been nursing hope. Hope that there was another explanation for the catalogue of events, hope that there was no foundation for his fears.

'Questions, yes,' he said.

'You're not surprised?'

He shrugged. 'This isn't the first time that this has happened to me,' he reminded them.

'And does this make you angry?' The man Rebecca called Comrade Kana asked.

'I'm too tired to be angry,' Alan said. He looked around him pointedly.

There was a chair standing by the door. Without asking for permission Alan walked over to it and picked it up. He took it to the centre of the room and then he sat on it. That felt better. He smiled.

'You find us funny?' Albert Kana asked.

'Comrade,' Alan addressed himself to Rebecca. 'Am I on trial for my sense of humour?'

'You think you are on trial?'

'Am I not?'

She looked down. Only after what seemed like an eternity did she speak. 'You were recently sent home to re-locate some supplies,' she said. 'You have written an account of your actions whilst in the country. Do you have anything further to add?'

The question ambushed him. 'No,' he said. His answer came fast, too fast.

'Think, comrade,' Rebecca suggested. Her tone was deliberately gentle. 'Think before you answer.'

Alan frowned. In his mind's eye he saw his report as if it were spread out in front of him. He saw it, every word as he had written it, laid out chronologically, exactly as he had been taught

66

to do it. It was accurate, he was certain of it. He had left nothing of significance untold. He shook his head.

'Kindly tell us what you did while in the country,' Rebecca said.

He looked her straight in the face, cutting the other two men out of his vision, concentrating only on her. 'I stayed in the safe house,' he said. 'As instructed. On the second day I located the weapons. I waited until dark and put them in my vehicle. I drove to the hotel, parking my car in the garage. I waited for my contact. I watched as he approached me. I watched as he gave me the sign.'

'What sign was that?' Albert Kana again.

'It's in my report,' Alan snapped.

There was silence in the room, a silence broken only by the distant sounds of movement outside. A tin was banged. Someone groaned himself out of sleep. Two people greeted each other and laughed. 'The new day has started,' Alan thought. 'And yet I am stuck in the old.'

'Continue, comrade,' Rebecca said. 'What was the sign?'

'My contact touched his right ear lobe with his right hand,' Alan said. 'The sign that it was safe. I waited until he left and then I abandoned my car keys in a folded newspaper. I took a bus back to the safe house. When the time was right, I picked up a new car and drove to the meeting point. I crossed the border at the time appointed for me.'

'Is that all?' Rebecca asked.

'Yes,' Alan said dully. He didn't understand. 'Did something happen to the weapons?' he asked.

'Did you go out at all?' is what Rebecca said. 'After you moved the weapons?'

Alan grimaced. 'Yes, I went out,' he said. 'Is there a law against that?'

'Where did you go?'

He shrugged. 'To the shops,' he said. 'I needed food. And to the car hire firm. I also made a couple of phone calls. From a public phone box. They've all been logged.'

The anger had all gone now and he was calm. I've nothing to fear, he thought, nothing to hide.

'You were spotted in Bryanston,' Rebecca said.

Bryanston – so that was it: the word deflated him. Bryanston, the place had come back to haunt him. Bryanston, how he hated it. How he wished he had never seen it. He had realized at the time that he was wrong to go back there, wrong to pay homage to a senseless past. He saw again the high wall, the wrought-iron gate, the technicolour, sprawling vines, the spreading jacaranda tree that seemed to soar above it all. He saw it with the eyes of a child and, at the same time, of an adult. It wasn't true what they said: the landmarks of childhood didn't grow smaller with age. That wall had seemed just as menacing to the man as it had been to the boy – more menacing and just as difficult to scale.

He would not think of it. He looked down at the floor. A lizard, lurid green, made its way past his feet and across the concrete. He saw it leave a trace of slime in its wake, a watery smear on the dirty grey surface.

'What were you doing in Bryanston?' Rebecca asked.

The lizard had reached the wall. It vanished down a crack.

'What were you doing in Bryanston?' Her voice was insistent, pulling him into the present.

He looked up at her. 'I was taking a walk.' Tears filled his eyes.

'A walk? Nobody walks in Bryanston,' Albert Kana said.

'I needed to stretch my legs. I got out of my car to walk.'

'And why did you not report this so-called walk?' Albert Kana barked.

Alan blinked the tears away. His face hardened. 'Comrade,' he said bitterly, 'when I first started my duties with the flying squad, I wrote the fullest possible reports. My commander told me to cut them down. His exact words were that he didn't want to know what I had eaten and when I'd shit it out. I was told to restrict myself to the basics. I never understood that innocent afternoon strolls were part of the basics.'

'If it was innocent.'

'Well, what do you think I was doing there?' Alan snapped. 'Meeting an enemy agent?'

They froze, all three of them. Froze in ludicrous positions:

Kana had his mouth open, Rebecca's hand was poised in mid air and as for the other, Alan had already forgotten his name, well his eyes bulged.

So that was it – an enemy agent. But how could it be? Alan frowned and the visit replayed itself for him. He thought of what had happened, of all that had happened. He had driven to Bryanston and parked. He'd sat in the car, searching for the courage to move and, when he found it, he'd got out and walked towards the wall, planning to look through the gate, to see how the house had changed. He didn't know any longer what it was that had propelled him there. A mixture of emotions, of curiosity, revenge and, oh yes, of love. It was Sarah's questions which led him to Bryanston, Sarah's probing.

But even the thought of Sarah and how proud she would have been, had not been enough. The closer he got to the wall the more it repelled him. It was a symbol of the mistake he had once made, a mistake he had long ago renounced. Or thought he had. As the wall exerted its power on him he knew that all these years, he had been deceiving himself. He was no different than he once had been: he was as corrupted. He felt, as he walked, as if he were dragging his own slime behind him. The closer he got, the slower he walked.

He remembered what had happened then. A shot had sounded in the distance – a shot or a car backfiring, he had not been sure which. The noise had flung him back to his youth and to the terror he had long ago experienced. He'd turned suddenly and fled, retracing his steps in blind panic.

And something else had happened. He had bumped into a man who had cursed at him and struck out with his arm, almost pushing Alan off balance. He didn't know how he could have forgotten the incident.

'That man,' he muttered.

Suddenly it was clear – all of it. The boat, the jeep, his arrival here. The man had been following him, he knew that now. He had turned too suddenly and the man had lashed out at him, lashed out at which had been his own incompetence. But that was not all. There must have been a third participant in this melodrama. Somebody else had been watching him.

As he sat still, reckoning it out, Alan knew that he had been betrayed – betrayed not only by an enemy but more specifically by his own love. He felt a wild desire to laugh.

He didn't laugh. He put his head into his hands and he began to weep.

CHAPTER TEN

South Africa

As he waited for his informant Captain Malan managed, for a moment, to forget himself. He sat perfectly still, his hands resting lightly on the steering wheel, his ears drinking in the concentrated intensity of Mozart's *Requiem*. The voices, soaring together high above mortal constraints, pulled him from himself. They offered him a window to a world where there were no Jansens, no spies, no pain; only sound, pure and beautiful sound, innocent in its simplicity.

He closed his eyes and concentrated. Good music, he thought, needed no accompaniment. At home while nursing his first drink of the day he would put on a record, but here, shut up in the car, without the diversion of a liquor cabinet, he realized that music was, in itself, a form of intoxication.

Perhaps, he thought, perhaps Ingrid is right: perhaps I'm drinking too much these days. When he got home, he resolved, he'd try to let the music work its magic on him, he'd lay off the brandy and use music instead. Except Ingrid would never allow him to play it as it was intended: if he turned it up she would soon claim that it was giving her a headache. Only here, alone in the car, could he find the right, the natural, volume. Only here, without the distraction of domestic life, could he rely solely on his senses.

He stretched his left hand over to the tape deck. The jolting that accompanied this movement brought with it sanity. What the hell did he think he was doing? He had chosen this deserted spot precisely because of security and yet he'd caught himself turning the volume up so high that he might as well have taken out an advert in the *Weekly Mail*.

He pushed hard on the tape's eject button. What he was doing was hazardous enough – he had no right to take unnecessary risks.

The music was abruptly cut off.

Just in time, for instead of silence he heard footsteps. He glanced at the luminous dials on his watch. Thank God he'd turned the *Requiem* off: a few minutes more and his contact would have arrived without warning, throwing him off guard. And that he could not afford.

The footsteps stopped. A man opened the nearside back door. As Malan turned a spasm of pain shot down his spine. He gritted his teeth.

'Get in the front for Christ's sake,' he snapped.

The man did as he was instructed. Quietly he shut the door, fumbled for the one in front, succeeded in opening it and then, at last, as he continued to rock his head from right to left, he managed to seat himself. Malan shifted away from him.

The man did not look at Malan: this man never looked at anyone. Instead he stared straight ahead, and Malan saw how pronounced was his twitching and how it contorted his facial muscles.

'Control yourself,' Malan said. 'We're safe.'

The man made an effort to obey but only succeeded in distorting his features still further. Silently, Captain Malan prayed his irritation wouldn't lead to the pitiful retelling of a life story that he already knew by heart.

'I'm sorry I'm late *baas*,' the man said. The man was not late but the man always started this way.

'Have you found out anything more?' Malan asked softly.

The man's head shook. Malan waited. The shaking abated.

'It's definitely a boat,' the man said. He grinned suddenly, inappropriately. 'Packed with soldiers.'

'Forty, you said.'

'Ja, man, forty soldiers,' the man replied and the grin turned first to a giggle and then to a full throated laugh.

The pain ricocheted down Malan's left side. 'Cut that out, you bloody *kaffir*,' he shouted.

The laugh was abruptly ended – replaced by a violent shaking.

Fleetingly Malan wished he had bitten his tongue off. He knew the man was unstable, an idiot who survived by selling scraps of information to the highest bidder. The man didn't even understand which side he was on – he certainly had no idea that if the soldiers managed to land safely then he might be one of their first targets.

And yet the man was touchy. 'I didn't need to meet you here,' he muttered. Coming from him this was a full scale rebellion.

Malan had made a mistake and he would have to pay for it. He reached into his pocket and pulled out a five rand note.

'Tell me again how you know about the boat,' he said gently.

The man closed his mouth firmly. Sighing, Malan dropped the note into the man's lap. It disappeared almost immediately into the recesses of the man's baggy trousers, into a tattered pocket stained with engine oil.

'Tell me,' Malan urged.

'I have a friend in Bagamoya, a docker, who saw them boarding,' the man said.

'And as he watched,' Malan suggested loudly, 'watched in secret mind you, he managed to count them – forty of them, not including the crew? Is that how it was, hey? Is it?'

The man's face became completely still as a look crossed it, a look of sly complicity. For an instant, Malan doubted himself: he wondered whether this man might be the hunter rather than the hunted. Had Malan been set up? No, it wasn't possible. Malan had used the man for too long to have misjudged him. The man was small fry, his information, apart from this latest piece, usually mundane but accurate. Malan had only kept him on the payroll because Malan needed eyes and ears independent of the department and because sometimes the most useless of creatures produced a gem.

A gem like an armed invasion by hand-picked MK soldiers. A gem that, if it was true, would place Malan in an unassailable position at the same time as it proved Jansen's undoing.

If it was true, Malan thought, and if he could get more information. Knowing that the enemy was about to launch an armed attack some time in the next ten days, and somewhere in the Transkei, was not good enough. If Malan was to go to Jansen with this information, or better still go over Jansen's head with it, he would be greeted by derisive laughter. The other side's disinformation campaign was working well these days: nobody would believe that, amongst the growing talk of negotiations, the ANC would dare to go on the offensive. Only proof positive would be enough to galvanize an appropriate response.

Yes, he needed more information and he needed it badly.

'. . . from a friend in the docks office who owes him a favour,' the man finished.

Malan nodded. He hadn't heard the beginning of the convoluted sentence but that didn't matter. The man was retelling, using identical words, the story with which he had first startled Malan. A story that pointed to mistakes in the past, and a story that, if true, could prove disastrous for an unprepared police force.

And the frustrating thing was that Malan could go no further with the Tanzanian connection. He'd asked the man to check and double check and the man said he'd done it. Short of sending an agent into Bagamoya, something that Malan couldn't contemplate without his superior's consent (which he knew, without asking, would be withheld), Malan had no way of checking the accuracy of the report. It would have to stand as it was: that a disaffected Tanzanian worker had observed unusual activity on the dockside and that a clerk in the docks office had gossiped about men and arms boarding a luxury yacht.

Except it didn't stand on its own. From other sources Malan had learned of peculiar activity at the ANC's Dar office, and on top of that there was another report: of a person sympathetic to the enemy registering a yacht in Liberia and of money changing hands. Jansen would read nothing in these coincidences but Jansen was a beginner. Malan was different. Every bone in his body told him that the ANC were about to pull off a major coup by forcing the government to the negotiating table while stepping up their armed attacks.

And only Malan could stop them. Only Malan. The thought of Jansen's face when he did so made him laugh out loud.

'Is that all *baas*?'

'No, it isn't.' Malan was surprised into talking too loudly. Deliberately he lowered his voice. 'You've done well,' he said. Out of his pocket he drew out a crisp new note – ten rand this time. 'This is for you.'

The man smiled eagerly. He stretched out his hand to take the money but before he could reach it, Malan withdrew it.

'You've got relatives in the Transkei,' Malan said.

Crestfallen the man nodded.

'I want you to go visit them,' Malan said. 'I want you to go to Port St John's.'

'But *baas*,' the man protested. 'My mother lives . . .'

Malan cut him off. He would tolerate no interruption, not when he was framing a strategy. 'I want you to go to Port St John's and hang around the beaches,' he said firmly. 'I want you to find out if anything unusual's happening. Anything, do you understand?'

'Yes *baas*.'

'And if nothing is, move along the coast. I want you to phone me twice daily at the usual number with messages. Twice daily, do you understand?'

The man nodded but his eyes were downcast, avoiding Malan as if Malan might infect him.

Perhaps you're right, Malan thought. Perhaps I have gone mad – perhaps it is sheer insanity to use you in this way. But what you don't understand, Malan thought, is that I have no other choice. Jansen has circumscribed my activities – I can't go through the usual channels.

Malan looked at the man and it struck him that perhaps the man did understand. He was an dullard, this man, but possessed of native cunning. Probably he had worked out long ago why Malan met him in such inhospitable venues: he must know that the subterfuge was for Malan's sake rather than his own.

Well, what did it matter? The man was merely a tool. Who cared what he thought? Malan wouldn't rely solely on him. He had other contacts, and more astute ones at that, whom he would also set to work. These other men would cost him dearly, especially if they knew that the money was coming from Malan's own

75

pockets, but Malan would pay it gladly. Anything to win this one. This last one.

'You can go,' Malan said. He joined another ten to the bill in his hand and shoved both notes at the man.

The man did not move.

'What are you waiting for?' Malan barked.

The angry tone was enough. Trembling, the man pushed open the door and loped lopsidedly away. Malan watched him go, watched as the man moved towards the murky shadows and then became one of them. And even after the man had disappeared, Malan sat, staring out and listening to the night.

He was no longer thinking about the man. His mind was concentrated elsewhere, making equations that still did not quite balance. What did he have? He had a boat heading for the coastline, a boat full of highly trained, highly motivated terrorists all armed to the teeth. And he had something else as well – something from Zonda, a source which could not be doubted – inside the country he had knowledge of an armed MK unit, already operating, already effective. He had both of these in his head, and experience had taught him that a series of coincidences was not to be trusted. They must be connected, they must.

They *were* connected, he suddenly realized, of course they were. That's what they were up to! It suddenly made sense to him – the whole ANC strategy.

Malan sat in his car and smiled. The ANC, he thought, was acting astutely, astutely enough to pull the wool over the eyes of men like Jansen. For what the ANC was doing was not launching a series of armed attacks as he had assumed but instead doing something even more sinister. The ANC was securing a more effective armed underground – an underground that might not act but which would always be poised to strike. The boat must represent the final piece of the plan: the forty men would join units already *in situ* – the men on the ground would orient those from the sea.

An underground, he realized, that would not strike, not yet. An underground that would lie not sleeping but in wait, its fangs at the ready, an underground that was the venom lurking behind the simpering face of negotiations.

Distractedly Captain Malan turned his car key. He stroked his fur-covered steering wheel as his engine purred into life. He knew that his conclusion was the only one. And he knew he was right and that also he would have them both: the boat and the armed unit as well. He would have them.

He let the car move onto the road, running for a while without lights. But then as a tree loomed up in front of him, he switched his headlights on and in that moment, when darkness was illuminated, his thoughts turned to something else that had been bugging him – to Alan Littell. It had been pure whim that had led Malan to have Littell followed, a whim that he himself did not fully understand. And when all Littell did was go to Bryanston, Malan decided that nothing was to be gained by further scrutiny and had called the watcher off. But now Sarah had got in on the act and Sarah too had gone to Bryanston. What could it mean?

For a moment all Malan's unanswered questions seemed to join up together. Was it possible – was there some connection between these visits and the boat? Was Alan amongst the forty and had he, in his last free moments, merely gone to pay his pilgrimage to his roots?

No, Malan was growing fanciful. The boat couldn't explain Sarah's visit and besides Malan knew much about Alan Littell and of one thing he was sure: Alan had left his past behind, he would never choose to visit his past.

So what the hell had he been doing in Bryanston? Why had he gone there?

Day Two

CHAPTER ELEVEN
Tanzania

'Why did you go to Bryanston?'
  'I told you, I felt like a walk.'
  'But why Bryanston?'
  'I . . .'
  'Why? Tell us why.'
  'I . . . I wanted to see my old home.'
  'To visit the Howards?'
  'Jack is dead.'
  'Were you planning to visit Girlie?'
  'No. I just wanted to see the house.'
  'Do you expect us to believe that?'
  'No I don't expect you to believe it. But it's still the truth.'
  'Who was the man you had arranged to meet?'
  'There was no man. I met no one.'
  'You were seen exchanging envelopes with a known enemy agent.'
  'Who saw me? Where is my accuser?'
  'You were seen exchanging envelopes.'
  'I've told you. I bumped into a man. If he is an enemy agent then can't you see that he must have been following me? I turned too quickly for him to take evasive action.'
  'Why would he follow you? How would he know about you?'
  'He's not apparently the only one. Somebody else was there, weren't they?'
  ''Why were you meeting the man?'
  'Who is my accuser? I demand that you name my accuser. I demand . . .'

81

Rebecca leaned forward and flicked a switch, cutting Alan Littell off in mid-stream. In the silence that followed she breathed a sigh of relief, arched her back and stretched. She yawned. She couldn't remember when last she had felt this tired.

'The man's unhinged,' Albert Kana said.

Rebecca grimaced.

'He's lying,' Albert continued. 'Our cadres don't stroll around Bryanston reliving their pasts.'

'Most of our cadres don't have a past in Bryanston,' Jabulani dryly remarked.

'You believe him then?'

Instead of replying Jabulani just looked at Albert. As Rebecca watched, fascinated, the men locked eyes. She looked from one to the other, drinking in their different appearances. She looked at Albert and saw a heavy man, grey-haired and dressed in a dingy brown suit, a man from the countryside whose stance proclaimed that he had travelled a long way from humble beginnings without ever really leaving them. She turned her head and looked at Jabulani – younger, city slicker, whose western suit was a trifle too tailored and a trifle too casual to be respectable.

They glared at each other these two as if this was a showdown, as if two generations of ANC militants were finally confronting each other. And, in a sense, that is indeed what was happening. Albert Kana was of the old school, a practical man who had served his time and who, through persistence and tenacious caucusing, had reached the upper echelons of the movement. Jabulani Dlamini came from a different stock. He had education, sharp intelligence and a thrusting ambition to back him up and he was aiming to go higher than Albert – if, and only if, he didn't make too many enemies on the way.

Rebecca, as she watched, saw that the vital issue, the only issue, had suddenly become which of them would be the first to break the deadlock.

'Men!' she thought, and for once she didn't try and censor herself for thinking thus. Instead, as the seconds ticked by, she began to feel strangely distanced from the conflict. Her mind wandered away from the room and for the first time since the interrogation had begun, she placed it in its surroundings. A

rhythmic sound from outside penetrated her consciousness. Somebody was drumming.

She glanced at her watch. It was too early for festivities – she
must be imagining things. She looked back at the men and saw
them still locked in their duel. How childish, she thought.

There was a knock at the door, and Albert looked away. The
moment was broken. A young man walked into the room, saluted
its occupants, handed a piece of paper to Rebecca and then
promptly left.

Rebecca scanned the paper before addressing her companions.
She frowned. 'Alan wasn't lying about one thing,' she commented.
'Peter has confirmed that Alan was spotted in the road where
Girlie Howard still lives.'

'That proves nothing,' Albert muttered. He hauled himself
to his feet and pulled his waistcoat down over his stomach.
'I'm going to rest,' he said. Slowly he lumbered out of the
room.

The drumming was louder now. Rebecca walked over to the
window and saw that the noise was no product of her own fatigue.
In the distance a group doing early morning calisthenics, stretching and bending to the sound produced by a young boy who was
beating a stick against a tin drum. Alan must be hearing that
sound, Rebecca thought and wondered if it was disrupting his
sleep. Well if it was – all to the good.

She turned abruptly. 'Albert thinks Littell's guilty,' she told
Jabulani.

'And you don't?'

Of course he's guilty, Rebecca thought. She frowned. 'I'm
keeping an open mind,' she said carefully.

Jabulani smiled. She read the smile for what it was and it made
her angry. It was typical of Jabulani, she thought. Neither of
them had mentioned it, their lost intimacy, but neither had
forgotten. He must know only too well what that wide flash of his
smile could do to her just as he knew how the small wrinkles that
the smile diffused served mainly to highlight those long, black
eyelashes and that red-brown skin.

He was enjoying himself, she thought and she resented it. It
was he, she suspected, who'd nominated her for this tribunal and

he, she guessed, was revelling in the way it agitated her. She felt a sudden urge to go up to him and shake him.

She shivered. That would be a stupid thing to do. Jabulani wasn't to blame: the future, looming up too fast, and not the past was what was dogging her. The time when she had wanted to shake him, when she had fought to resist the urge to jostle his entire body until he withdrew his words, was in the past. That time was gone: the way she felt was no longer of his making.

Carefully she stripped the irritation from her voice. 'Albert thinks Littell is guilty,' she said. 'Do you?'

'I'm here as an observer,' he said. 'It wouldn't be correct for me to voice my opinion – especially at this early stage.'

Even though she knew that he was right, the urge to shake him returned and this time it almost overwhelmed her. She tore her eyes from him and instead stared out of the window. One of the men on the periphery of the group was having trouble keeping up with the rest. He jumped in the air and landed heavily and when his arms met above his head he clapped a fraction too late, the desultory noise sounding above the successive beating of the tin.

'I'm like that,' Rebecca thought, 'out of step, out of time.'

She pushed the thought away. She was tired. That was it. She needed sleep. Stiffly she turned from the window and began to make her way to the door. She was more tired than she had imagined – those few paces felt almost insurmountable. She forced one foot in front of the other; all she wanted to do was sleep.

But Jabulani wouldn't release her. 'I think you should interrogate Littell on your own,' he said. 'Comrade Albert's manner is too abrasive.'

She nodded wearily. She wanted to sleep.

'So far what we have is inconclusive,' Jabulani continued. 'And Littell's question is a good one: exactly what was Peter's contact doing in Bryanston, on that particular day? A bit of a coincidence don't you think?'

'Who cares?' Rebecca thought. 'I'm tired.'

'You'll have to go into the past, reopen the Wentworth trial,' Jabulani concluded.

84

She was suddenly, painfully awake. Awake and full of panic. She was gripped by the immediacy of her sense of foreboding. A premonition, awful in its horrifying detail, descended on her.

'We must call back the boat,' she said.

Her words meant nothing to her; she did not know why she had uttered them. All she saw, as if it were taking place in front of her eyes, was the man on the outskirts of the group – the slow one. He fell to the ground. She saw how blood trickled from the side of his mouth. She saw him twitch once and then she saw how still he lay. Darkness descended on Rebecca.

She blinked. Her eyes were clear when she looked outside again and she knew that it hadn't been true. It hadn't happened. The man was still on his feet, panting quite visibly as he tried to keep up with the rest.

She shook her head violently, ridding herself of the treacherous image.

'We have time,' Jabulani's voice pulled her back into the room.

'I know we have time,' she shouted ferociously.

She was grateful that Jabulani did not react. When she looked at him she saw that he was staring at the ground, straight down at his feet.

'We're all a product of our pasts,' he said softly.

Rebecca scowled. 'I'm not completely ignorant, comrade,' she said. 'I just don't see the point in dwelling on what's gone.'

Jabulani opened his mouth to say something but she willed the words away from him. 'Don't,' she silently warned. 'Don't you dare.'

He hesitated. 'In a new South Africa the past will still live with us,' is what he finally said.

'In a new South Africa I will be able to refuse jobs for which I am unsuited,' she retorted.

She wrenched the door open and she walked out into the bright sunlight, away from the room, away from Jabulani, away from his words unsaid.

She was tired, that's all it was.

Alan paced the room. He was preoccupied by his thoughts but when he suddenly came to and realized he had been walking in

85

step with the drum beat, he deliberately re-shuffled his feet. He was determined: he wouldn't walk to their rhythm, his movements would never be tailored to theirs.

He knew that he should be conserving energy, that he should be asleep. But he had never been able to sleep in the day and the sight of the bed repelled him. Not that there was anything wrong with it. It was basic, an iron bedstead with a cotton covered mattress; basic, just like the rest of the room. He went to the window and opened the faded floral curtains.

His was the back view with the rows of tents laid out neatly before his eyes. He guessed that they were all empty now – all except one. In that one somebody would have been posted, somebody who would give the alarm should Alan attempt to flee. A necessary precaution perhaps, but made in the full knowledge that there was nowhere for him to run. He had lost his hiding place, his home. South Africa had once been this to him but he had forsaken it. In its place he had put the ANC but now it was possible that the ANC . . .

He could not complete the sentence because he didn't know its end. He was gripped by conflicting emotions; emotions of fear, of anger, and, overwhelmingly, of guilt. He blamed himself: he was trapped in a web that he alone had constructed. As soon as the thought crossed his mind, another contradicted it. It's not true, he thought, I'm confused. It's not my fault, it can't be.

He turned from the window and, going over to the bed, sat down on it. Leaning his back against the rough wall, he began to think.

Bryanston, that's what came to him. He should never have gone there. He'd known at the time it was a futile thing to do and a childish one as well. And yet, he had thought, what harm could it cause? An innocent walk was all it was, a saddened pilgrimage back into an almost forgotten time.

He stamped his foot on the ground. His visit to Bryanston had been innocent no matter what the ANC thought. It wasn't his fault: he hadn't shaped his own noose, somebody else had. He'd been getting too close, he'd been about to unmask the traitors and somebody had moved fast to stop him.

Not one somebody, he reminded himself, but two. They must

have assumed they were working in opposition to each other but in the end, they trapped him together. From their separate vantage points they'd been spying on him and, when the one bumped into Alan, the other went scurrying off to report the encounter. The only other possible explanation was that the set-up had been coincidental, that Alan and the two others had been in the same place at the same time by mistake.

No, he couldn't believe that, it was too unlikely. One of this own comrades must have betrayed him, must have notified the enemy of his presence in the country, must have followed him and reported back.

'Who?' he asked himself. 'Who hates me so?'

A list of names, of names attached to faces, came rushing into his consciousness. Robert Wentworth had hated Alan but Robert was long dead. Peter perhaps? Peter had kept his distance but Alan had always known that Peter disliked him, that Peter, in fact, disliked all whites. But Peter was a dedicated solider. Would he really create such a stir only to get back at someone of whom he merely disapproved? No, Alan shook his head, it couldn't be Peter.

Peter's face faded and it was replaced by Victor's. But that made no sense. Victor, like Robert, was dead. And Victor did not hate Alan: Victor was his friend.

Thabo, then. Yes, Alan thought, it's Thabo. Thabo hated Alan: they had never got on. From the first day of their training they'd been like wounded bears circling each other, each waiting for the other to commit a mistake.

Alan groaned out loud. His imagination was running out of control. How on earth could it be Thabo? Thabo was out of the game, Thabo was in prison, Thabo was in *their* hands.

Their hands! That was it. In a flash he had come up with another explanation and the more he thought about it the more likely it became. He jumped to his feet and began to pace again, thinking furiously.

He was the fly, he thought, there was no doubt about that. But had he properly identified the spider? Was it possible, he thought, that in looking to the movement for the traitor, he was doing what *they* wanted him to? What if there had been only one person spying on him, one of *them*?

Think, he told himself, think it through stage by stage. As he forced his racing thoughts to order, he reached the furthest wall.

Assumption number one, he thought, they know what I'm up to and they want me: want me badly.

He turned. Solution: they could have arrested me.

Yes, he thought as he began to walk again, they could have picked him up when he was transporting weapons.

But then he remembered he had been scrupulously careful and was sure that no one had been following him. The fact that the weapons had reached their destination meant that he was right. He must assume, therefore, that they had spotted him only after he had made the drop.

The wall once more. Assumption number two: they wanted me neutralized but they didn't have the evidence.

Once more he turned. Solution: they get somebody else to do the job.

The more he thought about it, the clearer it became. It was twisted but it was possible. They had channels into the movement, they had their own way of creating internal disruption.

And if anybody hated him, it was they. He was white and so were they. He had betrayed them by choosing sides. They expected blacks to work against them but they never forgave whites who did the same. And there was another point: he was on the point of unmasking their puppets. That was it, that was their motive for destroying him.

He had reached the wall again but this time he didn't turn. Instead he hit out at it, using his fist, hit it hard although he felt no pain. He had it. He knew he did. *They* were after him, *they* were bent on silence and on vengeance.

With this certainty came little consolation.

He imagined relating his conclusions to his interrogators and he could already see the expressions on their faces. Albert Kana would react with pure disbelief but then Albert Kana wasn't the problem. It was Rebecca Moisia who posed the greatest threat and it was her reaction he most feared. He had seen how she wavered between dislike of her job, which forced her to be more than scrupulously fair, and distrust of him, which made her want to condemn. He'd seen her face when he'd wept and he'd read on it contempt, writ large.

If he now presented her with his theory she would dismiss it out of hand. She would see it as sign of instability, of paranoia, of madness even. She would ask him why he had not spoken up before and she, a woman who abided by the rules alone, would find his explanation, that he wanted to be sure, so sinister as to be untrustworthy. One wrong move and he would tip the balance.

Sarah would have laughed to hear him think this way. 'It's because she's a woman,' Sarah would have teased, 'that's your problem: women.'

He threw himself onto the bed. He must push Sarah out of his mind. He must think: think as if his life depended on it. He smiled grimly. It was always possible that his life did in fact depend on it.

For the second time that day, Alan began to cry.

As if on cue the drumming stopped and the sound of relieved laughter rose into the air.

CHAPTER TWELVE

South Africa

The noise stopped abruptly, but there was no laughter here on the Island, only an unspoken sense of relief. Even though the men were overcome by heat, there was little point in seeking out shelter. They dropped where they stood, beside the hammers, picks, drills, wheelbarrows – the instruments of their long labour. They sat against the hard, grey stone, covering themselves as best they could against the onslaught of a blistering sun. Few words were exchanged. Conversation would soon re-surface, but for the moment each man dwelt within his own private domain, regaining his sense of self and preparing to re-enter the world of man. Gradually their breathing calmed and gradually did another sort of order begin to impose itself.

The men sat together in groups – all except Thabo. After the whistle blew, he chose to walk a few paces, distancing himself from the rest of his crew. He slumped down, his eyes closed, his mind mercifully blank.

The work had been arduous but Thabo didn't, for once, object. Hard work had its uses. It provided him with relief: relief from his thoughts, from his dreams, and from the spirit of Victor, which pursued him even in his waking hours.

Up in the sky, a thousand seagulls wheeled and screeched, their airy freedom mocking the prisoners below. They would cluster together occasionally, bunching so hard that they could block the light below, and then they would separate as suddenly as they had come together, and the sun would beat down again, unmoving, without mercy. Thabo pushed them from his mind:

he concentrated instead on spinning out his few moments' peace.

But in Robben Island, peace is a luxury that can cost a man dearly. A shadow passed in front of Thabo, blackening the grey in his closed eyelids. He knew what it must be and he opened his eyes but he was too late: the common law prisoner had already passed taking with him Thabo's precious ration of water. Thabo's peace was turned to dust: consumed by the aching dryness in his lips and by the lurching of his stomach.

'It's all right, comrade,' a soothing voice said. 'I've saved you some.'

The man who had spoken was sitting with the rest of Thabo's crew and holding a tin can up high. Thabo licked his lips. He put both hands on the ground, ready to lever himself upright. But the man beat him to it. He sprang to his feet and crossed the divide, bending down to deliver the water.

Thabo gulped at it gratefully. He downed the last drop and reached up to hand the tin back.

'Thanks, comrade,' he said.

The man smiled but didn't move away. He remained where he was, gazing speculatively down at Thabo.

Thabo frowned. The man wanted something in exchange for the water yet Thabo had no idea what that might be. All he desired was the chance to rest alone. Surely his comrade would understand?

It came suddenly to Thabo, the realization that although the man understood all right, he was deliberately flouting Thabo's wishes. This kept happening: many of his comrades had taken to intruding on his space, one way or another, engaging him in trivial conversations as a prelude to something else. It was as if they were watching him, watching and waiting.

His frown deepened. Why? Was there something he didn't know?

'Am I sick?' he asked stupidly.

The man squatted down beside Thabo. 'I don't know,' he replied. 'Are you sick?'

What a stupid question! Thabo looked away. 'Yes,' he said bitterly. 'I am sick. Sick of being here, sick of watching time pass so slowly that each minute feels longer than the last and sick of the way time races by, unrelenting.' He made a feeble attempt at a smile. 'But this is a sickness with which we are infected,' he said, 'and for this sickness there is only one cure: release.'

No there isn't, he thought. There is only one cure for a lifer and that is death. He pushed the thought away.

But the man caught it. 'The country is changing,' he said. 'We may be all soon be released.'

'So we may,' said Thabo dryly.

There followed a short silence. Thabo closed his eyes, hoping the man would take the hint. Let him believe that Thabo's problem was a simple resentment at being incarcerated. Nothing could be done with such resentment so let him believe it was that and then, let him go away.

The man didn't go. 'We hear you're not sleeping,' he said.

Oh, so that was it. His cell companions had complained about him. Thabo opened his eyes.

'I sleep fine,' he said. 'Occasionally I dream.'

'More than occasionally.'

It was true, Thabo thought, the dream was relentless. Once it had been sporadic but during the last month it had gripped him, gripping him so hard that he'd become afraid to close his eyes, afraid that if he did he would fall under its inevitable spell. Even just thinking about it filled him with a nameless horror.

Tears sprang to his eyes. 'What am I supposed to do?' he asked. 'I can't control my dreams.'

'Perhaps you should try talking about them,' the man suggested gently.

Thabo shook his head violently. He couldn't talk about the dream, he couldn't. 'You can't force me to,' he said.

'It's not a question of force,' the man said. 'It's a question of your sanity.'

'Sanity!' How melodramatic, Thabo thought.

The man beside him rose. From his near six foot he looked down at Thabo. Thabo was conscious how the seagulls formed a guard of honour above his head, swooping low as if they actually believed they were about to be fed.

'Prison can be a terrible place, comrade,' the man said, 'if unfinished business follows you into it. Such worries can eat away your soul and they can leave you without a moment's peace.'

Peace, Thabo thought, how I long for it. He shrugged.

'You're not alone,' the man continued, 'we've all experienced the terrible intrusion of the outside world.'

Well if you've experienced it, Thabo thought, why are you bugging me?

'There is only one solution,' the man continued, 'one form of relief. Talk to us about it and we can help you.' The man did not wait for a reply. He walked away.

Alone again, Thabo was tempted to spend the last few minutes of the break muttering to himself. But that would have been stupid, a waste of time. The man had after all only been trying to help. Thabo knew that, in prison, it was all too easy to turn self-pity into anger and then to direct this anger towards one's companions: the only people who could make life bearable.

Bearable, Thabo thought, but never pleasant. He wished he could be free again; constantly the ache pursued him.

That's what's wrong, he thought. I'm not free.

Even as the thought crossed his mind he knew it to be only partially true. Prison made freedom seem enormously seductive, and yet experience had taught him that freedom was not all one might imagine it to be. Life outside was fraught with difficulties, while the simplicity of gaol brought with it consolations. Looking back at his past Thabo sometimes thought that the period of freedom had been the most difficult phase to handle. Looking back the only time he remembered feeling truly happy was during his training in the camps.

What followed the camps seemed, in hindsight, to have been mere preparation for prison. Not that he was trying to undermine his achievements, or the achievements of his group. They had carried arms into a country that was crying out for someone to defend it: their actions gave hope to a hopeless cause.

After training Thabo had revisited a country that refused to stagnate under an oppressor's fist. And after training he was able to arm his people not with words, as he had formerly done, but with guns: with gestures still, perhaps, but with gestures that

93

came wrapped in a bullet rather than in rhetoric. Even the defeats – like Victor being shot dead – were of use, for Thabo knew that the fact that Victor's death preceded another round of township protest was no coincidence. Victor had died fighting and the people had taken his memory out into the streets.

Victor! Not that name again. Thabo pushed it away. Where was he? Oh yes – the happiness delivered by freedom.

Being involved in active service had been exciting, stimulating, rewarding. But it hadn't made him happy. It wasn't possible to be happy because, for most of the time, he'd been too damned scared.

Yes, he thought, it's true: the last time I was genuinely carefree was in the camps. And yet was his memory deceiving him? Had it ever been as carefree as he liked to imagine?

He let his mind wander back to that time. Conditions had been difficult, he remembered, food scarce, malaria rife. And yet there had been compensations: compensations in the form of a camaraderie that few would ever be privileged to experience. This feeling of belonging didn't only spring from difficulties jointly shared. It was a feeling created by the knowledge that at last they were taking control over their own lives, that at last they were fighting back at the system that had so oppressed them. True happiness was the feel of an AK in one's hands: that and the joy that came from hardships collectively endured, obstacles overcome, victories gained.

But, Thabo remembered, there was another side to it. There had been tensions in the group, personality clashes, accusations even between the closest members. Their training was partially responsible. When they had studied surveillance and counter surveillance they had become like young psychology students, each reading into each other's actions, the Judas curse – the sign of the enemy. They'd grown spy crazy, but at the time they thought it was just a game: they little realized that there was a foundation to their paranoia, a foundation that would later cost them the lives of those they loved.

No, thought Thabo. Forget Victor.

He summoned up the faces of the others. Alan, Peter, Robert, Thembi. Thembi was a distant memory, he had never known her well. And Peter also failed to withstand the test of time: there was nothing about him on which Thabo could reflect.

The whistle blew: break was over. Thabo got to his feet. He picked up his hammer and walked over to join the rest of his crew.

Wentworth and Littell, he thought as he raised the hammer in the air. Littell and Wentworth – the hammer smashed down on a slab of rock.

The two whites had never liked each other. From the start there had been between them an antagonism that grew into simmering hatred. They competed for everything, even though Wentworth never really stood a chance. He'd been all fingers and thumbs whereas Alan was a model trainee – quick to learn, slow to forget. The feud between them had infected the rest, forcing everyone to choose sides. Not the same side though. Even Thabo and Victor, the closest of friends, had disagreed on this issue. Thabo had disliked Littell, whereas Victor distrusted Wentworth.

Victor had teased Thabo about his dislike of Littell. 'It's your black consciousness background,' Victor would say. 'You'll put up with Wentworth because he's inadequate but you suspect Littell because you can't believe an intelligent white man could be on our side.'

Perhaps, Thabo thought, perhaps Victor was right.

The hammer was up in the air. He let it drop.

Victor had been right about one thing. Wentworth had betrayed Victor and both men had died.

A splinter of rock flew straight at him. He jumped to evade it. 'I will not think of it,' he muttered.

He raised the hammer again but before he let it drop a sense of dislocation stayed his hand. He looked to his right and saw that the rest of his team was still in the process of smashing down at the rock. He had, he realized, been working too quickly, far too quickly. He stood still, waiting for his crew to catch him up.

He wondered as he waited what had happened to Alan. He assumed that Alan was still in active service, going under his assumed name – what was it now? Thabo searched back into the recesses of his memory, digging out incidents that he had long ago buried. Yes, that was it. Alan had claimed his name early on.

He'd earned it because he liked engaging in philosophical disputations late at night. On those occasions, Thabo remembered, Alan seemed to unbend. But even then not all the comrades liked him; many of them felt intimidated by his intellectual prowess. After one of these sessions someone who had been tied by him into a particularly sophisticated Socratic knot had said that talking to Alan was like talking Greek. From the generalized hilarity that followed, Victor had invented Alan's code name. He'd named Alan Theodarakis – Theo for short.

'Comrade.'

Thabo jumped and turned. They were waiting for him, he saw, waiting for his hammer to join their sequence. It angered him, the way they stared at him. Why would they not leave him alone? He stretched his arm back and the hammer almost touched his shoulder. He breathed in and then, on the out breath, he launched it above his head and down on the pile of rock. He struggled desperately to rid his mind of all coherent thought. Remembering didn't help. It just brought back a feeling that he must at all costs avoid – a feeling that there was something inside of him waiting to explode.

CHAPTER THIRTEEN

Sarah stood directly under the shower and tilted her neck so that the full force of the water landed on her forehead, cascaded down her face and joined the small whirlpool at her feet.

Alan, she thought, was absolutely right: South African showers were second to none. White South African showers, she corrected herself quickly, thinking once again how everything in South Africa must be classified into either black or white.

She smiled and, opening her mouth wide, allowed the water to fill it. She didn't feel like thinking in terms of black or of white, she was in too good a mood to be that serious. This was a time of celebration for her and nothing could really alter that. She had finished, she was about to leave, and politics seemed a million miles away. She gargled and the water spurted from her mouth. All she wanted to do was enjoy her shower, enjoy the wastage of it without the guilt and, at the same time, contemplate going home.

Home, she caught herself naming it thus, and it made her smile the more. Since leaving England and following Alan to Southern African she had turned her back on it and her mind as well; although Mozambique and Angola could never quite be home, London just didn't beckon. Indeed, if it had been her choice rather than the ANC's, she never would have chosen to fly back in such a roundabout way through London.

And yet, now that she was going to, and now that she was ready to leave South Africa, she had caught herself thinking of England as home.

Perhaps I can do it now, she thought: because I've proved myself and so I can own up to my past.

She shrugged. Maybe that was right – maybe not. What did she care? She had done with calculation, with watching her every step, with endless self-scrutiny. She had done with all that because she was finished and because she had succeeded. She had done with it and the shower was a symbol of a new kind of abandon: when she reached London, she resolved, she'd go wild, have fun, stay up all hours and glut herself with luxuries that, during the last few years, had been almost completely denied.

She spat the water from her mouth. 'Now for the daring part,' she thought. 'I'll open my eyes.' She didn't know why she thought it, or why she even wanted to try, but having decided, she went ahead. She pushed her head back again and counted from one.

The moment she reached five she opened her eyes. In that split second, when the first sharp drop hit straight at her eyeball she heard a sound. The water and the sound seemed to collide in her head and to explode there.

They've come for me, she thought, that's all. They've come for me.

There was no time for further thought. She was out of the shower, and with a towel around her before she was even aware that she was in motion. In fact, by the time she was sentient she was out of the bathroom, through her bedroom and halfway to the front door.

She came to and stopped abruptly. What on earth was she doing? If the police were there it was crazy to confront them wearing only a towel. And, she thought, if they were there, and if that noise had been of their doing, then why could she not see them? She changed direction, walking over to the window and peering outside. There was nothing to see, nothing save for a lone black man who, in the distance, was mowing a neighbour's lawn. He must have hit a brick, she thought, as she retraced her steps towards the beckoning shower. He hit a brick or I imagined the noise.

She dropped the towel upon the floor and stepped into the

shower again. She knew what had happened: she had imagined the noise, just as she had yesterday and the day before as well.

She wondered at herself: she knew of this kind of counterfeit creativity but it was a new experience for her to be involved in it directly. She was usually in the observer's role, the person who sat patiently while others confessed that their imaginations led them down blind and fearful alleys. She was accustomed to listening and holding hands, and producing rational explanations that helped her friends be less reproachful of themselves.

She was usually that person and now she had suddenly changed. Now she was the one dogged by erratic thought, moving from euphoria to terror and then just as quickly back again. She had managed to peel away the first layer of her own sanity and catch a glimpse of the instability within.

As the water washed over her she decided that she didn't really mind. Seeing the dark side in herself was another step in growing up, in finding out who she really was. For who had she been until now? The woman her father saw – a spinster, a scientist, a chemistry teacher, good at her job but made all the more unwomanly by it? Or the woman Alan saw – a homemaker, his English rose, so constant in her love that she became the anchor for his volatility?

She laughed at herself for thinking this way: she, a confirmed feminist, judging herself through the eyes of her men. But, she thought, at least it was honest. For no matter how much she resisted it, she had always judged herself through male eyes. And there was no way of denying that she'd been both those women, the one her father saw, the other that attracted Alan.

No more, not if she didn't want to. Southern Africa had been good for her, it had shown her that she could be the rose and be exotic too, that she could feel the passions and act on them as well.

She stepped away from the direct gush of water and poured some shampoo on her head. Placing the bottle back on its ledge, she started to rub at her hair. I've changed, she thought, because I've been accepted. Finally, after all this time.

She stepped back into the path of the water, closed her eyes, and waited as the soap was slowly washed away. Then, keeping her eyes firmly closed, she groped again for the shampoo bottle. She misjudged the distance and it fell to the floor. She bent down to pick it up and it was then she heard the noise. A tentative sound it was, almost as if somebody was testing the knob on the outside door. She froze.

The water continued to flow down her back and that was the only sound she could hear.

'You're imagining things again,' she told herself sternly. Resolutely she grabbed the shampoo and, straightening up, applied it to her scalp.

There was no mistaking the second noise. It was a bang so loud that the whole house shook.

Somebody's broken the door down, she thought. The bastards. They were there all the time. They waited until I got back in the shower.

That was all she thought: that and the fact that they must not find her naked. She pulled the towel, the wet one, from the floor, and threw it over herself.

They were in her sitting room when she emerged. Four, no five, of them. The eldest, the one whose plain clothes – contrasting with those of his underlings – showed he was in charge, smirked at her.

'Miss Patterson?' he asked. 'Miss Sarah Patterson?'

Her imagination had been accurate, she thought. He looked just like she had predicted. 'What do you want?' she asked.

He shrugged as if to say that *he* didn't want anything. 'Under the powers vested in me by Section 29 of the Internal Security Act,' he enunciated slowly in a voice bored from repetition, 'I hereby order your immediate detention. Kindly follow my officers to the car.'

The bastard, Sarah thought. He doesn't even care. 'I'm not dressed,' she said out loud.

That's obvious, his eyes told her. She shivered.

'Get dressed,' he ordered. 'And make it snappy.'

She turned away from him heading for the bathroom. She heard him speak again.

'Kleynhaus,' he barked. 'Watch her.'

100

Sarah stopped abruptly. She had seen them, all of them: she was sure she had, and none of them were female. She didn't turn. She wouldn't let them see the tears that were welling up in her eyes.

'I will not have a man watching me dress,' she said.

'Then don't dress,' he said. 'It's up to you.'

She blinked and walked into the bedroom feeling the hot breath of a young policeman on her shoulder. She opened the wardrobe and pulled out a skirt, a shirt, some underclothes. Then she kept on walking, straight into the bathroom, shutting the door loudly behind her.

When he entered she was already in the shower, the curtain firmly drawn. She heard him shuffling in the background and held her breath while the water washed out the remaining shampoo. He did not open the curtain, not even when she shut off the shower and dried herself. There was no sound when she pulled each item of clothing off the rail and slowly put them on.

Once Sarah was fully clothed, apart from her shoes, she re-emerged. He did not look at her: he continued to stare fixedly at her cosmetics shelf. She leaned around him and removed a few items. Then she left the bathroom for the bedroom and pulled out a pair of sneakers from under her bed. She put them on and carefully tied the laces. She packed her handbag, filling it with everything that she might need. And then, finally, she was ready. She turned to see him still standing by the bathroom door.

'Well, what are you waiting for?' she asked.

He blushed and ran to the door, opening it for her.

'Round one to me,' she thought as she walked through.

She felt as though she had climbed from despair to light-headedness and back down into despair again, all within a couple of hours. Except she knew that she was wrong: the changes had occurred in a matter of minutes rather than hours.

Round one to me, she'd thought. That was the up. It had been downhill ever since.

They'd led her outside and then paused – willing her to get one last glimpse of freedom. She was determined to resist and yet she found herself staring round her greedily, consuming it all. She was dazzled by the detail and by the clarity with which she recorded it: everything was so vivid that she felt almost drugged. The light was blinding and yet it was the purples and reds of exotic flowers which sang in her eyes. The grass no longer looked uniform, she could see each spike standing alone, and on every individual leaf veins seemed to bulge. It was technicolour plus, a psychedelic experience. It was a world sprung anew.

It was all too much: she turned away from it.

The world reverted to black and white again. The man who'd been mowing the lawn stopped, leaned on his machine and looked first at her and then at her police escort. His face was blank and yet knowing. And then just as Sarah was bending down to get into the car, the madam of the house emerged. Sarah saw the look of inquiry on the white woman's face, a look that changed first to comprehension and then to hardened neutrality. The woman waved her hand at her gardener who bent down at his work again, and then the woman went inside and closed the door, shutting Sarah out.

Inside the car a policeman sat on either side of her. She struggled to ignore them, grappling with inappropriate and conflicting emotions. She felt terror but also a kind of exhilaration: denial and at the same time acceptance of the arrest. This was the nightmare that she could never have imagined, and yet she had anticipated it.

Her clarity of vision turned inwards, extending itself into the future. She saw herself wedged into a tiny cell which nevertheless dwarfed her. She saw herself in the dock, alone, unloved. She saw huge iron gates open in front of her and she heard them bang shut behind her. She felt herself dissolve into nothingness.

'Stop it,' she whispered to herself, 'stop it.'

A voice came floating into her head, the voice of her ANC instructor. *Guard against your imagination*, the voice advised. *It can unnecessarily frighten you. Don't think of the future: live each moment as it comes.*

Each moment was an age: each moment was too short. The city passed in front of her eyes, parts that she had never explored, that she would never explore. The drive into central Johannesburg was like torture and yet it was over too soon, far too soon. She saw a

102

flash of blue and then darkness and the interior of a padded elevator.

John Vorster Square, she thought. The elevator went straight up to the tenth floor. Corridors, that's what she saw. Corridors and fluorescent light and a man behind a glass booth. They held her by the elbow as if she might run – as if there was anywhere to run. A man passed her by, a tall grey-haired, grey-complexioned man, who walked with a limp and who continued on his way without a second glance at her. He doesn't care, she thought, I'm just another in a chain of others. And so is he. Somewhere there's a room, and in that room is a man like him, waiting for me.

The room was closer than she had imagined. It was a small, dull room empty of furniture save for a table and two upright chairs. A policeman pushed her into one of them, the one stranded at the centre of the room, and then he left. The other chair was occupied by a man who had been expecting her. He was not like the one she had passed in the corridor. He was young and healthy, a pleasant-looking man. And he had blue eyes. He reminded her of Alan.

Forget Alan, she thought. She had to forget him: she would not endanger him.

The man smiled. He got up and, stretching across the desk, lazily proffered his hand. 'Smit,' he said, 'that's my name.' And his tone implied that he was offering her friendship with his hand.

She refused the hand. Smit, she thought, you have struck a rock.

She had never felt less like a rock in her entire life.

CHAPTER FOURTEEN

Captain Malan waited in the corridor until the door closed behind Sarah. This is her moment of vulnerability, he thought: now Smit must pounce. He smiled at the thought, smiled as he willed his body back into motion. He walked determinedly through his pain, back into his office and closed the door carefully behind him.

The phone was ringing. He hobbled over to it and picked it up. 'A moment,' he said into it.

Placing the receiver on the desk he lowered himself into his chair. As he did so an image intruded, an image of a man, an image of his doctor. A recent image it was, culled from that very morning. The doctor had been talking on the phone but when Malan entered he'd hung up abruptly. Malan had known then, known that the news was bad.

Don't think of it, he told himself. 'Yes,' he barked into the phone. A voice, faint and blurred, issued across the line.

His doctor had talked softly. Malan remembered the slickness of his voice, remembered this along with his choice of words, and worst of all, the hateful look of sympathy on his face.

He would not think of it. 'Speak up,' he shouted.

The voice on the other end came through again, fractionally louder. 'De Vries?' Malan shouted. 'Is that you?'

Yes, it was de Vries, as incompetent as ever – the man couldn't even locate a properly functioning telephone!

'Where the *blerry* hell have you been, de Vries?' Malan asked. 'You were supposed to report in last night.' He picked up a pen as he spoke, and pulled a clean pad closer. He was nowhere as angry as he sounded: thank God de Vries had phoned; now he could really get things moving. He smiled.

But the pen never touched the page, and the smile became a scowl. For what de Vries said was not possible, it was not credible. Malan must have misunderstood.

'You've been where, man?' he asked.

De Vries repeated his story. He had, he said, been in prison, on the wrong side of the bars. He, an accredited policeman on official duty, had been arrested and held for sixteen hours on a trumped up charge.

As Malan opened his mouth, intending to ask for more details, words flew, unbidden, into his head – words from the past, words he'd chosen to disregard. *Don't act without me:* that's what he remembered.

He pushed the words away. 'What about our targets?' he asked of de Vries.

No, de Vries related, he'd never got a chance to find the target. He'd been arrested on his way there.

Don't act without me, because there's a delicate balance on this one that can easily be disrupted – that's what Zonda had said.

'Well go and find him now,' Malan shouted. 'Report to me as soon as you do. I'll deal with the rest.' He slammed the phone down.

He sat in his chair for only a fraction of a second and yet in that short time a myriad conflicting thoughts crowded in. He picked at them randomly: wondering whether he had been wrong to ignore Zonda's warnings, wondering why de Vries had been arrested and also who was involved – registering each item and then discarding it. They were thoughts but they were framed as questions: as questions without answers.

Well, he would find the answers. Pushing his chair hard away from his desk, he got up and left the room.

'What the hell's going on?' Malan demanded as soon as he had succeeded in gaining access to Jansen's office.

Jansen seemed unaffected by Malan's precipitant entrance. He looked up and smiled. 'Gert,' he said. 'I was just going to call you. You've heard about de Vries?'

'I've heard all right,' Malan said grimly.

'A disgraceful misunderstanding,' Jansen said. 'The district has extended a thousand apologies. But I won't, of course, let the matter rest there – I'll be taking it up at a higher level.' He smiled again and this time his face was poignant with concern. 'Gert,' he said, 'you don't look at all well. Come, please have a seat.'

Not at all well: that's how the doctor had started. He'd started gently, talking in euphemisms, before he finally came out with it.

Malan shook his head, and sat. To business, he told himself. 'De Vries was acting on my instructions,' he said. 'Someone stopped him.'

'Yes,' Jansen agreed. 'It's their fault, no doubt about it. Someone must pay.'

Someone must pay: that was Malan's first thought when the doctor stopped talking.

He blinked. He couldn't allow this train of thought to continue, he wouldn't. He had more important matters to deal with. Matters like the motive behind de Vries' arrest and the involvement of Jansen, and other matters too, matters almost too frightening to contemplate.

'Captain?'

Malan shivered: Jansen had been talking to him and he hadn't heard. He nodded as if he had.

'Are you planning to interrogate her yourself?' Jansen asked.

Her? Who was she? Malan frowned. And then it came to him. Sarah: of course. Jansen was talking about Sarah Patterson. 'No,' he replied. 'I've briefed Smit.'

'Smit. Well, if you think so.' Colonel Jansen nodded at Malan, nodded pleasantly enough but nodded to make it clear that he was summarily dismissing him.

Malan sat his ground, looking straight at Jansen.

His silence brought quick results, as he had known it would. 'About the other matter,' Jansen said. 'The unfortunate incident with de Vries. I'll pursue it, I promise you.'

Empty promises, thought Malan; he continued to wait.

'It was a mistake,' Jansen said. His voice was jovial and yet too loud to be really joking. 'It's not a conspiracy,' he said.

Isn't it? Malan thought. Interesting, then, that you should think to deny it. Satisfied he got up and made his way, without comment, to the door. He should have left more quickly, left while Jansen was still on the defensive but the ache in his leg slowed him down. Jansen was given another chance, which he chose to take when Malan was opening the door. 'Tell me again, Gert,' he asked. 'Why do you think Sarah Patterson is so important?'

Wrongfooted, Malan turned. 'Something big is planned,' he said.

'Involving Miss Patterson?'

Malan nodded, shook his head and then nodded again.

'Take your time, Gert,' Jansen said. His tone was gentle.

The bastard, Malan thought. He swallowed the bile that rose to his throat. 'Sarah Patterson is the link,' he said.

Jansen didn't blink. 'I see,' he said. The careful neutrality of his voice displayed the fact that he really did not see.

'Alan Littell holds the key,' Captain Malan said. 'And Patterson is my link to Littell.'

Jansen nodded. 'Littell,' he prounounced the name tentatively as if he disliked it. 'Littell,' he said again. He paused, wringing out the silence so that Malan would see him purging his face of doubt. 'You know, Gert,' he said when it was clear, 'you know I'm one of your most ardent admirers. Your work in the Sixties and Seventies is legendary. Your involvement in Rivonia – in paralysing the entire leadership of the ANC – did more than anything to buy us time. And your single-handed smashing of an armed terrorist unit in 'seventy-nine – well that's a text book case of exceptional police work.'

He spoke quickly to stop Malan from interrupting. 'No, don't be modest.' He stood up, reached across his desk and flicking a button on his dictating machine, removed a small tape.

'But then even old dogs must learn new tricks sometimes,' he said. He pushed the tape across the desk. 'Would you mind giving this to my secretary on your way out?' he asked.

*

107

She was ignorant as to the passing of time. They had taken her watch from her and the blinds were securely drawn. She was disoriented, not knowing whether what she felt was hunger or fatigue, fear or plain boredom. It was as if she had spent her whole life in the room and yet she knew that she'd only recently arrived. Inaction had numbed her body and for this she was grateful. All she could hope was that the fog that hovered over the room would completely engulf her.

Smit did not appear to have noticed the fog. He was relaxed: he had leant his chair against the wall and tilted it so that his feet were propped up on the table.

'Be reasonable, Sarah,' he said. The soles of his shoes, she saw, were clean.

His voice sounded soft, muffled by the fog. It was joined by another one. *They try to lull you into a false sense of security*, the second voice said.

Sarah blinked. The fog, she realized, was her enemy: it was clouding her mind. She must fight it. 'I've already told you, you have no right to call me Sarah,' she said.

'No right?' He smiled at her and raised an eyebrow. He paused.

The fog embraced her, its damp tentacles caressed her. She raised her voice. 'I'm a British subject,' she said. 'I demand to see my Ambassador.'

He inspected the nails on his right hand. They too were probably spotless, she thought.

'Your Ambassador,' he mused. 'You've said that before. And I've told you that under Section 29 you have no right to call anyone.' He touched a finger to his lips and glanced up at her as if something had occurred to him. 'Don't you find it sad,' he asked, 'that you look now to the British government for help?'

The fog was warmer now and she desired it.

Smit frowned. 'You're right,' he said, 'it isn't sad. It's depressing. You go running to the British because your friends won't help you.'

Friends, she thought. Which friends?

'What kind of friends are they?' he continued. He smiled gently. 'Not my kind, I can assure you. My friends wouldn't use me and then dump me.'

'I don't imagine you have many friends,' she said without stopping to think.

He reacted vehemently, dropping his legs to the ground and jumping up to glare at her, parting the fog as he did so. She felt a moment's triumph that, as his glare hardened, was turned to fear. She had angered him and that was a mistake. The fog was cold. She shivered.

He turned away from her, faced the window and, lifting a section of the blind, peered out of it. He was careful: she didn't see a thing. 'Looks like it's turning misty,' he commented.

She felt a moment's relief: so that explained the fog! But the moment was too short and quickly did it go. He was lying, he must be. He was paid to lie.

'You say you're here on holiday,' he said, and his voice was so low that she had to strain to hear it. 'Yet you don't act like a tourist.'

'Is that a crime?' Her voice was loud, too loud. 'Perhaps in this country, it is,' she said.

He turned and smiled at her, seeming genuinely amused. 'You don't like our country, do you?' He didn't wait for a reply. 'I don't like it much either,' he mused. 'Not at the moment.'

'Because you're on the losing side,' she said, enjoying the resonance in her voice.

Carefully Smit reseated himself. He folded his hands in front of him. He sighed. 'Now, now, Sarah,' he coaxed, 'do you have to talk of sides?'

What else is there to talk about? she thought.

'If you really want to know,' he said, 'I'm against apartheid. It's unnecessary and outmoded. And I'm not alone in my thoughts. There are many who feel as I do, who consider the time ripe for talks.'

'Even with the ANC?'

'You know about the ANC then?'

I'm talking too much, she thought.

He continued to look straight at her. 'Of course you know about the ANC,' he said and his voice had become the fog. 'Mandela, Sisulu. They're household names these days.'

She shrugged.

109

He frowned at her. 'If you refuse to answer even the simplest of my questions,' he warned, 'I'm going to have to assume you're hiding something. For Christ's sake woman, pictures of a free Sisulu have been beamed to every country in the world. You must have seen them. Surely you did?'

Don't lie when you don't have to, she remembered. She nodded.

'And they weren't new to you either,' he continued. 'You're an intelligent woman, you've been in Southern Africa, you must have known of the ANC.'

She heard the mockery in his voice and she knew it to be justified. 'I've known of the ANC,' she conceded.

'Known of them?'

'Of course I have.'

'Anything else?'

'No,' she said. The fog had gone. 'No,' she said again. She was glad it had gone.

'That's stupid,' he said flatly. 'I'm disappointed in you, Sarah: I didn't think you were stupid.' He took his arms off the desk and pulled a file towards him. 'You know of the ANC,' he said. 'And more than that. You've attended their functions.'

Slowly, agonizingly slowly, he opened the file. He frowned and began to read from it. 'You were first spotted at a New Year's party in 1980,' he began, 'and then again at a December 16th meeting in the same year. You frequented, on numerous occasions, pubs known to be ANC venues. You were pictured – oh yes, this is quite a nice one.' He pulled a photograph out of the file and waved it in the air. 'Taken, when? Let me see.' He read something off the back. 'During an ANC bazaar in October 1980. In addition . . .'

The fog closed in again. 'All right.' Her voice pushed it away. 'So I attended ANC events. That proves nothing.'

He threw her a dazzler of a smile. 'Yes,' he said. 'Of course it proves nothing.' The smiled vanished as quickly as it arrived. 'But you interrupted me', he continued, 'before I got to the really interesting part: your time in Mozambique and Angola . . .'

Old dogs, new tricks, the litany stayed with Malan for over an hour. He sat with it, not in fury, but in concentration. He rolled the phrase around his brain, focusing on its hidden meaning. It was on the face of it a flippant cliché, uttered so as to belittle. And yet, Malan thought, did Jansen ever enunciate a single word without first weighing it? Perhaps Jansen had been doing more than merely undermining Malan: perhaps Jansen was warning him off.

When it came, the second call from de Vries added weight to Malan's suspicions. For what de Vries told him was simple enough. As instructed by Malan he had gone to the place that Zonda had mentioned. He had gone there and found the place not only empty, but bearing the signs of a hurried evacuation. So that's how things stood: Malan had sent de Vries to watch one of their terrorist suspects, but de Vries had been deterred. Somebody had removed the target, imprisoning de Vries while he did so. That meant, Malan thought dispassionately, that the somebody was either part of the force or had influence over it. Somebody with power, perhaps, who'd heard that Malan was sending de Vries and who'd had de Vries neutralized. Somebody who was protecting an ANC spy and arresting a member of the Special Branch.

A spy in the ranks. A spy and an important one.

Was it possible: was it possible that the ANC had a spy high up in the force? Someone who protected the leader of the ANC's armed group and who moved him when threatened. A spy: was that why Zonda was being so careful, and so silent? Was that why he'd warned Malan not to act until he'd obtained all the information?

Malan frowned. He should have waited, should have listened to Zonda. It was Jansen's insinuations that had panicked him, Jansen's intrusive suggestions. His frown deepened. Jansen was worming his way into Malan's psyche: Malan had spent many years, most of his working life in fact, in the Special Branch and this was the first time he had thought he might have been panicked into an unwise course of action. The first time.

Perhaps Jansen was right: perhaps the country was changing so much that Malan no longer knew what was happening. Perhaps both he and Zonda had been outmanoeuvred. Perhaps they were both old dogs. But no, he would not have it that way. No matter

111

what his doctor said, Malan was not finished. Even if his doctor was right, he still wouldn't be beaten. Neither cancer, nor the likes of Colonel Jansen would get the better of him.

I still have the fight inside of me, Malan thought. And like the fighter he was, he looked to his weapons. He mentally counted them all, his network of agents, the impending report due in from Zonda, his suspicion of a highly placed spy. He could use them – each in its time. Oh yes, he could use them.

And more than that, he had another weapon, already in his control: he had Sarah Patterson. If he was finished, he vowed, then so was she: he would make sure that Smit milked her dry and, in the process, Malan's own doubts would be either abolished or confirmed.

Smit, on a winning streak, appeared suddenly to lose interest. He pressed a button and a uniformed policeman came into the room, put his hand under her elbow and propelled her out. The corridor was a blur, the lift a cage, the basement as dark as a coffin. There was a man who appeared to be waiting for her down there, a man who looked familiar. But he was not waiting for her, he turned away when she arrived. He was like an insect, she thought, inching his way along the walls.

She had thought that she would have done anything to flee Smit's insinuating voice. And yet, when they left her in a small cold cell, she found herself fighting an impulse to call them back, to ask for Smit, anybody at all – just as long as she had company. The yearning for human contact swelled until she found herself at the door, one hand up, ready to bang on it. But then she heard the sound of metal moving. She jumped and turned away, turned from eyes that studied her. She felt first self-contempt and then determination. She wouldn't, she resolved, give in so easily.

She moved away from the door, sat down in the middle of the concrete floor and crossed her legs. Placing one hand on each knee she began to breathe deeply and regularly. She imagined herself back in the safety of Camden Town, surrounded by her friends, listening to a voice bidding her to empty her mind. She constructed the room there in her head, the smell of incense, the large pink pillows, the feeling of women together.

It worked: gradually the panic lessened. She closed her eyes.

As soon as she did so, Smit's voice, that voice that she'd only a few minutes ago been desperate to hear, pursued her. 'What were you doing in Johannesburg?' He was relentless. 'What were you up to?'

'Nothing,' she silently screamed. 'I was doing nothing.'

'How do you think we know about you?' he asked. And then he answered himself. 'Your so-called friends betrayed you,' he said.

'No, they haven't. They didn't. They wouldn't.'

The questions came at her unceasingly, worse than they had in the room. She was bombarded by them, wanting the fog back again but unable to conjure it up. It was a waking nightmare, a dream from which there was no escape. Her eyes felt heavy, the lids sealing them securely.

She forced them open. In doing so she banished Smit. She could not, however rid herself of the fear. He knew all about her, his documentation was immense. He had photos, copies of letters, tapes even. He had her life, there on his desk.

She shook her head. She must think of something else, she must ground herself another way. Alan. That was it.

He could help her.

CHAPTER FIFTEEN

The place was London, the date the 31st December 1979. She was at an ANC party.

And the trigger? Oh yes, that was it: 'Across a crowded room Sarah Patterson saw Alan Littell . . .' Smit was no longer with her. She had Alan in her sights: she saw him as she had then.

She was at an ANC party, minutes away from the dawning of a new decade, and on the point of leaving. She had been like that then – quiet and yet independent, determined to go her own way. She had turned from her friends, laughing off their injunctions to stay until midnight. She had turned away, separating herself from the crowd. That's when she saw Alan.

That is when she saw Alan and when she fell in love with him. It had been as simple as that – one glance and her life veered off track. To think of it now, lying in a gaol, made it seem ridiculous. And yet that's how it had happened. He was standing on the other side of the hall, leaning against a wall. He was tall, lanky almost, but he projected strength. His skin was pale and yet not insipid – he had the look of a man who'd really lived. He was ranging his eyes around the hall and he caught her looking at him. For a moment he returned her gaze and in that moment a part of her dissolved. He looked away, but she could not.

'I'm off,' she told her friends. I'm off, she thought as she steeled herself against rejection. She dodged through the crowd, pursued by unfamiliar insecurities, telling herself it didn't matter and a casual word was all she would have with him before she left. But as she neared him, the attraction was magnified. Dropping all

114

pretence of indifference she went to stand in front of him. What he must have registered was a pretty, oval face, brown shoulder-length hair, friendly brown eyes, a charming smile and an awkward warmth. She had seen only one thing, the bluest eyes, and had wanted suddenly to fall into them, to lose herself in their intensity. She'd smiled.

'I don't usually approach strangers,' she had said. She had held out a hand, 'My name's Sarah Patterson.'

'Alan Littell.' His grip was strong and somehow familiar.

'You're South African,' she'd said.

He'd shrugged. 'What else?'

'It's midnight,' somebody called.

As Sarah lay still, savouring what happened next, the past and the present collided.

'*Voetsak*,' a hard voice ordered.

'She'll be floundering between the twin polls of insolence and anguish,' Malan told Smit, 'and she'll be exhausted. It's soon time to bring her up again.'

Smit, young and fit, was sprawled in the chair opposite his Captain. He nodded, content in the knowledge that his superior was pleased with his progress.

'Keep the pressure on,' Malan said.

This time Smit's nod was tinged with perplexity. He didn't understand why Malan was wasting so much time on Sarah Patterson: he thought of her as a low-key diversion who could be easily handled. He looked a question at his boss.

Malan caught Smit's look and he knew that Smit thought he was over-reacting, but he made no attempt to counteract this impression. For he also knew something else: he knew Smit's loyalty could be bought, and that the highest bidder was Jansen, the only man in a position to deliver promotion. So it would be disastrous for Malan to even hint at his suspicions. It would be disastrous to suggest that Jansen might have ordered de Vries' arrest or forewarned de Vries' target. Smit would never believe that: Smit would consider it unthinkable that a man of Jansen's calibre could be a traitor. Smit was inexperienced and his imagination was limited. He would balk at tales of insurgents

115

arriving by sea, of an officer in the police protecting a terrorist and of a mysterious silence from a master spy. Smit would balk because he hadn't lived, as Malan had done, with the unthinkable and he hadn't learned how to face it.

So Smit could not be used as a sounding board. But Smit was still important.

'Alan Littell is Patterson's only real contact with the ANC,' Malan told Smit. 'And her most vulnerable point. Press her on him. I want to know everything about Littell – where he spends his time, how he spends it, what he tells her and what he doesn't tell her. Get it for me, even if it means breaking her, get all of it.'

He nodded his head, dismissing Smit. 'Don't let up on her,' he said.

Alan's eyes had haunted her in those first weeks and in the months that followed too. They were so expressive, those eyes, so ever changing. They were the reservoir of a man who had lived life and of a man who knew what it was to feel deeply. And even though Alan kept himself distant he had much to offer; only when she was with him did she feel completely whole. Not that he ever promised security – far from it. Whereas her life was stable, his was ablaze with change. He lived on the edge of intensity and he took her to it. She talked long into the nights with him, she danced with him, she laughed and made love with him, and all the time she was afraid that one day he might vanish from her life.

Yet each step brought them closer together. He went away – that was still true – but on his return he would hurry round and hungrily embrace her. And she had begun to realize that it was not only physical attraction which bound him to her. The wariness that had once been ever present began to leave his eyes and she knew that she had finally won his trust. That was when she began to feel safe: that was when she had proposed living together.

The cell door opened abruptly and a man stood there, jangling a set of keys.

'You're wanted,' he said.

*

116

Arriving at the fifth floor, she was buffeted by fatigue and elation, and by fear and confidence as well. She stood motionless, trying to mentally catch up with herself, but the policeman behind her shoved her forward.

She took a deep breath and, with it, took herself in hand. She walked down the corridor thinking that anything was better than being alone. She walked into Smit's room and sat down on the chair, the one she considered hers.

'Who told you to sit?' he bellowed.

She jerked her head away as if he had hit her.

Never give up she remembered. She turned to look at him and then, keeping her eyes firmly fixed on him, she stood.

'Let's talk about your friend Alan Littell,' he suggested. His voice was mild.

A muscle in her leg quivered. She willed it into stillness. 'I have nothing to say,' she said.

Smit nodded. He stretched both arms, stretched them up high above his head before bringing them slowly down to his sides. He yawned. He got up and began to move, skirting around her, inscribing a circle until he came to a stop directly behind her. She felt his breath on her neck. He was tall, she realized, as tall as Alan and as well built. He placed one hand on each of her shoulders. She flinched.

'What's the matter Sarah?' he asked. 'Are you one of those women who don't like men?'

He pushed down, hard down on her shoulders. She gave way, sinking until she was seated. She felt him move away. He ended up standing straight in front of her, his arms indolently crossed.

'That's better,' he said, looking down at her.

'I thought you wanted me to stand.'

He shrugged. 'Stand, sit – what do I care?' he said.

You care, she thought.

'But you do like men,' he said as though nothing had passed between them since he had touched her. He narrowed his eyes. 'You like Alan Littell.'

Alan, she thought, I will not betray you.

'Tell me about him.'

She bit her tongue and the pain felt good.

117

Smit shrugged. 'You can't tell me about Alan,' he said. 'Because you don't know him – not really. But I do and I'll tell you. From the beginning, I'll tell you.' He looked her up and down and there was no mistaking the lingering of his gaze, nor the languor in it. 'Alan Littell pursued you,' he said. 'He followed you because he wanted to use you.'

Smit was wrong. Alan had never pursued her. It was she who had ensnared Alan, she who'd invited him to her flat and she who'd followed up after he'd left.

'You didn't know what you were getting into when you jumped into bed with him that night,' Smit jeered.

She smiled to herself. She hadn't jumped into bed with Alan, not that night and not for many others after it.

'I bet you thought he was serious about you,' Smit said. 'You, like all his women, thought you could change him.'

Like all his women – what did Smit know? She closed her eyes, shutting out Smit's venom, remembering the time, almost ten years ago, when she had first felt Alan's nakedness against hers. She remembered it all: how his reserve had melted as they made love, how she had seen his vulnerability and learned that, under his strength, lurked reserves of gentleness. She remembered how, at first, his touch was tentative, almost as if he were in awe of her, but how, as she grew bolder, so did he, until it was he who took the initiative, who took charge of both their bodies, who brought a certainty to their act of love. She remembered feeling that all his alertness was focused on that one interaction. She remembered him watching her with those blue eyes, being aware of his gaze on her all the time even as she came.

'Don't dream, Sarah,' Smit shouted. His face was close, revoltingly close, and a drop of his spittle hit her cheek. She turned her head away. 'You can't hide from me,' Smit hissed. 'No one will help you. Even your heroic Alan can't save you.' He reached out a hand and, grabbing her chin with it, pulled her face back to the front. 'I bet Alan said he could save you,' he said. 'But Alan's a liar. He kept you in the dark.'

She struggled to move her head away but his fingers were dug into her flesh and she couldn't budge them.

She moved her thoughts instead. It's true, she thought, Alan

118

did keep me in the dark. He never told me what he did, it was months before I guessed that he was involved with the ANC.

Smit had reached bone.

Alan had to be like that, she thought quickly. For others depended on him.

'Alan did nothing but take from you,' Smit jeered. 'And you accepted it.' He released his fingers and shoved her head away. 'You accepted everything,' he said.

She felt the imprint of his hand even though he had removed it. It wasn't true, it wasn't. What Alan took he bountifully returned. He'd ended by sharing his whole life with her: it was she, not he, who'd been transformed.

'He led you astray,' Smit said. 'He sent you here. He cares only for himself, not for you. He betrayed you.'

She shook her head. Alan had not led her astray. He'd never wanted her to come to South Africa, he'd fought with her to prevent her from volunteering. Smit was wrong. Alan hadn't betrayed her: he had tried to protect her.

She looked up defiantly. 'You don't know Alan,' she said.

Smit smiled and his eyes sparkled. 'But I do,' he said. Those eyes weaved a spell of magic, pulling her into them, just as Alan's had. 'I know him better than you.' He withdrew his eyes, strolled away in fact, slowly sauntering over to his desk and then sitting on its edge. He stretched a hand behind him and picked up a piece of paper. He began to read from it, pronouncing the words exactly as Alan might have pronounced them.

'I was born in a country that was not mine,' he read, 'and this fact has haunted me for most of my life.'

She knew those words: they had been long ago scorched on her memory. Everything about them: when she had read them, where she had been sitting, how she had felt . . . All this had remained with her. That sentence and the ones that followed had been the real beginning for her: they had led her to this place.

She swallowed hard, keeping her mouth firmly closed. Her head ached as she struggled to stop herself from blinking.

'I realize how this must sound,' Smit read.

How did Smit have those words? How had he obtained them?

Smit smiled at her. 'I don't need to go on do I?' He held the page up, high in the air. 'Alan showed you this didn't he? Alan knows how to get sympathy: he's clever that way.' Smit lowered his arm, crumpled the paper and threw it, now in a tight ball, across the room. It landed by her feet.

She let it lie.

'Alan would tell you enough to keep you hanging on,' Smit continued. 'That and no more. He kept secrets, from you, many secrets: they all do. Face it Sarah, you've been used. Alan Littell and the ANC sent you on a suicide mission: they were using you.'

'And you're not using me?' She laughed, briefly, mirthlessly.

He responded with concentrated seriousness. 'I am, of course I am,' he agreed. 'But at least I'm honest.' He picked up a pencil, it was sharpened to a point, she saw, and jabbed it in the air. 'I'll admit that you're insignificant,' he said. 'And I'll do more than that. I'll tell you plainly that if you answer my questions, I'll let you go. You're nothing to me. Talk and you're a free woman.'

He got up and stood for a moment, looking down at her. His eyes were cold and cruel. She didn't know how she could have seen Alan in those eyes.

'Don't talk,' he said, 'and I'll throw away the key.' His fist with the pencil attached hit down at the desk. The point broke and he dropped the rest. 'Think about it, won't you?' he asked.

He walked past her, making straight for the door. It opened as if somebody had been timing him, as if they had known that he was ready to leave. And then the door closed and she was left alone.

Alone she sat, aware she was aching but dismissing it, conscious of how her thoughts raced but powerless to grasp a single one of them. Alan's words kept repeating on her, his words and what Smit had said about them.

Smit's absence felt more poisonous than his presence. While he was in the room she had known he was lying; but once he left, what he had said remained with her. She could not discount it all. Smit had twisted everything, but his words were not all falsehood. Alan did indeed hide things from her.

She was pulled back into the past, resisting but still pulled back to a time, nine years previously. She had come home unexpectedly and Alan had been there, at the desk, his head bent

120

down in concentration. Planning to surprise him she had walked softly up behind him, put her arms around his neck and bent down to kiss him.

She had surprised him all right. He'd whipped round, his eyes ablaze with hatred. 'Were you spying on me?' he had snarled.

You don't know Alan, Smit said and at that time in the past, that's exactly what she had thought. I don't know this man, she'd thought, as he lambasted her.

'Can't I ever be left alone?' he had shouted. He was beside himself, unstoppable. 'You interfering bitch. You have to know everything.'

You accepted everything, Smit said, but it wasn't true. She hadn't accepted Alan then. She had stood there, listening while her incredulity was turned to fury. She had watched silently as the colour left his cheeks, silent as well when, seemingly surfacing from madness, he swallowed back the words that had issued from his mouth. She had felt no forgiveness, only anger. 'What were you doing?' she had asked.

He had been just like Smit then, driven by rage. He'd grabbed his note pad and stuffed it into his briefcase. 'I won't be questioned,' he'd shouted. He got up. 'I'm going out,' and, taking the briefcase, he left without another word.

She was left standing in the centre of their London living room, facing the dissolution of her world. Alan had become a stranger. What went through her head was something similar to what Smit had been saying. Alan, she had silently raged, you gave me nothing, volunteered nothing, met my questions with evasions. Alan, she had thought, you betrayed me.

But still Smit was wrong, she hadn't accepted everything. She had left the flat, taking none of her possessions, not even a shred of clothing, but resolved to return only when he had gone for good. Smit was wrong.

Alan Littell pursued you: that's what Smit said. Smit was right: Alan had come after her, tracking her down and turning up unexpectedly.

'I've come to apologize,' he had said. 'May I?'

She'd stood aside and let him in, leading him to the room that had become hers. When she had shut the door she looked straight at him.

Alan cares only for himself: that's what Smit said.

Two men, two white South African men, with piercing blue eyes, and yet they couldn't have been more different. Smit lost his power – Smit was lying. Smit had been talking about himself, not about Alan. For in that time Alan's eyes were moist with tears and she'd realized then how much he loved her.

She embraced the memory and it warmed her. She'd gone up to him, put her arms around him. They had stood there in the centre of the room unmoving for a while.

Alan had won the battle: Alan had banished Smit. She saw Alan, as clearly as if he were in the room. She saw him in his weakness and in his strength. He started to explain, but she sealed his lips with a finger. 'It doesn't matter,' she said.

He shook his head. 'I should have told you more.'

Smit was wrong: Alan had not lied to her. He'd reached into his pocket and withdrawn a document. 'This is what I was writing,' he said. 'I want you to read it.'

She'd taken the paper and glanced at the heading. 'Your life story?' she said in surprise.

He nodded. 'Read it,' he insisted.

And so she sat and so began to read. 'I was born in a country that was not my own . . .' she read, gripped despite his archaic turn of phrase, reading fast until the end, until the pieces of her Alan had been slotted finally into place.

'I knew some of it,' she'd said. 'But –'

Alan had silenced her with a shake of his head. 'I didn't give it to you so you could feel sorry for me,' he said. 'But because I wanted you to know why I reacted with such anger. I felt too exposed.'

She'd pulled him down beside her and, when his head was level with hers, she'd kissed him. Her body melted at the touch of his lips, of the hard and yet tender contact from a man she was only now learning to know. She undid the buttons of his shirt and she felt his hands behind her as they gently unzipped her dress. Slowly, gradually, tenderly they made love. The Alan of Smit's imagination could never have behaved so.

Only when they were lying side by side, joined together by invisible threads, did either of them speak.

'I know it's wrong,' was what Alan said, 'but until you left I believed we were living a charmed life and that the outside would never intrude.'

She turned to face him. 'So I was just a distraction between revolutionary acts was I?' she teased.

He didn't return her smile. 'Sometimes I wish it was like that,' he said seriously. He paused. 'I never loved anyone before I learned to love you,' he whispered. Again a pause. 'Anyone,' he repeated.

She thought of what she had just read and she nodded.

He got up and sat at the edge of the bed, his back to her. 'Do you know what my biography means?' he asked. He didn't wait for an answer. 'I had to write it as a first step to joining MK,' he said.

'MK?' She wished she didn't sound so stupid.

'Umkhonto we Sizwe. The ANC army. I can't justify staying out of it any longer: I have to play a more active role. I wanted to break it to you gently but when you walked in on me like that, I was taken by surprise.'

Sarah sat alone in the interrogation room and felt again the shock his words had engendered. The same anguish surged in her chest: the same stabbing pain she'd felt when he said he was going to leave. And then the shock left and the pain as well as she relived what happened next. She remembered how clear she had felt, how totally sure she was. She never doubted herself, not even when without informing Alan, she had left her job, her home, her country – all to follow him into the unknown. The memory warmed her: the memory of how startled he had been at her appearance, startled to the verge of fury. She had stood there, watching, trembling, waiting to see what his final response would be. She had stood there, counting the long seconds until his sudden, delighted acceptance released her from fear.

Smit entered the room, walked over to his desk, sat down and opened his mouth. She felt momentarily grateful to him, grateful that he had forced her to remember and that, in remembering, strengthened her. For what had happened after then was the beginning of everything, the time when she followed Alan to Southern Africa and into her new life.

123

'I've got nothing to say to you,' she told Smit. Alan had vanquished Smit.

Smit shrugged. 'That's a pity,' he said. 'But never mind. I have plenty to say to you.'

He reached into his pocket and pulled out a photograph. Lazily he tossed it over to her. His aim was true: the photograph made a high arc in the air before landing in her lap.

'Look at it,' he said.

She let it lie there on her lap.

'Look at it.' It was a command this time, spoken with a force that brought back memory of his fingers on her face.

She picked up the picture and looked at it, straight into the face of a young black woman, a woman with braided hair, large eyes and high cheekbones. The woman was smiling at the camera but her eyes were sad.

'Do you know her?' Smit asked.

Sarah shook her head.

'You wouldn't know her would you?' Smit commented. 'And even if you did you wouldn't tell me. Well, I'll save you the trouble, I'll tell you her name. Her name's Thembi. She was an MK combatant. She's dead.'

Dead, thought Sarah, the face has the look of death about it. 'What is this to me?' she asked.

'You really didn't know?' Smit's voice grew almost sympathetic. He had good range, she thought and she was glad she thought this before he spoke because, afterwards, there was no room for thought.

'Well, Sarah,' was what he said, 'believe it or not, I'm sorry to be the one to tell you. Thembi was a friend of Alan's. No, that's not right. They were more than friends. Thembi was Alan Littell's lover.'

Day Three

CHAPTER SIXTEEN

Tanzania

Transcript of interview between Comrades Alan Littell and Rebecca Moisia . . . (continuation page 12)
RM: Tell me about Thembi.
AL: Thembi is dead.
RM: I know she's dead. Don't you remember? I delivered her funeral oration. Tell me about her.
AL: What do you want to know?
RM: Were you lovers?

(The record here shows a long silence)

RM: Were you lovers?

(AL's answer not audible. Note to interrogator: please ask subject to speak into the microphone).

RM: Comrade, you do not help youself by being obstructive. We are investigating a serious charge against you, a charge that involves your activities in our movement in their entirety. Now tell me: were you and Thembi lovers?
AL: (inaudible)
RM: Was that a yes?
AL: Yes, I told you, yes. We were lovers. For a short while.
RM: Why did she kill herself?
AL: Because she was unrevolutionary — isn't that what you said at the time? You, I suppose, should know.
RM: Comrade, I'm asking you.
AL: What does it matter why she killed herself? She's dead. She

127

and Victor are dead. Robert Wentworth is dead: why don't you ask me why he killed himself? Oh yes, and there was a man who stuck to a hand grenade on our first day's training. He's dead too. Is he my responsibility? We could spread the net further if you like: those in death row – did I give them away?

(*Note from transcriber: AL's voice so loud that sound distorted*).

AL: (continued) ask me about – don't you. What I say will make no difference. I'm guilty because I'm white. You know that most spies are black but you think I'm guilty because I'm white. And you're right, of course. I'm powerful you know, I hold the balance of life and of . . . of the skull risen from the grave, the revenge of white South Africa, the harbinger of death. . .

(*Sound of loud banging. Tape appears to end here.*)

Pushing the transcript aside. Jabulani frowned. 'What happened?' he asked.

Rebecca sighed. 'Nothing much. Littell grew hysterical and kicked over a chair. The guards heard the noise and came rushing in and I decided to end the interview. There didn't seem any point in continuing: Littell had become completely irrational.'

Jabulani raised an eyebrow. 'Irrational?' he asked. 'Because he thinks you judge him guilty?'

'He is guilty,' Rebecca snapped.

The words flew unbidden from her mouth, those words she should not say. She registered Jabulani's shock but with recognition came the realization – and it was good – that she didn't really care. She was tired, bone-tired: tired of pretending, tired of concealing her dislike for Alan Littell. Her job was difficult enough without Littell doing his utmost to make it worse. On occasions, when she was alone with him, she felt as if he were, quite literally, driving her insane.

'He's so sorry for himself,' she said. 'So emotional.'

'If you were he,' Jabulani said softly. 'You might also react as he does.'

'No.' Her denial was absolute.

Jabulani smiled. 'You're right,' he said. 'You wouldn't react that way. But don't you think you're equating Alan's obvious sense of guilt with the assumption that he's guilty?'

He looked across the table at Rebecca. She was sitting still, completely impassive. As if she's been carved from stone, he thought, she has buried her capacity to feel.

What he didn't know — what he couldn't know — was that as Rebecca sat there it occurred to her that, if she were to rise from her seat and walk over to Jabulani, she could put her hands around his neck and squeeze before he had time to react. The thought came into her head as if it were a natural one, as if it had been queuing up politely, waiting its turn.

She shivered violently and pulled her cardigan around her. I'm being irrational now, she thought. Jabulani is not my enemy.

'Guilt,' she said quietly. 'I have no time for it.'

Jabulani looked at her, a question in his eyes.

She shivered again. I'm getting malaria, she thought. I need some quinine. 'How could Alan accuse me of labelling Thembi unrevolutionary?' is what she said.

Instead of answering, Jabulani activated the tape recorder on the desk. A disembodied voice, Rebecca's voice, issued from the machine.

'*Comrade Thembi's life was hard,*' the voice said. '*She suffered greatly.*'

Rebecca cut across her voice on the tape. 'What's the point of this?' she asked.

Jabulani put a finger to his lips.

The voice continued. '*She was young and at an age when she should have been at home with her parents,*' it said, '*playing childish games, learning what it is to become a woman. All this was denied her and it caused her great distress.*'

'We understand,' Rebecca whispered and it surprised her that she could still remember her words.

'*We understand,*' the voice said. '*And we mourn for her. She was our comrade. Every death in our movement we experience as a death in our family.*' The voice strengthened. '*And yet,*' it continued, '*Thembi was wrong to take her own life. Although it is true that revolutions are won so that individuals may live in peace it is also*

129

true that there comes a time in every revolution when the individual is no longer as important as the whole. That time has come for us. At home our people are fighting: their actions are superhuman and they require a superhuman response. Thembi should have listened to the collective pain of our people rather than concentrating on her own. Not only Thembi, but all of us. We must respond to our people: not with sleeping pills but with the gun, not by dwelling on our own petty problems but by daily renewing our determination to end apartheid.'

Stretching over the desk, Rebecca switched off the tape recorder.

'If I remember rightly,' Jabulani said, 'you ended by saying that apartheid killed Thembi and that we must abolish apartheid in order to save future Thembis.'

'And so?' Rebecca demanded. 'What's wrong with that?'

'You and I talked about it afterwards,' Jabulani said. 'Do you remember?'

The impulse to strangle him returned. She could almost feel the texture of his skin beneath her fingers: that soft skin she had once known. There had been a time, she remembered, when his words had pleased her, when the way he touched her had comforted her.

She was hot, too hot. She undid her cardigan and pulled it off.

She had been wearing the same cardigan on the day of Thembi's funeral. The day was cold and she had been grateful for its protection as she stood by the graveside watching the crowd disperse. She was thinking how familiar the cemetery had grown. Her fellow South Africans were dying regularly, too regularly, felled by malaria, traffic accidents, UNITA attacks, old age even. So many, she thought, who would never go home, so many casualties of the war against apartheid. She stood and watched as the groups of soldiers, foreign workers, Angolans, filed into buses and cars, walking slowly, without conversation, their animation dulled by the weight of Thembi's death. A chill wind was blowing through the graveyard bringing with it the scent of mimosa. She remembered thinking that she must be imagining the smell, that it was invoked by some incident in her past. She had turned away from the dusty grave.

130

Jabulani had joined her as she was walking towards her car. He must have been observing her, she'd thought, and even at the time she had felt irritated by his watchfulness.

'A good speech,' he'd said.

A simple enough comment and one that, from another's lips, could have been taken as a compliment. But although Rebecca and Jabulani were no longer lovers she was still attuned to the nuances in his voice.

'We agreed that the point had to be made.' She hadn't bothered to conceal the hostility in her voice. She increased her pace so that he was almost running to keep up with her.

'Yes, we agreed,' Jabulani said. 'But sometimes I wonder. . .'

She had stopped abruptly, cutting him off in mid-sentence. 'You think too much,' she'd said. 'You've spent too long in the west.'

Jabulani nodded, acknowledging the continuation of a running verbal battle. He had looked back at the grave and somehow he managed to pull her eyes there too. 'Thembi suffered under apartheid,' he had said, 'but apartheid exists only in our country while all over the world people choose to kill themselves. Personal distress is not always political.'

His eyes met hers. 'As you must know,' he concluded.

Those words had angered her. *As you must know*. What right did he have to utter them? What right to pry into her past, to hint at things unsaid, at feelings unexperienced? She had known then that cosy talk of a continuing friendship was dishonest. Jabulani was too pushy for her, too ready to assume a closeness that could never exist between them.

She had been so angry that she forgot to say goodbye. She walked to her car resolving to keep away from him. She had done exactly that, done it so effectively that she had almost managed to forget how he could make her feel. But Jabulani had not forgotten and he hadn't given up. She looked at him now, so handsome, so strong, so well satisfied with himself. His, she reflected, was the look of the new, self-assertive black South African – of the sophisticated, westernised black South African. His was the confidence from education in America rather than in the Eastern bloc, his the superiority stemming from a theoretical base rather than from a

131

simplistic passion for justice. His type would one day wipe out the unsophisticated Albert Kanas of this world: his type would win and perhaps, in winning, might displace her as well.

'Is this why you picked me to judge Alan Littell?' she asked. 'So you could play with me?'

'I did not ask for you to head this tribunal,' Jabulani replied. He talked slowly as if he were carefully choosing his words. Not carefully enough, however, to stop them irritating her. 'To be honest,' he concluded, 'I wouldn't have chosen you.'

Her anger returned. 'Am I not good enough?' she demanded.

Jabulani reached across and covered one of her hands with his. 'You're good at your job, Rebecca, you know you are,' he said. 'All I'm trying to say is that you if you are so unfair to yourself, how can you be fair to Alan?'

'I don't know what you're talking about.' She pulled her hand away.

'I think you do Rebecca,' he said. 'I think you do. Mzwanele. . .'

Is dead, she thought. She stood up, cutting Jabulani off in mid-sentence. 'Nothing is important', she said, 'except the struggle against apartheid.'

Her tone was final and it had its effect. The expression on Jabulani's face changed from a pleading sympathy to a brisk neutrality. 'There is one another matter to discuss,' he said in his trained voice, his bureaucratic voice.

She sat down, matching her expression to his.

'Have you thought it through?' he asked. 'What it might mean if Alan Littell is a spy.'

'Of course,' she said. 'The boat.'

'No, not only that,' Jabulani insisted. 'What it might mean about Robert Wentworth.'

'Wentworth admitted his guilt.'

Jabulani shrugged. 'You know how we used to do these things,' he said. 'Because we couldn't collect evidence from home, we found it difficult to identify spies. So we had to rely overmuch on personal pressure.' He paused as if he were waiting for her to object to what he had said. She didn't, she wouldn't give him that satisfaction. 'Wentworth was the type who might break from such pressure,' he continued. 'He could have been lying just to stop the questions.'

'But Wentworth killed himself,' she protested.

Jabulani nodded. He didn't comment and for that Rebecca was grateful. She got up, paused a second in case he wanted to say anything more and then, when he didn't speak, she left him sitting there.

The room was pathetic, that's what Alan thought. He gazed around at it, at its concrete outline and its contents – an old iron bedstead and heavy bucket. He looked at the zinc-lined window with its faded floral curtains and the pictures on the walls beside it – one of Thambo, one the youthful Mandela. From outside comes the sound of pounding: women are preparing mealie-meal.

And inside? Inside stood a man who was going mad.

It couldn't be true: he wasn't going mad. It was a plot, that's all it was, a plot launched to stop him from exposing the traitors. A plot, he thought, and he thought again of the look on Rebecca Moisia's face should he try and convince her of it. She'd never believe him, never, never.

He was going mad.

I need Sarah, he suddenly thought. I need her here.

But Sarah was in South Africa.

Or was she? He tried to figure out how long she had been there, and when she was due to leave. He had been in this place one, no two days. Or was it three? He tried so hard to work it out that his head began to ache – but all to no avail. The days and nights had merged, he couldn't put a number to any of them. For all he knew Sarah was already in England, waiting for him to call, worrying about what his silence meant.

Well, he must phone her: he must reassure her. He ran to the door and wrenched at it. The door was locked as he should have expected it to be. He was surely going mad for in all the time he had spent in this room, be it one or three days, it had never occurred to him that they might bar his exit.

How dare they? he thought. How dare they? He took a step backwards and then launched himself at the door, striking at it with his foot. It shook but did not budge. He moved back and hit

133

at it again, over and over until his foot ached and the wood showed signs of splintering. The door stayed closed. The door, he remembered, opened inwards not outwards. How could he have forgotten? In frustration he threw himself against it. He began pounding at it with his fists, calling out for help.

A tentative voice pronounced his name.

'Open the door,' Alan shouted. 'Open the door.'

He had to move away when they opened it, because he was in its path. There were three who opened it, three anxious black faces staring down at him.

'What's the date?' he asked. They took a step back, moving in synch as if they were connected to each other. 'What's the fucking date?'

The one in front mumbled something, a month, a day, and then, looking at his watch, the time as well. The words washed over Alan. He had forgotten why the date was so important, he was seized by another, more urgent desire.

'I want to go for a walk,' he shouted. 'I've got to get out of this room.'

The three shook their heads, shook them in unison. They are connected, Alan thought. In which case, they'll be sluggish.

He bent his head down and then he rushed at them, butting them out of the way. He stepped over the threshold of the room, stepping out into a kind of freedom. Three feet of freedom because that's how far he got before they recovered from their surprise, ran up to him and grabbed him by both arms. They were angry with him and unnecessarily rough. They pinned his arms behind him and threw themselves on top of him onto the dirt.

It felt good, the contact, the contact combined with the knowledge that they were going to beat him. Words, that's all they'd thrown at him, words, endless words. They had tied his brain in knots with questions, Rebecca's voice kept resounding in his head. How much better then was brute force: how much more real. Alan let his body go limp, waiting for the first blow to fall.

It never did. Instead Rebecca's voice pursued him even here. 'What's going on?' she asked.

Alan saw light again as the men got off him, stumbling their way to their feet. He didn't move: he lay on the dirt and, shading his eyes with his hand, he peered up at Rebecca. She was standing against the sun and her fuzzy hair was framed by a halo of yellow brightness.

'I need a walk,' he said.

He could not make out her features but he thought he saw a look of something – was it pity? – cross her face. I must surely be mad, he thought, to imagine that Rebecca Moisia pities me.

'Get up,' she said.

That was better. Her voice was harsh.

'Go for your walk.' She turned to the three who were standing sheepishly by her side. 'I want a full written report on what just occurred,' she said. She turned away.

Alan got up, dusted his clothes, and began to walk.

As for Rebecca, she went straight back to her room. She had been almost asleep when she'd heard Alan's shouts, and it was to her bed that she returned. She lay down on it, waiting for that blissful state of semi-consciousness to return, waiting for a brief time when she could slough off Alan Littell. And Jabulani. All men in fact.

But she was trembling. She thought about getting up to take some quinine but she couldn't be bothered. She couldn't be bothered and she no longer believed that she needed quinine. The trembling was a psychological manifestation, she was sure of it, brought on by the sight of Alan, lying on the dust. As she had stood above him it had felt almost like she was holding a negative to the light, seeing what had once been but this time in reverse.

She pulled a blanket onto the bed, and, wrapping it around her, she turned over to face the wall. She closed her eyes and waited for sleep to come.

Alan walked round the compound, giving its occupant a wide berth, feeling the sweat begin to trickle down from his forehead. The moisture was good, it sobered him: it made him feel alive.

Thembi: it was time he thought of her. She had been too easily dismissed. Her death, four years ago, was one of a string of deaths and it lost its way amongst them. First Victor had died and then

135

Robert Wentworth and then, before Alan could catch his breath, Thembi too. First Victor had been killed and then Robert and Thembi had dispatched themselves. A long chain of death but nevertheless Alan had been stunned by the news of Thembi's death: stunned but also unsurprised. He had trained with her, and he had slept with her, and he knew somewhat how things stood with her. Rebecca Moisia had been right to say that Thembi should have been at home: Thembi was a child launched into an adult world, a child who went through the motions without fully understanding what it was that was required of her. In the end the struggle to fit in must have proved too much for her.

Sarah had outlasted Thembi and always would.

Sarah had been there at Thembi's funeral. He had been glad to have her with him: she'd seen him upset and she'd comforted him. It had crossed his mind, he remembered, to confess to her then, to tell her about his involvement with Thembi, but the time passed before he could find the words. And, after all, what was there to tell? That he had slept with Thembi? Sarah would have been hurt by his infidelity — like all women she valued monogamy disproportionately. He would have been forced to explain that sex with Thembi had not sprung from desire, but rather from the fact that she happened to be there when he needed her. And if he had done that Sarah would have been offended on Thembi's behalf: she would have taken the other woman's part and thought less of him for using her.

But it wasn't like that: he and Thembi had both used each other. They had come together out of a common grief, they had fallen into each other's arms for nothing other than reassurance. The news of Victor's death was the precipitating factor. Thembi was devastated and so was Alan. Thembi had loved Victor. So had Alan.

He stopped in his tracks. Loved a man? Was it possible?

He looked down at the ground, at the red dust and the small pebbles that dotted it, the blades of rough grass struggling their way up through the uneven terrain. Victor, he thought, had been like a rare cactus amongst all this. A cactus that continues to flower through every season, defying botanical expectations. Victor had been the only one prepared to play with ideas with Alan but

136

Victor had not lived in the realm of ideas alone. Victor had been tough like a cactus but gentle as well. Alan could still picture Victor, audacious and yet caring. He could picture Victor, that time in Angola during his first combat experience. He could picture Victor, his hair streaming wild, caught combing it out, his black, black skin shining in the sunlight, his strong arm beckoning. Alan could see how the land lay, he could smell the stink of his own terror, and the knowledge emanating from the men around him that they were all about to die. And he could picture something else, he could picture Victor sprinting across uneven ground, throwing himself over a mound of dirt, spurting up again and running, running, shouting wildly as he launched himself upon the machine gunner.

And the silence that followed, that blissful, wonderful silence before Victor stood up straight, and Victor beckoned them on as they cheered him uninhibitedly.

Victor had been unique. And yes, Alan had loved Victor.

Thembi, Alan remembered, he was supposed to be thinking of her. Had she also loved Victor? He frowned. She had, he remembered, been Peter's girlfriend but when Peter was called into active service their relationship seemed to slowly fall away. But Alan was sure that there was no real involvement between Thembi and Victor. Perhaps Thembi and Alan had more in common than they had ever acknowledged. Perhaps she too thought of Victor as special.

Whatever the truth, they had made an unspoken pact on those few days after they'd heard of Victor's death and Thabo's arrest.

They had spent the days apart from each but, when night fell, they had moved into each other's arms. It had all happened, Alan thought, in a place quite similar to this one. Their encampment had been less well established but the land was as empty, surrounded by low scrub and by acres of unoccupied and infertile land. He and Thembi used to steal away, stumbling in the dark, until they were alone, out under the skies, entangled in each other's arms.

They had spoken little of what happened. Alan never knew how Thembi felt about their love-making. He had not, he realized, ever asked her. For his own part, the experience had disturbed him. There was something too familiar about Thembi: familiar and dangerous as well. He had not understood what had made her seem forbidden at the time but now, as he turned and began to walk back to the security of his room, the explanation dawned on him. Sarah, if he had told her, would have known immediately. She had been fascinated by an aspect of South African life that, to her, seemed inexplicable: the fact that whites learned to hate those that they once loved.

'Whites are brought up by black nannies,' she'd say. 'They've been given love by black women. How can they forget that?'

Alan had not tried to explain it to her, telling himself that it was too complicated. But now, as the low buildings came into sight, he realized that he had not explained because he couldn't. He had fooled himself into thinking he was an exception – his father had been too poor to afford servants – and yet he now realized that the wrongness he had experienced when sleeping with Thembi had been created by the fact that he had felt almost as if he were committing an act of incest. The Howards had got him a nanny, he remembered, a woman who had given him, before he met Sarah, the only warmth he'd ever received. But now he could hardly remember her name.

Well what did it all matter?

His mood had changed. He wanted to go into his room and shut the door, closing out the activity around him, the sight of African soil, the intrusion of useless thoughts raked up by the past. The room no longer seemed oppressive: it beckoned him and he summoned it up in his imagination. He was glad, he thought, that it was so empty. In that room he was safe, without trappings or memories.

He quickened his pace, driven by a compulsion to get indoors. When he passed another room like his and when he heard the sounds of someone protesting from inside it, he didn't even bother to slow down or to wonder what was happening.

CHAPTER SEVENTEEN

'Don't!' Rebecca shouted.

Her voice merged with her dream, became part of it, and, in doing so, it cut off her escape into wakefulness. The dream possessed her in its wordless frenzy, it sucked her down into a terror that had neither name nor face. It was all feelings, the dream, feelings and blackness: it was a dream of death. It had got hold of her and she feared that it would never release her.

Suddenly she was awake. She opened her eyes, opened them wide. She dealt first with the essentials. A fly had settled on her blanket and automatically, she brushed it off. The room was hot, stifling hot. Light filtered in through the curtains, which meant that it was still day. She glanced at her empty wrist and remembered she had discarded her watch. Well she didn't care. She didn't really need to know the time: by the pitch of the voices outside and by the brightness of the sun's rays she knew that she had not slept long.

She closed her eyes and the feelings in the dream returned.

She felt a sudden need to know the time: the hour, the minutes and the seconds too, anything that would pull her more firmly into the present. She let her hand drop to the floor and began to fumble there, searching for her watch. Her hand hit something solid. It was hard, unyielding, and worse than that, it did not belong. Opening her eyes she turned her head. Jabulani was standing there, beside her bed.

'What are you doing here?' she asked.

'I heard you crying out.'

She licked her lips. Her throat was burning. She heard Jabulani moving. She heard the sound of water and then he swam back into vision, holding a glass. She lifted her hand to receive it. He sat down on her bed and, gently putting his arm around her shoulders, he pulled her upright. He held the glass for her, held it as if she were a child. She gulped at it gratefully.

When she'd had enough, she pushed the glass away. Jabulani bent to place it on the floor, his arm still gripping her. She didn't try and resist. It was comforting to be so close to another, to feel supported. It was comforting and it was frightening as well. She began to shake. The words came out before she could censor them.

'I saw Alan on the ground with three men on top of him,' she said.

She felt Jabulani's arm tense. She frowned. Was there something else she had to say, something that was making her tremble? Her voice sounded faraway when she spoke as if it didn't belong to her and the words it used came out unbidden. 'That's what they did to him,' she said.

'To him?'

'To Mzwanele.'

Mzwanele: she had called his name.

She breathed out and only then did she realize how long she had been holding her breath. For thirteen years in fact. For the first time in over thirteen years she had called the name of her son.

And with his name came memory. Mzwanele had been twelve then: he should now be twenty-five. He'd been a handsome boy, charming, eager to please, quick to laugh. They were a pair, a working team, she and Mzwanele, united in love and by the fact that each had no one else. United always – except in his last hours.

His last hours: these had been the source of the dream. She remembered, so distinctly did she remember, even though she had not thought of that time in thirteen years. She could see it all clearly. It was an ordinary evening and they had been sitting together in their house, bound by a sense of comfortable companionship. Mzwanele was concentrating on homework while she had been busy mending something. In those days, she re-

140

membered, she had often sewn. When the knock came, that loud, unmistakable knock, Mzwanele glanced up at her. They were so close, she and Mzwanele, he knew her so well. He looked at her and he read the expression of fear in her face. He had smiled at her, a slow, reassuring smile. It was the last time he ever smiled.

What happened next?

What happened next was more than she could bear. What happened next was that they rushed into the house, five of them. This was no habitual raid: they were driven this time by fury. It was 1976 and their world was dissolving under the weight of street protest. After nights of stone-throwing phantoms they came for Rebecca, a teacher in a school which no longer functioned. They were half mad, seeing her as a target that they at least could grasp. They had done something to her to express their wrath. Hit her? Kicked her? She could not remember which. She had taken the blow and she had closed her mouth, cutting off a response.

But Mzwanele had responded. He had muttered a curse under his breath, a stupid, childish curse.

That's when they did it: that's when it happened. It all happened so quickly that she marvelled at the clarity of her recollection. They had heard his curse and set on him, knocking him to the floor. As two of them held her arms, the others went methodically about their work. They beat her son, beat him until he no longer cried out, beat him until he was dead. And then they'd taken her away, thrown her into a cell, left her there to rot as somebody picked up Mzwanele's broken body, as somebody washed him clean, as somebody buried him. As somebody mourned for him.

As for Rebecca: she did nothing. She didn't cry for Mzwanele. She sat in her cell, a woman devoid of feelings. She withstood interrogation and even torture: all without uttering a word. Only when they hit her did she feel alive. Only then could she accept what she rightfully deserved: the blows that her son should not have received, should never have received.

When they finally released her she had not gone home. There was nothing for her there. She had left the country, dry eyed; joined the exiled movement, dry eyed; worked for the destruction of apartheid, dry eyed. She had shoved the past behind her, fixing her mind on everyday details and on the time when there would be no more Mzwaneles.

No more Mzwaneles. The tears that she had held for thirteen years at last began to fall. They welled up inside her, spilling over, and dripping onto the bed. Tears of rage, of bitterness and, finally, of sorrow. They were not cleansing tears: they were stale. She had stored them up too long.

And all the while Jabulani sat beside her, the tears could not wash him away.

With the tears came words, words that she'd nursed for thirteen long years. 'It was my fault,' she sobbed. 'My fault.' She tried to pull Jabulani's arm away.

He gripped her tighter. 'How could it have been your fault?' he asked.

'Mzwanele was only a child,' she said. 'He didn't know.'

'He was a child,' Jabulani confirmed. 'And they murdered him.'

'It wasn't them, it was me,' she protested. 'I should have taught him.'

Jabulani squeezed her arm. 'Taught him what?' he asked.

'That it was not a game,' she said. 'I filled his head with slogans, I told him that we would win.'

'And what was wrong with that?'

'The sons of others, of those we call collaborators, they would have known,' she cried. 'They would have known that you do not toy with the white *baas*, that you do not insult him. But my son . . .' she heard something in her voice that should not have been there, but she could not control it. 'My son,' she repeated and the word had an edge to it, 'my son thought himself impregnable because I allowed him to think so. He didn't know what might happen, he didn't know.'

'Mzwanele lived in South Africa,' Jabulani said quietly. 'He was black. He knew.'

'Then why did he do it?' she shouted. 'Why was he so stupid?'

The question bounced off Jabulani and returned to her, piercing at her heart. Her tears stopped abruptly. She jerked her head around to look at him. But there was no shock in his face, no judgement either. He met her gaze straight on.

142

Say something, she thought. Go on, condemn me. But Jabulani merely lifted one hand and touched her cheek with it. His skin felt warm, she thought, warm and alive.

She looked away wondering, vaguely, what next to do. She was relieved to hear a knock on the door, relieved when Jabulani disentangled himself, got up from the bed and went to answer it. He opened it a fraction and spoke to whoever it was outside. Rebecca swung her legs onto the floor. She dipped a handkerchief – was it Jabulani's? – into the remnants of the water and wiped her face with it.

The door closed. Jabulani turned and looked at her. He was holding a piece of paper.

'Sarah Patterson's been arrested,' he said.

When he was halfway into the room Alan stopped in surprise. He hadn't expected all three of them but all three of them were there. Their presence, ranged as it was against him, should have frightened him but instead he felt as if a weight had lifted from his chest. An antagonism had grown up between him and Rebecaa Moisia, a hostility that was not entirely of his own making. And so, even though Jabulani Dlamini was an unknown ingredient and Albert Kana quite obviously hiding confusion with bluster, Alan felt that the men afforded him some kind of protection. They could go either way.

Rebecca was another matter: Rebecca was quick and Rebecca had already judged him.

He sat down on the chair that had become his and looked down at his feet. He was unafraid. The walk had done him good, it had brought back a sense of proportion. The madness that had been stalking him no longer seemed real and, as it retreated, his confidence returned. All he had to do was remain calm, answer their questions as best he could and thus convince them of the truth. The truth: which was that he was on their side.

The room was quiet. Outside dusk was falling. As he had been escorted from his room Alan had noticed the other occupants of the camp eating their evening meal some distance away. As the smell of meat wafted over to him he'd felt a vague sensation of hunger. With it came satisfaction. He had not thought of food since he'd arrived: the fact that it now attracted him meant he had turned a corner. The farce of a trial would soon be over, he knew it would.

'Sarah's been arrested.'

Alan looked up. One of them had spoken, one of the men. He did not know which one. 'Sarah?' he asked.

It was Jabulani who had spoken and who did so again. 'Sarah Patterson. Your girlfriend.'

Alan frowned. Sarah could not have been arrested for Sarah was back in England. 'Sarah's safe,' he said.

'She's in John Vorster Square,' Jabulani said. 'They picked her up yesterday.'

Alan looked down at his feet again. They were covered in dust from his walk. 'I don't believe you,' he said dully.

He heard the sound of rustling. When he raised his head again he saw that a piece of paper had been placed on the edge of the table, an offering to him. He didn't want to pick it up.

It's a trick, he thought, a stupid, lousy trick. He let it lie there and he heard it ticking. It's a bomb, he thought, but then he knew that he must indeed be crazy. The paper was too thin to be a bomb: the ticking was coming from his watch.

He snatched the paper, unfolded it and scanned the lines that had been transcribed there. 'It's a lie,' he said. His voice was quiet.

'Come now, comrade,' Rebecca urged. 'What purpose would such a lie serve? Believe me, Sarah's been picked up by the other side.'

So that's why there had been pity in her face: that was why. She'd known about Sarah then: she'd known and she'd kept the truth from him. A veil of despair began to descend, but before its cover was complete he slipped underneath it the knowledge that it was no lie: the regime was holding Sarah. In which case, he thought, there was only one question.

'Who?' he asked. 'Who betrayed her?'

'That's what we're wondering,' Rebecca said.

Distantly Rebecca's voice penetrated Alan's shock. He blinked. And then, slowly, the cogs in his brain began to shift, to move, to roll. As they gained momentum he sloughed off the veil and

144

concentrated solely on one thing and one thing only: the person behind Sarah's arrest. Numerous black faces rolled before his mind's eye and methodically he examined and then discarded them. It couldn't, he decided, be the leadership because the ANC had nothing to gain by Sarah's arrest. So how about a grass roots spy: one of his so-called friends with a grudge against him? Would such a person go to these lengths? Would they risk exposure over Sarah? No, he thought. Sarah was small fry and since every communication with the other side must involve risk, it wasn't worth it. What point then in wondering whether Peter had been the one to betray her? What point also in seeking for a leak outside of South Africa?

The faces changed their skin colour and began to sharpen into focus. He saw them ranged before him and he saw the malice written there. In a flash he got it. There was only one possible explanation and he knew immediately that it was right.

Those bastards, he thought, those bastards. They'd picked Sarah up to get at him. They were after him. Somehow they knew of his plan to expose their underlings and they wanted to stop him. They wanted their revenge.

'No one betrayed her,' he said softly. 'They had her on their lists.'

Somebody coughed and just as quickly stilled his cough. Other than that there was silence, a still, questioning silence. Rebecca looked at Alan, her eyes bored into him. 'How?' she asked.

He was certain of that as well. 'Robert Wentworth,' he said. 'Robert knew Sarah. I've always assumed that Robert gave my name to them: he must also have told them about Sarah before he died. As soon as she arrived at the airport they would have known who she was.' His voice had been calm till then, calm and sensible. But now it broke. He looked up at them and they could all see that his eyes were full of tears. 'They picked her up to get at me,' he sobbed. 'It's my fault: all my fault.'

Opposite Alan, Rebecca shivered. 'Comrade,' she said and her voice was sterner than she had meant it to be. 'Pull yourself together.'

But Alan was lost to them. He sat in his chair, his head hung down, his arms hanging loosely by his side, his body racked by sobs, an image of defeat. He sat there and he cried. Albert coughed. Jabulani walked over to Alan, and put one hand on his shoulder. Alan responded immediately. He got up, still crying, and he moved towards the door. When he reached it, he stood by it, waiting.

Jabulani opened the door and flicked a hand in Alan's direction. 'Take him back to his room,' he said softly. Two men appeared in the room, one on each side of Alan and Alan, his head still low, began to walk. Jabulani closed the door behind the three.

Albert was the first to break the silence. 'I don't trust Littell,' he said loudly. 'He's too emotional.'

Rebecca turned her head away and looked out of the window. Night was almost upon them and the sky was streaked with memories of the setting sun. A deadened tree stood in the distance, its branches turned blood red by some trick of the light. She forced herself to speak.

'It fits with what we know about Wentworth,' she said. 'He wasn't a very good spy.'

'Not good,' Albert muttered. 'He managed to kill Victor.'

Rebecca grimaced. 'What I mean is,' she explained, 'that the investigation held after Wentworth's death concluded that he must have relied on gossip and tittle-tattle. The man with the camera – that's how they referred to him. Alan's right: Wentworth could easily have supplied the other side with lists of our people's contacts.' She turned her head again to look outside.

The red was fading and the black of night beginning to take its place. In the gloom, Rebecca could just distinguish the form of a young woman, taking, pehaps, an evening stroll. As Rebecca watched the woman passed the tree, stopped, leaned back and lifted her hand to a lower branch. It must have broken for the next thing Rebecca saw was the woman standing with a piece of wood in her hand. The woman looked around her guiltily, dropped the branch, and hurried off.

Rebecca turned to look back into the room. 'How could we be so stupid as to send Sarah Patterson into the country?' she asked. 'We should have assumed that Wentworth would report on her. We should have protected her.'

She had been looked at Jabulani while she talked and she saw a look cross his face, a look of understanding. 'Like Mzwanele,' she thought she heard him say. She spoke before she had time to think, before she had time to realize that Jabulani had not spoken. 'Leave Mzwanele out of it,' she hissed.

Confusion replaced whatever had once been there on Jabulani's face. He opened his mouth to reply but Albert Kana beat him to it. 'Who's Mzwanele?' he asked.

Rebecca was seized by an urge to reach across and physically shake Albert. She resisted the urge because she knew that it was misdirected: the person she really wanted to shake was herself.

'I apologize,' she said quickly. 'For a stupid diversion.' She waved her hand in the air, pushing away both the apology and the feelings that had provoked it. 'Let's concentrate on the matter in hand,' she said. 'We know that the regime would not automatically pick up somebody in Sarah Patterson's position. She was only doing routine surveillance and, if they were alerted to her presence, they would be more effectively deployed by watching her and then arresting those who followed up.'

She got up and began to pace the room. 'In addition,' she said, 'Sarah is British and the regime is trying not to make waves. So what do we think of Littell's contention that they've taken her to get at Littell?'

'To get at Littell,' Albert said. 'Precisely.'

'Or to vindicate him,' Jabulani said.

Rebecca stopped in her tracks. 'What do you mean?' she asked.

'If Alan is theirs and they learned that we suspected him,' Jabulani said slowly, 'what better way to clear him than by arresting Sarah Patterson and throwing us off the scent?'

'The comrade has a point,' Albert said.

Rebecca frowned. What the hell did Jabulani want? First he pushed for Alan's innocence and now, at the point when she was coming round, he argued the other side.

'They don't work that fast,' she protested. 'They couldn't know that we've arrested Alan.'

'They might know we suspect him: it's a risk we cannot afford to take,' Jabulani said.

'So how do we now proceed?' Albert asked.

'We have a few days left and we must use them to the full to try and complete our investigation,' Jabulani replied. He frowned as if something had just struck him. 'If the Boers were to charge Sarah Patterson,' he said, 'or, alternatively release her, then we might know.'

'They won't do that.' Rebecca said. 'Not so soon.'

'So it's up to us,' Jabulani replied. 'As it has always been. Sarah Patterson's arrest changes nothing.'

'Precisely,' Albert said. 'It changes nothing.' He got up from his seat, stretched, patted his stomach and sighed. 'We must think on this,' he said before walking out of the room. He left his companions in silence, a stiff, uncomfortable silence, each locked in their own thoughts.

Don't, Rebecca was thinking. Don't say anything.

And yet it was she who broke the silence, who was the first to speak. She was unable to stop herself. 'What do you want?' she burst out.

'Want?' Jabulani asked. 'Me? I want justice.'

Justice, thought Rebecca. Such a simple word.

'And I also want', Jabulani continued, 'to prevent forty of our men from sailing into wholesale slaughter.'

Do you think I don't want that? Rebecca thought. She shut her mouth and forced herself to meet Jabulani's scrutiny.

It was a long time before he spoke and in that time the world kept moving. Laughter could be heard outside and the sound of dishes being scraped.

'You no longer believe Alan's guilty,' Jabulani said. Or was it asked?

'I don't know what to think any more,' she answered.

Jabulani smiled. 'Which, in your position, is the right way to be,' he said. 'And now I'll join Comrade Albert at supper. Coming?'

She shook her head. You're patronizing me, she thought, as she watched him walk out of the room.

Alan was no longer hungry. He had only one sensation and only one thought, the thought of Sarah and of what she must be going through, and it pursued him no matter how fast he paced the room. It's my fault, he thought, I should have known this would happen.

And then another voice spoke to him, an inner voice. You did your best, the voice said, you tried to dissuade her. He cursed this second voice: it was unfair. True — he had tried to dissuade Sarah but all the time he'd also been proud of her and so had not tried hard enough. He had let her go without ever really getting through to her, without ever really forcing her to understand.

Alan was guilty precisely because he knew one important fact that nobody else did: he knew that Sarah was an innocent. She took each person at face value, she refused to judge another, this quality of innocence was what had first appealed to him. And yet innocence could be dangerous. Even though Sarah knew the stakes were high she didn't understand how far people were prepared to go in their attempt to win. And now his worst fears were realized. Sarah — his unselfish, his good Sarah — had become a pawn in a game that she could not play, that she never would have been able to play.

It was his fault and he must remedy it. I'll give myself up, he thought. I'll offer myself in her stead.

He stopped in the middle of his room and hit himself on the head. He must be insane, to think this way. What good would his sacrifice do? They'd take him and Sarah too and the consequences would be even worse.

They. He must think of *them*. He must think of them and so outwit them. He must name them in his mind and, having named them, work out how to save Sarah.

Malan. Gert Malan. That was the name.

Alan had met Malan only once but he remembered each detail of his face, each line etched on it. Their encounter had occurred in a prison cell, a cell similar to the one where they were holding Sarah. Malan had come in smirking, knowing that Alan was in his power. Malan had been confident. He had tortured Alan: with words and blows and other things beside.

Alan had been weak then and he had cried for mercy. But Malan did not know the meaning of the word and Malan persisted. Alan still bore the scars of their encounter. Even as he thought of it the line on his back began to itch. He lifted his hand above his shoulder, ready to scratch at it. And then he dropped his hand. The itching was good, it would remind him. It would remind him and so would force him to think. To think of how he was going to beat Malan.

CHAPTER EIGHTEEN

South Africa

Smit was in full swing, contempt dripping from every word. *'You're so* blerry *naïve,'* he was saying. *'You should never have come. This isn't your struggle, this isn't your country.'*

'It's not yours either.' Sarah was fighting back. Or attempting to. Her voice was shaking.

'Face it, Sarah,' Smit said. *'Alan betrayed you. He slept with Thembi.'*

'You don't understand.' She was crying now, her words were muffled.

'Look up, Sarah, look up,' Smit shouted.

Smit paused and, then, when he spoke again, he'd lowered his voice. *'I understand,'* he said. *'My question is: do you? Do you know what type of man Alan Littell is?'* Another pause, another notch down the register. *'Because I also know Alan. I've followed his career carefully. And I know something which you don't: I know that Alan is not to be trusted.'*

'He told me about Thembi.'

Bad acting, thought Malan, bad acting. He glanced across his desk to where Colonel Jansen was sitting, a picture of concentration. Malan smiled inwardly. Colonel Jansen and Sarah Patterson have something in common, he thought: a shared tendency to overdo everything.

As Smit's voice droned on Malan reached for the picture on his office desk. He licked his finger and carefully wiped away the faint smudge on the silver frame. Squinting, he saw himself thirty-seven years younger, smiling with his wife beside him. He and

Ingrid were decked out in their Sunday best, on this their wedding day. He'd been a young policeman then, a young man from a poor background on the threshold of a successful career and a happy marriage. His back was broad, the colour of his cheeks deepened by time spent outdoors, his stance that of an able and energetic man.

The Gert Malan he faced whilst shaving was no longer even a faded version of this youth. His hair and his complexion had both gone grey, and as for his frame – well it was shrunken, shrunken by age and by the fear of constant pain.

He shifted his thoughts away, looking not to the past but to the future. Now that their sons had left home he and Ingrid could savour their togetherness. The two of them, in tune with each other's little ways, inhabiting the same space without resort to raised voices or even suppressed irritation. The two of them.

His smile faded.

It wouldn't be the two of them for long: not if his doctor was to be believed. And what then would Ingrid do? They had never had much time in the past and they had intended to start serious socializing once the children were gone and Gert retired. And now, even if he reached retirement, Gert had used up his time. Ingrid would be left alone, financially secure but friendless.

No, he thought, it can't be so: it won't be. He had friends, many of them in the department. They would visit Ingrid, they would console her.

Friends, he thought, except where were they now?

For those he had once considered his friends were retreating. Something was happening in the department, something which concerned him but from which he was simultaneously excluded. He didn't have to be a genius to have noticed it: to have intercepted glances being passed above his head, to have detected conversations drying up on his approach.

My friends have gone, Malan thought, my friends have gone.

He shook his head and the spasm that followed this gesture was positive. It was the reminder he needed, the reminder to be

152

vigilant. The present was threatening enough: he could not afford to indulge in self-pity. There were questions that had to be answered, and answered now.

And the first of these was why had de Vries failed? Malan had trained de Vries and Malan knew that, although de Vries was no intellectual, his tracking skills were second to none. And yet when de Vries tried to trace the man Zonda had fingered, the man who was a member of the ANC's terror gang, he'd met one blank wall after another. The suspect had been forewarned, that was certain. And what was increasingly clear was that he'd been warned by someone in the Special Branch, someone who had the resources to move quickly and to cover his tracks as well. The question then became – the million-rand question – was this someone as high up as Jansen? Or was it Jansen himself?

Malan looked across his desk. What, he thought, was Jansen doing there? Jansen possessed his own tape recorder, his own comfortable chairs, his own – and better – view. The fact that he had deigned to walk down the corridor and enter Malan's office, 'to review the situation' as he'd said: all this was significant.

If it was significant then Malan needed to concentrate. He placed the picture back on his desk and closed his eyes, listening to words he knew almost by heart and to voices, Smit's and Sarah's, which had become as familiar as his wife's.

Smit had returned to Alan's lies. *'He told you about Thembi, did he?'* Smit laughed. *'But sleeping with Thembi isn't the only way that Alan betrayed you. He let you come here, didn't he? He let you come knowing full well what was going to happen to you.'*

'He didn't know. He didn't know.'

'He knew all right,' Smit said. *'Alan's one of us. He plays the game and he plays it by the rules.'* His voice hardened. *'For Christ's sake, woman,'* he said, *'wake up. Alan Littell is a South African. He understands. The only reason he chose to share his bed with you is because you don't.'*

'Alan loves me.'

'Alan Littell loves nobody. Nobody but himself. Can't you even understand that? Alan Littell –'

Smit's voice was unexpectedly cut off.

Malan looked at Jansen and saw the Colonel settling back in his chair, a bemused smile on his face. Jansen was too enamoured of his own opinions, Malan thought, to listen until the end. Well, what did it matter? Malan had heard the interview before and he knew the interrogation of Sarah Patterson was going well. Smit was on the point of cracking her. All he had to do was give her time to ponder what had been said to her before presenting her with their trump card, their last turn of the wrench. Then they would have beaten her and so discover what pieces of knowledge rested in the crevices of her confused brain.

Sarah, Malan knew, would probably tell them little. But at this point in time, and with so many unknowns to balance, every little piece was vital. For what did Malan have? He had a boat heading into the country, a boat carrying forty armed men who would land and then divide into groups, each group setting up a separate base in the country, before embarking on a programme of military training. An armed underground, that's what the men would form, an armed underground more organized than anything previously encountered. And what made the whole thing more sinister was that it was happening at a time when all talk was focused on the prospect of negotiations.

The ANC was being clever, fiendishly clever. They were planting a fourth column inside a country, lulling suspicions with one hand whilst building their base with the other. All this Malan had gathered or guessed.

And he had other pieces of information to contend with as well, many of them worrying. He had Sarah Patterson's unexpected arrival in the country – something that, if his networks were working properly, should have been impossible. He had nothing from Zonda – a fact not yet in itself ominous but worrying nevertheless. And he had Jansen, here in front of him – a Jansen who could no longer be trusted.

'What does Smit think he's doing?' Jansen suddenly said.

Malan took a deep breath. 'Interrogating the suspect,' he answered.

'Ah.' Jansen shared the out breath with Malan. 'He's interrogating her by telling her that her lover shared a bed with another?'

'We know her type,' Malan explained. 'She'll be loyal to the point of perversity. We have to force her to doubt Littell before we can move her to a more profitable area.'

'A more profitable area,' Jansen repeated. He narrowed his eyes and looked at the man sitting behind the desk. 'This being your so-called sea landing of an MK group?'

So-called, Malan noted: so that's where we stand. Jansen — Malan was not convinced of it — Jansen wanted to avoid the subject of the boat. Yet connections (or more to the point, deliberate disconnections) between the boat and Jansen kept surfacing. Every time Malan was ready to trust Jansen, Jansen would say something to fuel distrust anew. Which side are you on? Malan nearly asked. Which side?

He didn't ask. He merely nodded.

'I've looked further at your involvement with Littell,' Jansen said, 'and I can't help noticing your obsession with the man. You met him once didn't you?'

You know I did, Malan thought: it's in the records.

'Not your usual technique,' Jansen commented. 'Meeting them.'

'Littell was a student at the time, a nothing really. I met him because I judged it necessary.'

'Ah.' That word again. Jansen paused to allow it to do its damage before changing tack. 'You know I'm worried about Smit,' he said, 'he seems to have become carried away with this psychological mumbo-jumbo he's using on Sarah Patterson.'

'But Smit's doing well,' Malan protested.

'Smit's doing his best,' Jansen corrected, 'in a difficult situation. But Smit is young.'

Jansen paused and smiled. He looked straight at Malan and, although his posture was as relaxed as it had formerly been, the smile faded and as it did so his face grew almost sinister in its intensity. He looked unwaveringly at Malan, held the look for what seemed like forever, held it until he finally deigned to break the silence. 'Perhaps we should vary your

155

usual technique a second time,' he said. 'Why not give Smit a break?'

The words were uttered as if they had only just occurred to Jansen but Malan knew at once that Jansen had come here, had walked the length of the corridor, had broken with routine, precisely in order to issue this one instruction.

'What about Patterson?' Malan asked quietly.

Jansen furrowed his brow as if it was indeed a problem for him, as if he were thinking furiously. Then his face cleared and he smiled a smile of absolute innocence. 'Perhaps you could have a crack at her?' he asked. 'You might enjoy it. We old hands can grow to miss the nitty gritty, don't you think?'

We old hands, Malan thought. 'Is that an order?' he asked.

Jansen smiled. 'Come now, Gert,' he said. 'Take it as a suggestion: a strong suggestion from one colleague to another.'

Having said this Jansen leaned forward as if he was about to get up. But he stopped halfway, stopped as if something else had just occurred to him.

And if you believe that, Malan thought, you'll believe anything.

'Oh yes,' Jansen said. 'I almost forgot. I've asked one of our men in the Cape to pay a visit to Thabo . . .' Jansen frowned as he searched for the name. Then his face cleared. 'Mjali. Yes, that's it, Thabo Mjali.'

The shock worked its way from Malan's head downwards.

'As I've said, I've been reviewing Littell's history,' Jansen continued. 'And as far as I can see – do correct me if I'm wrong – your especial interest in Littell dates back to the incident which led to Mjali's arrest: the incident when the man they call Victor was killed resisting capture. I thought an interview with Mjali might well help to clarify matters. I'll keep you informed of course.'

With that, Jansen got up, threw a brief smile in the general direction of Malan's desk, and walked from the room: walked so easily that Malan thought that Jansen might be taunting Malan for his loss of mobility.

Malan was left alone. Alone and in a rage.

How can he be so stupid? he thought.

Or so treacherous? – the word entered unbidden.

He shook his head in disbelief. He must not dwell on this alone. His desk was piled with other cases, each at different stages, each needing his careful attention. And yet his mind kept going back to Jansen.

Jansen must know that Robben Island was no longer inviolate and that to question Mjali was therefore risky. If Jansen had read the files then he would have seen that Mjali might hold the ANC's missing key: Mjali's hidden knowledge combined with Robert Wentworth's legacy could destroy Malan's network. All Malan needed was for some idiot to tip Thabo Mjali into consciousness. That's all he needed: one clue and the wires would begin to hum, the ANC would work it out, work it out and act on it. And in acting, destroy all Malan's carefully planned work.

Which perhaps, Malan thought, is what Jansen really wants.

For Jansen couldn't be so stupid that he didn't know that pulling Smit out was a way to inflict untold damage on the interrogation of Sarah Patterson. An interrogation was a delicate thing – a balance between pressure and action, between possibilities and escape routes. So what would Sarah think if in Smit's place, Malan suddenly appeared?

Malan knew what she would think: she would think that she had won, she would think that Smit had been called off because Smit was wrong.

And if she thought that, they would lose her. She would retreat back into girlish ignorance, she would give them nothing.

Well, Malan would not allow it: he would not allow Sarah Patterson to slip through his fingers. Viciously he pushed at his intercom.

'Get Smit,' he snapped into it.

Smit appeared within two minutes of Malan requesting him. He came into the room and sat down when Malan indicated, by a nod of the head, that he should do so. Malan waited until Smit was comfortable. 'I've just consulted with Colonel Jansen,' Malan eventually said.

Smit blinked, that's all he did, but Malan saw something in

157

Smit's eyes: knowledge perhaps of what was about to happen. In which case Malan must needs change strategy. 'You've done a good job on Sarah Patterson, Piet,' he said.

Smit was good but not that good. He flinched under Malan's scrutiny and Malan knew for certain what had happened. Jansen had got to Smit, got to him before he'd visited Malan. Jansen had planned his strategy carefully: that's why he'd come to Malan's room – so Malan would not get a chance to guess his move.

The question then became: which way would Smit jump?

Malan could guess that too.

'You've done a good job,' he repeated. 'And I thank you for it. But I am in complete agreement with Colonel Jansen that it is now time for me to take over from you.'

Smit was not that good. Malan saw relief cross Smit's face.

Well, the relief is mine, Malan thought: if I'd asked you to continue you would have refused. He got up and offered his right hand to the younger officer. 'Thank you, Piet,' he said formally. 'You may go.'

And then Malan was alone again and this time he understood how truly alone he had become. With Smit in his pocket, Jansen had finally succeeded in isolating Malan.

Well, thought Malan, and his resolution strengthened him, I will not let Jansen beat me. I will not.

Jansen had said Malan should interrogate Sarah Patterson and so he would. But not in the way Jansen expected, no, not in that way. He would shake Sarah up all right, that's what he do. He flicked through his notes, reached across for his telephone and began to dial a number.

Thabo stood still, adamantly refusing to look at the policeman. When he'd been shown into the room and when he'd seen this man the size and width of a pig, he'd fixed his eyes on the ground in front of him. He wouldn't sit and neither would he talk. He spent the time instead examining a pair of large, shiny black shoes, a fitting contrast to his own apology of what prison regulations deemed was adequate footwear.

The policeman had come full circle. He had started pleasantly enough until, faced with Thabo's resolute silence, he'd grown frustrated. His voice rose and his words changed from promises to threats, from wheedling to downright bullying. When those tactics in turn proved ineffectual he'd made an effort to calm himself, dropping into a posture of innocent friendship.

'Come on, Thabo,' he said. 'What would it cost you to unbend a little? Victor's long dead, you can't harm him.'

Victor is dead, thought Thabo: murdered by your hands or by the hands of your brother.

'All I'm asking is co-operation,' the policeman continued. 'If you co-operate I'll do everything in my power to bring about improvements in your life.'

Improve my life? Thabo thought, and he smiled. The only improvements on the Island have been a result of our struggles.

'But if you refuse to co-operate,' the man continued, his voice indicating he was about to launch his way on to the circle of anger again, 'if you don't – it will the worse for you.'

And that, thought Thabo, is the biggest joke of all. He bit his tongue. I've been worked over by men much tougher than you, he wanted to say. You're soft: look at the flab around your middle, and the useless way your arms hang by your sides. What could you do to me that I have not already withstood?

He did not say the words because he had already decided that, no matter what the provocation, he would refuse to talk. And he did not say the words for another reason: because it was too painful to relive what they had once done to him. His memories of that time, that time shortly after his arrest, were in a special category in his mind: restricted viewing, available only for limited periods. He could remember their faces as they inflicted it on him, the *sjamboks*, water, electricity, the smell of his own body as it evacuated. He could remember these things but only vaguely, for the real memory of what they had done to his mind and to his body was unimaginable even for one who had been there.

I didn't break then, he thought, why should I do so now?

'Listen to me when I'm talking to you,' the man barked.

Bark on, thought Thabo. I will not speak.

He heard a sudden sound, the sound of wood scraping against concrete. He did not move his eyes although he knew that the man had got up and that the man was heading straight for him. He steeled himself against the inevitable blow, thinking to himself, watch out, you pig, I have nothing now to lose.

But the blow never landed. Instead Thabo felt the air move around him as the man passed him by. He felt the atmosphere in the room lighten as the door was opened, and then he heard a familiar voice.

'Get moving, *kaffir*,' his warder said.

When Thabo was taken outside, the van was nowhere in sight. As his warder swore loudly Thabo stood on the pavement and looked around him. He had no time for buildings, it was on people – ordinary, passing people – that he concentrated.

What he experienced was a visual feast. He found himself examining an everyday scene where people hurried past on their way perhaps to work, to sleep or to their children. But these people, these ordinary people, did not look ordinary to him. The colours, he thought, the colours of their clothes. He realised that he had grown more accustomed to the uniformity of prison attire than he'd thought. As a result, his comprehension of the sheer range of the spectrum had been diminished. But now it all came flooding back to him: reds, pinks, magentas, greens of varying shades, all manner of colours each subtly different from the one beside it, each speaking of another life.

But it wasn't only the colours which were so different: it was the expressions on the people's faces. At the Island the comrades laughed together; they joked, they sang, they frowned and sometimes wept but no matter what they were doing the reality of their imprisonment and their isolation pursued them and this reality was etched on every face.

Out here in the free world there was a tangible difference. Poor these people might be, but defeated, no, not defeated. They noticed Thabo in his prison uniform, they knew where he was from and they showed their knowledge by quick smiles, illicit gestures, the occasional burst of whispered conversation.

And all the time the warder grew more agitated, uncomfortable with this reversal of roles where Thabo, handcuffed as he was, breathed freedom while the warder's only desire was to return to his imprisoned sanctuary.

The van sped round the corner and stopped abruptly. Thabo was roughly bundled into it. Into it and its darkness, heading back to the island of rock.

The transition into almost complete blackness was a frightening one and Thabo thought for a moment that he had been struck blind. But soon his eyes grew accustomed to the gloom and his imagination took over, delivering uncalled-for images to him.

Images of Victor and of their last morning together superimposed themselves on remembered faces of policemen. Images he could not understand. Images which came from a time he'd resolutely forgotten.

What made him think of policemen? Did it mean that Victor had been a spy?

No, it was inconceivable. No spy would stand passively by, waiting for his own death.

And there was a stronger reason why it was inconceivable: to say the words Victor and betrayal in the same breath was an abomination.

But Thabo remembered, and it was the first time he'd allowed himself to remember this, that there had been something wrong with Victor. Not on the morning, not when Thabo left, but before then: the night before. It was then that Victor had told Thabo that he'd changed the plan; it was then that Victor ordered Thabo to leave the house the next morning; it was then he'd told Thabo to check the arms cache.

Thabo, in all the four years since Victor's death and his incarceration, had never remembered this before. The policeman, pressing him, had brought back the recollection. And there was something else lurking there in the back of his mind, just out of reach: something else he didn't remember.

The van stopped abruptly and he was thrown across it, landing by its door. Goodbye, Thabo remembered, goodbye was the only word the two men exchanged after that night: goodbye, little knowing that it would be for ever.

161

The van door opened. On the warder's face was a look of victory. The tables had been turned. It was the warder who was free and Thabo who was once again imprisoned.

CHAPTER NINETEEN

There – it was done. Although the old woman had protested, she was no match for him and the rest was easy, the car dispatched to pick her up. All Captain Malan needed to do now was to work out how best to face Sarah with this new actor in her personal drama.

And even that was simple. With a few well-chosen words he would introduce himself and then follow through with the evidence. As simple as that: simple, but it should be the first step in finally breaking Sarah Patterson. As he thought about it, Malan absentmindedly twisted the pencil in his hand.

There was a sound of wood cracking and the tension left his hands. He looked down at where the two pieces had fallen. They lay there on the desk – a warning to him. He must detach himself: breaking Sarah was not the goal. She was just a means to an end, a weapon in his fight for information about the ANC boat, a weapon, as well, in his more important battle with those who opposed him.

Those who opposed him: they were, he thought, growing in number. They were too cowardly to come out into the open but their presence could be made visible by the trail of malice that followed them: a trail in the form of office memos dropping on all desks but his, after-work drinks of which he only vaguely heard, and important briefings from which he was 'mistakenly' excluded. Sometimes the signs were so subtle and yet so vicious that Malan suspected that, inside his body, it was paranoia that was festering there, festering like a cancer, summoned up only by his imagination. But then he would remember that de Vries' failure was not his imagination and neither was Jansen's refusal to take the boat seriously.

These days Jansen criticized Malan at every turn, but in an indirect way. Jansen obscured his language: his warnings sounded in Malan's ears but Malan didn't know what they meant. Jansen, Malan was certain, was laughing behind his back – saying that Malan's problem was that he dwelt in the past, unable to come to terms with the changing present. But what Jansen, with all his university education, could not understand was that it was the Malans of this world, the guardians of the past, who had kept South Africa safe. And what Jansen further could never know was that in the past lay the seeds of the present – not least so tied up with Malan's current dilemma.

The men of the past – the men from each side of the great divide – were better men. They were not one-dimensional but they were sure. They knew where each other stood, they had respect for each other and a knowledge, too, of how to treat each other. Men like Malan – schooled by experience. Men like Victor – unusual, talented, self-taught men.

Victor.

That was it. The starting point was Victor: he must think of Victor and of the manner of Victor's death, he must exhume the past.

He redistributed his weight to his left and mentally began to recall it. It had happened, he remembered, in 1985. It was in 1985 the trough of the dark time; as the police doused each successive insurrection, another sprang up to take its place. A time when columns of smoke hung over black townships and when even white cities began to hear the first sounds of their insulation crumbling. It was in 1985 that young hot-heads came out into the street, yelling their support for MK, while arms and personnel filtered into the country. It was 1985, and Malan was clear: his task to rid the country of its terrorists and, in doing so, make an example of them.

And so the ambush of infiltrators had been carefully, painstakingly planned. Malan was explicit: he didn't want a row of captured terrorists who, parading in court, would stir the populace to further acts of madness. No, what Malan wanted was a salutary death, a warning to those who might otherwise risk armed defiance. They were at war, and Malan felt no scruples: he selected his target, struck his bargains and set the operation into motion firmly convinced that nothing could go wrong.

But it did go wrong.

Victor was not meant to die in the crossfire: in fact, Victor was not meant to have been there at all. Yet Victor had been there and Victor had died.

Malan had his reputation to consider and, after it was over, he had questioned and cross-questioned his men. They were too frightened to lie to him, and he could find no chink in their insistence that they had carried out his instructions to the letter. They had, they said, watched a man leave the shack, watched him turn the corner, and then they had waited a good half-hour before they opened fire. Malan eventually believed them: believed them even though it was Victor, not Thabo, in the shack and Victor, not Thabo, who had died. And yet, here he was, so many years after such a triviality, worrying about it.

'Fuck it,' he said suddenly to the empty room. He would not think of it for what did it really matter? There were worse ways to die than suddenly. And Victor hadn't died alone, he'd taken others down with him. Victor was the type who would have enjoyed the irony. Victor would have seen that his aim was true and Victor was probably smiling as he fell.

Yes, there were worse ways to die. It was a mistake to dwell on it. 'Forget Victor,' he told himself.

He put two hands on his desk and pressing down on them he managed to get up. Slowly he inched his way to the door.

By the time he arrived in the basement he had straightened up and he was walking easily. Perhaps it was mere backache after all, he thought: perhaps the doctor was wrong. Impatiently he jiggled the money in his pocket while he waited for a uniform to let him through. Then he walked quickly down the corridor, shaking his head at the offer of a cell key. He would meet Sarah soon enough: all he currently wanted was to look at her.

When Sarah heard the sliding of steel she wiped her eyes and turned to stare defiantly at the chink of light. Let Smit look his fill! This time she was ready for him.

The grille slid shut. She turned away, almost disappointed, to face the wall.

I must look terrible, she thought. I'm glad there's no mirror in the cell. *I must look terrible:* what a stupid way to think! Her tears began to flow again.

She had been crying on and off since they had last dumped her in the cell, crying because Smit's poison had infiltrated her veins. No matter how hard she tried she could not rid herself of it. His voice pursued her and the thing that hurt the most, the one she could hardly bring herself to acknowledge, was his contention that Alan didn't love her.

She told herself Smit was wrong and yet his insinuations continued to worm their way through her bloodstream. She stamped her foot on the concrete floor. 'Enough,' she shouted. The word returned to her like an echo. She ground her teeth together until they hurt. She took one step and ended up sitting on the bed. A strand of hair, of lank and dirty hair, trailed down her forehead, blocking her vision. She was seized by inertia: too tired to shake the hair away. She sat quite still, her mind a blank.

Smit's voice spoke even then to her. *You're passive,* it accused. *Your thoughts are not your own, your actions come from others not yourself.*

She tossed her head defiantly, ridding herself of the hair. Smit was wrong. She was not passive, far from it.

You're passive, Smit said. *You followed Alan because he wanted that.*

Smit was wrong. She had followed Alan in clear defiance of his wishes. She'd acted alone, impulsively, going against the advice of friends and movement alike.

But why? Smit had asked. *Why then did you follow Alan?* and this time he seemed genuinely interested.

What answer could she give? What answer was the truth? Every time she started to respond, she stopped herself halfway. 'I met Alan' was the simple answer but it wasn't good enough. Other people met Alan, her friends in England for example, and none of them ended up in a South African gaol.

166

Think it through, she urged herself. You can do it.

The first step was their meeting. The second, and more important step: her decision to follow him. And that's what she no longer understood. It had seemed so obvious at the time but, as she thought it over, and as she pulled the details together, it began to make less and less sense.

The facts, she thought. What are the facts? The bare facts were that she had caught Alan doing something he wished to hide, that he had turned on her, that they'd had their first serious fight. She had left their flat thinking that it was over and then, having discovered that what he was doing was leaving her, not only had she forgiven him, she had also pursued him to Africa.

Once there each move was followed by another. Hearing about apartheid was one thing: seeing it was different. The longer she stayed in Africa, the more she learned of the thousands that streamed across the South African borders and the angrier she became. Her anger had been genuine. Smit accused her of being a movement groupie but, no, it wasn't true. Her decision to volunteer for a mission was not part of a sick compulsion to be closer to Alan. It stemmed instead from her urge to get involved, to throw off the role of sightseer on the edges of a war.

A sightseer, that was it. That's why she'd followed Alan: because she no longer wanted to be bonded to the routine of her ordinary life. And there was another truth, hiding behind the first. And this was that while Alan endlessly repeated that he loved Sarah for her strength, she had only just realized that she had loved him for something other than himself. She had loved him because he needed her and because, in her world, he was unique.

Alan needed her but then so had all the others. But Alan stood separately from the men she had known before. True, she thought, he shared certain characteristics with his predecessors: men, all the men she had met, never really grew up, they were all children at heart. But in one aspect Alan was different. His eyes, those eyes of ice and of fire, said it all. They demonstrated how his energy was always there, just below the surface, waiting to explode. His life was driven by drama and by intrigue – by hushed conversations held in uncomfortable venues; by mysterious guests who smiled and said little but who brought with them strange documents that were quickly spirited away; and by fun as well, fun that only a community living by its wits could create.

Alan's community – through him she was offered a window to it. And what surprised her most of all was how much she yearned to be part of it. She liked the mystery, the drama, the sheer unpredictability of each hour. She liked it so much that she didn't even mind when, instead of turning up for supper, Alan phoned her from 'somewhere in Europe' (somewhere where the phones didn't function too well) and told her it could be days or weeks before he saw her again. She liked the life and she liked the way she was in it. She began to blossom and in blossoming she grew to like herself the more. She no longer judged herself a typical, boring Englishwoman: she agreed, secretly, with what Alan used to say – that she was free of the English compulsion to have everything neat and labelled and coldly parcelled. She'd embraced the unknown and it had transformed her.

Let Smit laugh – she didn't care. She *had* been a movement groupie, she *had* been in love with the revolution. But what had once been foolish sentiment had now become solidified: what she had once done for adventure's sake she now did because it was right. She would not regret volunteering: she would never regret that. And neither would she regret loving Alan because she also did love him.

And, it wasn't true what Smit said. Alan did have the capacity to love. He had loved Victor, his commander, and mourned for Victor. There were times, after Victor's death, when Sarah thought that Alan was on the verge of breaking down, so great was the weight of his sorrow. Yes, Alan had loved Victor.

And Thembi: had Alan loved her too? Sarah had been at Thembi's funeral and she had spent time with Alan after it. So many funerals, she remembered, each one fuelling her hatred of the apartheid state.

No, she told herself, don't evade it.

She had watched Alan at the funeral, drinking in the sight of him because she assumed he would leave soon after it. But, when the formalities were over, he hadn't gone. He had been allowed home with her, to spend the night as if they were an ordinary couple. She remembered clearly how Alan looked that day, how alone he had seemed. No wonder, she thought. He was mourning his dead lover.

She didn't try to deny Smit's words: she knew them as the truth. Alan and Thembi had been lovers: that explained his grief that day, his incoherence, the way he had looked at Sarah and started sentences without finishing them. Her memory, and the image contained within it, sharpened. They had been sitting outside, on a balcony, overlooking the sea, watching the sun go down. She had offered him a drink and he'd refused.

'It's funny,' he'd said. 'When I'm in the camps I dream of alcohol and how much I'm going to drink when I get out. But once I'm away from there it no longer seems so important.'

'I hope the same doesn't apply to me,' she'd said.

He'd turned to face her. 'How could you think that?' he'd whispered. He'd touched her cheek with the back of his hand. 'I . . .'

She hadn't asked him to finish his sentence. She'd suspected then what it was he was trying to say. She'd suspected it then and she knew it now.

She smiled suddenly. She no longer felt ugly. Thembi meant nothing to her. What was important was that Alan did have the capacity for love. Of this one thing she was positive. Alan had loved Victor and he loved her, too. When she was released she would look him in the eyes and see his love written there.

When she was released – when would that be? What did it matter anyway? She rested her head in her arms and began, once more, to cry.

It was the same room to which they took her, the same room. And yet it felt completely different. Smit had been the room, he had filled it and in his absence it was transformed, its power diminished.

In Smit's chair sat a man Sarah didn't know. His face was impassive when she entered and it remained impassive as she sat. The seconds ticked by while Sarah thought, where is Smit? The seconds turned into minutes while Sarah thought, I'm safe. They've taken Smit away because he couldn't win.

'Malan,' the man suddenly said. His face was turned from hers. 'Captain Malan.'

Captain Malan. She had heard that name before. She knew it in its entirety: Captain Gert Malan. In the dead of night, Alan had called out that name, and in the dawn that followed he'd spoken of that man. But Alan had described a big man with red hair, a man with fists like hams, not this shrunken, grey-haired specimen. This man doesn't look well, she thought.

But when he turned to look at her she saw that one detail of what Alan described had still remained the same: this man could read minds. He looked at her and some tiny change on his face told her that he knew she knew of him. He knew and didn't care.

'You don't scare me,' she said.

He raised an eyebrow. 'Scare you?' he said. 'I'm not trying to. I never resort to bullying or violence: that's not my method.'

'Not your method,' she scoffed. 'I've seen the evidence of your handiwork on Alan's back.'

Malan shows no emotions. Alan had told her, but as she spoke she saw Malan's eyes flicker and his mouth twitch. *Malan shows no emotions other than the ones he uses to deceive,* was what Alan had said and Alan was right. The twitch lengthened into a smile and the flickering to a twinkle.

'Is that what Alan told you?' Malan asked. 'That I beat him? Inventive of him.'

Malan uses few words but those he employs are there to set you talking, Alan had said. Sarah clamped her lips together.

Malan shrugged. 'We'll talk later,' he said. 'For the moment, I've brought somebody to see you.'

He got up slowly. *Malan's every movement is deliberate,* Alan had said. *He slows himself down, conserving his energy until it is time to pounce.*

This is different, Sarah thought. This man can't pounce. For he was walking past her with ill-concealed difficulty, his face puckering in concentration. If I stretched out my foot, I'd trip him up, she thought. She kept her feet inert while she turned her head to watch him.

He opened the door and gestured with his hand. Then he stood and waited, leaning against it for support, waited until hesitant footsteps sounded outside. He stepped back. When an old woman walked slowly in, a woman leaning heavily on a walking stick,

170

Malan took her arm and led her to his chair. He waited while she used her stick to help her sit and only after she was settled did he speak.

'Allow me to introduce you,' he said. 'Sarah this is Mrs Girlie Howard. Mrs Howard, this is Sarah Patterson – your adopted son's girlfriend. I'll leave you two alone, shall I?' And with that, Malan crossed the room again, quickly this time, and, closing the door softly behind him, he left.

Sarah's jaw went slack. She looked silently at Girlie and saw her sitting upright in her chair but dwarfed by it, her eyes were fixed firmly on her stout brown shoes. The hand that held the walking stick was trembling. Girlie Howard. If Alan was here, Sarah thought, he would have trouble believing this. Alan talked of Girlie as a woman in her prime, a woman capable of making him feel twelve years old, a woman who held, out of his grasp, the power of the world. A woman who had rejected him.

But Alan wasn't there and Girlie was no longer that woman. She had aged beyond measure. The tailored clothes Alan had described were of the past: now Girlie wore a simple skirt, a cotton shirt and both were faded and both were garments manufactured for a much younger woman. If Alan could only see Girlie now, Sarah thought, he would see her for what she was. I was right, Sarah thought, to send him to Bryanston: the past loses its sting when viewed through adult eyes.

Girlie coughed.

'What are you doing here?' Sarah asked.

'Captain Malan invited me.' Girlie's voice was hesitant. For the first time she looked up at Sarah, looked at her through eyes that were moist with age and lined with sorrow. 'How is Alan?'

Rage: that's what Sarah felt. How dare you ask? she wanted to say. How dare you? You've forfeited all right to know about Alan, you deserted him when he needed you.

'How should I know?' was what she said, looking pointedly at the locked door.

'He's a grown man now,' Girlie said softly. 'He's thirty-seven.'

'He's thirty-five,' Sarah's voice was brisk.

Girlie nodded her head, nodded in defeat. And Sarah knew then that, should she refuse to say anything more, then Girlie would also remain silent. Sarah could leave it there, she could outsit the older woman and, in doing so, spoil whatever it was that Malan had planned. Yet something impelled her to continue. Not just something but Alan. This was a meeting that Alan never could have and so this was a meeting that Sarah must have for him.

'Malan calls Alan your adopted son,' she said. 'But you never officially adopted him did you?'

Girlie blinked. 'Yes, we did,' she protested. And then her face grew uncertain and her voice was vague. 'Jack looked after that,' she said.

Girlie is weak, Sarah remembered Alan saying, *she'd do whatever Jack demanded of her.*

'I suppose Jack was the one to evict Alan from your home?' Sarah asked.

'Jack never evicted Alan,' Girlie said.

Sarah smiled. Time sanitizes everything, she thought.

'Jack never evicted Alan,' Girlie's voice was louder on the repetition. 'He wanted him to stay. We both did.'

'A funny way to show it,' Sarah said. 'You turned your back on Alan when he needed you. You – '

Girlie banged her stick on the floor, not once but twice, and the force of her action stopped Sarah in mid sentence. Girlie's eyes displayed neither age nor defeat but instead a flashing blue. Girlie was Alan's aunt by blood, Sarah remembered.

'Alan was not an easy child,' Girlie began. 'I didn't blame him for his tantrums,' she said, softening her voice. 'His early life was more difficult than any of us could imagine: shut up with that brute of a father, brought up in a hovel. The things that man did to Alan – and to my sister. Alan had nothing when we took him in: nothing but the rags he wore.'

'Only in this country,' Sarah interrupted, 'is poverty such a heinous crime.'

'You don't understand,' Girlie said and her voice had changed again, becoming reasonable, persuasive, ingratiating.

Girlie is a consummate actress, Alan had told Sarah. *She had to be. She had no work and, therefore, got her way by assuming a number of different roles to suit her mood.*

172

'It wasn't the poverty I minded,' Girlie said, 'although I can assure you that Littell's poverty was purely voluntary – we offered him money many times but he refused it. It wasn't the poverty, however, it was the brutality.'

My father never raised a hand against me: that's what had been written.

'Alan's father never touched him,' Sarah said.

'Oh, he did,' Girlie answered. 'He certainly did. When Alan came to us, he bore the scars of his father's whip.'

No, thought Sarah, you're wrong, just as you were wrong about his age. The scars came later. You don't want to face this fact because you don't want to acknowledge that the scars were your responsibility, were a direct result of what you did to Alan. The thought fed her initial anger. She was driven by an impulse to punish this woman, to make her suffer just as Girlie had made Alan suffer.

'Alan hates you,' she said. 'For what you did to him.'

Girlie blinked and the fight drained from her face, returning in its wake, old age.

'You never wrote to him,' Sarah said. 'You couldn't even do that.'

Girlie grasped blindly for her stick. 'Jack wouldn't let me,' she whispered. She found the stick and she fumbled for its head with arthritic hands. Gripping it tightly, she pushed on it, pushed down to get herself upright. Then slowly, head bent, she walked past Sarah and to the door. It opened before she could make contact with it.

So Malan was listening, Sarah thought.

Girlie turned to face Sarah. 'If you have the chance my dear,' she said. 'Send Alan my love.'

'Shame on you, Sarah,' Malan said. 'Punishing an old lady like that. Have you no compassion?'

'I did not bring her here,' Sarah said. 'You did – although I've no idea what you hoped to achieve.'

'To achieve?' Malan said mildly. 'The truth, that's all. Alan's been lying to you. Alan's whole life, his very personality is a lie.'

He held up one hand, high in the air. 'No,' he said. 'Don't

173

interrupt me. What I'm going to do is give you time to think. And after that we'll meet again, and this time I'll have something else to show you.'

Day Four

CHAPTER TWENTY

Tanzania

'I've gone through it before,' Alan mumbled, 'not once but many times.'

'Well, this time you'll have to go through it for me,' Rebecca said. She sighed.

Alan leaned back in his chair, folded his arms and then he echoed her sigh, emphasizing and mocking it. 'After I returned I was debriefed,' he said, 'I wrote a full report. In addition I had many meetings with the rep from the PMC. And then,' his voice rose and he leaned forward, 'and then I went through the whole fucking process again when you people first chose me for a scapegoat.'

Rebecca's eyes flashed. 'You people?' she said. 'You do not consider yourself one of us?'

For a fraction of a second there was silence in the room. In that time suspended Alan stared straight at Rebecca, his face blank, and in that time he picked carefully between a number of different responses. In the end the one he chose was laughter. He threw back his head, opened his mouth wide and laughed. He did so ostentatiously enjoying the largeness of the sound and the way it filled the room. And yet there was no mirth in his laughter, no joy whatsoever. It was an automatic response, that's all, a set piece amongst set pieces.

As he laughed, his mind continued to work, sorting through the grim realities. The outward display of hostility between himself and Rebecca had dimmed: ever since she'd told him about Sarah, she'd changed (or perhaps he had) and yet every now and then she shot out one like that – one that showed she still suspected him and was still trying to entrap him. It was almost, but not quite, worth laughing about.

'You find me funny, comrade?' Rebecca asked.

His laughter was abruptly stanched. He yawned. 'No, I don't find you funny,' he said.

'So can we proceed?'

'I entered the country from Swaziland,' Alan said. His voice was monotony itself. 'The river was at its lowest and my comrade and I had little difficulty carrying the arms. In our possession were eight AK 47s, two rocket launchers, hand grenades and ammunition. The car was waiting for me on the other side. I parted from my comrade who returned to Swaziland. I drove the car, as instructed, towards Johannesburg. I was stopped once on the way but I was lucky: the car wasn't searched. The safe house was in order when I arrived, I hid the arms and after two days, began to look for a suitable DLB.' He stopped and glanced at Rebecca. 'Dead letter box,' he said.

'Yes, comrade,' she answered patiently. 'I know what a DLB is.'

'I found the perfect place,' Alan continued, 'accessible to me but near enough to the township to make a black comrade's presence there explicable – we needed that for afterwards. I buried the weapons in an abandoned building site. This process took me three days.'

'You were taking a risk,' Rebecca commented. 'Returning over such a long time period.'

'Not as much a risk as I would have taken had I tried to hide them in one go,' Alan shot back. 'Have you any idea how bulky my consignment was?'

'Yes, I have an idea,' Rebecca said. 'Proceed.' She was not looking at Alan. She was writing despite the recording, meticulously transcribing everything he said.

'On the fourth day,' Alan continued, 'I spent some time working out the exact co-ordinates of the DLB, I had to move a few landmarks to make it absolutely clear. When I was finally satisfied I abandoned my car and picked up the other, which was waiting at its designated location. I drove back to the border.

178

After crossing at night I was transported to military HQ, debriefed and returned to base.'

'To base,' Rebecca said, after a pause, 'where you told Victor about your mission.' She did not look up, and neither did she bother to frame her words into a question.

'Yes,' Alan confirmed. 'I told Victor.'

And still she refused to look at him. 'There were others to brief Victor,' she said. 'Why did you tell him?'

Alan stretched his mouth into a second, and more prolonged, yawn. 'I told Victor because I was instructed to do so,' he said. 'The location of the DLB was complicated and it was thought that, given the importance of the mission and the danger attached to it, that a verbal briefing should also be given.'

'And who else did you tell?'

'Nobody.'

'You told Thabo,' Rebecca suggested.

'I told nobody,' Alan insisted. 'Nobody but Victor.'

Rebecca raised her head, slowly and deliberately. 'But it was Thabo, not Victor,' she said, 'who went to check on the weapons.'

'Yes it was Thabo.'

Her tone was even but her looks belied her pretended non-chalance. Something akin to ferocity shone out of the eyes she locked to his. 'How did Thabo know where the weapons were?' she asked.

Alan blinked. Sarah once looked at me like this, he thought: on the day of Thembi's funeral, across the grave she looked at me. He averted his eyes, dropping them to the ground. 'I don't know,' he muttered. 'I don't know.'

'Try and think, comrade,' Rebecca urged so gently that Alan thought he had imagined the intensity of her concentration. 'Suggest something, even if it's only a guess.'

Alan kept his eyes firmly downcast. He took a deep breath. 'Victor must have told Thabo,' he said softly.

'Impossible,' Rebecca snapped. This time the ferocity could not be denied.

But Alan had expected it. Slowly he let his gaze move from the floor, up the desk and to face level. He looked calmly at Rebecca.

179

You didn't know Victor, he thought. You claim him but you didn't know him.

Although Alan's face was blank, Rebecca sensed something in his silence and it provoked her. 'Our comrade, Victor, had an exemplary record,' she insisted. 'He was one of our highest-ranking commanders, renowned both for his courage and for his ability to give and follow orders. Victor was told to keep the information to himself and he would have done so.'

Alan listened to Rebecca's assertions, noting how her voice rose in anger, so strident, so full of conviction. He felt nothing but contempt – contempt for her fervour and for what lay behind it.

When she had finished, he spoke without thinking. 'You deny the truth,' he said. 'Even when death rams it down your gullet.'

'What do you mean?'

He didn't answer her, not immediately. He turned his head away, running through it logically. Rebecca is blind, he thought: can't she see that Victor defied orders by giving Thabo permission to go out, and, then again, by staying in the house while he waited for Thabo to return? It didn't take a genius to know that's what must have happened. And yet Rebecca, with her reputation for pragmatism, didn't seem able to figure it out. She didn't even stop to wonder why it was that Victor deviated from the plan. Instead she remained fixated on the step before, on the weapons, and thus she ended up running round in circles trying to find the name of the traitor who'd given away their location. And all this because she couldn't face the thought that Victor might have made a mistake.

'Comrade.' Her voice was full of anger.

He turned back and he opened his mouth, almost at the point of telling her. But he never did: he changed his mind. There was no point, he decided, in arguing for he knew only too well why she blinded herself to the truth. She did so because she needed to: she needed to ignore Victor's infraction and so keep the myth of Victor intact. She, along with all the others, was driven by an urge to keep Victor's halo firmly on his head.

Alan heard her do it. And Alan thought, that's what you want to believe. That's what you *need* to believe – that Victor was perfect. Everybody thinks so: Victor's been deified. Only I know the truth. Only I know that Victor was a man not a god. And you, all of you, you helped destroy Victor by refusing to acknowledge this. You destroyed him because you would never allow him his humanity.

He shrugged. 'You asked me to guess and I did,' he said. 'I cannot be blamed for guessing wrong.'

'What about Wentworth?' Rebecca asked. 'When did you tell him?'

'Wentworth,' Alan spat the name out like a curse. 'What has Robert Wentworth got to do with it? Why the hell do you keep talking to me about him? He was no friend of mine. He was a spy.'

'If Wentworth was a spy –' Rebecca began.

'*If!* What do you mean, *if*?' Alan shouted. 'Wentworth left a note. He admitted he was a spy.'

Rebecca banged her fist down, hard down on the table. 'If Wentworth was a spy,' she said evenly, 'then where did he get his information?'

'What information? Wentworth knew nothing about the arms cache.'

'To betray our comrades,' Rebecca said, 'he would have had to know what they were doing. But since he was uninvolved in the mission, he should have known nothing. So who told him?'

Alan shrugged. 'Not I,' he said. 'Not I.'

'It would have to have been somebody who was involved in the first phase of the operation,' Rebecca said, 'somebody like you.'

Like you, the words rebounded on Alan pounding at his brain. Except the words that attacked him were ones delivered by a voice and face other than Rebecca's: by Robert Wentworth in fact. Those were Wentworth's last words to Alan: *I wish I could be more like you – like you*. He'd repeated the couplet as if he were already fading into death. In his face had been an appeal, a mute kind of longing.

At the time all Alan had wanted to do was flee Wentworth's desperation and all he could think was that Wentworth was crazy. He and Wentworth were not alike, they weren't. Wentworth had been asking for help but Alan had felt no pity for a snivelling wreck of a spy, who'd probably given the other side nothing of worth. Nothing that is, he thought in hindsight, except Sarah.

Like you. Sitting in the room and hearing Rebecca say those words, Alan for the first time wondered what Robert Wentworth had really meant by them. Had he known that Alan wanted to unmask him, to expose him as a spy? Had he known this and, because he felt himself powerless, had he envied Alan his capacity to carry through?

No, no, Alan thought, Robert hadn't known, he couldn't have. The truth was that Wentworth was desperate at the time. Guessing that exposure was near he'd cast around for friends, and then, finding none had settled on one of the few other white faces amongst the comrades. That was it, that was why Wentworth had picked Alan to envy. Because Alan was accepted. Because Alan was one of them in a way Wentworth could never be. Because Alan had Victor as a friend.

Jumping to his feet, Alan strode across the room. He stopped when he reached Rebecca's desk. He leaned over it, leaned so far that his face was all but touching hers.

'Don't you understand, you stupid woman,' he hissed, 'that what I knew was irrelevant. It wasn't the location of the weapons that finished Victor. Victor was killed in the house and Thabo, who went to check on the weapons, survived. Don't you understand anything?'

She was so close to him that when her eyes flared in alarm he felt almost as if it were his eyes that moved, and when she breathed to calm herself and then became still, he felt her as a rock against him. She's just like Sarah, he thought. What is it about women that gives them courage?

He was suddenly ashamed of himself, ashamed of coming so close, of intimidating her. He backed off, muttering. 'I didn't cause Victor's death,' he said. 'I wouldn't. I loved Victor.'

'But Victor died,' Rebecca said.

'Yes, Victor died.' He raised his head but his eyes were faraway, focused on the distant past. 'I have mourned for him,' he said, 'I have cried for him. I owed Victor, I owed him. If there was anything I could have done to prevent his death, even if it meant sacrificing my life, then I would have done it.'

He stood in the middle of the room, his arms hanging by his sides, and it was as if he were seeing Victor in front of him – Victor laughing, joking, comforting Alan. That face that was almost as familiar as his own, swam in front of his eyes.

'What did you owe Victor?'

The question pulled Alan into a present that seemed less real than the past. He started in surprise. His eyes came back into focus. 'Why do you ask?'

'Because you said you owed him.'

'I didn't,' Alan said. He shook his head wildly. 'You misunderstood me.' He went back to his chair and slumped down in it. 'What's the point?' he muttered. 'You wouldn't understand. None of you understand.'

As Rebecca gazed at the man opposite her she was filled with a boredom so strong that it was oppressive. She had watched Alan's collapse into sullenness too many times before and she knew it signalled long hours of silence. To proceed would mean frustration as Alan dismissed questions with a flicker of his eyes, as he retreated into himself, into a place to which she couldn't follow. She had hoped that he'd discarded such childish posturing and indeed, since the news of Sarah's arrest, he had seemed more amenable. But now she saw that the old Alan had returned – the hostile, suspicious, paranoiac Alan. If she questioned him further, the result would be predictable. He'd resort to one of two phenomena: fury or tears.

Well, she was tired, she had no inclination to start on the circle again, and besides, she needed time to think. She closed her exercise book and stood up.

'That's all for now,' she said.

A twig snapped under Alan's foot, surprising him. He had been lost in thought, he realized, walking under the night sky, unaware even of the soft voices of the guards behind him. He turned his head and saw their figures some distance away. Their heads were touching as they stood together, the low voice of the man resonating through the dark, his urgent speech interrupted only by the sounds of his companion's giggles. A romance, he thought. They probably volunteered so they could sneak away from the others. Well, at least I'm doing somebody some good. He almost smiled.

There had been a time when he and Sarah had walked like that, into the night. Not here but in a landscape like this one, and in a climate similar as well. Sarah had linked her arm to his and he had thought at the time how well she'd managed it, keeping close without leaning her weight on him. The warmth of her skin against his bare arm had been comforting, life had been with him in those days.

There was nothing to smile about. Now Alan's only companion was death. Three of them had died: Victor, Robert Wentworth and Thembi. Wentworth and Thembi were history but Victor would never leave Alan. The question that had haunted him since Victor's death continued in his mind: the question of who had been responsible for Victor's death.

Rebecca wanted him to think it was him.

Not me, he thought as he walked a step.

He stopped when another, and equally menacing, thought struck him. Victor, Wentworth, Thembi. Would Sarah be the next in line? She was incarcerated in his enemies' gaol: would she fall from the fifth floor, becoming another to add to unreal suicide statistics? Or would she be left there to rot, isolated amongst a group of petty criminals, in danger of losing the thing that he valued most in her – her sensible equilibrium?

He shook himself back into motion. Worrying about Sarah's fate could not help since he had no answer to these questions. Only one thing was clear: *they* would never let her go because *they* would never forgive Alan.

Behind him the woman laughed again. Alan began to walk fast, away from their intimacy. He saw, in outline, a tree, a dried-up, broken tree struggling between life and death, its gnarled branches reaching up for rain that never seemed to fall. Somebody had helped it on its way to death: somebody had snapped off a branch since he was last here.

The tree reminded him of another time. Of a time with Sarah, perhaps, was that the time? No, he thought, the tree was from a different time.

The tree seemed to change shape before his eyes, transforming itself into the one before. The first tree had also been battling for its life and yet it was a symbol of life. Victor used to sit under it and play the penny whistle there. The pied piper that's what Victor seemed to be. He sat and played while other, younger, men crowded around him as if this proximity was what would keep them safe.

Alan had not been then amongst Victor's acolytes. Alan, like so many others, had been attracted to Victor but in his case this very attraction was the precursor to fear. Victor was dangerous to Alan: he was too sure of himself, too in control, his repertoire ranging from joker to counsellor, from warrior to friend.

The tree was in southern Angola, in the depths of bandit country. They were fighting the same enemy in a different form – in the form of South African-backed UNITA troops. The severity of military life was made worse by the constant threat of ambush. The countryside was mined and every step outside the camp was a step into the unknown, with routes of escape carefully charted, with warnings never to stray from designated paths.

To the men, Alan included although he would never admit it, Victor had been security. His calm and his experience had kept at bay much of the claustrophobia that threatened always to overcome them. But even Victor could not stop all the symptoms of the men's sense of entrapment. Tempers grew frayed as they sweated under the sun by day, and were devoured by mosquitoes by night, plagued by killers who were not their enemy.

Alan had suffered especially because Alan used walking as a way to calm himself and walking there was a virtual impossibility. That's what they had in common: that's what started it. Victor too had also liked to walk. It was that which finally united them. Victor hadn't attempted to befriend Alan but Victor was observant and he'd noticed Alan's restlessness. Or perhaps it was something else, perhaps Victor guessed that Alan was a person who would understand why Victor kept part of himself so concealed. Whatever the truth, one afternoon, one late afternoon, Victor had approached Alan and spoken to him unexpectedly.

'Let's make tracks,' he said.

Bewildered by this unexpected approach, Alan shot a silent question at Victor.

'Come on man,' Victor said. 'Let's go for a walk.'

At that point a cloud passed in front of the sun and Victor's face, dark as it was, became blacker still. Alan caught a glimpse of something in Victor's eyes – a hint of wildness and of desperation – that he'd never imagined could be there. Suddenly he understood why it was that Victor made him feel afraid.

The cloud moved on and Victor's face cleared. If Victor had not staggered Alan might have thought that the change had been illusory. But Victor did stagger and for a moment Alan thought him drunk. He pushed the thought away: there was no alcohol to be had and besides Victor never drank.

Alan shivered.

'Are you scared of walking?' Victor asked.

If anybody else had asked this of Alan, he would have denied it. But Victor was not like anybody else and for some reason Alan felt impelled to tell the truth. He nodded.

Victor laughed and pushed Alan's arm. 'Go on then,' he said. 'Fetch your weapon. It and I will protect you.'

They had moved away from the camp together, not furtively, but without drawing needless attention to themselves. And then, when they were out of earshot, Victor, the perfect cadre, did something else to break the rules. Instead of walking along the designated track, he chose another. He turned deliberately from what was relative safety into the unknown.

When Alan protested Victor turned on him. 'Ag man,' he said. 'Don't you ever get bored of treading the straight and narrow? Come on, let's move.' Victor walked off, not waiting to see if Alan would follow.

Alan followed. They walked a long way together, in silence mostly, tramping through the bush. Victor, who was superbly fit, set the pace and at times Alan had to struggle to keep up with him. But the effort was worth it for as yards turned into miles the tyranny of forced confinement began to lift from Alan's chest. Victor must have felt it too, because the ferocity that Alan had glimpsed on Victor's face gradually faded and in its place, in the twilight that descended on them, returned the gentle, sensible Victor. Peace, Alan realized, that's what Victor had been hoping for: that's why he'd suggested a walk.

As dark replaced dusk, they'd turned back and walked towards the camp. They were within a mile of it when it happened, happened so quickly that Alan could barely summon up the details.

186

A twig had cracked at the time too, he remembered, that was the first sign that they were not alone. The second sign was not at all furtive. It came as a whining of a bullet that flew close past Alan's ear.

'Shit,' Victor had said, that one word only, or was it shoot?

Victor had no gun and Alan no time to think. His reflexes tested only previously in training took over and he spun round to shoot into the bush, once, twice, three times. He'd cocked his gun, ready to shoot again but Victor gripped his hand.

'There's no returning fire,' Victor said.

As Alan stood and waited, his heart thumping, he heard a sound, a faint, slow release of breath. And then nothing more.

They found the man a few feet away, a man whom life had already abandoned. He lay there, sprawled on the ground, his mouth open, two holes in his chest but his body clean of blood. He was not quite a man but young, poised on the threshold of adulthood, the first signs of stubble only recently arrived to blot his face.

Alan had never killed a man before. The sight of this warm corpse sank to his stomach. When he saw the first trickle of blood, coming from the man's chest, he tasted bile. Alan had cried out, trapped in the horror of what he had done, unable to step away. But Victor was there, and Victor had led him from it. Victor held Alan's head while Alan vomited and then Victor straightened Alan up and looked him in the eye.

'You have given me the gift of life,' he said.

It was dark but when Alan looked into Victor's eyes, he saw a warmth there, an expression of gratitude and of something else as well – of fellowship. He nodded and Victor embraced him, held him in his arms, while one of the two had sobbed. Alan could not remember which of them had cried, in that moment he and Victor were one.

'A snake,' is what they'd told their comrades who had come out to investigate.

'A big snake,' Victor laughed before picking up his penny whistle again.

Neither he nor Victor ever spoke of that night but the incident was a turning point for both. Victor became Alan's friend and, in this way, Victor opened doors. Not doors of influence or of power but doors of love. For Victor taught something to Alan that the younger man had never had the chance to learn. It was a lesson by example: if a man like Victor could be both strong and vulnerable then Alan could be strong and vulnerable too.

Sarah, Alan thought, had taught him love for a woman but Victor, Victor taught him something more precious. Victor had taught him the beginnings of love for himself. He and Victor had been brothers in arms, friends, comrades.

'Comrade.' The sound reached him from afar. Alan turned and saw his guards gesturing frantically at him. 'You're going too far,' the woman called, 'we must return.'

Wearily Alan began to walk back towards his own confinement. As he walked he remembered Rebecca's question. *What did you owe Victor?* she'd asked. He realized suddenly that she hadn't made it up, that he must have said something about a debt to Victor. Is it because of what I gained that night – he wondered – that made me say I owed him? Is it because of Victor's friendship? But even as he asked himself the question, the answer came to him. Victor's friendship was worth much, but that wasn't why Alan owed him. It was something different, the source of the debt. Rebecca would never have understood but Victor did. Victor knew that if you save a man's life then that life becomes your responsibility.

'And I let him die,' Alan shouted into the night. 'I let Victor die.'

CHAPTER TWENTY-ONE

South Africa

The sounds issued out into the night not smoothly but in bursts, each volleying up before being arbitrarily cut off. Curses, laughter, sections from unfinished arguments, all these rose staccato-like, clashing as they descended with the sounds of metal hitting concrete, of glasses clinking and of the untamed, raucous guffaw of the *shebeen*'s owner.

Peter stood only a few feet from the Umtata *shebeen*, there in the middle of the Transkei, and he was hiding in the shadows. He watched patiently, ignoring the stench of urine, which issued from the alleyway. As he watched he concentrated on the activity around the *shebeen* – on that and on the prospect of what he would find inside. When the door swung open he licked his lips expectantly.

A man came out of the *shebeen*, and stood by the door: a man framed by the light and also waiting.

That's him, thought Peter. He took one step forward.

What the man on the *shebeen*'s doorstep saw was a startling transformation in the blackness beyond – what had once been still and uniform, separated and a figure emerged from a place which accommodated no life. The man staggered backwards and put a hand up over his eyes – a shield against an imminent blow.

'It's me,' Peter said softly.

The man dropped his hand. 'Ag, Archie, you gave me a fright,' he said. He smiled sheepishly. 'I've been waiting for you,' he said. 'Come in, come in. We're wasting valuable drinking time.'

The man turned and lurched his way into the *shebeen*. 'My friend Archie,' he told the rows of expectant faces. The occupants of the small room nodded and their faces dulled again as they re-applied themselves to their disparate conversations.

Peter followed his contact to the end of the smoke-filled room. He saw how the man tottered, almost losing his balance at several points, and how, once he was seated in front of one of several rickety coffee tables, he looked expectantly up at Peter.

'Four beers and half of Viceroy?' the man asked.

Peter grimaced. Life is shit, he thought. This man only invited me here so he could drink my money. But then, he thought, I only talked to him because I knew I couldn't walk into this place alone without inviting trouble.

A grin replaced the grimace. 'Four beers and a half of Viceroy,' he called to the mama of the place. He pulled one of the steel chairs closer.

The first of the beers was quickly consumed, chased down by a slug of brandy. His companion reached for the bottle. 'Viceroy's the stuff,' he commented.

'Ja,' Peter agreed, 'Viceroy is the stuff,' agreed even though what had provoked the grin was not the taste of the liquor but rather the surfacing of the memory of where he had just been and what he had just done. The boat, that's what had made him grin: the boat with its freedom fighters soon to be disgorged.

While he gulped down the second beer he pushed the memory aside. Tonight was a time to forget about work and the secrets which drove him through life. Tonight was his alone. He raised a can, the sign that he was ready for a refill. The room, he realized, had lost some of its sharp edges. I'm already half drunk, he thought.

A man emerged from another room – one almost directly behind Peter – and glanced sharply at Peter before going back in again. This man was one of the privileged, belonging to the *shebeen*'s inner circle. Before the door closed, Peter craned his neck and peered quickly into the other room. What he saw was a space of far superior quality than the one he inhabited. It was larger and emptier too, and instead of only murmured conversation, drinking was done to the accompaniment of the latest township hits – all under the rather sombre colours of reproduction Picassos and Matisses.

The door closed on Peter, shutting him out and something in his brain closed too.

His companion leaned closer. 'Nice place,' he commented. He whispered in Peter's ear. 'Nice people, too,' he said. 'Committed people.'

A comrades' *shebeen*, thought Peter. I guessed as much. He took a swig of a fresh beer. I should be in that room, he thought. He stomached the beer along with the bile that had risen unbidden to his throat. On the outside looking in, that was the thought that had brought with it nausea.

He saw his companion smiling quizzically at him and he gritted his teeth. Would you still smile if you knew I had a gun under my shirt? Anger and self-righteousness jostled secretly with each other. I deserve it, he thought, deserve to be in the inner sanctum. I could go in, he thought, and claim my place amongst the comrades.

He must be really drunk to think of that for the irony of his life was that if he had barged in and boasted about his achievements they would be more inclined to take him out and beat him up than to welcome him. Enemy infiltration, both within MK and internal structures was a desperate problem, and so a stranger in a comrades' *shebeen* who said he was a member of the ANC's armed wing would be treated with a combination of incredulity and naked hostility.

I'm alone, Peter thought, completely alone. He grabbed the brandy and drank straight from the bottle.

'Mandela.'

The name roused Peter from a state of semi-consciousness. He looked blearily at his watch and saw that some hours had passed since he'd entered the place. The *shebeen* was in its last nightly phase: animated conversation had long since died down, as had the drunken quarrels that invariably follow sudden friendship. Now what Peter saw was dissolution – a time when alcohol would only produce *angst* in those who imbibed it. Most of the occupants of the room had escaped this fate by falling asleep. Peter glanced to his right and saw his companion was amongst these – his mouth open wide, his chair tilted precariously back against the wall.

Who's talking of Mandela? Peter wondered. As sleep filtered from his brain he identified the source: the name had come from the direction of two of the heaviest drinkers, two who sat amongst the wreckage of others sporting the bright looks of men poised between the loquacity of a second wind and an imminent alcoholic collapse.

'Ag, don't be so stupid, man,' one of them was saying, 'de Klerk will never release Mandela.'

'But he says he will.'

'Can't trust a snake like that,' muttered the first. He lunged forward, grabbed a bottle from the low table, and tilted his head back as he guzzled its contents. He drank until the bottle was finished and then he carefully put it back on the table. Having made sure the bottle was secure he sank, almost in slow motion, down onto the floor. There, he curled and there began to snore. His companion glanced only once at him, frowned in bemusement and then turned away to stare contentedly into space.

I'm the only person awake in the world, Peter thought, the only person who can never properly let go.

A laugh sounded from behind him, a laugh which issued from the inner room. My comrades are also awake, Peter thought. He kept his head still – if they as much as suspected he was eavesdropping they would immediately shut the door.

'Our great African peoples,' a soft voice said, 'solid until the last drink.'

'Ja,' another agreed. 'But he's right, you know, we can't trust de Klerk.'

'And we can't ignore him either,' a third voice chipped in. 'Or we'll lose the initiative. We must believe it: we must believe that Mandela will be released before Christmas.'

Peter nodded and then, catching himself, hid the nod under a low cough.

'Whether you believe it or not, we'll soon be going legal,' continued the third speaker.

Legal, thought Peter. Here was one of those eager for compromise. Watch out, he thought.

192

'We must move with the times,' the man's voice grew louder. 'And we must listen to our leaders. The time of the gun is over.'

Peter narrowed his eyes. His hand moved inside his shirt and he felt the metal there.

'Don't be in such a hurry,' the first voice scolded. 'Our people still need defending. You only have to look at what's been happening in Natal to know that. And the police – you think they're ready to make nice with us? We'll need our own army for a long time to come . . .' and then, as he continued to speak, his voice grew softer until, although he was straining his ears, Peter could distinguish only the occasional word. 'Plans,' he heard and 'tactics', 'MK' and 'underground', too – words that spoke of conspiracy and of belonging. Words that plumbed a life in which Peter was vitally essential while being simultaneously excluded.

I should have known, Peter thought. He should have known that there was no end to the pain of his loneliness and that drinking with others would do nothing to staunch it. He should have remembered that, while outside the borders of South Africa thousands of exiles waited for admittance, he had a different problem – his was exile from within.

How long, he thought, how long has it been since I had a conversation without first working out what I can and can't say? How long, he thought, how long will it be until I can walk into a room like that one, and hold my head up high, and say – here I am – your defender. Bitterness rose to sour his mind.

He closed his eyes and drove out the rancour by imagining it, his triumphant entrance. He saw himself standing by the door, smiling at the sight of their outstretched arms. Acceptance, that's what he'd bask in – acceptance instead of subterfuge, belonging instead of separateness. The image of himself, the people's champion, raised his fist up high in a clenched salute – high and firm, without apology.

He smiled and turned without thinking, turned to face one of the speakers in the inner room. For a fraction of a second two sets of eyes met, and then the door was shut firmly in Peter's face.

Fantasy, thought Peter, nothing but fantasy. He blinked and the image of himself as hero dissolved. In its place came the outline of another, of a man who yesterday had skirted the edges of his consciousness. A man with a twitch, who Peter had noticed not once but thrice. A man spying on me? Peter wondered. No, he thought, no one could use a spy with such a marked disability.

He pushed the image away from him and slowly he got up. It was still dark outside but by the sounds of distant stirring and by a glimmering blush in the darkness he knew dawn was not far off. He must hurry. He must use the cover of the remaining darkness to find a way of getting to Cape Town and to his next rendezvous. He glanced down at his companion.

The man was out completely. Whipping his head quickly round the room to check that no one was watching him, Peter put his hand into the man's pocket. There it was, a set of car keys. Perfect. He removed his hat from the floor and tipped it in the direction of his unconscious companion. 'Sorry,' he mouthed. 'But it's in a good cause.'

Picking his way carefully through the debris, Peter walked to the outside door. And then, just before he left, he heard another fragment issuing from the inner sanctum.

'Discipline,' a voice said. 'That's what's needed now.'

Discipline, Peter thought, as he slipped the key into the car door. Discipline, what do they know of it? Discipline, this was the daily drill by which he alone abided. Discipline and his respect for it kept him alive and on the move: discipline separated him from his fellow man and cut short his relations with women. Discipline the word by which he lived.

Except, he suddenly thought, that to have Alan Littell followed was not disciplined. Nobody had instructed him to do it, he had acted on his own. Was it because of Thembi? he thought. Was it because Thembi had rejected him and slept with Alan? Was that why he didn't trust Alan?

As the car moved away from the *shebeen* Peter wondered, for the first time, perhaps whether what he'd done had been wrong.

CHAPTER TWENTY-TWO
Tanzania

Alan stared out into a night of such unrelenting blackness that it might have been conjured out of his deepest imagination. Even the stars seemed to have retreated, obscured by clouds which, holding out the illusion of rain, only made the atmosphere more oppressive. The dark and the silence were suffocating. Alan struggled to free himself from their embrace but at first he could find no way to dent the shroud that had covered his room. And then, as he continued his vigil, noises came to fill a space which had formerly been lifeless.

His ears began to hum with the impact until he could hardly believe that the room had so recently felt quiet. Now the shrill chirping of cicadas rose in intensity until it was almost deafening. At that point another sound took over; the scratching of a small animal, a rodent perhaps, right below the window as if it were trying to break in.

But the worst, and the loudest, of the sounds was human. Outside in the tented city, somebody coughed, somebody cried out and somebody else groaned and turned. Over and above these sounds, and more horrible by far, was the breathing: uniform, rasping breathing, which pulsated through the night, bearing down on Alan, snatching the very air from his lungs. It was more than he could bear. He blocked his ears. The sound swelled and prepared itself to surge again. His shoulders heaved as he gasped: dizziness almost overcame him. Desperately, he covered his face with both hands.

The sound reached a peak before slowly subsiding. As it faded,

Alan realized that what he'd heard was not the sound of others' breathing but rather his breath alone. His gasps turned to sobs and he sank down, foetus-like, to the floor.

The light from a bare, hundred-watt bulb temporarily blinded him. He shut his eyes, held them closed for a fraction and then slowly reopened them. In the transition between an inner view and the artificial illumination, he realized that, just as it was the sound of his breath that had filled the air, so was the darkness his – the black that oppressed him was not the shadow cast by his soul. He was lost.

But he was no longer alone. He was a child, there on the floor, while ghosts towered above him. 'Get away,' he shouted, blocking his eyes with his hands. He couldn't stand the dark. Shuddering, he removed his hands. Victor was there and Thembi too, close together, two lonely people each needing contact. They were both smiling but not at him – rather they looked at each other and, as Alan watched, they nodded as if confirming something they already knew.

He shifted his eyes to the right. Robert Wentworth was also there, standing alongside the other two but separated by the colour of his skin and by his fateful decision. Robert, no longer pleading, stared accusingly at Alan.

Alan turned to the fourth spectre in attendance and saw the shape of a woman round and smooth and somehow half dissolved, a woman without features. Of the four only she moved. She stretched out her hand but then, before she could make contact, she had vanished.

My mother, Alan thought. She appeared again, behind the other three, standing at a distance as if resisting the temptation to reach out again.

He frowned. There was somebody missing from this parade, somebody else who should have been in attendance. Who was it?

No, he was wrong: of course she wasn't missing. Ghosts came from the grave, and Sarah could not therefore be present. And yet she should be here for here assembled were the people Alan had destroyed. Each of them had – in their differing ways – touched him and each of them had died soon afterwards.

Somebody like you, that's what Rebecca had said. Somebody like him had sent Victor to his death. But was it he? He didn't know.

He shivered violently. Not to know the truth – therein lay madness. Ever since that moment when his whole world collapsed, he had ignored the dictums of others, sticking to his own resolve, policing himself solely through his ethics. His only proviso was that he must always remain truthful to himself. In the four years that followed he had stuck steadfastly to this resolution and it had kept him sane. If, however, the truth became blurred, then he risked losing his anchor on reality.

A voice accused him: *You don't known what you believe, you stupid boy. You don't know what,* it hissed. The voice belonged to his adoptive father, Jack Howard, the fifth phantom to appear. Jack, pointing at Alan as he had done during their last encounter, and uttering those same words.

It was no effort to conjure up that time – Alan remembered it as if it existed in the now. To reproduce it entirely, Jack should be standing a few feet away and roaring at Alan, while in the background Girlie would be hovering, wringing her hands as she ignored embarrassed guests. At that time Jack's craggy face was reddened by fury, his mouth open as he volleyed insults at Alan. It was Jack, rather than Girlie, who had reminded Alan of his father: it was Jack who bore the stigma of a disappointment so strong that it fuelled a tyrant's curse.

'It's not fair.' Alan cried out the words for the boy he'd once been.

Jack was a big man and Alan, only just sixteen, had been dwarfed by the accusations raining down on his head. He had said nothing while Jack cursed him, nothing when Jack ordered him out.

Leave my house, Jack had yelled, *Leave my house.*

As the words reverberated through Alan's brain, the ghosts lined up beside Jack, their mouths wide open. They weren't shouting, like Jack, they were laughing.

Why were they laughing?

He knew the answer. They were laughing because they had caught him out, caught him lying to himself. Jack hadn't ordered him from the house. What he'd done was tell Alan to go to his room.

It was Alan who had chosen to exile himself. The fiction he had created for outside consumption – created because it was simpler than the truth – was that Jack and Girlie had turned their backs on him. The reality was that he had walked out on them. But in a sense the fiction was more accurate because it was they who'd made him do it. He wasn't the transgressor, he was the victim! After all he had only been trying to please them, to give them what he thought they'd wanted – what they and what his teacher, Mr Garfield, had wanted.

He closed his eyes and it all came flooding back. He was sixteen years old and his reward for excelling at school was the opportunity to deliver the end of term speech. He was sixteen years old and on top of the world – too innocent to know that after pride comes a fall. He had stood by the lectern and smiled while school friends and parents waited patiently for him to begin.

'I'm going to talk of our brave country,' he began.

Their response was normal, a few coughs, a rustle of paper, a yawn from the back – all signs of an audience settling down to an average, and largely anticipated, speech.

'I'm going to talk of our brave country,' he repeated. 'And of the cruelties daily committed in our name by those who are our agents.'

As soon as he finished the sentence, the atmosphere was transformed. He saw it, in their faces, in the way they looked at him, and he felt it in the air, an unease so strong that it was almost as if the room hummed with static. For a moment, he had faltered.

They're not all as enlightened as us, is what Jack had once said. Believing Jack in everything, Alan had gone on with his speech. He had expounded ideas that he had thought were held by his parents and teacher alike: ideas of what constituted injustice and of the solutions too – of the need for whites to be divested of their wealth and for blacks to plunder it.

Driven by the force of his own rhetoric, his voice had grown more confident. Good, he'd thought, as he noticed how each sentence was more radical than the last, I've shaken them up. That's exactly what Jack used to say: *This country needs a good shake,* Jack would say, and now Alan was giving it one.

'Step aside, or die,' he told his audience.

And then, just then as he nearly reached the end, he had happened to glance up. His eyes landed accidentally on his teacher, Mr Garfield. He saw Mr Garfield's uncharacteristic stillness and the way he was staring glumly down at hands wedged uncomfortably between his knees. Alan willed his teacher to look up but Mr Garfield's eyes remained fixed on the floor.

Uneasily Alan searched the audience for Jack and Girlie. When he found them his suspicions turned to certainty. Girlie was blinking rapidly, a sure sign that she was upset. But Jack – well, Jack was the worst. He was staring at Alan, his lips narrowed to a straight line, his brown eyes blazing a message. A message of aversion.

Alan had read awkwardly through to the end of his speech, and then, in the silence that followed it, he had walked down from the platform and out of the school. Nobody stopped him and so he made his own, slow way home. When he arrived he pushed the imposing gates open and thought: why have these barriers if you're not shutting someone out? He walked slowly up the white pathway, between a parade of trees and thought, those who are willing to share, don't grab so much for themselves. He walked past carefully manicured lawns and ebullient flower bushes and thought, if God had made flowers black, they would have been sure to weed them out.

He reached the doorway of what had once been home but what now seemed like a mausoleum to his rejection. He saw the Howards standing there, under the imposing white doorway and he thought: That's it. I'm finished here. They hate me, all of them. What should have been his hour of victory was transformed into his moment of defeat. It had taken him years to learn to trust the Howards, but it only took a second for his trust to collapse.

And Jack, never a subtle man, had confirmed Alan's foreboding. Not by words alone, although the words Jack later employed were harsh indeed, but through the simple narrowing of his eyes. Alan had seen Jack do this once before, when a black beggar had the temerity to ring insistently at their bell, and so he understood what it meant. He was an outcast, an untouchable who, in challenging the way they lived, had broken their unwritten rules. He was an outcast and there was nothing he could do. He hadn't bothered to defend himself against Jack's accusations of disloyalty. He had left the room and the house as well.

He had never gone back.

Never gone back, that is until recently. Until he had given in to Sarah's entreaties and driven to Bryanston just to see the house – and perhaps to catch a glimpse of Girlie. *I'll never see this house again* – that's what he'd thought when he'd jumped from his window with nothing but the clothes he wore. He had kept his resolution for almost twenty years and only Sarah's persistence dented it.

He had gone back because she told him to. He'd gone back, and the visit – so brief and so insignificant – might mean his downfall. It was Sarah's fault. She'd got him into this mess.

No, it wasn't her fault: she wasn't to know. The failing was his alone. He loved Sarah, more than he'd ever loved another, and yet he wasn't blind to her faults. He knew that her cherished openness could lead to *naïveté*, and her ability to trust could sometimes make her inattentive. He knew this and should have guarded against it, but instead his love had made him careless. He had allowed himself to be led on by her enthusiasm, to be carried forward by her conviction that the past could actually be mended.

It was his fault and he deserved to be punished for it. He'd known it was wrong as soon as he'd got out of the car and walked to the gates. To say that the visit was insignificant was to deceive himself. It had meaning all right – it had hauled buried feelings to the surface, feelings that were so hard to bear that he'd deliberately forgotten them.

These emotions, and not the sound of a car backfiring, that's what had made him forget where he'd parked his car – that's why he'd rushed away blindly, and bumped straight into his shadow. These emotions were sensations of the beginnings of insanity, the same kind that haunted him now. By merely being in the vicinity of the house, everything he'd once felt – the doubt, the rage, the fear of being on his own again and of being white and poor – returned in all its intensity. He remembered, clearly he remembered, how close he had once come to the edge of madness.

The memory was strong because he had been there not once,

but twice in his life. It had happened again when he'd started at Witwatersrand University, doubts had insinuated themselves into his mind. The isolation had all but destroyed him but he had eventually survived it by managing to win the trust of first one radical and then another until the whole network accepted him. That's what had saved him: finding a sense of purpose. He'd grown strong in the belonging and strong in the knowledge that the others with their drugs, their talk of free love, and their revolutionary posturing were playing games while he was deadly serious.

Some of his former comrades had withstood the test of time. Some of them were still involved. But as for the majority, having had their fling, they retreated back into suburbia, joining the Howards in bemoaning the state of South Africa while they grasped its rewards in their sticky hands. Their panic must be tangible now: their knowledge of the change to come devouring their artificial security.

Alan had never been like them and, of all his group, he had gone the furthest. He'd joined the ANC and he'd been completely accepted.

Until now.

Now, for the third time in his life, he must fight his way through hostility. And now he was no longer a youth. He was pursued by his past, by Victor and by Sarah as well, each in their own way, staying his hand. And the truth was that he no longer knew whether he was strong enough to win. Worse than that, he no longer knew whether he actually wanted to win.

He looked up and the ghosts were gone. For a moment he wanted them back, anything for company. But then he remembered that he had conjured them up and that he could do so again. He took a few deep breaths. His face was wetted by tears that had fallen without his knowledge. He wiped his eyes with the back of one arm, not once but twice and still the tears kept coming. He hugged his head close to his knees and gave in to his grief, sobbing his confusion out into the night.

'Haven't you taken enough punishment?'

Rebecca jumped and turned. She saw Jabulani standing a few

201

feet away, smiling quizzically at her. He must have crept up on her and, for all she knew, he'd been watching for some time. She experienced a moment's irritation, which she pushed to one side. Her behaviour was no better than Jabulani's: she was doing the same thing, standing in the dark, suppressing the sounds of her own breathing, as she eavesdropped on Alan.

She turned away from the door and a feeling of relief took the place of tension. Jabulani was right: she'd been punishing herself. She had already spent too much time with a sobbing Alan – it was a kind of sickness that had pulled her out into the night so she could endure more of the same.

'I couldn't sleep,' she explained as she began to walk back.

Jabulani fell into step beside her. 'Come to my room,' he suggested. 'I'll give you something to help.'

Stopping abruptly, she turned her head and glowered at him.

He smiled. 'A nightcap – that's all I meant,' he said. He raised his hands in the air, palms upwards, in a gesture of surrender.

Mortified by her assumption, she nodded her consent. Together they made their way past her room and into his. Which was, of course, in chaos. Standing in the middle of it, Rebecca reflected that Jabulani's rooms inevitably reverted to type – they were always littered with more books, papers and folders than one could reasonably expect from a man who was constantly on the move. His desk, she saw, was buried, the floor covered and even his bed hadn't escaped the devastation. It was unmade and covered with pages of what looked like an unfinished manuscript hastily discarded. And yet none of it was dirty. Another thing Rebecca remembered was that Jabulani was a fastidious man. Should the bed be cleared, she knew the sheets would be clean and fresh smelling. Not, of course, that she would give him any excuse to clear the bed.

'Whisky?'

He looked so innocent standing by the desk, a bottle raised in his right hand. She nodded more brusquely than she should have done. He poured two fingers into a plain glass, placed it on the desk, carefully removed the books that were lying on the chair and gestured to her. When she went to sit on it, he moved away and poured himself a drink. She took a sip and felt the whisky hit the back of her throat. It was a long time since she had bothered with hard liquor – tears sprang to her eyes.

Jabulani lifted his glass into the air. 'To drive away the devils,' he said before taking a swig.

The devil, she thought. 'You think Alan is evil?' she asked.

Jabulani walked to the bed, swept some of the papers to one side and sat. He frowned. 'I was speaking metaphorically,' he said. He paused and held her gaze, held it so intently that she, against her will, blinked. Out of the side of her eyes, she saw him smile.

'It's not funny,' she said, looking up but taking care to avoid facing him directly.

'What's not funny?'

His tone of gentle inquisition revived her irritation. What am I doing here? she asked of herself. She put her glass, still mostly full, on the ground and then straightening her back, she stared at Jabulani.

He shrugged. 'I am not the enemy,' he said.

He was right. She felt ashamed.

'The real question,' Jabulani continued, 'is whether Alan's the enemy.'

What if he isn't? she almost blurted out. What if we're wrong? She stopped herself for this was no time for rhetorical questions.

But she needn't have bothered to still her tongue. 'You've changed your mind about Alan,' Jabulani stated.

Yes, she'd changed her mind. Alan was innocent – that's what she now believed. That's what kept her from her bed, that's what drove her to spy on Alan when it wasn't required – her sense of his blamelessness.

For a moment she wondered whether she was going crazy. Ever since she had arrived in this place she'd found herself splitting her thoughts one from the other in an effort to be fair to a man she considered guilty. And then, without noticing it, her position reversed itself so that, even as she interrogated Alan, she now felt like his defender. Ever since she'd left South Africa, she had turned a practical bent into an obsession. Problems she encountered were dealt with briskly and without the need for introspection. But suddenly she was awash with conflicting emotions. She could hardly stand it.

'If we continue to apply the pressure,' she said tentatively, 'we're going to break Alan.'

Jabulani nodded. He'd read the transcripts.

'What if he isn't a spy?' she asked.

Jabulani shrugged. 'Then he isn't,' he said. 'But we need to be certain. What other choice do we have?'

'If he's an agent, we'll uncover him,' Rebecca argued. 'But if he isn't we still stand the risk of destroying him. How can we do that?'

'We've no other option but to continue with Littell,' Jabulani replied. 'We have only two days left to act. Two days before the boat will be too close to South Africa to be recalled. It's one against forty.'

'It's one against forty,' she said, 'only if Alan is a spy. If he isn't . . .' She could not find a way to complete her sentence. 'I refuse to be party to the wanton destruction of an individual,' she burst out.

Jabulani raised an eyebrow. 'We've reached a time,' he said, 'when the individual is no longer as important as the whole.'

She heard the mimicry in his voice. He was quoting her, paraphrasing from her speech at Thembi's funeral. The anger that had been bubbling below the surface burst out. 'Don't patronize me,' she hissed.

'Come on, Rebecca,' Jabulani said firmly. 'You're no mere beginner. You must know this has happened before. This and worse than this, in fact. Without direct access to the country one of the only ways we can uncover the truth is by direct confrontation.'

'I don't like it.' She hated the hint of childishness that had invaded her voice.

'Nobody said you had to like it,' Jabulani replied. 'You have to do your best – more than your best – because it's necessary.'

Those three words, so simple and so poisonous. Because it was necessary Rebecca ran a department with a tenth of the resources she needed; because it was necessary, she attended meetings and listened patiently while people she despised discussed ideas that were not only ridiculous but also sometimes dangerous; because it was necessary she worked towards an uncertain future. Because it was necessary, she had once carried on in the knowledge that her son was suffering.

Because it was necessary she had watched Mzwanele die.

The mist that obscured her vision could not be blamed on alcohol. She forced herself to speak. 'We consider ourselves better than the enemy,' she said. We say we're fighting against injustice. And yet where is our justice?'

Jabulani shrugged. 'We're not perfect,' he said, 'but look around the world and show me perfection, or even something close to it. I bet you won't find it, especially at this time, when the sands of time are shifting so rapidly. South Africa is on the move but the traps are everywhere. We have to keep our footing because our task remains the same: to do our best for the next generation.'

Not for Mzwanele, Rebecca thought. Mzwanele was of the next generation and Mzwanele was dead.

Her thought must have been openly displayed on her face because Jabulani responded to it. 'Mzwanele was one,' he said. 'There are many others to think of now.'

How could he dismiss Mzwanele so casually? She hit out at him. 'You and your books,' she shouted, sweeping her hand to encompass the room. 'You use them to separate yourself from life. You're a theorist posing as an activist, you talk of emotions and yet they are alien to you. How have you suffered? Tell me, how have you suffered?'

She bit her tongue, drawing blood. She wanted to snatch the words back. How could she have said them to this man, to a man who had once been her friend? For Jabulani had indeed suffered. She had seen the scars of his long-time incarceration, a time when they had brought him close, if not to madness, then at least to death.

She spoke before he could. 'Oh, Jabulani, I'm sorry,' she said. She got up abruptly and she made her voice as friendly as she was able. 'It's Alan Littell,' she said. 'Either he's a spy and a clever one at that, or he's merely close to the edge of insanity and taking me with him.'

There – she had admitted it.

'Did you hear what he said about Victor?' she asked. 'He said

205

none of us knew the man. His implication was that Victor was responsible for his own death.'

Jabulani nodded up at her. He appeared to be thinking. 'Do you know,' he said after a pause, 'that I always wondered whether Victor was gay.'

Her anger violently resurfaced. 'How dare you? How dare you blacken the name of one of the fallen?'

Jabulani looked straight at her. 'Blacken?' he said. 'Blacken. An interesting turn of phrase.'

'You know what I mean. You're accusing a man who can't answer back for himself.'

He shook his head sadly. 'That was the source of Victor's tragedy,' he said. 'And that is our mistake – to say a man is gay is to be seen to be accusing. If Victor was gay, then, no wonder he kept it quiet.'

She did not want to listen to him: she did not want to hear. 'Are you trying to say that Victor might have disobeyed orders because of sexual involvement?' she demanded.

'All I'm trying to say', Jabulani softly responded, 'is that Victor was almost certainly gay. That would be difficult for him in the camps – especially with such a macho reputation.'

Almost certainly gay – Jabulani was hardening his phrases. Fatigue washed over Rebecca. She never should have left her room, she should have stayed and slept there. She made her way to the door.

Jabulani's voice pursued her. 'I'm here if you need me,' he said.

She looked back at him, remembering a time when she would have stayed in the room, when she would have found consolation in his embrace. 'Oh, I need you,' she wanted to say. But she couldn't bring herself to utter the words. Instead she pressed down on the door handle and pushed it open.

'I need sleep,' she said. 'We all do.'

Day Five

CHAPTER TWENTY-THREE

When Rebecca arrived in the interrogation room she found Albert Kana already seated. He was reading out loud, haltingly stressing every syllable as if only that way could he squeeze the meaning from the words. Rebecca stood by the door and listened.

I can't live with myself, Albert read. *I did the things of which I stand accused. I am a spy, recruited whilst at university. I was caught taking drugs and they said I was finished unless I agreed to work for them.* Albert frowned. *I was never much good as a spy,* he continued, *but I suppose that makes little difference. If it's any consolation, I've finally seen my former masters for what they are. They betrayed me – they and others.*

Albert paused, took a breath and then continued as if he hadn't registered Rebecca's presence.

I won't name those who double-crossed me, he said. *They know who they are. I only hope that one day they'll suffer for what they did to me.*

Still holding the single sheet of paper, Albert looked over his glasses straight at Rebecca.

'Wentworth's suicide note?' she asked.

He nodded, returned the paper to the pile in front of him and glanced pointedly at his watch.

'I overslept,' she said.

Albert shrugged. 'I'm going through the Wentworth papers,' he said. 'Why don't you start on Littell?'

Rebecca made her way over to the desk and seated herself

opposite Albert. In front of her was stacked an array of files, each neatly labelled.

'I sorted them out,' Albert said, before addressing himself pointedly to his own pile.

She knew he was reproaching her for her lateness, but she was too tired to care. Ignoring her shaking hands, she opened the first of the folders. She began, wearily, to read.

It was a good hour before Jabulani arrived.

When she heard him open the door, and when she heard him reply jovially to Albert's greeting, Rebecca's heart began to thump.

She kept her head deliberately bent down to her work. She found herself battling for concentration. Instead of reading, she was waiting: waiting for Albert to reproach Jabulani for his tardiness. When Albert failed to comment, her resentment resurfaced. Men! Why do they let each other get away with the things they hold against us?

She felt Jabulani hovering behind her and so she turned and nodded. His unspoken reply was so cool as to be almost glacial. Okay, she thought. Let it be war.

Jabulani seated himself on the chair next to hers. She shifted away a fraction. The gesture was unnecessarily childish, and she scolded herself for it.

She tried again to concentrate but again to no avail. The words danced in front of her eyes. She found herself reliving the night. All through it, she had been obsessed with Jabulani and why she hadn't stayed with him. Tossing and turning she'd spent each moment caught between the twin extremes of anger and regret. At one point, she had told herself that she'd imagined his intentions. She had tried to convince herself that his words had been purely innocent, without any sexual significance. But having made herself vulnerable to memories from the past, she found it impossible to shut down again. She knew she hadn't misread his look: he had been inviting her into his bed. And she had refused.

That's when the anger took over. How dare he play with her? How dare he exploit her vulnerability? He cared nothing for her –

he'd merely wanted a companion in this desolate place, a brief respite from the knowledge that forty of their number might be heading to their deaths.

But so what? she suddenly thought. He wasn't being machiavellian, merely human. She knew she also would have benefited from such comfort: she also needed respite from the images of each of those forty men, and of Alan Littell, which dogged her waking hours.

She should have consented.

She glanced at Jabulani and immediately contradicted herself. Look at how rested he was: he'd obviously lost little sleep over her refusal! She'd been right to say no. He'd been using her, and, what's worse, he'd been doing so half-heartedly. He hadn't tried to stop her from leaving. For all she knew he'd gone outside and picked himself another consolation prize. That's probably why Albert hadn't reproached him for his lateness – men always sided with each other in matters of love. Not of love, she thought, of sex – pure and simple.

She shivered. What on earth was she doing, worrying about sex? Anxiety began to pulse through her, almost propelling her from her seat. 'We're wasting time,' she burst out. 'We should be interrogating Alan.'

Jabulani smiled. 'What? And risk breaking him?' It wasn't a smile, she thought, it was more like a sneer.

'Do you care who breaks?' she demanded. 'Do you care about anybody?'

Fury had made her face him and she saw him flinch. She noticed, for the first time, how bloodshot were his eyes and how deep the purple pockets beneath them. He'd suffered the night as well. That's why he'd been late. She wanted suddenly to take back her words, to reach across and with some simple gesture, make friends with him. She struggled with her pride and she almost managed to overcome it. She lifted her right hand.

But Albert was in the room and Albert, oblivious to the undercurrents, spoke before she could move. 'I've reviewed the records of the Wentworth trial,' he said. 'And I've come to the conclusion that its findings were correct. Robert Wentworth was indeed a spy.'

'Because of his confession?' Rebecca asked.

211

'Wentworth's letter was certainly unambiguous,' Albert replied. 'But there is another factor. Our people found a document in Wentworth's room – a document typed on a machine to which he had access – and which was a report on a variety of our operations. Since there was no good reason for him to be either cataloguing our activities or listing our personnel, the document became a crucial piece of evidence. Our people faced him with it and, soon afterwards, he killed himself.'

That's how it happened, Rebecca thought. How could I have forgotten? 'Wentworth said he was a terrible spy', she said out loud, 'and he was right. He must have been mad to keep incriminating evidence in his room.'

'Except, if you remember,' Jabulani said, 'Wentworth denied ever having written it.'

'He also denied being a spy,' Rebecca said. 'Until the very end.' Jabulani was looking directly at her, one eyebrow raised.

'It stands to reason', she said, 'that, when first he is confronted, the spy will do everything to protect himself. Wentworth must have started out on a strategy of complete denial and thus he automatically repudiated all knowledge of the document. And then later he realized the game was up.' She was thinking as she spoke but when she'd finished she decided that what she'd said was incontestable.

But Jabulani continued to look, questioningly, at her. 'It stands to reason,' she repeated.

'Reason,' Jabulani said softly. 'Are we still within its domain?'

Anger flooded its way back through her body. Was Jabulani telling her that she had become irrational? The anger strengthened into fury. 'What do you mean?' she snapped.

His smile enraged her further. 'I'm merely considering the possibility that someone might have planted the incriminating evidence on Wentworth,' he said.

'You mean that Alan Littell planted it on Wentworth?' Jabulani didn't reply. 'Why would he do that?' Rebecca demanded.

'Because, if you remember,' Jabulani said, 'Wentworth accused Littell of being a spy.'

If you remember – that was the second time Jabulani had uttered that phrase. What was he trying to say? It struck her suddenly what it was. He was saying she was incompetent, that she was caught between extremes of contempt and sympathy for Alan both of which were clouding her mind. Well it wasn't true. It was Jabulani who acted out of his emotions.

'Are you suggesting that Wentworth wasn't a spy?' she asked coldly.

Jabulani shrugged. 'No. He almost certainly was.'

'You can't have it both ways then,' she said. 'What you've suggested is the stuff of pure fantasy. If you remember,' she smiled in an approximation of sweetness, 'if you remember, Wentworth was the first to be suspected after Victor's death. Wentworth reacted by accusing Alan Littell. Now you're saying that Littell's response was to plant evidence on Wentworth. It's farcical.' She transformed the smile into a laugh. 'You can't have it both ways,' she said.

'Seemingly, I can't have it any ways,' Jabulani softly replied.

The glare Rebecca shot at Jabulani was strong enough to affect even Albert. 'Let's move on to Littell,' he said hastily. 'Rebecca?'

She forced herself to look down at her notes and to give her voice a businesslike efficiency. 'I've combed through Alan's training record,' she said, 'and confirmed that Alan was of the highest calibre. His instructor cannot speak too well of him.' Her voice strengthened: she was no longer pretending. 'Alan is said to have been a quick and eager learner, careful to consider the feelings and abilities of others, ready to reach those less skilled than himself and, although several of the youngsters complained that they did not like him, generally a good mixer. I have, in all my time in the movement, read only one report better than Alan's — and that was Victor's.

Victor was gay: Jabulani's voice from the night before intruded itself. She pushed it away.

'As to Alan's operational record,' she said. 'It is admittedly patchy. Several notable successes, combined with some failures. The last occurred just before Victor died. Weapons Alan had concealed in a dried-up river-bed, were washed away after unexpectedly heavy rain.'

'Washed or taken away?' Jabulani asked.

Rebecca tapped one finger impatiently down on the table. 'The men who went to pick them up', she said, 'returned to base untouched. If Alan had informed on them, they would have been arrested.' She glared at him but he was no longer concentrating on her. On his face was a faraway, concentrated expression.

Rebecca tapped the table briskly. 'Comrade,' she said. 'Perhaps you'd give us the benefit of your attention?'

Jabulani blinked and refocused his eyes. 'I was just thinking', he said, 'that it was a pity Wentworth died when he did. A pity,' he paused and swallowed. 'Or was it deliberate?'

'Alan couldn't have done it,' Rebecca said quickly. 'At that point he too was in custody.'

'I wasn't suggesting Alan killed Wentworth,' Jabulani replied. 'Just thinking that because Wentworth killed himself we never found out how he obtained the knowledge to betray Victor. In an ideal world the inquiry should have sat until it had the answer to the question but at the time the country was up in flames and there were other priorities.' He shook himself and smiled straight at Rebecca. 'I'm sorry, comrade,' he said. 'My mind was wandering. I didn't sleep well last night. Please continue.'

His smile pierced her and she shivered. She was being unfair. She shouldn't be taking out her own bewilderment on him.

Albert coughed. Rebecca looked down again. 'The lost weapons was the last time that one of Alan's missions failed. He wasn't given much for a while, Wentworth's accusation was still uppermost in the Political and Military Committee's mind, but gradually he was reintegrated. There was no reason to doubt him until, that is, he was spotted in Bryanston. Which', she said, 'is the crux of the matter. Do we believe Alan's explanation for his presence there?'

She almost had to bite her tongue to prevent herself from answering her own question. He's telling the truth, she wanted to say. She knew Alan. She believed him.

She wondered suddenly at her conviction. Alan had changed her: in interrogating him, and listening to his obsession with his early years, she had ended up looking at herself. She had been forced to face the memory of Mzwanele and acknowledge how firmly the past had trapped her.

They were waiting for her.

'If we believe Alan,' she continued, 'then our problems don't

214

end. For Alan bumped into an agent which means, if we believe him, that he was being followed. And yet other members of the same mission weren't endangered. It's a puzzle.'

She waited, this time genuinely, for a reply. But none was forthcoming until Albert, who had grown visibly more irritated, expressed his anxiety. 'We have only two days,' he said. 'We must know.'

'Yes,' Jabulani said. 'We must know.' He looked straight at Rebecca and his look was friendly. 'I'm afraid you need to have another go at Alan.'

She nodded and got up and so did Jabulani. Albert, however, remained seated. 'I have a report to write,' he said.

Together Rebecca and Jabulani walked towards the door. Rebecca reached it first and she opened it. She glanced back at Jabulani and saw him waiting for her to proceed. 'It's now or never,' she thought.

'I'm sorry about last night.' There, she had said it. And it wasn't that bad.

'Last night?' Jabulani replied. He shrugged. 'Nothing to be sorry about. Nothing happened.'

Rebecca moved quickly through the door. I suppose he's right, she thought, nothing did happen. She bent her head down to prevent him from catching the expression on her face – an expression that he would surely have identified as disappointment. 'I'll get Alan,' she said.

This time, Alan thought, I won't break down. This time I'll answer her questions openly. This time I'll make her see that I'm the victim, not the predator. And I'll tell her about the traitors – if I tell her right she'll know I'm telling the truth.

He was seated in the same room and in the same chair and yet he felt completely different. He experienced a moment of absolute and eerie calm. His crisis was over. He had come perilously close to cracking – the ghosts were the manifestation of how close – but he had survived and would go on surviving. It crossed his mind that he should be grateful to the ghosts; they'd forced him to see the immensity of the precipice on which he was standing. Their appearance had shown him that unless he controlled himself, he was lost. It had been a long night but he'd eventually managed to

215

fall into a dreamless sleep. When he awoke he was cleansed of anxiety, his mind focused only on what he had to do. It was almost over, he knew it was.

He looked straight at Rebecca and what he saw in her face strengthened his resolve: she was focused on him in a way she had not been before. This time she was also deadly serious.

'How did you feel,' she asked, 'when Robert Wentworth said you were a spy?'

Alan frowned. How had he felt?

He closed his eyes and visualized the scene. He had been in Zambia at the time, in a courtyard, amongst a group of about fifteen MK soldiers. There was little conversation. They were all at a loose end, waiting for a meal, but the atmosphere was strained. They had only just learned of Victor's death and each was silently experiencing the weight of what had previously been unthinkable. What Alan remembered feeling at the time was something close to self-hatred: Victor was dead and yet he wasn't able to cry for him.

Somebody (was it Thembi?) began to sob.

At this exact moment two men from security materialized. They walked into the courtyard and the manner in which they looked over the assembled company showed they meant business. They examined each person in turn. When their eyes alighted on Robert Wentworth, who was standing on his own in a corner, their faces did not change. They moved quickly though. They walked straight up to Robert and arranged themselves on either side of him. The man to Robert's left placed a restraining hand on his arm.

They all knew what the visitation meant. Silence, there was a silence more deafening than noise. Despite the fact he felt he should, Alan couldn't tear his eyes from the tableau. He watched while Robert's body sagged, almost as if he were about to fall, and he watched as the men moved in closer to their prey.

But Wentworth didn't fall. Not then anyway. He started instead to shout. To shout and to move. He freed himself from the man beside him and he began to twist and turn, whirling round as if at the centre of some dervish dance. Alan found himself moving closer and he was not the only one. Each of the witnesses was drawn towards Wentworth and, at last, they formed a circle around him. Wentworth rotated at their centre, faster and faster as if he might never stop. But he did stop. He stopped abruptly in front of Alan. Momentum propelled him to the ground and he landed in a jumbled heap. And it was then that he'd lifted his head, pointed one shaking finger at Alan and spoke: 'There's your spy,' he said.

'I was astonished,' Alan told Rebecca.

It was true. So astonished had he been that a chink to the past was opened. He was thrown back, far back, into his childhood. A part of him left the courtyard and was drawn into another. He heard the taunts of his school friends as they too pointed at him: *Littell by name*, they jeered, *Littell by nature*.

He had blinked. He was no longer a child. He remembered staring incredulously at Wentworth, unable to comprehend yet what he had heard. He even turned around to see if Wentworth was pointing at someone behind him. But there was no one there. He felt the circle dissolve and he registered how the others recoiled from him. It was then that his astonishment was converted into something more ominous. He was at centre stage and he was in trouble.

'I was at first astonished,' he told Rebecca. 'And then afraid.'

'Afraid?' she asked. 'Afraid of what?'

'Of somebody believing Wentworth,' Alan said simply.

Rebecca's eyes were boring down on him. 'You were afraid of somebody believing Wentworth,' she stated. 'Because it was true.'

'Robert was speaking bullshit,' Alan said loudly. 'He whirled round and round, playing some kind of childish game, plotting to accuse the person who happened to be standing in the place where he landed. He landed by me and so he fingered me.'

'But why were you afraid?'

'We all were,' Alan said. 'Somebody had done the unthinkable. Somebody had betrayed Victor. There was a blood lust about, not only a desire but an urgency to identify and punish the traitor.' Or at least that's how I felt, he nearly said.

'I was scared people would believe Robert,' he continued bitterly. 'And they did, didn't they?'

'What they did was correct,' Rebecca said. 'They had to investigate all possibilities.'

'Funny how all the possibilities were white,' Alan said.

'What do you mean?' Stabs of anger brimmed up and out of Rebecca's eyes.

Alan shrugged her disbelief away. 'Just an observation,' he said airily but then he remembered his earlier resolution. Nothing could be gained from deliberately provoking her. 'I'm sorry, comrade,' he said. 'My comment was unwarranted.' He paused and smiled. 'Although Robert probably chose me because I was white.'

'Why would he do that?'

'He might have thought he would be more easily believed,' Alan said.

Rebecca's face twitched, and then, unpredictably, she changed the subject. 'Your training instructor gave you the highest possible recommendation, especially in the fields of surveillance and counter-surveillance,' she said.

Alan smiled.

'You'd done it before, hadn't you?'

The smile cracked. She's gone on the offensive, Alan thought, because I spoke a truth she considers a heresy. He saw her waiting. 'Yes,' he said, 'I'd done it before.'

Rebecca's lungs seemed suddenly to deflate. She gasped for air. So Alan was a spy. She didn't want to believe it. But she must. He had betrayed Victor. She'd felt sympathy for this man and all the time he was a traitor.

She hated him at that moment, she really hated him. 'How?' she barked. 'When?'

It was then he realized how well he knew her. Just by looking at her he could tell she had turned against him. The hostility in her voice was mere confirmation – she hated him. Well, she was not alone in her hatred. He hated her. He had regarded her almost as a friend but she was no different from the others: she had smarmed up to him in order to entrap him. She wasn't interested in the truth: only in getting at him. Well, she was in for a big disappointment.

'I learned counter-surveillance skills when I was at Witz,' he said, 'and a NUSAS member. We had all sorts of grandiose ideas. We considered ourselves the vanguard of the revolution and revolutionaries had to be properly trained didn't they? We set up classes at one of our number's father's estate. Rich kids playing war. I was good at it then as well.'

'At playing war?'

'At surveillance and counter-surveillance,' he said. I'll never tell you just how good, he thought, good enough to find an armed group of those who have betrayed our cause. I'll not tell you of them now.

And Rebecca, watching him, knew she had lost him. Her hatred shrivelled, replaced by disenchantment. For a moment she had thought that Alan was going, for this the first time, to co-operate. But she'd been wrong.

As for herself, she was exhausted: futile hatred had drained the energy from her. She forced herself to concentrate.

CHAPTER TWENTY-FOUR

South Africa

They stood together at the top of a small hill, on a path surrounded by green lawns, overlooking a manicured stretch of water.

'It's good to get out of the office,' Jansen said.

Malan clamped his teeth down – hard down – on his tongue. It was Jansen who had proposed they come to Zoo Lake and Jansen who had made it clear that refusal was not really on the agenda – the implication being that the outing was part of an elaborate security precaution. What Malan felt like saying was that if Jansen couldn't stop his bloody office being bugged, then nobody in South Africa was safe.

'I always think more constructively when freed from the constraints of routine,' Jansen was saying. He smiled, waiting for his subordinate to catch up. 'You field men are lucky,' he said. 'You're given the opportunity to buck the rules. Whereas I . . .' He let the sentence hang, unfinished, in the air. His concentration had shifted: he was busy moulding his expression, previously calibrated for frivolous small chat, into profound concern.

Here it comes, Malan thought.

In front of them two children, accompanied by their nanny, were squabbling over a ball. The younger one grabbed it and was rewarded with a punch. When the nanny tried half-heartedly to intervene, both children began to yell.

Jansen strode away from this scene of domestic strife, heading towards an expanse of grass. 'I've been reviewing the Wentworth files,' he said.

Wentworth? thought Malan. Why Wentworth? The Wentworth thing happened four years ago – before Jansen was promoted. There was no reason why Jansen should review the files, no reason at all. Malan limped over to where Jansen was waiting. 'I'm sure you found the files in order,' he said.

Jansen didn't bother to conceal his irritation. 'Nobody ever faulted your paper work,' he said. He began to walk, more slowly this time. 'I'm an ardent admirer of orderly files,' he continued, 'but there's nothing like an informal chat for really getting to the bottom of things.'

He stopped abruptly. 'Look at that,' he pointed excitedly at a clump of trees, and at a blur which flew past them. 'Was that a humming bird?'

'No, it wasn't,' Malan replied. 'It was a starling.'

If Jansen noticed derision in Malan's voice, he chose to ignore it. He looked straight at Malan. 'And that I gather,' he said, 'would aptly summarize your opinion of Wentworth. You'd categorize him as a common starling rather than as anything more exotic, wouldn't you?'

Malan took a deep breath. 'Robert Wentworth only supplied us with the most basic of information,' he said. 'He had his uses – he confirmed our general picture of the opposition – but he never gave us anything original. From the very beginning his controller . . .'

'That's right,' Jansen interrupted. 'You didn't recruit him did you?'

Malan shook his head.

'In fact,' Jansen continued, 'Wentworth was recruited by the security services whereas you were, before its untimely demise, in BOSS.' He put on his thinking face, his careworn, juggler-of-difficult-issues face. 'We couldn't be getting into the thorny province of inter-departmental rivalry here, could we?'

Malan narrowed his eyes. 'I'm a career officer,' he said. 'I think my record speaks for itself.'

'Of course.'

'But then my record isn't at issue,' Malan continued dryly. 'Robert Wentworth's is. And Wentworth's files confirm that, no matter which agency ran him, his information was always low priority.'

Malan took a few painful steps. You only have to look at Wentworth's photograph, he thought, to see how weak he was. The thought provoked him into impatience.

'For Christ's sake,' he said, 'Wentworth was panicked into working for the police after they found him with one lousy joint of *dagga*. What could we expect from such a coward?'

'So you betrayed him.'

Malan stopped abruptly. 'I did not betray Wentworth,' he said quietly. 'I was forced to sacrifice him.'

'Ah! I see.'

'And it was little sacrifice at that,' Malan continued.

Jansen smiled. 'You mean he was worth so little?'

'No, I don't.' Malan made a deliberate effort to control himself. 'I mean that Wentworth would have cracked,' he said, 'sooner or later. Sooner in my reckoning. The reason Wentworth was suspected by the ANC was because of his vast number of stupid mistakes. He was already lost to us – he never would have stood up to interrogation.'

'So you had incriminating evidence planted in his room.'

Malan's anger had worked its way through his frame. Nothing, not even mild resentment, remained. 'It's all in the files,' he said. 'Wentworth went crazy when accused. He started pointing fingers at others, all at random. He had to be stopped before he did some real damage.'

'Before he exposed your agent Zonda you mean?'

Your agent: Malan heard and noted the pronoun. If that's how things stand, he thought, then why ask the question?

'A worthwhile consideration,' Jansen continued as if Malan had replied. 'In his day Zonda really delivered the goods. I can't help noticing, however, that he's been quiet of late.'

'Zonda is the best we've ever had,' Malan retorted. 'And he's about to present us with a major victory.'

'Ah yes,' Jansen said. 'Ah yes.' He paused, frowned and bent down to the ground. When he straightened up again Malan saw he was holding an old sweet wrapper fastidiously between his thumb and index finger, holding it away from him as if it might contaminate him.

'Kids,' he muttered. 'No respect these days.' He took a few

steps and dropped the paper into a nearby litter bin. 'Tell me, Gert,' he said, 'talking of kids and do forgive me for being so dim, but how does Sarah Patterson fit in with all this?'

'The boat.'

'Ah yes,' Jansen said. 'Another big operation. So Miss Patterson's somehow involved with that is she?' He smirked. 'No, that's wrong isn't it,' he said. 'Miss Patterson's involvement is restricted to Alan Littell and Littell, according to you, holds the key.'

Suddenly he yawned. Just like that he yawned. Instead of covering his mouth, he deliberately widened it. He glanced at his watch. 'Time to go,' he said. 'You know how prickly the Minister can be.' He walked a couple of paces away from Malan and then he stopped abruptly. He turned as if something had only just occurred to him. 'About your so-called terrorists,' he said. 'The ones you sent de Vries to track.'

So-called: Malan heard.

Jansen's face became suddenly still. 'Leave them alone,' he said in a voice pitched so low that only Malan could have heard it.

Malan frowned. Had he heard wrong? 'Why?'

Jansen smiled a smile of pure, uncontaminated malice. 'Because they're ours,' he said.

Ours, the word echoed in Malan's brain. Ours, it made no sense. 'Ours?'

'Wake up, man,' Jansen said impatiently. 'They're ours – Askaris. Keep away from them,' his voice rose, 'I'm ordering you,' he dropped it and hissed, 'keep away.' And then he lowered his voice yet another notch and smiled. 'Could I get my driver to drop you on his way back, Gert?'

'No, thanks.'

Jansen nodded. He took another step, stopped and frowned. He lifted one shoe up in the air and peered at it. The frown turned to a scowl. He looked straight at Malan. 'That's the trouble with shit,' he said. 'It sticks.'

He lowered his foot. 'Good idea of yours, Gert,' he said, 'walking back. You should relax: get out more. You're not looking well.' With that he marched away.

223

Malan stood perfectly still and watched Jansen. He watched Jansen walk to the edge of the park and through the gates. He watched Jansen nod to his chauffeur as he climbed into his official car. And, even after the car had been driven out of sight, Malan still remained rooted to the spot, watching he knew not what.

They're ours: that's what Jansen had said. They're ours – and Jansen was telling the truth. It all fitted, all of it – de Vries' failure, Malan's exclusion, Jansen's self-importance and now this meeting in the open air. They're Askaris, Jansen had said. Askaris, the department's hidden time bomb. The men Malan had been tracking, the ones Zonda had said were ANC, belonged to the police.

The existence of such men – ex-ANC personnel formed into killer squads and then aimed exclusively at their old comrades – was no secret to Malan. But he didn't know them, and he wouldn't have, because he had avoided working with the lot of them. Askaris were habitually drawn from the lower ranks of the ANC, men recruited by blackmail or by terror, men who had no allegiance to either side. Malan had no moral objections to them but he had one rule from which he wouldn't budge: he wouldn't work closely with amateurs. He would use them as informants or to do simple jobs but not in anything major because he knew that men like they could too easily turn traitor. One day, Malan was accustomed to saying, the whole Askari business would blow up in someone's face.

Not in my face, is what Malan had thought, and so he'd steered away from them.

Now he found himself alone and the finger was pointing at him. Jansen's message was unambiguous – not only had Malan exposed incompetence by stalking men who were in the pay of the department, but the fact that he had done so on a word from Zonda meant that Zonda's loyalties were also in doubt.

And there was another part to Jansen's message: that if Zonda did turn out to be a double agent, then Malan would be carpeted over the issue of Wentworth's death. Not carpeted, Malan thought, but sacked. Or even worse: sacked and then prosecuted. Two years ago this latter prospect would have been unthinkable, but now anything was possible.

Well, does it matter? Malan suddenly thought. I'll be dead before they can do anything to me. He began to hobble towards the exit.

Askaris, he suddenly thought. Was it possible that Zonda was playing a double game?

Surely it was unthinkable. Malan knew Zonda and he also knew that if Zonda had defected, he'd have gone underground. The last person he'd contact would be Malan. So Zonda must be true.

But if Zonda was true what had happened? Was it possible that the ANC had secretly uncovered Zonda and were using him as bait with which to trap Malan?

No, Malan thought, that couldn't be right either. Zonda was too clever to be tricked.

Zonda, Malan thought, the Zulu word for hate. An appropriate code name for one so consumed by revenge. There could be no greater contrast than that between Zonda and Robert Wentworth. Wentworth, a reluctant spy, selected by chance and kept in place through sheer inertia; Zonda, a unique and dedicated agent. Wentworth's information had been mundane but Zonda's was like gold dust, scarce but absolutely and dependably genuine. Only once had Zonda faltered and that was years back at the time when . . .

No, Malan told himself, there was no point in dwelling on the past. The present was already pressing its nose to the window of his future. And, unless he unravelled the mystery of the boat, and of Zonda, he was finished.

The boat, he suddenly realized, was another factor and one he had almost missed. Jansen didn't believe in the boat because Jansen no longer trusted Malan. Well, thought Malan, suddenly cheerful, this might work in my favour. He knew the boat was coming, knew it for a fact, and he would play on Jansen's uninterest.

Jansen had made a mistake to underestimate Malan because in doing so Jansen would have failed to hear of the existence of the man with a twitch. And it was this man who, in Zonda's absence, was about to deliver the goods. His last message had been bursting with staccato excitement. There was, he said, something happening just north of Port St John's. There was a man there making preparations that couldn't be explained. So the boat was on its way. And, by the sounds of the rather garbled description, the man in St John's could very well be the elusive Peter. Malan experienced a momentary flash of enthusiasm. Peter had managed to evade Malan but the boat would prove his undoing. Malan had him now.

Except Peter, if that's who he was, had moved on. Gone to Cape Town, the man with the twitch had told Malan. Cape Town, Malan thought. What on earth would Peter be doing in Cape Town?

It came to him suddenly. Of course, Peter would be in Cape Town because of its proximity to Robben Island. Visiting day was imminent and a courier of Peter's stature would be in place to transmit to the exiled leadership any gems passed through the prison gates. Fucking Jansen! Everything Malan had heard about Thabo confirmed Malan's suspicions that Thabo had buried knowledge of the past deep in his unconscious. But now Jansen had sent someone to interrogate Thabo, and, in doing so, risked prompting Thabo into remembering.

Well, Malan would cover his own back – and Jansen's as well. He would instruct his men in Cape Town, those he could really trust, to search out Peter. If that failed, as it might well do – the underground network in Cape Town was proving dangerously effective these days – Malan would still get Peter. He'd swamp the Swazi border, he'd make sure that not even a tadpole would penetrate his net.

Malan realized suddenly that he had reached the perimeter of Zoo Lake without having experienced the pain of getting there. He smiled joylessly to himself. Remission, that's what the doctor called these episodes. Malan knew differently: he knew that only sheer and bloody-minded concentration on other matters could ward off his bodily frailty.

Well, he would concentrate: and he would win, and perhaps, just perhaps, in doing so he would vanquish that most powerful of opponents – death itself.

Suddenly images of death would assault Thabo. They would descend on him without warning and, at the same time as he labelled them phantoms, he'd experience them as if they were real. He might be waiting for a consignment of rock and he would hear a rumbling noise. This isn't happening, he would tell himself, while the sky darkened and the air as well, and while he cringed down against the crushing onslaught. Or he would be walking to his cell and be overcome by a desire to run – and then he'd hear the bullet impacting on his flesh, or the white silence as he plunged down, far down into the sea.

The images were fleeting but what puzzled Thabo was that they should come at all. When he had been in MK, in situations a thousand times more dangerous than this one, he'd never worried about dying. Not consciously, that is, for even though he had lived hourly with the knowledge of his peril, death in the abstract had not entered his mind. And yet now death daily grew more present, repeating on him unceasingly.

It's the dream, he thought.

He looked at the food in front of him, scowled and pushed it away. It wasn't the dream alone, he realized, for it was only after his interrogation in Cape Town that these images of death had begun to dog him. His time in Cape Town had changed everything: whereas before it, the dream had seemed to be the worst that could happen, he was now haunted by the thought that it might be concealing an even more disastrous reality. Why else had they taken him to Cape Town, sent a high-ranking officer to interview him and raked up an incident that had been closed years before? Why else but that it was important to them?

And if it was important to them, then Thabo must appraise it too. And if it was important he must find the answer to the question that dogged his waking hours.

The question was a simple one: what was Victor trying to tell him?

Traitor, that's what Victor in the dream had used to say. But last night Victor's ghost had acted differently: when he'd opened his mouth no words issued from it. Thabo had awakened abruptly and for a second, a thought hovered on the edges of his conscious mind. He had tried to grab at it, but it flew away and no matter how he searched for it, it continued to evade him.

Sitting at the table, no longer hungry, his frown deepened. The same thought, he realized, was always with him but always elusive

227

– it was a memory that pressed upon his brain, a memory without name or explanation, a memory more important than any other. And he couldn't locate it.

You've got to trust yourself. The words came to him.

He whipped his head round, but all he saw was his exhausted comrades, heads bent as they finished their meal.

You've got to trust yourself. He'd heard those words before. Victor had uttered them. When was it?

He remembered when. Victor had said those words after Thabo had failed the test.

The test – it was more in the nature of a trick. They had been told to watch a sequence of events and then report back on what they'd seen. Victor went first and his report was so at variance with what Thabo was about to say, that Thabo changed his story. Only later did he learn how thoroughly he'd been trapped. For Victor had been the straight man: his role to see if the others trusted their own eyes.

Believe in yourself, Victor's voice echoed in Thabo's head. *Believe in yourself. Not in me.*

Not to believe in Victor – what could it mean? Was this the thought locked somewhere in Thabo's brain, the one he couldn't reach. Was it possible that Victor had betrayed them?

No, it was impossible. Except, thought Thabo, Victor was no saint. And Victor had done something, said something on that night before his death, something . . .

Thabo dropped his head down on the table and buried it in his arms.

Peter waited as the train from Cape Town disgorged the first of its commuters. When the pressure had partially lifted, but before the train could fully empty, he joined the throng. As the stale human smells of the train's interior were replaced by a whiff of Khayelitsha, the atmosphere lightened. Passengers, weary from a full day's work, began again to smile, the occasional joke was cracked, somebody called out loudly, promising a night of revelry ahead.

Peter also experienced a glimmering of relief, but before it could solidify he pushed it away. Experience had taught him that the moments before reaching sanctuary were dangerous times:

many of his comrades had been caught precisely because, judging themselves safe, they dropped their vigilance.

Pulling his hat harder down his head, Peter walked at the same pace as a group of men also clothed in workmen's dungarees. As they pushed through the narrow gate, making their way towards the city in the sand dunes, he engaged one of their number in hurried conversation. It was something at which he was expert: talking to strangers as if they were good friends, talking incessantly while his eyes continued to dart from left to right, looking for the police.

There were four of them at the gate – four, which was normal. Behind these four were, however, another four and behind them a group of men too well dressed to be part of the train's offspring. Peter cracked a joke, one of the best in his repertoire, and when his companion threw back his head and roared with laughter, Peter slapped him ebulliently on the back. That got him safely through the first row. The second line-up was more dangerous: they had the pros to back them up. Peter saw immediately that they were concentrating hard and for a moment he thought that all was lost. For the eyes of one of them which had been flickering aimlessly from left to right, settled on Peter and focused.

He's looking for me, Peter thought, and in one more second he'll know it's me.

Just then, a petty thief, in the act of picking somebody's pocket, spotted the police. Panicked, he began to run. The eyes on Peter were drawn away as the uniformed policemen acted instinctively. They tackled the thief, all four of them, tackled him to the ground before gazing up at the plainclothes men.

Peter was not among those who loitered, waiting for the outcome. Only when a few yards away did he risk a backward glance. He saw the crook rise to his feet, mutter something to the police and then, as if he could not believe his luck, quickly walk away from them. Peter nodded to himself. He was right, the police were not there to net one of the train's many thieves. They were after bigger fish.

He swung his arms in as relaxed a fashion as he could muster, walking at an even pace into the depths of Khayelitsha. The elements were working in his favour. The south-easterly wind that blew over the sand dunes and straight through the settlement was enough to explain both the positioning of his hat and the way his eyes were focused on the ground.

Over cluttered debris, past tents of black plastic, whose lining of cardboard rattled in the wind, ignoring children bathing in milk crates or playing with torn rubber tyres, Peter went. It took him some time to reach his destination, but when he finally managed it he didn't slow down. Instead he circumnavigated the small dwelling, one of many constructed from corrugated iron. With his hand on his trousers he whistled softly as he walked. If anybody had noticed him they would have assumed that he was a man urgently looking for somewhere to empty his bladder.

Whistling continuously he reached the front of the hut for the second time. He was rewarded by the appearance of a woman carrying an old tin can. Ignoring Peter she stood in the doorway and emptied the tin of its dirty water. When she had finished she returned indoors without as much as a glance in Peter's direction.

But she had played her part efficiently. The gesture had given him plenty of time to see that she was wearing a simple shift dress and that she had covered her hair with a sludge-brown *doek*. Peter did not even pause. He maintained his steady pace and walked straight past her dwelling, further into the depths of Khayelitsha. No one watching him could have guessed that his heart was beating hard, and that his mind was working overtime, planning where to go.

The *doek* had been the giveaway – the sign that the woman had recently been questioned by the police and that her house might no longer be safe. And Peter had read something else from her warning. The very fact that she was still at liberty confirmed a growing suspicion – that police surveillance had been stepped up and that Peter was its probable target.

So Peter's first impression had been accurate: somebody was on to him. That man in St John's had been watching him. He must have known that Peter had left Umtata and he'd wasted no time telling his superiors.

They must be desperate, Peter thought, feeling somewhat reassured. The man with the twitch was so inept that whoever hired him must surely be scraping the bottom of the barrel. It was a coincidence, that's all it was – there was no way that they could know about the impending arrival of the boat for if they did they would have used a professional, not a stuttering idiot. He was safe, his stolen car long discarded, he could go on.

He would, of course, mention the man in his next report but he saw no reason to either abort the mission or risk sending an emergency communication. He would hide in Khayelitsha, collect the communications from Robben Island, and then, and only then, he would cross the border.

In the meantime, he would take nothing for granted: he'd call his contact the next day and set up a check meeting, just to make sure that the whole network was not already infiltrated.

CHAPTER TWENTY-FIVE

—

A metallic clanging shook Sarah out of her state of semi-trance. She shuddered and turned to see a plate, which had not previously been there, lying in the meal hatch. She frowned. She wasn't hungry. And, besides that, hadn't she just eaten?

The smell of over-cooked vegetables assaulted her. She had just eaten, she knew she had. It was all part of their plan: first they'd deprived her of food and now they were showering her with it. They were trying to drive her mad, warping time for her, scrambling her stomach and her internal rhythms alike, clicking the light on and off, looking and laughing at her.

'And knocking,' she said out loud.

No, an inner voice contradicted, *they* weren't knocking: her friends were.

Friends, she thought, I have no friends.

A knock again upon the wall and whispering too, low voices shimmering in the atmosphere, tugging at her, pleading softly in a language full of sibilance, hissing words she couldn't understand.

The other prisoners, she thought, that's who it is. Well, she would ignore them. Her thoughts were all tied up. She was having trouble organizing her mind into the simplest of sequences. Memory, feeling, intuition, jostled with each other and she could find no relief from them. She was pursued by a vicious self-doubt: examining herself in the piercing light of their interrogation, she grew increasingly uncertain. Voices, men's voices, Smit's and Malan's kept insinuating themselves into her mind and, as they wafted through, they took with them more and more of herself.

Even the thing that had sustained her in the beginning – her conviction that Alan loved her – had begun to fade.

Alan betrayed you: that's what Smit had said.

Was it true? Had Alan slept with Thembi? Of course he had, she knew that now. She had probably always known it. But then, what did it matter? Thembi was dead. It wasn't Alan's affair with Thembi that caused her to doubt his love for her.

What was it then? Something Girlie said?

Send Alan my love, those were Girlie's parting words. Simple words, easily said, and just as easily dismissed but they'd stuck in Sarah's mind because they were so unexpected. Alan had constructed such an unforgiving picture of his adoptive parents that Sarah assumed they'd cut him from their hearts. And yet Girlie's words showed this wasn't true.

Well, this was easily rationalized. Time had passed and Girlie, without Jack, might have regretted what she'd done so long ago. And besides that, Alan was young when it all happened, he could surely have misjudged their anger.

Something in her head clicked. Why, she thought angrily, why do I have to rationalize Alan's behaviour? She, not Alan, was the victim. She hated Alan.

Another click. It wasn't Alan's fault: it was Malan's.

Malan. What was it he'd said? Oh yes, he'd denied ever touching Alan. So what? Nothing Malan said could be believed.

But Girlie, what about her? Girlie had said quite clearly that Alan's father was a brute and that Alan bore the scars of his whip. Why should Girlie lie – what reason could she have?

Sarah's head began to pound. She was suddenly awash with fury. She wanted to be away from this place, she wanted to be safe, secure, separated from her raging doubts.

And then a thought came to her, as clear as a voice: *This is what I asked for,* she told herself. *This is what I asked for – all the drama I could handle.*

Her inner voice was more unbalanced than either Smit's or Malan's, it was a voice imbued with rage, a voice that mocked. It rolled around her head and an image came with it, an image that was calm and happy, which contrasted with it: she saw herself, a few years younger, in a car, Alan beside her; they were driving somewhere. She embraced the image and cut out the voice. She remembered the time. They were in Maputo, on the way to the beach in the days when it was still safe to travel outside the city. They were going out for the day, together, carefree, singing, revelling in their unaccustomed freedom.

It didn't last long, for just as they reached the outskirts of a city a car hooted. Sarah saw one of Alan's comrades draw up alongside them, point at the pavement, park and get out. She had sat, patiently, while Alan also left their car; and she had carried on singing softly while the two men talked in low whispers, their heads touching conspiratorially. She'd smiled and waved when the other man got back into his car and drove off and she'd nodded her head in understanding when Alan said he must return. She hadn't felt angry. Not then and not on any of the other occasions when their plans had gone similarly awry. She had never balked at the inconvenience: she had never complained about the dangers inherent in Alan's life or about the un- predictability. She had endured visits held at the dead of night, unexplained disappearances, books which she must not open, weapons that frightened her, grunted phone calls and the endless talking out of earshot. She had endured it all for this was the stuff of her new life.

No, that was wrong. She hadn't just endured it, she had positively enjoyed it.

The drama, the voice cackled. *You loved the drama.*

She saw herself running down a flight of stairs, running in the darkness, her heart pounding. She saw herself arriving at the bottom in time to catch Alan climbing from his car. She saw what happened next, watched as she flung herself into his arms, as she muttered words of joy, of relief that he hadn't been caught up in the attack, and she experienced anew the sense of sheer jubilation that she'd felt then.

Jubilation that he was safe, the voice said. *And that you were included in the action.*

The voice was clear and unimpeachable; and she knew suddenly that it came only from inside her. *Love,* it continued scornfully, *you think only of love but what has love to do with anything? You needed Alan because he made you feel alive. You grounded him but he, he gave you drama.*

Yes, Sarah thought, the voice speaks truth. I wanted his lifestyle, I needed his excitement.

Except now, the voice mocked, *you've got too much*.

She stood up abruptly and began to cross her cell. It was too small. She reached the door and stopped. She moved a few inches and leaned her head against the concrete wall. Oh, how cool and solid it was. It felt good. She started to rub her head slowly and rhythmically up and down the rough abrasive surface. This is what she had been missing – some, *any* contact with an object other than herself. Only when she felt wetness on her face did she stop.

She wasn't crying was she? She put her hand up to her face and saw that it was streaked with blood.

It didn't surprise her at all.

'There have been reports,' Jansen said by the door.

Malan glanced up and smiled. Jansen had come into Malan's office unexpectedly and was standing uneasily by the door. Something had happened to ruffle Jansen's calm and that something could only be good. But then he recalled what Jansen had said. Reports: what reports? Had Jansen uncovered Malan's search for Peter?

'Reports that Sarah Patterson is on the point of breaking,' Jansen snapped.

So what? Malan thought as relief washed over him: that's exactly what I want.

'This is a sensitive time and Patterson is a British citizen,' Jansen said.

'Who happens to have knowingly involved herself in terrorist activity,' Malan replied.

'You have no proof of that.'

I have no proof, Malan thought, but I know it. And if you don't, then you're stupider than I thought.

'I've given orders,' Jansen said.

Malan narrowed his eyes.

'I've ordered her release.' Jansen said.

It was no less shocking for the fact that it was expected. 'You did what?'

'She's collecting her belongings now.' Jansen's voice seemed to issue from far, far away. 'She'll be escorted to the airport where her passport will be endorsed. And that's the end of it.' Jansen looked peculiar up there, towering over Malan, his features peculiarly distorted.

'Leave her alone, Gert,' Jansen said. 'Just leave her alone.' He left the words hanging there while he marched straight out the room.

And he didn't even close the door, Malan thought.

Malan shut his eyes and then rapidly opened them again. The door was still a gaping hole, he could see ugly neon from where he sat. He pushed himself to his feet, inched his way across the room, shoved the door shut and slumped against it.

The policeman stood by the door of the cell and grinned nastily at her.

'Your things,' he said. 'Don't forget your things.'

Sarah's eyes misted over. She wiped at them with the back of her hand but the gesture only further obscured her vision. She turned away from the policeman and picked up the few items they had allowed her to keep. By the time she turned back she had managed to control herself. She looked at the man and breathed in resolutely.

But once out in the corridor her courage deserted her. They were moving her, that much was clear. She watched her feet, treading ghostlike against the neon, one in front of the other. Moving to a space, which, because it was unknown, was more frightening than the one she had been occupying.

The policeman was in the lift and waiting for her. He leered again at her. She took one step back, one tiny step back to safety but she felt the breath of the second man, the silent one, behind her. She felt his breath and she heard the sounds of the corridor, a groan issuing from a cell, the banging of a distant door, the thump of an object without a name. She walked into the lift.

In no time at all, she was stepping out again, into another corridor, eerie in its silence. She was marched straight down its dingy outline to a room where a policewoman ran uncaring hands along the outline of Sarah's body. Another room, and her bag, complete with all that had been confiscated, was handed to her.

'This way,' her escort barked.

She emerged finally into the light, into open, bustling light. She stood by the doorway and her eyes shut automatically against the sheer busy-ness of it all. She opened them again, blinking. People, so many people, all moving in different directions. People occupied with themselves and not with Sarah. She was led up to the desk.

They gave her a plaster for her face and a form for her to sign. She didn't understand what it was they were asking but automatically she did as she was bid. Her sprawled signature looked anarchic against the neat order of the typewritten page. Before she could read what it was she had attested to, they removed the paper. In its place they put a bag, a purse, a comb, lipstick and a small red book. She recognized them all as hers. She looked first at the desk and then at the man behind it.

He sighed and shoved her bits and pieces into the bag. 'The car's outside,' he said.

She looked again at him.

'You're being released, Miss Patterson.' he said. He'd said those words before, hadn't he? 'The car will take you to your rented accommodation', he was enunciating each word separately, 'and give you time to pack. You will then be taken to Jan Smuts and escorted onto a plane.'

'Where am I going?'

He paused and looked at her.

'Where am I going?' she asked again.

'Go where you want,' he said. 'Moscow or Beijing for all I care. But just get the hell out of here will you?'

They were laughing, laughing at her and it was their laughter that propelled her from that place. She stood outside of it and blinked: she could hardly tolerate the brilliance of the sunlight and the way that everything except for it was blurred. There were sounds she registered but did not know, sounds that might once have been ordinary but which now seemed utterly foreign.

A shadow crossed in front of her. 'Miss Patterson,' it said.

That's what you should always have called me, she nearly said, not Sarah as you have been doing.

'The car's here, Miss Patterson.' The shadow had taken the form of a policeman. But it couldn't be a policeman, it was smiling at her, making an obvious attempt at politeness.

She hesitated, seized by an impulse to march away. Images of death squads came to her, along with memories of the way people in South Africa had begun to disappear. What would they do if she refused to get into the car?

What could they do? They could force her in, that's what they could do.

She walked the remaining few steps to the car and seated herself in it. The policeman closed her door and then got in beside the driver. She was driven along a route that was both strange but also strangely familiar. After ten minutes she realized that they were returning her the same way they'd once removed her.

When the car stopped outside the house she didn't wait for them. She jumped out and ran to the door and then had to stand there while they brought the key. As she stood, her neighbour emerged.

How long had it been since this scene had been played in reverse? She had no idea. She only knew that where had once been fear and antagonism on her neighbour's face, there was now a hint of pity.

I must look terrible, she thought. No worse, however, than her house. Even with the door only partially open she could see the havoc therein. She pushed her way to the centre of it. They had ripped the place apart. Cushions lay scattered on the floor, lying amongst the other debris of torn papers, broken bowls, overturned jars. She didn't care, she continued into the bedroom. The same devastation here. They hadn't gone as far as to rip her clothes if those were her clothes – they didn't look right to her. But they'd done everything else – destroyed the bed, pulled the curtains from their railings, smashed the matching table lamps to the floor. And still she didn't care: she wanted out.

But she wanted something more first: she wanted a shower. She needed a shower. She would not budge without one.

She picked her way over the wreckage, grabbed a towel and started towards the bathroom.

'We have no time,' a voice behind her called.

She kept on moving. If he wanted to stop her then that was his, and only his decision. He didn't stop her.

Once under the cascading water she remembered how she had stood in this same place, reflecting fondly that Alan was right about South African showers. There was no point, she thought, no point in dwelling on what Alan had said and what Alan thought. Pulling a towel around her, she walked to the bedroom. The man had gone from there – she heard him coughing through the door. She rummaged through her fallen clothes until she had picked herself an outfit, a bright, inappropriate travelling outfit – a sun dress clashing with garish oranges and reds. Years ago she had bought the dress in London but, until this moment, she had never felt quite bold enough to put it on.

She towelled her hair dry, ran a comb through it, and then she began to pack. Slowly and methodically she set about her work, including only those items she truly liked. The rest she would leave behind amongst the mess – slough it off along with her old self.

She was carrying her suitcase when she returned to the living room. 'Where's my passport?' she asked.

He patted his breast pocket but he didn't speak. She marched straight past him and got back into the car.

There was a man waiting for her at Jan Smuts airport. A solid smiling man who spoke in the measured tones of Sarah's childhood.

'Cook from The Embassy,' is how he introduced himself.

From The Embassy. She had wanted such a man to come to her when she was in John Vorster Square and it was all she could do to stop asking him why he had not.

'I'm glad to see that our efforts have paid off,' he said. 'The authorities here can be rather over-vigilant. But I expect you'll put it all behind you once your feet touch British soil.'

British soil: how she longed for it. In Britain she could become ordinary again.

But wait, she thought, Britain – that's where she was supposed to have gone. That's where the ANC wanted her to go. If she went there, would she be trapped by them?

239

No, she needn't obey them there, in Britain she'd be safe. She could fly there as if following ANC instructions but refuse to be debriefed. In fact, she suddenly thought, she could easily refuse to have anything more to do with the ANC. She could merge back into English life, construct fables from her time in Africa and watch her friends looking at her with new respect. She could visit her father and tolerate his parochialism without feeling that it threatened her. She could get a job in a London school, teach science to kids who didn't feel as if their life depended on what she could give. She could attend sporadic union meetings and keep her mouth shut, no longer haunted by the fact that she might not really belong. Without guilt she could spend money on herself. She could update her photo albums, stick her last years into them, relegate them to their proper place as suitable subjects for late night reminiscing.

Or she could be a good girl, go back to England, invite the ANC back in, tell them what she knew and wait for them to deploy her again.

All this was in her grasp, all this was possible.

'I'm not going,' she said.

Mr Cook frowned kindly. 'You can't stay here,' he said.

'I don't want to stay here.'

'No,' he said, 'Of course you don't – not after what you've endured.'

'I don't want to fly to England.'

'Come now,' he argued, as the first hint of discomfort showed on his face. 'Your ticket has been booked. I've cleared it all for you.'

'It's an open ticket,' she said. 'I can change it.' She nodded to herself. 'Yes, it's open. They made sure of that.'

'Who's they?'

'The travel agent, of course,' she said. She disengaged herself from the beam of his curiosity and concentrated instead on the departure board.

'I'll go to Dar,' she said.

'Dar es Salaam? But you can't even fly there direct.'

From somewhere, far in the past, she pulled a piece of information. 'I'll fly via Nairobi,' she said. She pointed at a flight number.

'But why Dar?' His voice was angry, pulling at her. 'Have you friends there?'

'I'll go via Nairobi.'

CHAPTER TWENTY-SIX

Someone pushed at Malan's door and someone swore when their way was blocked. The pressure, along with the sound, was enough to rouse Malan. His first thought was of his wife. He must call Ingrid and tell her to come fetch him. He didn't know how long he'd been lying on his office floor – all he knew was that a black-out had put him there. A black-out – his first. The first of many if his doctor was to be believed.

'Captain Malan.' It was Jansen's voice.

Keeping a hand firmly on the door, Malan pushed himself to his feet. As quietly as he could he turned the key in the lock and then, having made it secure, he limped his way to the nearest chair. He slumped down into it.

'Malan.' The voice was growing impatient.

'A moment.' Malan called, as he smoothed one hand through thinning hair. He got up slowly, returned to the door, and unlocked it.

'What the hell were you doing, man?' Jansen demanded as he burst into the office. He followed through with a *non sequitur*. 'She went to Dar,' he said.

'She?'

'Sarah Patterson. For God's sake, man, what's the matter with you?'

Sarah went to Tanzania, Malan thought and he nearly laughed out loud. Round two to me, he thought.

'Why would she do that?' he asked. His voice was one of neutral interest.

Jansen narrowed his eyes. He knew Malan was goading him and he also knew that the only way he could discover why Sarah Patterson had gone to Tanzania was to ask. He toyed with the prospect. In the end, he was too pig-headed. He made an obvious effort to calm himself; he even attempted a smile. It came out like a grimace.

'Probably couldn't face her relatives,' he muttered.

Malan shrugged. 'Perhaps,' he said, his voice indicating that he thought otherwise.

And once again, Jansen refused the challenge. 'Oh, well,' he said, 'what does it matter?'

He lingered for only a few minutes after that, talking over other, inconsequential matters, which he presented as if they were important. He didn't fool Malan. And yet, even though Malan was enjoying Jansen's discomposure, he would have preferred him gone. He got his wish eventually. Jansen assumed his commanding face, looked at his watch, and then, and only then, did he leave.

Malan's smile, the one he'd installed for the duration of Jansen's visit, dissolved. Thoughts, the ones that he had renounced while Jansen was in his office, surfaced. They weren't pleasant. Why, he thought, had Sarah Patterson gone to Dar es Salaam? She was a mere pawn caught up in a larger game – he was sure of that. But pawns were predictable: they moved in only one direction. They followed instructions: if their tickets said they were going to London, then they bloody well went to London. They didn't take off on their own initiative, they didn't fly to a country where they had no friends other than the ANC.

He reseated himself abruptly. Was it possible that he'd committed an appalling blunder? Was Sarah the real thing? Had she outwitted him? Had she outwitted him on her own or had she and Zonda planned something together?

He struggled for calm. There was no point, he told himself, in becoming emotional. Instinct led him to the conclusion that Sarah Patterson was indeed the small-time player he had taken her for, but proper research might well prove otherwise. He wouldn't let this bother him: he knew all about setbacks and how to proceed from them. He knew exactly what he must

243

do. He must comb through the records, not only of her interrogation but of her past and Alan Littell's as well, and only when he had done this would he be in a position to make a full reassessment.

All thought of Ingrid had left Malan's mind. He pushed hard down on the buzzer on his desk and then swivelled his chair round to open a filing cabinet. He pulled a batch of thick files from it. When a policeman finally answered his summons he ordered coffee and lots of it.

When she stepped from the plane a blast of sticky heat almost overwhelmed Sarah. With one hand shielding her eyes she stood on top of the rickety steps and began the process of physical acclimatization. She felt absolutely no inclination to move. Her fellow passengers pressed at her back. This is silly, she thought and she was on the point of giving in to their impatience, when a separate emotion, a sense of rigid anger overtook her. She whipped her head round.

'Can't you wait a minute?' she snapped. 'Can't you see I'm ill?'

The man behind her looked at first startled and then, as she continued to glare at him, apologetic. He turned away and addressed the person behind him and so, while Sarah stubbornly blocked the stairs, a chain of anger and recriminations was activated. She didn't care. She was past the point of caring. All she knew was that she was in Tanzania. An impulse of sheer bloody-mindedness had brought her here, an impulse that evaporated almost as soon as she was safely on the plane. Into the vacuum its leaving created, had flooded uncertainty and fear. She had lost the ability to make decisions – how quickly, she reflected, these skills could go.

'Madam. Please, madam, come down.'

An airport worker was waving wildly at her. She toyed with the idea of ignoring him, of using passivity as a way of determining what next would happen, but in the end she decided against. She took first one step and then another and soon, far too soon, she was on the ground and walking towards the airport. The other passengers hurried after and overtook her.

It felt good to move. She even enjoyed the fact that the others avoided her. How long had it been since she had last walked alone?

She shook her head violently. Every time her mind fluttered on to the subject of her imprisonment, despair and the vindictive voice would overwhelm her. She would not think of it: she could not, for therein lay danger.

Before she knew it she was inside the airport building and at the front of a queue. She handed her passport to an immigration official because that's what was expected. He looked at it and then at her, a question clearly written in his eyes. She realized why — he'd seen the endorsement placed there by a South African counterpart and he was wondering what it meant. Well, let him wonder.

'What are you planning to do in our country, Miss Patterson?' he asked.

She stopped herself from yelling at him. Why does everybody want to know what I do? she nearly shouted.

'A short holiday,' she said. 'I have money.'

He nodded, pressed his stamp firmly down on the open page and then she was free of him. Holding her suitcase by her side she walked away, heading through the lounge and out into the oppressive Dar es Salaam air. She didn't bother to look back.

If she had bothered, she would have seen the immigration official wave the next in line away, beckon to a colleague and, when he approached, whisper something in his ear. And if she had watched further she would have seen how this second man walked quickly away, straight into an office and to a telephone. She didn't actually need to look back because if she had thought about it, she would have known that this might happen. But she did not think about it and she did not look back: her mind was concentrated only on the immediate future and on a place where she might hide.

Rebecca stepped out into the midday heat. She walked, her head bowed but uncovered, her forehead creased in bewilderment. She walked towards the main compound. She walked forward automatically until she walked straight into Jabulani. He laughed and, touching her elbow, made as if to steady her.

She moved away without really being conscious that she had done so. 'Jabulani,' she said. 'I was coming to get you.'

The laughter died. 'News?'

'Sarah Patterson's been released.' She looked at him as she said the words and she saw him nod, nod as if had already known. He couldn't have known – the message had only just been received.

'Is she still in Jo'burg?' he asked.

Rebecca shook her head. 'No, Dar. She flew there this morning.' Dar, she could see him thinking – Sarah shouldn't have gone to Dar. 'I've told HQ to pick her up,' she said. 'To pick her up, no matter what.'

'Then we must wait,' he said.

Wait, thought Rebecca: wait in the hope that she'll tell us what we need to know. And what if she doesn't? What shall we do then?

She blinked and remembered what else she had to say. 'There was another message,' she said. 'For you. It has been decoded.' She handed him the slip of paper and she stood there, wondering about Sarah, as he unfolded it. The look on his face distracted her – she saw his eyes flash, not once but twice. She remembered, from their past, what that look signified. She stepped away.

But Jabulani took no notice of her – he was lost to himself. He wheeled round and marched away from her, his arms swinging, driven by a paroxysm of rage. As he walked she saw him crumple the piece of paper, and throw it on the ground.

She knew he'd acted involuntarily but she didn't call him back. She knew him too well for that – she must give him time to calm. So she went and picked the paper off the ground and made as if to put it in her pocket. But then, instead of doing that, instead of behaving circumspectly as she had been trained, she found herself unwrapping the paper and she found herself reading it.

'OUR MEN DISAPPEARED,' was what was written there. 'SOME-BODY TIPPED THEM OFF.'

Rebecca stood alone, with the sun blazing down at her, and she watched the space that Jabulani had just vacated.

Malan closed the folder. It hadn't taken him long to read through the plethora of cross-connecting files. It hadn't taken him long which was just as well since his scrutiny had yielded little. He had found a better description of Peter somewhere, which was to the good, but as to the other principals in the drama, there was nothing there that he had not already guessed.

He had concentrated mainly on the transcripts of the Patterson tapes, reading the transcripts and occasionally listening to the actual tapes in order to hear her tone of voice. This process brought with it reassurance. Smit had done his job well. He had shown that Patterson was no high-ranking spy. Her denials, her inability to pick from amongst the irrelevances the really important things that were being said to her, her petty deceptions – all these proved to Malan that Sarah was irrelevant, of value only because of Alan Littell. So Sarah Patterson could be discarded as a threat. It might have been better if he had wrung her dry, but Jansen's stupidity in releasing her could now be used to good effect. Jansen was irrationally panicked by Sarah's decision to fly to Tanzania. That meant that Malan had room for manoeuvre.

The boat and Peter, these must be Malan's main and only points of focus. He would step up his vigilance on the Swazi border and in Cape Town as well. In the meantine he would do something that seemed even more risky. Risky – but Malan was willing to bet his life on this last throw of the dice. He was now, more than ever, positive that there was a boat headed into South Africa and it was going to land armed men on the beaches of the Transkei.

If Jansen had his way they would ignore the boat: Jansen's stupidity would allow terrorists to play havoc with the fragile order in the country. Well, Jansen was vulnerable and Malan could act. He would send men to guard the beaches, as many as were necessary, hiding them until the time was right. This action was something Malan had longed, but not yet dared to do. But now he could. If Jansen found out, as he surely would (Jansen's strength seemed solely to be derived from spying on his own), then Jansen, having grown uncertain about Sarah Patterson, wouldn't dare countermand Malan's orders.

It was so simple: it was sweet. Malan picked up his telephone and began to dial. He was smiling when he heard a ringing tone.

'Good for you Sarah,' he said. 'Good for you.'

*

247

She sat by a palm tree on the white sands beside the blue water of Dar's coral reef. Her eyes were closed but, although they had crept up on her, she knew, almost immediately that they were there. She experienced their arrival as a slight darkening in front of her eyes, almost as if a cloud had passed in front of the sun. But that notion was ridiculous: when last she'd looked up at the sky it was a sheer blue-white, its uniformity indented by a single cloud. A waiter then, that's who it must be, come to ask her if she required another drink.

'I'm fine thanks,' she said.

'Sarah.' It was a woman's voice. And one that she distantly recognized.

'Go away,' she said.

'Sarah.' The voice was urgent now.

She opened her eyes. Zandile Theyise was standing in front of her, blocking out her sun. In the near distance was a man whom Sarah had not met before.

'I don't want to talk to you,' she said. 'I need time,' she said.

Zandile crouched down beside her and stretched out a hand. She began to speak, quietly as if to an invalid. 'I know you've had a rough time,' she said. 'But we need you.'

'I don't care,' Sarah said defiantly. She closed her eyes again.

Zandile's voice pursued her even into darkness. 'I know what you must be feeling,' she said. 'I too have suffered in John Vorster Square. Let me help you.'

Tears welled up in Sarah's eyes. She forced them back down her throat. She felt a deep hatred for them and for the person who had provoked them. The new Sarah would not cry from self-pity, the new Sarah was stronger than that. It was Zandile's fault: she'd come too soon. Well, Sarah would not obey Zandile: she would never again obey someone other than herself.

'Go away,' she said. 'I'll help myself.'

The sand shifted as Zandile tood up. The darkness was deeper now.

And Zandile's voice had lost its sympathy. 'We need you, Sarah,' it said. 'You must come with us.'

Sarah opened her eyes. 'And what will you do if I refuse?'

In answering, Zandile used no words – all she did was flick her eyes to the side.

Sarah understood. She shivered when the man began slowly to move towards her. He had no expression on his face, she saw, no expression save for sheer determination. She looked down the deserted beach, at the closed glass door in the distance, at the miles of shallow sea. And then she looked at Zandile.

'We're your friends,' Zandile said. 'Come with us.'

Yes, thought Sarah, you are my friend. It was clever of them to send a friend. I might as well go with her, she thought, for what else am I to do? She got up and nodded at Zandile. And then together, followed by the man, they walked off the beach and to the awaiting jeep.

'Where are we going?' she asked, after the man had started the engine.

'I'll drive awhile with you,' Zandile replied. 'And then I must leave. You'll be taken to one of our settlements.'

For debriefing, Sarah thought – another word for interrogation. She turned away and stared out the window.

But Zandile was too quick for her. 'It was bad,' she stated.

Sarah nodded, not trusting herself to speak. She blinked once, twice, three times. And in blinking she held back the tears that would once have fallen freely.

'Your clothes are in the back,' Zandile said after a long silence. 'You can change when he stops to let me out.'

Sarah nodded. So they had packed her clothes. She looked at Zandile. 'Would you really have kidnapped me?' she asked. 'If I had refused to come?'

Zandile shrugged and smiled openly. 'How could we have done that?'

The old Sarah would have accepted the denial, taking it at face value, delivered as it was by a friend. The new Sarah was wiser.

They were playing for mortal stakes, all of them.

'I apologize for my outburst,' Jabulani said.

Rebecca nodded. She reached into her pocket and pulled out the note. 'I didn't think it wise to leave it there,' she said.

He took it from her outstretched hands, shamefacedly at first but then something in her eyes must have given her away. His face hardened and he locked his gaze on hers.

He knows I read it, she thought. The thought shocked her. How could she have been so ill-disciplined? Her life had been steeped in secrecy, her own and others', and she had learnt not only to restrain her curiosity but also to welcome ignorance, Never before had she stepped over the boundaries, never had she contemplated reading a decoded message that was not meant for her.

I read it, she thought, but he was the one who dropped it.

'You know what it's about?' he asked.

'I can guess.' Her voice was even. 'I've heard rumours that you were tracing a group of men inside the country.'

'But now they've disappeared,' he said bitterly and she knew that his anger was not meant for her. 'Somebody's given us away,' he said. 'Somebody betrayed us.'

As he said the words an image formed before her eyes, an image not of the men that Jabulani had lost, but of a boat she had never seen, and of the men who sailed in it. We have to decide she thought: we have to know. And if we get it wrong, she thought, then they will all be killed.

CHAPTER TWENTY-SEVEN

They were in the same place, Sarah Patterson and Alan Littell and they came, at one point, within a few feet of each other. Her footsteps passed his door but he didn't recognize them. She saw food being delivered to his room but, although she fleetingly wondered why the person within did not emerge, she failed to draw the obvious conclusion.

Alan pushed the passing footsteps out of his mind. He had heard a jeep arrive, he had even thought it odd that this one did not stop as it normally did within sight of his room, but he didn't dwell on it. There had been many visits since he had been brought here, and none of them had yet affected him. He dismissed the jeep: he was conscious only of a pressure of time and of a need to nurture, rather than disrupt, the fragile balance in which he existed.

And so, instead of preparing himself to meet with Sarah, his mind was focused on other things. On another woman in fact – on Rebecca. He thought over their last encounter. The last time he had been with her he had started full of good intentions. As he'd been marched to the interrogation room, he had promised himself to give her what he wanted – to tell her the truth. And yet, in the end, it had all gone badly wrong. They had parted more at odds than they had ever been and Rebecca's final words were full of dissatisfaction.

Had it gone wrong because of something he had done?

No, it hadn't. She was to blame: she'd stopped him from speaking out. She didn't really want the truth. As soon as he had said something that she found hard to countenance – in this case that it wasn't easy to be white in the ANC (a truism that she would readily concede in theory) – she'd turned against him.

She'd turned against him because he spoke the truth. She'd turned against him like her predecessors.

He couldn't bear it. He sprang to his feet and began to pace the room. A picture of Rebecca, so strong in his mind, began to waver, her face changing subtly into others. He had meant to think only of her, but now, in mid flow, he reflected on how like the rest she was. His theory of how people behaved could be encapsulated thus: humans only saw what they wanted to see, only learned what they thought they already knew, and, finally and most disastrously, only loved what had already been made safe.

This view of life, he had garnered at an early age. His father was the first to fit with it. Mr Littell was embittered and he judged people accordingly. When he looked at the world (and his only son was included in this general category) he saw himself reflected back. He thus considered people as enemies to be fiercely combated. If Mr Littell had been the only one to act that way then Alan might never have developed his theory. But it didn't stop with Mr Littell. Jack and Girlie Howard were the next in line and they suffered from a similar delusion.

The Howards' version of unreality centred around Alan. They boasted quietly that they'd welcomed a foundling into their house. Yet what they'd in fact done was incorporate into their static lives an image of themselves. Their fantasy – that they'd given an unloved boy love and an insecure youngster security – was a view seen only through their own eyes. They'd built a picture of him, played God by creating a form in their own image and then they'd wanted him to conform to it. He had tried, God knows he'd tried. But he was imperfect and when he'd made his first mistake, they'd turned on him. He had worked so hard to please them, to be the son they craved, but he was given only one chance. When he failed they rejected him.

Rebecca – where did she fit in all of this? Rebecca. He'd thought she might be different. He'd been proved wrong. He'd thought her different because, during their short acquaintance, she'd changed. At first she'd labelled him a traitor and was trying to prove it. But gradually she'd reversed her first impressions and he had caught her looking for the good, rather than the evil. That's what made him decide to tell her the truth. And then, when he spoke it, she proved herself to be like all the rest. One glance at her had been enough to show him just how much she despised him.

The memory of her disdain pursued him. He was in full swing, prowling round his room, baring his teeth. All people are the same, he thought: they're all like that.

No – he stopped abruptly – not all. There were two who'd been different. Victor was the first. Sarah the second.

It was funny he should think of them in that order – Victor first, Sarah second – since he and Sarah were established lovers long before he'd even heard of Victor. But, as he began to walk again, more sedately this time, he realized that the order was correct. He had trusted Victor almost from the start. With Sarah trust had taken years to grow. And even that was not the truth. For what had taken years was not trust itself but the realization of it.

He remembered the moment almost exactly. He had come into Sarah's arms warm from Thembi's embrace. His mind and his heart were both in turmoil and guilt pursued him into her room. He was convinced she'd know what he had done – certain that one glance at his face would be enough to expose the fact that he'd betrayed her. She had glanced at him and her pleasure had changed first to doubt and then anxiety. She'd known all right: Sarah always knew. But, miraculously, she'd forgiven him. Her face had cleared and she'd walked right up to him and she'd put her arms around him.

There were times in his past when Alan had thought of women as predators – even Sarah – but this time was different. He felt her warmth enfold him, he felt her love support him, and he collapsed. She wasn't strong enough to prevent the fall and yet he remembered experiencing no impact when they both hit the floor. She had cushioned him, he realized, and yet she'd given no sign of pain. She'd kept her hold on him, comforting him, there on the ground.

And there, on the bare concrete, they began to make love.

What Alan had experienced with Thembi was a mutual seeking of comfort which left both feeling bereft. Sarah, however, seemed to give and give and ask for nothing in return. Desire, passion, lust – these were words Alan used previously to describe the act of making love, but these were words that, this time, did not apply. What he experienced was a joining, a real and endless joining. He no longer thought in terms of 'her' and 'me' but only thought of 'us'. Her breath and his had no barrier between them, her touch and his were the same touch. His outer skin, the layer of protection that had travelled with him, perhaps, since the time when birth had deprived him of a mother, dissolved and it left him naked, vulnerable and . . . and human.

Alan in the present laughed out loud. Of course he was human, he always had been. What he was remembering was a great fuck – no more than that.

The past pulled back at him and his laughter died as abruptly as it had arrived. He was lying to himself – it had been more than pure sex. It was the time when he had learnt to trust Sarah, when he realized that she was the one who'd helped him break the past.

After it was over he had looked into her deep brown eyes and he had admitted to himself for the first time that he loved her. He said as much to her and she saw her smile. And then he opened his mouth again to tell her more: to tell her about Victor and Thembi, all of it, trusting that she would understand.

'But surely Alan talked to you about Victor?' Rebecca asked.

'Yes,' Sarah said frowning. She looked at them, the three of them ranged in front of her, each darting questions at her, questions which made no sense.

'He talked well of Victor?' This from the shorter man, the man they called Albert.

'Yes.' There was nothing in the room to look at, nothing on which she might focus. It was empty, not bright and empty like John Vorster Square, but empty nevertheless.

'Sarah.' Rebecca's voice was soft, cajoling. 'We know how difficult this is for you, but believe us, it's important.'

'Important? What Alan thought of Victor? How can it be?'

She didn't know whether she had spoken the words out loud because they seemed to diminish in her head. And then they were replaced. She was assailed suddenly by a noise, a roaring, rushing noise, that besieged her eardrums. The table in front of her seemed to sway and tilt. She shut her eyes quickly.

'Sarah..'

Rebecca's voice filtered vaguely through her thoughts. She resisted it even as her sense of balance returned to her. She was still caught up in a memory that had only now come to her, of a time in another age when she had been with Alan. They were lying on a floor somewhere and it was uncomfortable: she had his arm to cushion her but the intensity of his gaze only added to her discomfort.

What had been happening? Of course, they'd just made love. It came back to her now, the place and what had preceded the act.

Alan had walked into the room and she'd been there, waiting for him excitedly. But when she saw the look upon his face, that look of sadness and of preoccupation with his other life, her joy had turned to disappointment. Disappointment and anger too that he should come to her caught up in the world from which she was excluded. She'd made up her mind. She'd gone up to him, intending to shake him out of himself and to deliver an ultimatum. But before she could do anything she'd lost her footing and they'd both stumbled to the ground.

What next occurred was not of her making. He had reached for her, in a kind of wanton desperation. She'd responded instinctively, stroking him into quiescence, hushing him with her lips and with her touch. She had been too caught up in the act of love to separate herself from it. But when it was over she felt ridiculous. The ground was cold, her arm bruised from when she'd fallen. She had wanted to get up and wash herself, to comb her hair and use words to normalize her discomfort and to distance herself from Alan.

But he'd spoke first. 'I love you,' he'd said, and some other words – a few of them – had followed. These she had forgotten. All she remembered was the lustiness of their interaction and the need to escape its spell. He'd opened his mouth to say something more but she had stopped him. Nicely stopped him with a kiss, but stopped him all the same.

'Sarah.' Rebecca's voice was insistent.

Sarah blinked. For a moment she couldn't recall what it was that had prompted the delivery of such a powerful memory. She looked at the faces ranged in front of her, all three waiting for her to speak. What had they been asking her? Oh yes, about Victor. They'd asked whether Alan might have unwittingly betrayed Victor. That's what had made her remember, for the incident that had been burned on the back of her brain had occurred just after Victor's death. And now with hindsight she understood Alan's intensity that day, and what it was that he'd been about to tell her. Thembi. He had been going to tell her about Thembi. Perhaps she had always understood: perhaps that's why she'd tried to shush him.

She took a deep breath and addressed herself to the present and to their insistent questioning.

'Alan would never have betrayed Victor,' she said. 'Alan loved Victor – perhaps more fully than he ever loved me.'

She saw the embarrassed look that crossed Albert Kana's face, the heightening of interest on Jabulani Dlamini's, the flash of denial on Rebecca Moisia's – all these she saw and registered for what they were without understanding any of them.

She didn't try and understand. She was more concerned to work out what they wanted from her. She'd expected them to ask about her time in gaol but instead, after a brief touching on it, they'd concentrated on Alan. They seemed to know less than the South African police: they asked her how she'd met Alan, about the progress of their relationship, about him and how he was and how he had changed and what he did and more even than that. While Smit had been relaxed, as if he had all the time in the world, they were anxious, pressed, falling over each other in their efforts to get an answer to a question that they never really put.

She had no idea what that question might be: she was only conscious of how she had deceived herself. When she had left South Africa she had told herself that she was going to live only for herself. But the old feelings, the ones she had first experienced when imprisoned, had returned and with a vengeance. All she wanted to do was to see Alan. The same feeling but no longer amorphous: it had a goal this time. She was certain now that Alan held the key to her dilemma. It had all started with him and with him it must end.

'What's happened to Alan?' she asked for what must have been the fourth time.

And for what must have been the fourth time they did not reply. But this time was also subtly different. This time the men looked at Rebecca while Rebecca looked at the floor. And then, at last, Rebecca raised her head.

'You'll see him soon,' she said.

CHAPTER TWENTY-EIGHT

They took her to out of that room and to another. She watched as a brown hand put a key into the lock and turned it. She watched as the door was opened and then she felt the hand gently prompt her into movement. She stepped forward into the room. She heard the door close after her.

I'm alone again, she thought, the room is empty.

And then, across an empty room, Sarah Patterson caught sight of Alan Littell.

She knew it was him before he turned and yet, because she had not been expecting him, she doubted the evidence before her eyes. She took a second step forward. He turned and it was indeed him. Nobody else had eyes like those, nobody on earth. They jolted her, making her realize how memory had muted their intensity. The shock in his face was palpable. He didn't know I was here, she thought, and she wondered why that was. She took another step, feeling a physical pull into his orbit. He echoed her motion, joining her in the middle of the small room.

They didn't touch. They stood, close to each other, just looking. She could hear his heart, beating hard, loud against the sounds from outside the room. She felt the years join up, experiencing this moment as she had the first. She was sure: he was the man for her. She reached out a hand to touch his face. His hand covered hers. She felt the warmth of his skin, the bristle prickling through it, and she felt something else, a pulse below the surface, a pulse that vibrated against her hand.

'Sarah, I'm in trouble,' he said.

You're in trouble, she thought, *you're* in trouble!

He put his arms around her and buried his head on her shoulder and her bitterness dissolved. She slipped her arms under his. How familiar he was, how strong, how alive. She felt his tears falling against her skin and she remembered feeling them before.

He moved his head backwards and looked at her. 'Are you all right?' he asked.

She nodded. Of course he cared for her, of course he would look after her.

'I met Malan,' she said. She was going to say more but instead she paused and watched as his face changed, not once but many times, watched as alarm, pity, fear, despair bisected each other. She frowned.

He saw her frown and he struggled to contain himself. She was in need and he must help her. He wanted to squeeze her anew and bridge the gap between them: he wanted to be strong for her.

Yet Malan stood there between them. Malan stood there, solid, safe, sure of himself, threatening and cajoling. Alan felt himself thrown back into the past, towards the youth he had once been, alone, unkempt, uncared for. He refused to be that youth: he refused to be so vulnerable. His face hardened.

Sarah shivered, she blinked and, in a moment out of time, she saw the two of them upon the floor. We made love on the floor because that was what he wanted, she thought. It was a thought that made no sense and it was followed by another. I love him, an inner voice protested.

Why? Why had it protested?

She needed him, she could not afford to doubt him. She needed him. She moved from him and she stood, inches away, just looking at him. She wanted him to re-approach her, to enfold her, to use his love to wipe away her time in John Vorster Square. She wanted him to make her safe, to join his world to hers, his thought to hers, himself to her. She wanted him.

He didn't move. 'Malan,' he said. 'Malan has always hated me.'

'Me', she heard it echoed once and then once again, 'me'. And suddenly she realized that that was the way that Alan thought and those were the words that he used. He appeared to be looking at her but his eyes did not register: he was looking at her but seeing himself reflected. Her fatigue paled in comparison to his desparation, her loneliness was a mere foil to his essential aloneness. He was thinking of himself, only of himself not of her.

And she thought: have I been deceiving myself? Has Alan always been this way?

No, a voice inside her shouted: it wasn't like that, it couldn't have been.

'Malan would like to destroy me,' he said.

His words turned in her stomach and her love settled there alongside them. She heard the voices of Smit and of Malan and Girlie Howard, intertwined, delivering only a single message. Alan had used her: she was his casualty.

'Why did you do it?' she asked in a voice that did not sound like hers. 'Why?'

Alan heard the hostility in her voice and he felt his heart stop. He knew again that he should be thinking of her but the questions in his head were too insistent. What did she mean, *why did you do it?* What did she mean? He heard a distant bang which came from inside of him.

And with the bang came voices.

Jack's voice: *Why did you do it? Why did you humiliate me?*

His father's voice: *Why did you do it?*

Bang. His body ached from the impact. He held his arms above his head to ward off the blows.

His father's voice again: *Why did you trip over that suitcase?*

Bang.

He couldn't stand the pain, he crouched on the floor, drawing his body up tight, wishing himself invisible.

She looked down on him. He looked so small. She wanted to comfort him, she wanted to stretch out her hand and offer it to him but the distance between them seemed almost insurmountable.

She took a step, and the distance grew shorter. 'Alan,' she said.

He looked up at her and she saw his eyes flash. Those eyes – she'd seen them before, she'd seen them on another man. She wanted to kick out at him, she wanted him to suffer. Smit's eyes that's what they were. Smit and Alan had become one. She heard

Smit's voice. *Alan cares only for himself:* Smit had said that. And there he was, Alan, her Alan, grabbing the monopoly of suffering.

'Why didn't you tell me about Thembi?' she asked.

Thembi, he heard. The room refocused. Thembi – so that was all.

He was an adult again, and a man who could not be beaten. But he was a man betrayed. Rebecca had double-crossed him more fully than he had imagined. She had told Sarah about Thembi.

Rebecca – he would deal with her later. In the meantime he must answer Sarah's question. 'I'm sorry,' he said. 'I was going to tell you.'

She heard the words come out, each enunciated slowly and separately, and she believed him. He'd been going to tell her something that day and she had stopped him. It was her fault that the news, coming from Smit's mouth, had cost her so dearly.

She took a step towards him. She put a hand out to him.

He saw the hand and he wanted to bridge the space between them, to stretch out and nourish it. But he saw something else too – he saw how tired she looked and how thin. She had suffered, and because of him. She had been arrested because Malan wanted him.

He flinched away from her hand: he could not take the responsibility, he would not.

She dropped her hand and as it fell her anger came flooding back. Thembi was not the point, she thought, there were other lies between them.

'Girlie Howard sent her love,' she said. She watched in satisfaction as he blanched. 'I saw her,' she said. 'They brought her to me.'

He looked at her, a question in his eyes. In the days before, the days before everything, she would not have waited for the question to be articulated, she would have answered it because that's what she'd do for him. No more, she thought, those days are gone.

Alan's inventive: that's what Malan had said. Malan was wrong, Alan was not inventive. Look at him there, struggling to find words, to find a way of getting what he wanted. She looked at him and at herself, looking with a dispassionate eye. Alan's in pain, she thought. And I'm being sadistic, she thought.

She shrugged. 'Your father beat you up,' she stated. 'That's where the scar came from.'

He saw her look, he heard her icy condemnation and he knew that she despised him. He took a deep breath, relaxed his limbs, and unfolded them. He got up, stood tall, looked straight at her.

He weighed her up, seeing her as if for the first time. She was, he saw, like all the rest. She did not want the truth. She would never understand that he had lied to her because he was ashamed – because he thought she would think the worse for him if she knew how he had been humiliated. She was like all the rest but she was worse than them for she had led him into this mess. It was she who'd persuaded him to confront his past, it was she who'd encouraged him to go back to Bryanston. It was she who'd made him vulnerable.

'You lied to me,' she said.

Why shouldn't I? he thought. You too would ignore the truth. 'They think I'm a spy,' he said, 'because of you. I'm here because of you.'

The last three words rebounded on her. She looked around the room and she remembered how they'd locked the door behind her. She was slow, too slow; she realized only now where their questions had been directed. They wanted to know whether Alan was a spy. They wanted to know whether her Alan was a spy. It was ridiculous, ludicrous, inept. How could Alan be a spy? He loved nobody but the struggle. She threw back her head and she began to laugh.

Rebecca looked at Jabulani. Sarah's laughter, picked up and transmitted by microphone, was echoing round the room. Rebecca felt ashamed. What was she doing, eavesdropping on the two? It was distasteful, this was real life not an episode in a serial. It was distasteful and the laughter made it worse. The laughter was horrible, eerie: it contained no humour – only a kind of deep despair.

She got up and walked away from the loudspeaker as if that way, she could escape the noise. But the laughter pursued her to the window. She stood and waited for it to fade, waited for words to take its place. She had a long wait, she could hear Alan trying to do what she would have, trying to stem the laughter, but to no avail.

'Sarah,' she heard. 'Sarah, calm down.'

The laughter rose and rose and rose. And then eventually, when she thought she could stand it no longer, the laughter was abruptly stanched. She looked at her watch and was taken aback to find that it had only lasted a matter of minutes.

'I'm sorry.' It was Sarah's voice, or was it Alan's?

'No, I'm sorry,' this was Sarah. 'I'm more tired than I thought possible.'

Rebecca heard the sounds of footsteps, Sarah's footsteps. Sarah, Rebecca guessed was walking away from Alan – or was it towards him?

'How can they think you're a spy?' Sarah asked.

'I went to Bryanston,' he said. 'And I was followed there. By one of Malan's men. He implicated me.'

'Malan is after you.'

'Yes,' Alan sounded relieved. 'He hates me. He always has. I defy his idea of what a white South African should be.'

Sarah must have walked towards, towards rather than away, because they were both standing close to the microphone. When they reached across and touched each other, the impact reverberated loudly.

'They captured you because of me,' he said. His voice was softer now, he must have moved away from her. 'You should never have gone to South Africa.' No sound from Sarah. 'Somebody told the Boers you were going to South Africa,' he said. 'Or did they?'

And still no reply from her. 'Sarah?'

Speak, thought Rebecca – and perhaps Alan, too. But Sarah did not oblige.

'Thembi meant nothing to me,' he continued. 'I think we were both, in our different ways, trying to get in touch with Victor. Thembi loved Victor, you see.'

A pause. A long pause.

'But Victor, of course, would never have a relationship with a woman,' Alan said.

At last Sarah spoke. 'Victor was gay?'

It was his turn to hesitate. He spoke softly when at last he spoke at all.

263

'Victor was unique,' he whispered. 'And Victor was a fool.'

Rebecca found herself almost touching the loudspeaker so close was her ear. Ask the question, she silently told Sarah.

'Why a fool?'

'He was too hidden,' Alan said. 'Too much the individual: he had made himself completely self-sufficient and he lost something in the process.'

'How do you know?' Sarah asked the question Rebecca would have put but her voice was friendly rather than antagonistic.

'Because I know,' Alan's voice grew louder. 'Because I am like him. Because I also hid things, hid them in fear of what discovery might do to those who loved me.'

Hid things, Rebecca heard, hid things. She looked at Jabulani.

'How old are you, Alan?'

Rebecca saw her look reflected back. *How old are you?* What kind of question was that?

'You know how old I am.' Alan sounded as confused as Rebecca.

'Do I? Do I?' Sarah's voice was low.

'I'm thirty-five.'

A pause and then her voice again. So soft. 'Girlie said thirty-seven.'

'Girlie doesn't know. Girlie's old.'

'Yes,' Sarah whispered. 'Girlie was old. And tired.'

A pause.

'I'm tired,' she said. So loudly that Rebecca jumped.

'You need to rest. Come, I'll call them to let you out.'

Rebecca waited until she heard the sound of banging, coming from the machine and from outside and then she leaned forward and switched it off. She looked at Jabulani.

'One step forward,' she said.

'And one back.'

She sighed. 'We have no proof that he's a spy.'

'And none that he isn't.' Jabulani frowned and then, almost instantly, his face cleared. 'I believe him about Bryanston,' he said. 'I think he was telling the truth when he said it was a stupid trip back into the past.'

'Which raises the question –'

'Yes,' Jabulani concluded as if her mouth was his, her thoughts, his thoughts. 'It raises the question of why Alan was being followed. By our side and theirs.'

CHAPTER TWENTY-NINE

South Africa

The dream had come again. But it was different.

This time when he left the shack Thabo could see Victor standing by the door and he could also smell what he was leaving – the dregs of coffee and porridge, the smoke that curled from the chimney and the smell of Victor himself, that sweet, strong, manly smell. And when he walked down the crumbling pathway he watched his feet move forward and he also saw how they trampled on an insect and how they created a spray of dust to bury it.

He journeyed automatically arriving soon, too soon. The weapons were there as they had always been, both in reality and in the dream. But this time he noticed something else. He noticed a flower growing from the rock, saw its delicate violet hue, its light blue veins, the way its stem twisted round in search of sunlight. He saw it and reached out for it but he could not get at it. It looped away from him and he saw that it was no longer violet but a deep blood red.

'Wake up, wake up,' he told himself.

The dream gripped him too securely: he couldn't wake. He could only watch as his feet turned away and headed slowly towards their doom. When he was nearly there a child passed by, just as one had done in reality. A child prematurely aged, dressed in tattered clothes who grinned at Thabo, sizing him up. Thabo shot a look at the child, just as he had so many years ago. 'Don't try it on with me,' the look said, 'I am a soldier.'

He wasn't going to be a soldier for long.

This was the worst part of the dream – the way it happened so unexpectedly. He walked back, dreaming of Victor's face and Victor's smile, dreaming of these at the same time as he knew he would never see Victor alive.

The end was upon him. As he stepped towards the shack a hand pulled out at him and knocked him to the ground. The child had accomplices he thought, before realizing that the hand that held him down and the boot that kicked him belonged, not to a child but to a soldier.

Victor, he thought. Victor have you betrayed me?

A sack descended on his head and he could smell it. Of dung it stank and sweat, too – but perhaps this was his own. He felt cold metal dig into his flesh – a gun against his head. He gasped desperately for breath. The sack was suddenly removed, his vision all at once clear. He saw the hand, the white hand attached to the gun, and he saw it point up into the air.

One shot was fired. One shot and all hell broke loose. Victor, he knew, Victor had not betrayed him. Victor was still in the shack.

A grenade was thrown, heading for the shack. But no, the dreaming Thabo saw, that wasn't right. The grenade came from inside the house and when it fell it took one of the enemy down with it. He heard the sound of gunfire, from beside him and in front too. Another groan amongst the army ranks and the dreaming Thabo experienced a moment of pure joy. Victor was fighting back. He would as well. He and Victor would get out alive.

But Thabo was shackled, bombarded by sound. He saw the bullets inscribe their deadly arc, he saw, in the dream, each single one fly up and in the dream he could trace their path straight to his comrade's heart. He watched the deadly bullets drift long after the point when no more sound issued from the house, long after the time when the house began to burn.

He waited in the dream. Waited for the inevitable. He waited while Victor walked from the house unscathed, while Victor walked through the ranks of jubilant soldiers, while Victor came up to him and while Victor smiled.

'Traitor,' that's what Victor would surely say. 'Traitor', straight into Thabo's face.

But this time when Victor smiled and when Victor looked Thabo in the eye and opened his mouth, blood spilled out and so did words but the words were not of betrayal.

'Beware of Greeks bearing gifts,' was what Victor said. And then he fell to the earth and disintegrated.

'No,' shouted Thabo. 'Come back. Come back.'

No, he shouted in his sleep again and again until he had wrested himself from its grip. He opened his eyes, immediately awake. I must catch the words, he thought, before they can disappear.

Beware of Greeks bearing gifts: that's what Victor had said. He had said it in the dream and before it too. He'd said those words the night before he died. He'd said them on his way to bed. He'd irritated Thabo by the puzzle of that phrase. But why? Why Greeks? Traitor, that's what Victor had once said in the dream. A Greek perhaps as traitor? But Victor knew no Greeks.

Something prodded at Thabo, something that tried to nudge its way through. He hauled at it, hauled it to the forefront of his mind but each time it nearly arrived, it evaporated. He banged his fist against the metal bunk. The thought had gone.

Thabo frowned, he remembered Victor saying something: what was it? Oh yes, that was it: *You must learn to relax or else you'll die young.* Victor had said during another time, a time of terrible danger. Victor had said that and Thabo had burst out laughing at the irony, laughing so hard that he risked giving both of them away.

He smiled at the memory. It was pure Victor – pushing a joke down the very jaws of death. A joke: Victor had many in his repertoire.

Suddenly it came to Thabo, another joke. A code name created by Victor. Theo after Theodarakis. Theo: Alan. That's how Victor had named him. Alan the philosopher. Alan the Greek.

It was Alan. Alan was the spy. Alan Littell had betrayed them. Alan had arranged for Victor's death.

But no, Thabo thought, that wasn't right – it couldn't be. Alan liked Victor, loved him even. Alan would never have wanted Victor dead.

Victor, Thabo realized, Victor saved my life. Victor knew that Alan would never kill him. Victor was briefed by Alan, told again and again that he must be the one to fetch the weapons and thus Victor had known the timing of the attack. Victor had sent Thabo out and Victor had waited for the inevitable.

The dream was clear. Alan was the traitor.

It was dark outside and quiet as well. Captain Gert Malan stood by an open door and breathed in the heavy perfume of the summer flowers. He smelt their scent and as he did so, a pain, intense as if a thin knife was chipping its way down his spine, assaulted him. He knew with sudden certainty that his pain would be gone long before the flowers faded. And yet the pain was not merely physical. The anguish that tore at him had brought with it knowledge that was itself unbearable. It can't be true, a voice inside him screamed, it can't be true. His throat constricted. He turned his head away as if by doing so his world would transform itself, making his conclusions seem like nonsense. But certainty continued to pursue him. He had finally been forced to face the truth: he had finally acknowledged that Alan Littell had betrayed him.

He'd spent the whole night poring over reports he'd read before, sifting through documents he never should have brought home. In reading them he'd seen what for a long time he had refused to face. Alan Littell, code name Zonda, had betrayed him. Alan Littell, the best spy the department had ever had, had turned tail, gone over to the other side, deserted the man who had created him.

Malan looked down at the photo of Alan in his hand. It was one taken a long time ago, when Alan was not yet a man. Alan was staring straight at the camera, half smiling, demanding something. Demanding to be pitied, thought Malan. How dare he?

Alan had been a nothing when Malan picked him up – a poor white facing a life of toil and unprepared for it. He'd been adrift, heading straight for the sewer, unable to survive in the streets but prevented, by stupid pride, from returning to security. He was, in fact, in the process of crucifying himself – poised on the self same precipice over which his father had once fallen. He had left the Howards' house in a fit of childish pique and his stupid pride had prevented him from returning.

Malan had rescued Alan. Malan had been clever and had understood Alan. After hearing from a schoolchild, a son of a friend, of Alan's garbled radicalism, and of Alan's abrupt departure from the Howards' house, Malan had sent someone to interview him.

Malan's action was well timed. When they offered him a lifeline – education in exchange for information – Alan had jumped at it. Malan had been well satisfied, categorizing Alan as another name for the department's files, another bank account to top up, another gatherer of minor information which might, just might, one day be useful.

But Alan Littell defied Malan's expectation for Alan was no ordinary spy. He was talented, Christ he was talented. His skill was innate, his judgement impeccable. From the outset he could tell the difference between those who would never be more than an armchair radical and those who might one day pose a real threat to the state. He knew instinctively which of his fellow students was serious, which could be recruited, which would never amount to anything and he was never wrong.

And he was special in another way because he was no Robert Wentworth – no reluctant recruit. Instead he actively enjoyed his work. In fact he fitted the persona of a spy more perfectly than anybody Malan had ever met – or would ever hope to meet. At their single encounter Malan had almost been overcome by awe for the man. Alan was a true chameleon, able to change persona from student radical to police confidant without appearing to even notice he was doing so.

Oh they had worked well together since then even though they had never met again. Through carefully layered intermediaries, Malan had smoothed the path for Alan, suggesting new roads for him to tread, grooming him to do the things that Malan, because of over-exposure, could never do. It was Malan who'd sent Littell to London, Malan who'd suggested a permanent relationship as cover, Malan who'd picked Sarah out from a group of anti-apartheid women, Malan who'd told Alan when to go for membership of the ANC.

It had been sweet, so sweet, it was perfection in an imperfect world. And Malan had been good to Alan. He had taken risks with his favourite spy, keeping quiet about operations in which Alan was involved in order to safeguard him. And he'd paid Alan – double, no triple, the going rate – and he'd put up with Alan's foibles, interrupting his sleep to get Alan out of childish scrapes. In the end he had done even more than that. He had sacrificed Wentworth. For Wentworth, in a moment of desperation had pointed the finger at Alan. Wentworth had not even known that Alan was a spy (Malan would never have trusted him with something as important as that) but he must have sensed something in Alan's reaction to Victor's death. There was no proof against Alan, and in normal times Alan could have withstood any investigation. He had been trained by a professional after all – in their one meeting Malan had taught him the most vital of interrogation techniques. But those weren't normal times: Victor was dead by then and by the tone of Alan's garbled communication, Malan had realized that Alan was on the verge of cracking. Malan had no choice: he had to divert suspicion away from Alan. And so he had intervened in the only way he could. He had instructed Alan to write the report that condemned Wentworth, and he'd told him where to place it.

He'd had no doubts then about his actions. They had so perfect a relationship. They were as one. Malan had studied Alan, watched him grow, nurtured him, until he knew Alan better than his wife, better probably than he knew himself. And in return Alan's gems had smoothed the way for Malan, helping build his reputation in the department. A perfect relationship.

Except so perfect a relationship should never have ended this way. With a betrayal that could finish Malan. With a betrayal that was unimaginable.

The stench of the flowers was overpowering, it turned his stomach. Malan went inside, slammed the door shut, limped back to his desk, to where the papers lay – those papers of death. He threw the photo, face down, amongst them.

It had taken him a long time to realize the truth. It had taken him a long time to realize that ever since Victor had been mistakenly killed, Alan had been worse than useless. Malan couldn't, in hindsight, explain his own stupidity. At first it had been explicable – Alan had kept up a pretence of passing informa-tion, and in the beginning he had the excuse that he was under

271

suspicion and therefore must be extra careful. But as time went on, and as Alan wormed his way back into the enemy's affections, his reports grew thinner.

But the mistake, Malan suddenly thought, went further back than that. It had started when he, Captain Gert Malan, a realist to the last, a player in the big league had been stupid enough to agree to save Victor. He had needed a casualty at the time, he had needed an MK death and he would have preferred two – Thabo and Victor both. But Alan had pleaded with Malan, don't kill Victor is what Alan had said, don't kill him.

Malan had agreed. Malan had let Alan find a way to get Victor from the shack. Against his own better judgement he had given in to Alan, persuading himself that Alan would find a way. Except Alan never found a way. Victor must have suspected – had probably suspected ever since that time when the cache of arms that Alan was supposed to hide had been picked up by Malan's men. Victor had stayed in the shack and Victor had been killed. And since that time Alan had been useless.

Malan was not stupid: suspicion of Alan had begun to slowly worm its way into his mind. He had dwelt on Alan over the years: his twinges of mistrust slowly increasing. But Alan had been clever. He had learned from his mentor and he'd given just enough to keep Malan in happy ignorance. And then he had gone one further. At the point when Malan's doubts had reached their height, Alan, almost four years after Victor's death, had thrust some bait at him – the bait of an armed ANC group just waiting to be plucked. Malan had grabbed it with both hands.

Greedy, that's what I've been, Malan thought. Too greedy to wonder why it was that, contrary to past practice, Alan had come to him with the information almost fully formed. Too greedy to examine why Alan told him to stay his hand until Alan gave the signal.

But not so greedy, nor so stupid, as to obey Alan's precise instructions. If he had, if he had waited and then attacked at Alan's signal, he would have been responsible for killing Askaris – men directly under Jansen's control. At least he hadn't done that. And at least he hadn't relied on Alan for everything; he'd kept alert, plugging his multitude of other sources. That's how he'd heard about the boat.

272

The boat. It had been the beginning of the end. When Malan learned of it and when he realized how big it was, he knew that Alan also should know of it. It was then that he had begun for what he assumed was the last time, to re-examine Alan's records. It was then he had set a man on Alan, watching to see whether Alan forbore to mention anything else in his reports. But even then Malan had been unsure. When Alan went to Bryanston, Malan had been lulled into inactivity. He'd told himself that Alan was merely displaying his only weakness – his inability to face the past square on – and that this might explain Alan's wavering contribution.

The final giveaway: Sarah Patterson's unexpected arrival at Jan Smuts. This should have told Malan that not only did Alan no longer trust him but that he had also stopped taking him seriously. It should have told Malan that Alan no longer knew who was his friend and who his enemy. And yet, Malan thought, it had still taken him time to acknowledge what had been shoved in front of his face. Why was that?

He picked Alan's photograph up again and looked at it, at that face more familiar than his own sons'. It had taken him time, he realized, because he hadn't wanted to believe it, because a spy of Alan's calibre did not change sides. Alan was looking straight at the camera; smiling smugly. Because he, Malan had lost his grip. Alan's eyes were oceanic blue. Because he wanted something more for Alan – because he felt for Alan, because he . . . he loved him?

No, that was not true. Malan pushed the photo and the papers, all of them upon the floor. Love was irrelevant to his job and he had not lost his grip. Dying he might be, but he was still in charge. He knew of the boat, and of Peter too. He would catch them both, would do it as surely as there were armed men on the Transkei beaches and all over the Swazi border. He would mop up these last, most glorious moments of his career.

And then?

Then he would settle his score with Alan Littell.

CHAPTER THIRTY

Tanzania

Alan stood in almost total darkness, staring out into the night. As he continued his vigil, his eyes grew accustomed to the blackness. Whereas at first everything had seemed uniform, he was able now to distinguish shapes, forms moving in the dark, the deadened tree in the distance, the outline of the encampment laid out before him. He registered all these but they were unimportant. His concentration was focused elsewhere, on something inside of him – on a feeling that was threatening to overpower him.

He had switched out the light because he couldn't any longer bear either its glare or the ugliness of his immediate surroundings. And he had switched out the light for another reason: because he thought that in doing so, he might escape the knowledge of what had happened to him.

In Tanzania the transition from day to night is a sudden thing. One minute the bright light illuminates the harsh landscape, and then, a few minutes later, that light is gone. It is something that occurs quite unexpectedly and yet, as Alan had once reflected, it's difficult to pin-point exactly the moment of transition. But this time Alan had no trouble doing so. For this time, just as night descended, Alan realized where he stood. At that moment, at the point where he lost the day, he realized he'd also lost something far more important. Sarah, he'd lost Sarah.

It was a fact of which he was completely certain. Sarah herself might not yet have realized it but that didn't make it any the less inevitable. He had lost her because she'd changed and because, in the end, she would reject him. Alan had always known that their

274

love was only possible because of who Sarah was. He had known he was unlovable, that it required a leap of faith on Sarah's part and a blindness as well to keep her tied to him. And this was only possible because Sarah was a calm, grounded, sure human being – because Sarah could tolerate his life and could forgive him for it too.

And now she'd changed, and now she would no longer put up with him.

This is what he'd been thinking when night fell, this and nothing other. But as he stood at his window another thought came to replace it. Not a thought exactly, that wasn't right: it was more a feeling. A feeling that hatred was being beamed at him, that out of the ether came shafts of poison, directed at him alone.

Where did it come from? It couldn't be Sarah: Sarah would never be so vindictive. It couldn't be Rebecca: she didn't know what he'd done. It couldn't be Victor: for Victor was dead. It was somebody other, somebody else.

He frowned. Why should anybody hate him so much? He frowned and then immediately he smiled. Why shouldn't they hate me? he thought. I'm a spy, he thought. I've always been a spy.

The words came naturally to him despite the fact that it was the first time he had ever used them. It was strange how blind he'd been, how thoroughly he'd split the two sides of himself. Spies were men like Robert Wentworth, men who looked on from a distance, unhappy men who passed on information for a price, and who did not know where their true allegiances lay. Or spies were white supremacists, confirmed in their beliefs, working for a cause for which they were prepared to die.

Alan was neither of these – he never had been. He wan't a spy. He was a skilled worker, good at his job, toiling in a Marxist sense to reproduce his own labour. That's how it had started, after all. He had agreed to work for the police because they were his only option: because his ability to insinuate himself in any environment was the single commodity he had for sale. It was a simple enough decision, made easier by the fact that the people he was to spy on were like the Howards – white liberals preaching what they would never practise, spouting revolution from behind the safety of hefty bank balances.

Perhaps not a skilled worker, he thought, more an intellectual. For he'd enjoyed his work much more than a mere skilled worker. He'd had no difficulty separating his two functions – the one of participation the other of reporting – and he was good at both. He was a consummate organizer, efficient, capable, canny and keen – the student radicals needed him. And a good spy as well – dispassionate, accurate, farsighted.

Oh yes, he'd enjoyed his job and had been well paid for it. Not that this mattered. The money itself was irrelevant. It had once been important: it had bought him something vital – an education, a ticket out of poverty. But after that, money took second place. What Alan had needed instead was the feeling of belonging.

Of belonging? a new voice in his head said, the voice that was finally confronting reality. *Of belonging?* The voice was scornful. *But you were a spy.*

Of belonging and not belonging then. Or more appropriately, of seeming to belong. That's what it was – the fact that he fitted the image of the world he had chosen.

And something else was important – power was important. Power made more real because its name could never be spoken. Power as exercised by the anonymous men who ran the world. Power that would only be diluted if anybody guessed at its existence.

It didn't bother Alan that Malan was the only person who knew about his power. Alan had never wanted to be a hero for heroes needed to be known – they needed an external stamp of approval to classify them. Alan hadn't needed this. His sense of self-esteem was enough for him, his sense of superiority in the world of blacks and whites alike, was what sustained him. He despised heroes.

But wait a minute, Victor was heroic. And Alan had loved Victor for it. He closed his eyes remembering how in Victor's face strength and vulnerability had been intermixed. He could see it even now. Whereas he had forgotten entirely his father's face, he could remember Victor's in all its details. Yes, Alan had loved Victor.

He opened his eyes abruptly. The Alan who had started spying would never have allowed himself to love his victim. That Alan was invulnerable, that Alan had been safe. But the new Alan had lost his footing, the new Alan was disarmed. How had it happened? Why had he been changed?

The answer came to him as he stood by the window, slowly it settled itself on his mind. It came in the form of an image, so strong that he could not avoid it. He saw himself a child again, a child in a playground surrounded by people bigger than he. He was sitting on a see-saw, not on either side but in the middle, at its very pivot. Somebody sat on each of the ends – Alan looked from left to right, trying to make out who was there.

It was dark, he couldn't see their faces. And then a movement from the left. The see-saw tilted and Alan gripped the wood. There was somebody at the left, on the ground, and that somebody revealed themselves. It was Sarah, poised to push off again.

It's all Sarah's fault, he thought, she changed me.

The see-saw moved and she was in darkness again. In his mind's eye he saw her differently. Her face from earlier that day loomed up at him. How could he blame her? How could he blame her when she'd suffered so much because of him?

It wasn't her fault, it was his. He was to blame, the more to blame because he had known that this might happen. When Malan had instructed him to form a permanent relationship and when Malan had suggested Sarah Patterson, he'd heard the warning bells sounding in the far recesses of his brain. They were faint those bells but they were clear. He had known of their existence and told himself to keep away from her.

The see-saw moved again, again it fell to the left and again he saw her face.

It *was* her fault. He would have managed to avoid her if she hadn't approached him. He would have looked elsewhere for companionship, searched in another place for a partner to give him the illusion of normality. And, even when she'd approached him, he'd almost escaped. He had rebuffed her, making some sarcastic comment when she, in her embarrassment, had said something trite. A part of him had watched in satisfaction as she blushed, as the light faded from those warm brown eyes and a

277

part of him had admired himself for dealing so easily with temptation.

He was tilted to the centre again and he knew that he was deceiving himself. It wasn't her fault. She'd turned away and left the hall. He was the one to blame: he should have let her go. He knew this at the time, knew it even as he followed her out, as he walked up behind her, as he suggested that he accompany her home. He knew it was a mistake when he reached her flat, when he asked her about herself and liked what he heard, when he bade her a reluctant goodbye.

He knew it was a mistake and he had resolved to leave well alone. He never would have phoned her, he never would have suggested another date.

But she pursued him just as later she followed him to Africa. She'd phoned him and when he heard the hesitation in her voice he was unable to resist the prospect of meeting her again. Still he had struggled with himself. He had blown hot and cold, he had done almost everything he could to put her off. But in the end her persistence, and his feeling for her, had been stronger than his rational mind. In the end he had to admit that he was in love with her.

What a ridiculous notion! That he, Alan Littell, a man who had never loved another person, who laughed at the very fallacy of love, should fall in love with Sarah Patterson.

Who was she after all? A nothing, unimportant, not only to his life but also to her own. Her attraction to him was based on her romanticization of the South African struggle. She was as all the rest – swept up in a fantasy in which she could take a central part. She was like other human beings, inhabiting a playground in her mind.

And yet he hadn't been able to resist her. He had seen her fantasy and he had wanted to make it real for her. He'd even, at times, got swept up in it. He had caught himself wishing that he was the man she thought he was, that the trust she so foolishly placed in him, could have been truly earned.

He had lain awake long nights, tortured by his own deception. He had almost told her about himself, then, before it was too late. But each time he was about to confess, something would stop him. He was trapped, unable to either commit or detach himself.

Military training seemed to offer an escape. It happened so conveniently. When she'd caught him writing his life history, she'd triggered the part of him that was having difficulty knitting the lies together. He'd reacted spontaneously, displaying the full force of his anger. The fact that she'd walked out on him confirmed what he'd always known – that she loved the image of Alan Littell, not the reality.

It should have ended there. That's what he told himself, over and over again. But he was too far gone, too caught up in his own madness. He couldn't stop himself from pursuing her.

But wait a minute – she was to blame. She'd closed her eyes to the reality. It was her fault. She'd followed him to Africa. It was her fault. She wouldn't let him tell the truth – she'd closed her eyes and her ears as well. She was too trusting. She was his downfall.

For many years he had been at peace with himself. For many years there had been clarity in his mind. Sarah had driven those years away.

He saw her face again, smiling at him. He remembered how she had been that day, so soon after Victor's death, and how he had learned that day how much he trusted her.

Victor.

It wasn't Sarah's fault. It was Victor who had ruined him. Victor who'd used his charm to entrap him in this world. Victor who'd been the first to catch him off guard, to make him believe that he couldn't second guess everybody. Victor who was not the man he seemed, and who offered to Alan the possibility of complete acceptance.

Until the moment when he'd fallen for Victor – because fallen was the only word he could think of to describe how he had felt – his difficulties with Sarah had been under control. He'd split his concentration, his double life with the ANC becoming multiplied as he continued to see Sarah and continued to love her. He could have managed it all right, for separating the parts of him was second nature.

He could have managed it if it hadn't been for Victor. It was Victor's fault.

How could he blame Victor? Victor was dead, killed by Alan.

279

It *was* Sarah's fault. She'd made him vulnerable because she'd made him love her. And once he loved one person, why draw the line at a second?

He had loved Victor and, at the same time as he knew he must rid himself of Victor, he'd done his best to protect him. He'd loved Victor and he'd split himself again, loving the man at the same time as he worked against all that Victor held dear.

All this he could have accomplished. All this he could have survived. But then Victor had been killed.

Victor's death almost destroyed him. Victor's death exposed the fact that Malan, whom Alan hated but admired, was as untrustworthy as all the rest.

Malan — Malan, not Sarah or Victor — was the one to blame. Malan had killed Victor and after that Alan could no longer enjoy his work, his real work. After Victor's death he could not be a spy. It wasn't a question of right or wrong, it never had been. Alan had never believed in apartheid — that's not why he'd sided with Malan. He had chosen Malan because Malan suited him, because Malan put in his grasp that intangible sense of power. And so his change of heart was nothing to do with politics: Alan cared little for politics of either side. It was instead a question quite simply of betrayal. Alan had never been able to abide it. The Howards had betrayed him and he'd left them — taking the escape Malan had proffered. He had worked tirelessly for Malan until Malan, in turn, betrayed him. Until Malan failed to keep Victor safe.

Since Victor's death Alan had been haunted by himself. Since Victor's death he had given Malan nothing of value and even lied to him. In doing so glimmers of the old joy returned. He'd realized that Malan was in the dark and he'd reverted to his double life — except this time with Malan, and not the ANC, as his target.

He didn't fool himself, he knew that, without protection from either side, he would soon be eliminated. He knew he'd have to give himself up to the ANC and he planned his defection carefully. What a coup they would have — a spy who'd turned and who was not known to his masters to have done so. They could have used him well; they could have used him to avenge Victor's death. It was all planned out — except life never worked that way for Alan.

Before he could confess, Wentworth intervened. Wentworth had outstripped him, pointing a finger at him, cutting off his options. If Alan had owned up then, they would have shot him. They never would have believed that he regretted what he'd done or that he could be trusted in the future. They would merely have thought that his confession was a result of panic at Wentworth's accusation.

So Alan had been forced to rid himself of Wentworth. He didn't regret doing so. He'd no feeling for the man other than to despise him. Wentworth was pathetic, even as a spy. They were in separate categories, Littell and Wentworth, irrelevant to each other. Just as Wentworth had never known that Alan was a spy, had chosen Alan through what must have been his first stroke of dumb luck, so Alan had been likewise ignorant. Only when Malan's instructions were sent to him, did he realize the truth. Feeling nothing, he had followed Malan's orders. No, that wasn't right, he had felt something – he had felt justified for Wentworth had destroyed his chances of building a new life.

Wentworth was in the past – but one memory of him continued to eat at Alan. Almost every minute of his waking hours, he remembered the look on Robert Wentworth's face when confronted with the planted evidence. Robert had been surprised, unbelieving and quite obviously guilty. It little mattered whether he had or had not written the document – the point was that he knew he'd been exposed and there was nothing he could do about it.

Alan remembered Robert's look and he'd resolved that never would he be so vulnerable. He'd made new plans. He would tell the ANC of his own betrayal, one day for sure he would. But he would tell them only when the time was right, only when he was prepared. And so he bided his time, waiting, plotting, planning, looking for the signs that would be good for him.

And then, it was then that he had spotted Slim inside the country – Slim who, with others, had turned and who was working for the police, Slim who'd been hiding out in Hillbrow. Through intermediaries he'd mentioned the name to Malan and by the transmitted response, he'd learnt that Malan was ignorant of Slim's new loyalties. A perfect solution to his dilemma, perfect!

He would set these traitors up, that's what he'd do, he would set them up and have Malan murder them. That would kill two birds with one stone, surely it would. For it would mean Malan's downfall and it would mean something else as well — that Alan would repay Victor and that Alan would be able to re-establish himself in the eyes of the ANC.

The thought came again: it was Sarah's fault.

It was her fault he never got the chance to wipe the slate clean. It was her fault because she'd sent him to Bryanston, just at the point when his plan had reached fruition. He had been discovered there and therefore couldn't finish what he'd started. And then, to make things even worse, she had, against his wishes, gone into South Africa where, presumably, she'd blown his cover. It was her fault.

He stood at the window and nodded his head in confirmation. He nodded but he didn't smile. The fact that he had decided where to place the blame was little consolation. He hated Sarah, more than he had hated anyone before. He hated Sarah but he loved her too.

He hated Sarah because he loved her and because his love for her had destroyed him.

Day Six

CHAPTER THIRTY-ONE

South Africa

Peter lived constantly with danger. He was always conscious of the threat that lurked around the corner, and of the moment, which must one day arrive, when he would be uncovered. Like all successful soldiers he had learnt to deal with these feelings. His technique was simple: he put them off, that's what he did. As soon as they grew stronger he'd tell himself to worry about them later, that the outcome could not be as bad as his premonition suggested, and that soon he would either have escaped the danger or would no longer be in a position to care. His technique had worked so far and he had emerged, strengthened, at the other side. But this time was different. This time the fear was so strong that each successive stratagem proved ineffective.

He walked down the street, knowing he was displaying his inner turmoil. He was no longer in control. He paused to tie his shoelaces and then he couldn't stop himself from raising his head, searching each passer-by for that giveaway bulge in a jacket pocket. He stood by the street corner waiting for his contact and he could assume neither of the safe poses that he'd long perfected – the one of good natured dawdling, the other of busy impatience. Instead he knew that, to any sharp-eyed observer, he bore the hall-marks of a deeply troubled man.

It was hard to know what it was that had raised the stakes. He had done everything by the book, taking special care not only of himself but of his comrades. Robben Island visiting hour had long since passed but he hadn't acted precipitously. He'd arranged a check meeting, going to the established venue two hours ago to wait for the woman to appear. He had seen her as soon as she rounded the corner and he'd watched her approach the post box. He'd watched her pass it, and he'd had a clear view in both directions. He was positive that she was not being followed. And yet to make absolutely sure, he'd waited before approaching her.

It was lucky that he waited. No, it wasn't lucky, it was right – that's what he'd been trained to do. But it was lucky as well for, as he continued to watch her unseen, he saw her stop suddenly on the pavement as if she'd forgotten something. He saw her turn and march straight back to the post box. He saw her push an envelope through its slot. He watched as she strolled away. She was doing what he could not manage: she was acting her part to perfection. They both knew what her turnaround signified – it was a signal to him that she was being followed. He had to keep away.

The signal astounded Peter. He couldn't understand how he could have missed the clues. He had taken all the right precautions – watching her walk down the road and scanning those around her for the tell-tale signs. But he'd spotted nothing, either when she was in vision or long after she'd disappeared.

Deliberately he set self-recrimination aside. He couldn't, when he thought honestly about it, believe that he had somehow missed the tell-tale clues. He was too highly experienced and his nervousness had increased his vigilance. Which meant one and only one thing: that they'd poured resources into their surveillance of his contact – that they were using many men to follow her, doing it so efficiently each man, and each car, would pass by only once, making outside detection an impossibility.

He nodded to himself – that was the right explanation. So be it: he must now stop worrying about them. His contact had behaved with remarkable maturity, doing exactly as he'd once instructed her. She'd told him, twice now, that she was under surveillance and she'd told him something else as well. By holding the envelope, just before she rid herself of it, in her left hand, she'd signalled that she'd set up an emergency meeting.

He had two hours to reach the designated spot. Two hours to check and double check that they weren't following him. Two hours to buy the necessary prop by which his contact – this one probably unknown to him – could recognize him.

Two hours and it felt too long. He bought a can of cola and immediately regretted having done so. If they'd spotted him, they'd see he wasn't drinking it and they'd know something was up. He drank the cola, threw the can away and began to walk.

For two hours he trod the streets of Cape Town, twisting and turning, stopping in front of shop windows to check reflections, memorizing number plates of passing cars, scanning the faces of those who shared his route. Two hours later, and in possession of a second cola, he was as sure as he could ever be that they'd not spotted him. Two hours and he was in place. He leaned against a wall, took one swig from the can and then placed it by his feet. He leaned against the wall and crossed his arms, half closing his eyes, the picture of an exhausted man – a picture that was hardly at variance with reality.

Half closing his eyes he filtered those coming towards him. Half closing his eyes he saw a woman, a white woman, with a yellow scarf knotted around her neck, come towards him. He belched.

She played her part to perfection. As she passed him her foot kicked against the can, knocking it over. With a word of timid apology she leaned down to straighten it and then she was off again, walking briskly down the street, her heels clicking as she went, her eyes focused in front of her.

He waited until she had gone. He waited until long after she had gone. He waited, his heart beating wildly. And then, when he was positive she was unaccompanied he bent down and picked up the can, pocketing at the same time the tiny piece of paper she'd pushed underneath it. He didn't unfold the paper right away. He wanted to but he didn't. He stuffed it into his trouser pocket and he walked slowly down the road, stopping briefly to discard the can amongst a pile of rubbish. Only then, when his hands were completely free did he pull out the paper and carefully unfold it. As he continued on his way he glanced casually at it.

His heart missed a beat. He almost stopped in mid stride. For the message was dynamite. What he had long suspected was written there, clearly, unambiguously, without frills or elaboration. Six words only it took to say it, six simple words:

'THABO SAYS THEO IS A SPY,' that's what was written there.

Thabo says Theo is a spy – that's why an unknown contact had risked exposure in a difficult time.

That bastard, Peter thought, that bastard.

He looked again at the paper and then cursed himself for doing so. If ever he needed his wits about him this was the time. He must act now, act decisively and rechecking the message was exactly the kind of time-wasting he must no longer indulge in. Instead he had better start planning. He must work out how he'd cross the country, he must work it out and execute it without delay.

No, that wasn't what he must do. He must first rid himself of the message. He must make sure that if he was caught the enemy would never know what it contained. He must make sure because if he was caught then others would have the chance to transmit it. He must make completely sure because what he now did could seal the fate of many of his comrades.

He reached into his pocket and pulled out a packet. The cigarette that he'd prepared ahead of time, the one with some strands of tobacco missing from it, was there in front. Carefully he withdrew it. Into the space he'd previously created he pushed the piece of paper and then, without missing a beat, he flicked a match against his fingernail. He had done it and he watched it burn. He took a puff. Inhaling, he breathed the news of Alan Littell's treachery straight into his lungs. He coughed – he was no natural smoker – but he could not cough it up. It lay there, the news, heavy on his chest, his sense of victorious confirmation buried by waves of trepidation that threatened to overwhelm him.

He could not push the waves away but he built a dyke against them. The materials he used to pack its walls were items on a list, items attached to each stage of his journey.

He must get a car, a safe car, and he must leave immediately, driving through the night, up towards the Swazi border, stopping only for petrol, keeping his eyes focused not just on the road in front of him but on the one behind. He must go, go now. He must succeed.

*

Malan couldn't stop himself from planning what he was going to do to Alan Littell. The night before, when he had finally faced the truth, he had told himself that he should put all thoughts of Alan out of his mind and concentrate instead on the boat and on Peter. The news from the Island, that Thabo had been overheard shouting about Victor, only strengthened his resolve. It confirmed to him that a moment that came once in a lifetime only if you were supremely lucky, had finally come to him. He had outguessed them all: experience and intuition had combined to deliver victory all the sweeter for its two-pronged nature.

Fact one: the boat was on its way, heading to its doom on a Transkei beach.

Fact two: Thabo knew Alan was a spy and had transmitted this information.

Fact three: Peter, who, because of absurd sexual jealousy, had always disliked Alan would be over eager to carry it.

Fact four: Malan would catch Peter.

Fact five (and this was the clincher): once the boat and Peter had been eliminated the other side would understand how deep had been Alan Littell's betrayal.

It little mattered that Malan didn't know Peter's face. He had organized roadblocks on every route from just outside Cape Town right up to the Swazi border, giving strict instructions that any lone black man (for Alan, when he could still be trusted, had told Malan that Peter always travelled alone) fitting Peter's general description should be instantly detained. It was a flamboyant step. There would be chaos, and it would take some considerable time to process all of the suspects. But in the end, Malan would have Peter and he would have the boat as well.

These were the facts on which he must concentrate – these and no others. Yet thoughts of Alan kept insinuating themselves into his mind. They crowded in on him and there was little he could do to keep them at bay. What happened, he suddenly thought, if even after Peter was arrested and the boat destroyed, the ANC was too stupid to guess that Alan was a traitor?

The solution came to him and it was sweet. He'd feed the flames of their mistrust, piling layer upon layer of false information over the border, enmeshing Alan in a web so thick that Alan, in thrashing around in it, would only further deepen their suspicions. The ANC would never forgive one who had turned against them twice, they would slaughter him without mercy.

And there was a further sophistication that occurred. Perhaps he could sow the seeds of distrust and then rescue Alan from their clutches. That would be the best he thought: he would allow his victim to experience anxiety and then relief. And then, just as Alan thought he was safe, Malan would face him with this final betrayal. Yes, he nodded, this option was definitely the best – the most satisfying of all. Even if it proved risky internationally, Jansen would not be able to refuse Malan. Jansen would be in no position to refuse Malan anything, not after the boat was found and every man on it was either dead or imprisoned.

Jansen! Of course! What had he been thinking of? Malan was due in Jansen's office a good ten minutes ago. He pushed himself up from his chair, and in doing so he experienced a stab of pain more acute then ever before. He did not fight against it, he used it on himself. It was a reminder to him – each thing in its place. First Peter and then the boat. Only after these could he concentrate on Littell.

Peter wasn't sure what had inspired him into picking up the hitch-hiker. He had done it automatically. He'd slowed the car, leaned across the front seat, opened the door and beckoned to the man all without really thinking. Only when the man was safely inside did Peter come to his senses. At this point it was too late. He couldn't very well chuck his passenger out, not without creating the kind of scene that he must, at all costs, avoid. So instead he'd lied about his destination, saying he was not even going as far as the outskirts of Cape Town. The man beside him had easily acquiesced: he was only too happy to get out of the harsh sun, he said, to rest his feet a moment in the comfort of a car, before continuing his journey. He stretched back in his seat, closed his eyes and began to hum.

The sound inflamed Peter's already jangled nerves. He remembered suddenly why he had picked up the hitch-hiker. It had happened in a moment of uncharacteristic hesitation. He had slowed the car, not because he was seized by either charity or loneliness, but because he'd spotted a phone box. He had slowed down, wondering whether it would not be better for him to phone headquarters and transmit his message.

At that point an image of Alan Littell intervened. An image of Alan's face when faced with Peter's evidence. An image of the time when, at long last, Peter could not only avenge Thembi's death but also be present at the denouement. I deserve it, Peter thought. I knew all along that Alan was a spy. That's why he had disobeyed the rules and had Alan followed. And now he held the final corroboration. They couldn't deny it like they had once before. If Thabo said Alan was a spy then Thabo would be believed. No one would dream of telling Thabo – as they'd once told Peter – that it was simple jealousy that caused him to make his accusation. No one would take Thabo aside – as they'd once taken Peter – and tell him that Thembi had not killed herself because of Alan.

Thinking of all this had thrown Peter off balance. He wouldn't telephone, he decided, he would take the news himself. He wanted to be there. He wanted to be there at the kill. And so instead of leaving the car, Peter had gestured at the waiting man.

The man's humming grew louder. Peter gripped the steering wheel hard, hugging his irritation to himself as he stared grimly through the windscreen. The sun was high in the sky and yet Peter was not wearing glasses – he was not wearing anything that might serve to separate himself from a crowd. As a result he was having trouble seeing, he was forced to squint down the road, to concentrate on driving when he desperately wanted to think of something else. Of someone else. Of Alan.

'Hey, what's that?'

Peter jumped at the sound of the voice beside him. He was so accustomed to travelling alone that he hadn't been expecting his passenger to speak. Now he looked in irritation to his left.

The man was staring straight ahead, and his hand was pointing up the road. Peter followed the gesture. He saw something that he should never have missed, that he could not have missed. Yet he saw something that he hadn't seen before. He saw the familiar sight of a roadblock.

Peter glanced at the man who was grinning beside him.

'I'm clean,' the man whined. 'Legal, official, stamped up. Yes *baas*, I'm clean.' He held up two hands in mock supplication.

Peter framed his mouth into a smile which, though expert, contained no real mirth. His mind went into overdrive. Part of him was dealing with his own negligence and with the fact that he'd not seen the roadblock – the other part was thinking, thinking furiously, whether there was any way to escape.

There was no way out. Even though he had lifted his foot from the accelerator, he was still too close to the obstruction to turn around. There would be mobile units serving the road blocks, their sole purpose to pin-point and pursue those vehicles which suddenly avoided them. If Peter were to turn, then he would be finished. This certainty strengthened him. He would have to brazen it out. He applied his foot gently to the accelerator and watched the distance between himself and his possible doom diminish. When he was within five yards of the road block, he slowed and then finally stopped the car right by the side of the waiting policemen.

They did not approach immediately: they were occupied with others. Peter sat still, waiting, staring straight ahead. He felt beads of sweat forming on his brow, and when the man beside him commented on how hot it was, he wiped them away with his hand. He rolled down the window.

The policeman, when he finally reached Peter's car, hardly gave its occupants a second glance. Instead he lifted his hand up lazily in the air and waved them on. Peter's leg had cramped and it was with effort that he managed to press it down on the pedals. The car jumped and then moved into motion, passing the obstruction. The sweat continued to spill down Peter's face and it was only after he had rounded a corner, leaving the roadblock far behind, that he felt able to breathe again.

His passenger must have sensed his relaxation. 'You're lucky you picked me up comrade,' he said.

Comrade, Peter heard. He glared at his passenger. 'What do you mean?'

The man shrugged good naturedly. 'Didn't you notice?' he said. 'They were looking only for single men. They arrested each one that was alone.'

*

292

Malan was enjoying the meeting with his boss.

Jansen's manner had changed subtly but not subtly enough for the change to escape Malan's notice. Not that Jansen had apologized, he would, of course, never bring himself to do that. But he was doing something unanticipated, he was giving information to Malan as if he really wanted Malan to help him with it.

That's how Jansen had told Malan about Sarah Patterson's disappearance into the depths of Tanzania. He told his subordinate straight, showing that he concealed no ulterior motive, that he was wanting Malan to shed light on it. Malan had played the game. He had frowned gently as if he were thinking about it. Then he had made a suggestion.

'She was on a minor operation,' he said. 'That's all. She probably went for debriefing.'

Jansen had seized on Malan's suggestion, saying, of course, that he'd thought that as well. Malan knew that all Jansen wanted was to be let off the hook: he wanted to be told that, in letting Sarah go free, he had not made a mistake. Well, Malan was willing to give Jansen that much: nothing would now be achieved by antagonizing the man.

'Patterson was a mere pawn,' Malan said. 'I got everything I needed from her.'

Jansen smiled. He was so relieved he couldn't conceal it.

Now's the time, Malan thought. I must hit him with it. As the thought crossed his mind a spasm, more intense than he'd felt before, shot through his entire body. He gasped involuntarily, saw a look of concern cross Jansen's face, and desperately struggling for control, gripped the sides of his chair.

'I . . .' he stuttered.

What had he been about to say? That *Zonda* was a traitor? No, that wasn't it; that he would never tell Jansen. It was something else, something that the agony consuming him was obscuring. He would not give in to the pain, he wouldn't.

'I have ordered roadblocks to be set up around Cape Town,' he mumbled. 'In order to trap the terrorist Peter.'

He breathed out in relief. The pain was less fierce now, it was waning. He saw Jansen looking at him. Had Jansen spoken and not been heard? No, Jansen hadn't yet spoken. The pain must have distorted Malan's sense of time because Jansen was only now nodding. Had to get the rest out. Had to.

'There are men on the beaches in the Transkei,' Malan mumbled. 'They'll catch the boat.'

Jansen's face was no longer in focus. Malan closed his eyes and faced a blackness that was unimaginable. He felt how his hands were going slack on the arm rests, but try as he would, he could not get his muscles to obey.

A voice penetrated his darkness. '. . . insurbordination,' it said. 'I will leave the men there for another twelve hours. After that . . .'

The voice faded. Malan didn't know whether Jansen had finished speaking. Malan didn't care. For the pain was not waning, it was coming again, tearing at every fibre in his body. He opened his mouth to let it out and the last thing he was conscious of thinking was how undignified it was to fall to the floor when one had one's mouth wide open.

He had abandoned the car. He'd dropped the hitch-hiker and abandoned the car. He had known that he must do this almost as soon as his passenger had spoken, as soon as the realization hit him that they were out looking for him. It was the only explanation for the road block: the only explanation for the growing sense of catastrophe that had plagued him ever since he had reached Cape Town, the only explanation for his one public contact to be so carefully watched.

They were on to him. For the first time, they were really on to him. He'd ditched the car and caught a bus, excitement and anxiety each battling with the other. This was what he'd been trained for, this is what his experience had taught him to overcome. He thought about the airport, about the room he knew was safe and the place where he could change and get his new documents. He thought about it all and he smiled.

The bus was packed with airport workers and so when he disembarked he was able to merge with the crowd. He walked into the building almost carelessly but before long he'd learned that the airport was no place for him. The room that spelt security was locked – a sign that danger lurked. Peter slowly began to prowl the airport, his eyes alert.

294

He knew two of the comrades there and both of them knew him. The first caught one glimpse of him and walked quickly away. The second was braver. Wielding his mop as protection he had swished his way up to Peter and then bent down as if to wipe a patch on the floor.

'Get out of here *com*,' he said between gritted teeth.

'I have to go to HQ. I need documents.'

'Get out of here,' the man repeated. 'There's no way we can supply you with documents. The whole fucking police force is looking for you.'

Peter nearly cried out with rage as the man moved away from him. Frustration welled inside of him: frustration that he knew now that what he had was crucial. And yet without help, he couldn't get it out.

Across the room, a black policeman was looking at him. Peter swallowed and stared back defiantly, locking the man's eyes to his. When at last the other broke away and turned to his companion by his side, Peter acted. He got up, wheeled round and began to march away, fast but smoothly. He walked into the centre of a crowd of passengers, blending with them, using them as protection until he had reached the door.

Abandoning all thoughts of Alan Littell he concentrated on self-preservation. As he climbed onto a bus he saw a silver plane rising gracefully beside him. For an instant it seemed to tower above him, a thing of beauty offering freedom. He turned his head away from it, focusing only on his next move – on survival.

CHAPTER THIRTY-TWO

The sun was high in the sky but, inside the room, it felt as if it was still deepest night and as if night might stretch into infinity. They had been up all through it, searching the transcribed material. The three of them, Rebecca, Jabulani and Albert had swigged strong coffee, started sentences without finishing them, argued back and forth, putting one fact against the other, building equations that in the end refused all resolution. They had searched through everything that Alan Littell had ever said, through Victor's life, through Thabo's and Peter's too, combing the documents as if the answer lay there waiting simply to be uncovered.

They had staggered from weariness to fatigue and then on still further into total exhaustion. They'd snapped at each other, gone outside to breathe in the oppressive night air, closed their eyes and then quickly reopened them, haunted by the thought of the boat imminently approaching South African waters. All this they had done and still they had no answer.

Someone tapped on the door and then, without waiting for permission, entered the room. It was a man Rebecca knew only too well, a man who didn't bother to say anything but who merely glanced at his watch. She understood at once what he meant. He was the radio operator and he had come to tell them that they had fifteen minutes in which to finally conclude. In fifteen minutes the boat's commander would break off radio contact with the outside. In fifteen minutes the only way to stop the boat would be to phone their contact in the Transkei and risk exposure not only of him but of the boat as well. In fifteen minutes they would have passed the point of no return.

'Comrades,' she said. 'We must decide.'

They looked at each other but no words passed between them. The decision rested with them and yet they couldn't make it. They looked at each other equally but for Rebecca the final decision lay with her. If she didn't act they would step in the breach but she could not allow this to happen. She must decide: she alone. The responsibility pressed down on her like mud. She couldn't breathe.

She got up abruptly, walked over to the window, undid the catch and pushed it open. The air outside was as still and as suffocating as in the room. There was no relief to be found, no relief until it was finally over. She leaned out of the window, turning her head to one side. She watched, unthinking, as a figure emerged from one of the adjacent rooms, emerged hesitantly, stood by the door and then, slowly began to move.

It was Sarah Patterson. Sarah dressed in the same clothes as she had worn the night before. As Rebecca watched, Sarah reached Alan's door. She stopped and, as Rebecca watched, she lifted her hand as if to knock on it.

Sarah lifted up her hand and watched it, made white in the glare of the African sun, as it hovered there. In that moment, when it was poised, suspended in the heat, her thoughts began to race. As if she were hallucinating she saw herself dispassionately from a distance. She saw her crumpled clothes and bent posture. And she saw closer as well, she saw her hand, and the faint brown spots upon it, spots which had once not been there. She realized that they were spots of age.

Not only of age, she thought, as she dropped her hand and glanced around her. It was the sun, that harsh African sun, that had transformed her.

She turned round and with her back against the wall she stood, her limbs quiescent but her head moving, transcribing a semicircle. She drank in the sight before her, the long low horizon, that flatness of the earth and the sheer size of it. She stared, past the signs of habitation, to the land which stretched beyond it –

that vast arid land, brown and stony, with no green to relieve its uniformity save for the drab olive of low scrub and the thin leaves, spreading pitifully from low branches.

This is the sight, she thought, that Alan used to speak of, that he used to miss while he was in England. And this is the sight, she thought, that I've professed to love.

She was seized suddenly by an uncharacteristic sense of loathing. I hate this place, she thought, I hate this continent, this landscape and all the pain it carries with it. She closed her eyes and groped for home. She saw in the darkness the land in which she had been born – that lush land of seasons each different from the other, of extravagant springtime colour and grey, foggy winters. She longed for it: she wanted to be there.

I'm tired of Alan, she thought, I'm tired of living through him.

She opened her eyes and memory came flooding in. She registered the times that she had once buried: the times when Alan had turned his back on her, when he'd fobbed her curiosity away, and when (and the memory of it made her shiver) he'd touched his lips in a gesture of self-importance. I used to like that, she thought, I used to like the danger and the secrets he carried with him.

She stood, unshaded by the sun, and felt how much she had been changed. She judged his actions differently: she saw with different eyes. All that mystery seemed now to her like the parched desolation of the landscape. What had once beckoned because it was different and exciting now appeared bleak and lifeless.

Forbidden, unthinkable thoughts flooded in on her. Alan lied to me, she thought, about Thembi, his age, his scar across his back. Alan lied to me, she thought, and I accepted it. I welcomed it, embraced the lies as part of him. I loved it all, I needed it to feel alive. It's my fault, she thought, that he lied to me.

She turned back to the door and raised her hand again. I needed the excitement, she thought, and the truth would have interfered.

Well, I've had my own excitement now, she suddenly thought. She stopped her hand in mid air. And I know that Alan will never stop lying, she thought, because he can't, because South Africa has made of him a liar. She felt relief flood into her and her hand edge forward again. That was it, that was the explanation! It was South Africa which was to blame, South Africa with its self-obsessions, its single-minded pursuit of opposing ideas, its centuries of blood and anguish. Alan was not to blame: he was a victim of South Africa.

But if this was true then Alan still needed her help. She moved her hand once more. The old Sarah would have let momentum carry the hand, would have watched as it moved almost without her consent and landed on the door. But the new Sarah could not be so passive and the new Sarah was fighting with herself. Me or Alan, she thought, Alan or me.

Her hand hovered for a while and then it fell, but not on wood. It fell down limply by her side. Slowly, as if she were a hundred years old, she pushed herself into motion, turning from Alan's door, past Rebecca's room and past Rebecca without even noticing her.

She passed him by, Rebecca thought. I wonder why she did that?

She passed him by, Rebecca realized, because she no longer trusts him.

Rebecca didn't pause to doubt the thought. Sarah did not trust Alan — she knew it intuitively. She withdrew her head from the window. She turned to stand with her back to it and stared at a spot on the floor.

Sarah didn't trust Alan. But then that didn't mean that Alan was a spy. Of course he'd lied to Sarah, lied foolishly about Thembi, his background, his activities, his feelings. Sarah had good reason to mistrust him. But a soldier in MK must learn to lie. Only through lies could a soldier survive in the jungle of South Africa. And Alan was a good soldier — that much was no lie.

So Sarah's case was special: she distrusted Alan not as a judge, but as a lover. Her mistrust could not be Rebecca's guide. How then, thought Rebecca, should I decide? Which one of my conflicting feelings can I trust?

She couldn't choose because she was no longer sure she knew herself. Too much had happened. She'd come here settled in her ways, convinced that her decision had always been correct. But the process of interrogation had changed her irrevocably. The Rebecca, who only a few days before had seen the world through rules, was no longer the same woman. The Rebecca who'd pushed her dead son away from her no longer existed. The Rebecca who thought she could manage on her own had gone for good.

Leaving what in its wake? Leaving uncertainty, confusion and fear. Leaving someone who did not want to take the responsibilities she'd always worked so hard to carry. Someone who was no longer strong.

Her eyes misted over. She shook her head in denial of the tears and of the thought that had provoked them. It wasn't possible – this couldn't have happened in a few days. She was deceiving herself.

She thought back to the beginning. She had considered Littell guilty merely because he was accused. That's how she'd felt at first. She'd considered him guilty and their first meeting had confirmed her in her beliefs. Alan was a man bereft of reason, he broke down for nothing, using tears to protect himself from questions. Alan was guilty, that's what she had thought.

And then she'd changed. Not all at once but slowly – slowly it crept up on her. It was Jabulani's hectoring which had allowed the change but Jabulani was not to blame. It was doubt about Alan Littell, also, that had inched her forward but Alan Littell could not be admonished for it. She alone must accept the responsibility. She alone must face the fact that the change had happened, not in the present, but long ago in the past. It had happened when she'd cut herself off from the pain of Mzwanele's death and when, in doing so, she'd buried her capacity for love. It was then that the new Rebecca had been born, the one who, having outlasted her only son, had no room for uncertainty. The one to whom efficiency was all and feelings a mere distraction. The one who laughed with her mouth but not with her heart. And now that one had in its turn been driven away. It had gone and complexity had taken the place of its endless simplifications. It had gone and the need for innocence had replaced cynicism, the need to believe in Alan.

Rebecca shivered, gripped by sheer astonishent at her thoughts. What was she doing? It mattered little whether she wanted to believe Alan. The only thing that really mattered was whether he had been speaking the truth.

Sarah, she thought, Sarah holds the key. Their voices, Alan's and Sarah's, came back to her as she had eavesdropped on them. Sarah had been bitter then, Sarah had been angry with Alan.

And how had he reacted? He had reacted defensively – well that was understandable. It did not make him a spy. He had reacted as Sarah had – he had tried to share the blame between them. He had taken no responsibility, he had owned to nothing. And he couldn't take the first step, he couldn't console her, he had shoved his own need in the space between himself and Sarah. He had spat in the face of reality, he had displayed the real Alan Littell, the man who refused to abide by the morality of others.

Rebecca breathed out. 'Recall the boat,' she said.

'Recall the boat,' she said again, louder this time.

She watched as Albert Kana, belying his bulk, sprang to his feet, sprinted to the door and was gone.

She watched the space that he'd vacated.

Jabulani's voice penetrated her silent vigil. 'I think you're right,' he said. 'I'll back your decision.'

She almost laughed. 'Do you think I care?' she wanted to shout. 'Do you think I need your backing?'

She didn't shout those words, she didn't say anything. She thought instead of what Jabulani had once meant to her. She felt something tug at her. She felt an impulse to make a gesture: an urge to wipe away the intervening years, to try again with him, to grab a chance for, if not love, then companionship at least.

'You've done well,' Jabulani said.

Her sense of urgency, of a need to act, waned. Yes, she thought, I've done well. I, Rebecca Moisia, have done well, I've faced myself and Mzwanele too: I've learned to like Alan and also to condemn him. I've learned, finally after all these years, how to cry. Yes, I've done well.

She nodded at Jabulani and then she began to trace Albert's path, heading for the outside.

'Rebecca.'

She turned and looked at him, looked at him sitting there, a mute appeal upon his face.

'I'm tired,' she said.

She walked away with shoulders bowed. But as she walked another thought descended. If I have learned to cry, she thought, perhaps I can also learn to laugh. I have been weakened, she thought, and strengthened at the same time.

CHAPTER THIRTY-THREE

Ingrid's face swam into view. Malan had long since stopped worrying about the strange angles at which his wife appeared and disappeared. He had accepted these just as he had accepted the fact that he would never again stand on his own two feet, that he would never leave this bed, that he would never . . .

He had grown used to Ingrid's strange appearances but what he couldn't accept was the way his mind kept wandering, the way sentences slipped off the edge of consciousness, never to be brought back. He wondered, not for the first time, whether Ingrid was disobeying his orders and filling his body with pain killers so strong that he could no longer control his mind. He wondered this, but he was too tired to ask.

He closed his eyes and heard a rushing sound. An unfriendly sound it was, it scared him. He winced and cried out.

He had no voice with which to cry. And the sound was not unfriendly, it was the sound of surf and sea. A sound from his childhood, a sound from a time when he was young and strong. He could almost see it now, the breakers coming towards his canoe, he could almost feel that excitement tinged with fear as he knew that the next one would be big.

But wait a minute, the sound *was* unfriendly. It swept in on him, not from his past but from a moment in his present. There was no canoe, in the scene he was imagining and it was no longer daytime.

It was night. And he was waiting for something.

'The boat,' he said.

He did have a voice and Ingrid heard it.

'Shush,' she said and he felt her hand on his forehead. It reminded him of when he was a child, sick with a fever, his mother beside him, comforting him.

The sound returned.

He was no child and Ingrid was his wife. He pushed her hand away and struggled against the pillows.

'The boat,' he said.

'Shush!' That word again.

'There is no boat.'

No, of course, there was no boat. How could there be? He was in bed, in Jo'burg. There was no boat and there was no sea.

There is no boat. That wasn't Ingrid's voice, it was a man's voice. A man's voice raised in anger. Jansen's voice.

Malan opened his eyes. 'Jansen's been here,' he said.

Ingrid placed a spoon against his lips. Roughly Malan pushed her hand away, watching as the scarlet liquid spilled over his chin and onto the fresh white sheets.

'Jansen was here,' he said.

He did not need an answer. By the alarm in her eyes and by the rigid line of her lips, he knew he had not imagined it, he knew it for the truth.

'Jansen has been here,' he said. 'And there was no boat.'

Ingrid turned away from him. Her shoulders were shaking. How like Jansen, Malan thought, to terrorize a man upon his death bed. The thought, that at least Jansen had remained consistent, comforted him. He relaxed back into his bed. He closed his eyes.

There had been no boat.

The men had waited but no boat appeared.

The ANC had outguessed him.

Alan Littell had outguessed him.

Alan Littell was safe while he, Gert Malan, was dying.

The pain came straight and sure but Malan no longer cared for it brought with it a thought illuminated, crystalline in its clarity. Alan and I are both unimportant, he thought, have always been unimportant. It is the game alone that matters.

And the game had changed. The game had changed even though nobody was yet aware of how much it had changed.

Jansen thought he knew the game had changed and was covering up the past in preparations for its new rules. The ANC thought they knew the game was changed and had tried to send a boat as a last minute gamble – an end and an opening simultaneously.

But Malan alone knew that both these gestures were futile. Malan knew that nobody, no human being, no organization built with human hands, could control the game. De Klerk might make his promises; Jansen might sweep the department clean; Mandela, even, might soon walk free, but no one could predict the outcome and no one could control it.

Captain Gert Malan closed his eyes and smiled – smiled at the irony of it all.

CHAPTER THIRTY-FOUR

There were four of them in the room and the fourth was Sarah Patterson. Alan saw her as soon as he entered, saw her sitting quietly by a wall, saw her eyes flick away when he looked at her, and then he felt rather than saw how they returned to dwell on him when he turned to face the others.

I've lost Sarah, he thought, I've lost everything.

No, he thought, it's not like that, it can't be – I still have one last card to play. He stood in the middle of the room, stood straight and tall.

'I have something to say,' he said. He savoured the way his voice rang out in that space and the silence, the expectant silence, that followed it. He smiled.

'I have catalogued a group of traitors,' he said, 'operating from inside the country. They were once part of us but they've been turned. They track and kill our cadres, they are Askaris. I have their names. The first is Slim.'

He was going to list them, each in turn, to list them and give their location too. He was going to tell them all about it, to tell them how he had Malan lined up to pounce on them – a bastard ready to kill bastards. All of this was he going to tell them.

But instead a sharp intake of breath prevented him from continuing. He focused his eyes in front, just in time to see a glance pass between Rebecca and Jabulani, a glance poignant with a kind of understanding.

But they couldn't possibly understand. This was his mission, his alone.

'I have their names,' he said insistently. 'I collected them. And their locations. All this can I give to you.'

'They've gone.'

Who was it that had said those words, who was it? Those words – *they've gone* – what did they mean?

'I have their names.' His voice was high pitched, unfamiliar, frenzied.

'We've been watching a group of Askaris for a long time.' It was Jabulani's voice and it was hardened. 'We were about to isolate them,' the voice continued loudly, 'when they disappeared. Somebody tipped them off, somebody who knew we were on their track.'

No, thought Alan, no it can't be true.

No, he thought, even as he knew that Jabulani could not be lying. It was Malan. Alan had told Malan to hold off until he had all the information but Malan had ignored him and somehow the men had escaped. It was Malan's fault: for the second, fatal time, Malan had betrayed him.

Alan groaned out loud, groaned for all to hear. He was lost.

'Sit down, please.'

Rebecca's voice was cold as gravel. Alan had no choice: taking the folder she shoved at him, he sat. He sat and looked and saw his Book of Life. Inside it he knew was a copy of a document thirty-seven years old – of his birth certificate.

'You lied about your age,' Rebecca said.

He glanced at Sarah, once only, a glance that registered the depth of her treachery.

'You lied about everything,' Rebecca's voice pulled him front-wards.

Not everything, he thought. He held his tongue and stared straight at Rebecca because in doing so he could cut out any part of Sarah that threatened to intrude into his vision.

'You are a spy,' Rebecca said. 'Recruited before you joined the ANC.'

Her voice was certain even though she could not have known this for sure. Well – let her condemn him, let her condemn him without ever knowing the truth: he wouldn't give her the satisfaction of confirming it.

'You betrayed your comrades,' she said. 'You betrayed Victor.'

No, he thought, not Victor. He shook his head involuntarily.

'You killed Victor.'

'No.' It was torn out of him, that word.

'Explain yourself.'

Her voice was devoid of all emotion and it mocked him. He set his jaw closed tight against it.

'Victor befriended you and you had him killed.'

That was too much, too much indeed. He threw back his head and laughed. He laughed and then he looked at Rebecca, looked her full in the face.

'Victor knew,' he said. 'Victor knew.'

'What do you mean?'

By the incredulity in her tone and by the question that she asked, Rebecca showed how little she understood – how little any of them understood.

I was the only one who ever knew Victor, Alan thought. I knew he was a whole man, perfect and yet, at the same time, full of imperfections. But they – the Rebeccas of this world – they are different. They refused to see the man as he really is. They idolized Victor and in doing so withheld from him the balm of human weakness. It was because of them, because of their blindness, that Victor chose to die rather than expose Alan.

Alan closed his eyes and saw again his last glimpse of Victor. Victor had been sitting across the table, smiling slightly. He continued to smile as Alan briefed him. I knew then, Alan thought, I knew then.

He nodded to himself. He had known then that Victor had guessed he was a spy. No, that was overstating the case. Victor might not have guessed. But he certainly had been suspicious, Alan had known that at the time. He saw it clearly once again: the wariness in Victor's eyes, the glimpse of something nameless. Victor had smiled when Alan insisted that he alone be the one to check on the weapons, Victor had smiled and nodded and there was again a flash of indecision and of sadness in his face.

'Victor knew,' Alan repeated to himself. But if he'd known then why hadn't he acted? One word from him would have been enough to begin the investigation that would have ended with

Alan's death. Yet instead of speaking out Victor had given Alan back his life. Why?

Sitting in the silence of the room the answer came to Alan. Victor had known all right but his friendship with Alan had neutralized him. Like Rebecca, Victor had not wanted to believe the obvious: he had gone into the country hoping to disprove his suspicions. Once Alan had unwittingly saved Victor: now Victor tried to repay the debt.

Cradling his head in his arms, Alan rocked himself against the impact of the knowledge.

'Alan.' It was Rebecca's voice, distant from him. 'Alan.' It came again, gently.

He opened his eyes and looked at her. He saw in her face that the thoughts which he had assumed were his alone, he had in fact said out loud. He saw in her face understanding and he saw something else: the knowledge reflected back at him that he had reached a point of no return.

He struggled to save himself and as he grappled for balance, the rest of the room dissolved. He saw only Rebecca, this woman who was his adversary, this woman who was the only one who had ever really tried to understand.

'Alan,' she said. 'Why did you not tell us?'

Tell you what? he thought: about my father with a *sjambok* in his hand? About the Howards who rejected me? About Malan who trapped me? He looked at her.

'After Victor died why did you not tell us what you had been doing? You were so grief-stricken, you were having second thoughts, you must have wanted to tell us.'

'How could I?' he mumbled. 'How could I? The blood hate was too strong – Wentworth saw to that.'

Rebecca lowered her eyes. Her voice came out, almost as a whisper. 'And when you learned of the Askaris, why did you not come to us then?'

He dropped his head.

'We might have been able to help.'

Help, he thought: no one could help me. No one could ever help me.

He shook his head and raised it once again. 'It was something

309

I alone had to do,' he said. His voice grew loud. 'Malan was to blame,' he said. 'Malan killed Victor. I owed Victor that: I had to get Malan.'

'But why?'

That word – why. Alan couldn't stand it. He put his hands up to block his ears.

'Why did you not involve us?' he heard. The hands tightened and a roaring came and still he could not blot her out. 'Malan is also our enemy,' he heard.

He had to speak. He had to stop her talking. 'You would not have accepted my way,' he muttered. 'You never accepted me.'

'Our movement is not like the other side.' It was Albert Kana's voice, ponderous and complaisant. 'We accept everyone, all colours, all religions, all creeds.'

Alan dropped his hands and narrowed his eyes, narrowed them against a slogan that was propaganda. His thoughts sharpened and he revelled in them. You never would have accepted me, he thought: an uneducated, confused, neglected child – a white child who didn't know which side he was on. You never would have accepted me. Malan knew that and that's why he helped me change. There is no room for those like me, the thought, no room at all.

He turned and he looked straight at Sarah, looked at where she sat shrunken against the wall.

'Get away from these people,' he said. 'For in South Africa only two sides are important. Those in the middle, those like you or me – we will be ground to dust.'

She blinked as if she hadn't heard – as if he wasn't there. Well, he no longer cared.

He shrugged. 'What will you do with me?' he asked the others. 'The bullet or the noose?'

'We are not barbarians,' Albert Kana. 'We will not kill you as your former masters would. We do not do things like that.'

Alan smiled. He smiled and then, as something inside of him shattered, he began to laugh. Not at this point in history, he thought – with the world's eyes on you. But before it was different, nothing used to stop you then.

His laughter rose up in the air, higher and higher, filling the room with a kind of twisted hilarity, soaring above them, mocking until it turned to something else.

Sarah stood outside the room and watched the man inside. I used to know him well, she thought dispassionately. She watched him sitting there, his chest unclothed and she saw the scar so familiar and yet so alien to her.

I never really knew him, she thought.

He must have known that she was there, he must have known. But he sat, still, stock still as he had been sitting for the past two hours, not moving, not even a muscle, not even to shake off the flies that were gathering on his back.

He's as good as dead, she thought. A gasp escaped her throat unbidden. I must go away, she thought, I must go away.

And yet she could not tear herself away: the sight was one that would always fill her days and therefore one that she must accurately remember. And so she didn't turn. She stood instead, as still as he, prepared to match his agony with her own.

And then she was interrupted. She heard a footstep behind her, and she felt a hand upon her back. She turned and saw Rebecca there. Their eyes met.

Sarah saw her own coldness reflected back and she fought against it. 'Alan lied to me,' she said. 'Lied continuously. But I don't believe the rest.'

'Alan was a spy.' Rebecca's voice was harsh. 'Purely and simply a spy.'

Never pure, Sarah thought, nor simple either – but I loved him. And I wasn't the only one. 'You grew to like him didn't you?' she asked Rebecca. 'I heard it in your voice, I saw it in your face.'

'Yes, I liked him.' Rebecca's voice was reluctant.

'And yet you can discard him now, so easily, so carelessly.'

'Like he discarded Victor.'

'No, not like that, not like that at all,' Sarah protested, 'and you know it. Again I say I don't believe it.' She saw something twitch in Rebecca's face, a muscle behind her cheek. 'You don't believe it either,' she said. The muscle was stilled and Sarah pressed on.

311

'You're not like them,' she said. 'You're not prepared to sacrifice everything for an idea alone. You feel for people.'

Rebecca looked straight at Sarah and nodded. 'Yes,' she said, 'I have learned to feel for people.' She paused and in the silence that seemed to stretch forever she did not blink. 'But I am like them,' she finally said, 'because I know that they're right, that their struggle, my struggle, cannot be surrendered.'

Sarah saw the certainty in Rebecca's face and only with effort did she resist it. 'Then it is I who am not like you,' she said softly. 'It is I who have failed.'

'Alan's betrayal was not yours,' Rebecca insisted. She faced the room. 'You do not have to suffer for his treachery,' she said.

'But if it's the truth then it was my betrayal,' Sarah said. 'I betrayed him by not listening. And by not listening, I betrayed Victor as well.'

'You didn't.' Rebecca's voice rang out loudly.

Alan in the room did not look up. Rebecca shivered and moved her eyes away from him. 'You weren't to know,' she said, gently this time. 'I too have made the same mistake. I too lost somebody because I would not face up to reality.'

I don't want to know, Sarah thought. Leave me alone. I don't want any more of your pain.

She did not speak the words aloud but she didn't need to. Rebecca understood. 'Don't let Alan's defeat affect you,' she urged. 'You are part of us. Stay with us.'

'I can't,' Sarah shouted. She glanced inside, to see whether her shout had roused him. He sat quite still. 'I can't,' she said. 'I'm not strong enough. You'll sacrifice everything for your cause — even your son.'

'It doesn't happen like that,' Rebecca said. 'You don't set out saying I will sacrifice this or that. You don't say, "I'll give up my job for the struggle", or "I'll go one better and give up my son." No one makes that sort of pact, no one on earth. But when it happens anyway, what are you to do?' She looked at Sarah, looked at her hard, gripping the other's eyes with her own.

She's trying to persuade herself, Sarah thought. I should help her.

But Sarah turned away. She turned and stared at a landscape that did not belong to her.

312

Rebecca's voice pursued her. 'You could be part of it,' she said. 'It's your struggle as well.'

Sarah's eyes were dry. 'No,' she said. 'It's not my struggle. It never was.'

She took her last glimpse of Alan, saw him sitting there, his back now ram-rod straight. Even in despair, she thought, Alan has dignity. She saw him sitting there and the image aligned with memories reflected back at her: his cool blue eyes, his smile, his secret heart. He had always been alone, she realized, and yet he had always struggled to break his solitude.

And only then, only after all this time, did a tear fall from her eye. That's all it was – a single tear, a tear of love, of hatred and of confusion. One tear to hold all that – one tear for a man who was lost.